LESSONS IN TIMING

SYLVIA BARRY

RIPTIDE
PUBLISHING

Riptide Publishing
PO Box 1537
Burnsville, NC 28714
www.riptidepublishing.com

Lessons in Timing

Cover art: L.C. Chase, lcchase.com/cover-design
Editor: Carole-ann Galloway
Layout: L.C. Chase, lcchase.com

ISBN: 978-1-62649-994-2

First edition
April, 2024

Also available in ebook:
ISBN: 978-1-62649-993-5

LESSONS IN TIMING

SYLVIA BARRY

To Iliana:
who read 600 versions of this book and still loved us by the end of it.

Everything you do irritates me. And when you're not here, the things I know you're gonna do when you come in irritate me. You leave me little notes on my pillow. Told you 158 times I can't stand little notes on my pillow. 'We're all out of cornflakes. F.U.' Took me three hours to figure out F.U. was Felix Ungar!
—Oscar Madison, *The Odd Couple*

"And they were roommates!"
"Oh my god, they were roommates."
—Vine

TABLE OF
CONTENTS

1

ARMAND ATTEMPTS TO
LEAVE AN AIRPORT

July 15th - One month until the convention

I think it was Douglas Adams who once wrote something along the lines of how it was no coincidence that not a single language on earth had produced the saying "as pretty as an airport."

This is because an airport is a bloody miserable place to be, no matter what language you speak or whatever your culture's concept of *pretty* entails. Airports are designed to suck the life force right out through the pores of your skin and use it to fuel the neon and fluorescents, not to say the automatons known as airline employees.

The flight from Heathrow to New York had been downright awful, but somehow the flight from New York to LAX had been just as ambitiously unpleasant. The plane was smaller, which meant the turbulence had been worse, as had the food, the service, and the quality of people. The middle-aged man sitting next to me, whose muscular bulk all but obscured the aisle beyond, appeared to have eaten something pickled prior to boarding, which had turned on him, and he'd shared his misfortune with the rest of the passengers in a variety of ways. I had tried to disappear into my corner, staring out the window, then had remembered in the nick of time my lack of fondness for heights and small spaces.

But that business had been over and done with for some time now, and I was once more standing on solid ground. Armand Demetrio, intrepid cartoonist stepping boldly into the land of the free and home of the brave.

That was, of course, assuming I'd clear customs.

After explaining to the severe, steel-jawed men in uniform that despite my complexion and accent I was not, in fact, a terrorist, but, as previously mentioned, an intrepid cartoonist, I was unceremoniously tossed back into the passenger hall, having been searched, interrogated, and implicitly admonished for not having the decency to be a god-honest terrorist. I could only imagine that the good bruising of a man's dignity was a cherished and prestigious art form in this country.

Eventually, I managed to locate the carousel which (so promised an assortment of lighted dots) would soon furnish me with my luggage. I found a place to stand, maneuvered my muscles into an autopilot arrangement designed to instantly wake me if and when I began to tip over, but otherwise was left free to lose a degree of consciousness.

I was quite happy to hold this position for as long as it would take for my luggage to appear, but I soon became aware of some sort of . . . humming nearby. Far from an electronic or mechanical hum, this was the sound of a happily atonal *Homo sapien* unintentionally sharing their self-satisfaction with the rest of the world.

I couldn't help myself; I glanced over.

He was a radiant specimen of as-seen-on-TV America: the delicately sun-bleached hair, the taut and lightly flushed skin over a sharp jaw and respectable cheekbones, straight nose, perfectly white teeth, and eyes that were so full of joy they might as well have been shooting laser beams of glee.

He was texting, shoulders hunched and chin buried in the folds of an expensive-looking scarf; he grinned down at the phone as if it held all the wonders of the universe and had promised to share. His thumbs fluttered rhythmically. He then waited a moment, giggled to himself upon receiving a reply, and once again clickity-clacked and beepity-booped away as he all but wriggled with the pleasure of communication with some other, obviously beloved, entity.

At one point, while presumably awaiting a reply, he glanced over and flashed a blindingly joyful grin in my direction. "Morning!" he chirped.

Unprepared as I was to be addressed by such a young American Adonis in my present condition, I managed a grunt and a bit of a half shrug. He did not seem to mind or even process this response and turned back to his bliss-giving sliver of shiny machinery.

That seemed like it was going to be the extent of our interaction, but a few moments later he stepped forward to pull a powder blue case off the carousel, turned to me again, and said, "Have a great day!" With that, he floated toward the exits, all but dancing along and whistling as his body language proclaimed in thundering overtones: *I am young, I am in love. The world runs deeper than its crust and its filling is a sugary goodness of affection and mutual respect. Watch me take a big bite.*

I watched him as the happy squeak of his trolley wheels propelled him through the lobby and out into the world, where he would undoubtedly go on to live a charmed and cherry-flavored life, and I would never lay eyes on him again.

An eternity of ten minutes later, with my luggage safe and finally in hand, I bade a relieved farewell to the carousel and turned toward the arrivals hall. I vaguely remembered that I was to be met or collected by someone from the university, so I made the effort and raised my head a little, just enough to take in the crowd waiting at the edge of the hall. Then I froze, riveted to the spot in disbelief.

My name, written in sparkly gelled ink and surrounded by stickers and stars, was on a piece of cardboard. This was held in a delicate right hand, the counterpart of which was holding and waving a tiny honest-to-god Union Jack.

I blinked, but it was still there.

A slight body, by all appearances connected to the hands that held the sign and the flag, wiggled and shoved its way through the crowd, and turned out to be topped by a grinning ginger head replete with freckles and gleaming green eyes.

"Armand!" it squeaked as it pushed toward me. "Mr. Demetrio, I'm Robin Finch!" It was strange to hear an American accent emanating from such an uncannily Irish face.

He managed to extract himself from the crowd and stood, bent double for a second, catching his breath. Swallowing my dread, I took the opportunity to search the crowd for the chaperone I hoped would be there.

This was a child; perhaps his chronological age would contest that, but it was a fact nonetheless. Anyone who believed gel pens and stickers to be a valid form of communication should not have been allowed out sans their name and address pinned to their coat lapel.

Robin Finch, Boy Wonder, had apparently regained his wind and composure, seeing as he was now both walking and babbling. Once it became clear that the noises emitted by him were intended to convey information, I took care to listen for a few moments, was reaffirmed in my assumption that it wasn't worth the effort, and tuned him out again. I nodded a few times and even grunted once but, most importantly, followed him out of the airport and into the car lot.

Well, I say "out of the airport," but the car lot was, of course, part of the airport. This might seem a mite nitpicky to some, but as anyone who has ever attempted to leave an airport knows, the car lot is naught but a false hope—you think it means you're almost out, but the truth is that there are long tunnels, endless spiral ramps, and incomprehensible, asinine road directions still ahead. In fact, you will not have *left* the airport until you have returned all the liquids in your possession to their natural state within bottles and tubes larger than the miniscule amount allotted to air travelers. Or perhaps, the official moment is when you see a small shop and do not instinctively want to burn it to the ground.

Robin Finch had led me to what was definitely a car of some sort, though arguments to the contrary were probably a regular occurrence. It was a yellow, old-fashioned Volkswagen, rusted and scratched but also polished to within an inch of its life, and it looked more like a child's toy than a vehicle. Robin patted her bonnet fondly before tossing my luggage in the boot and opening the passenger-side door for me. "This is Camille," he said proprietarily.

Hunching myself as much as possible, I managed to cram myself into "Camille." The driver's side was not only placed in a disorienting manner on the left but also disturbingly flush with the steering wheel and piled high with no less than three cushions.

I was going to die in a tiny yellow car in America.

Robin bustled into the driver's seat, still prattling as he shifted the car into gear. I waited for a rare pause in the torrent of blather, then said, "*Camille?* The Greta Garbo movie?"

Robin beamed at me. "You *are* an artist, aren't you?" he squeaked happily.

I tried to smile and managed a grimace as he administered a punch of camaraderie to my arm.

"I'm going to be an actor," he informed me. "I love comics and storytelling and that's why I'm excited about your workshop and all, but I really think I'm destined for the stage, you know? I'm actually the lead in this season's production. There's so much more complexity in theater, you know? It's so physically and mentally engaging, so I feel like I can really—"

I gently tuned him out again and tried in vain to see if I could spot the thoroughfare or any other indication of the real world past the cement spaghetti which was the airport parking complex.

I did not care to listen to Robin, and I did not care to think about the workshop I would be teaching. Norsemen University had hired me to teach a month-long summer workshop on . . . well, the proper name of it was along the lines of "Deconstructionist Themes as Expressed in Use of Monochrome and Non-Linear Narrative." My agent, Lakshmi Ranjit, had likely come up with that name; what I would *actually* be teaching these young people, if anyone showed up, could be summed up as, "How to Draw Broody Fucking Comics."

Lakshmi had been forced to practically knock me unconscious to get me onto the plane. And yet here I was, in a tiny yellow car in America, being told I was an artist and expected to actually teach others whatever it was they thought I could do.

The car puttered to a stop at some sort of toll booth, and then merged onto the thoroughfare.

Despite my obvious impending death, I closed my eyes and leaned back against the threadbare headrest, as we finally, officially, *truly* left the airport.

2
ROBIN MEETS
HIS HERO

July 15th

A rmand Demetrio smelled like someone who'd just come off a nine-hour flight. He seemed a bit crumpled too, as if he'd been used to mop up a spill and then tossed in a corner.

Despite all this, it was clear to anyone with eyes that this right here? This was one smoking-hot section of buttocks. He was very, *very* pretty. There was a lot of hair trying to hide it, but underneath the scruff and lack-of-sleep was a man almost too handsome to be British—all due respect to Messrs. Darcy and Bond.

It was a good thing I knew the way back by heart.

He was younger than I'd expected. From the amount of tech-splaining I'd been prepped for and his absence from social media, I'd assumed I would be dealing with a cute little grandpa. This guy was probably *just* kissing thirty.

The job, which was part of my Norsemen University work-study—count my blessings, I could be in a hairnet right now—was as follows: basically, be the personal assistant, gofer, and overall brain of the venerable Armand Demetrio, the oh-so-famous and oh-so-absent-minded artist who was teaching a comic workshop offered by Norse-U this summer. The workshop had been hyped up like a new hard seltzer flavor, and there was a deal with the DQ Comic Convention later in August, where Mr. Demetrio was an invited speaker. Which was amazing because a year ago no one had even heard of *Surrogate Goose*—his wonderfully weird comic.

My job, as savvy college sophomore-elect, was to assume that he knew nothing about the United States. He was, after all, British, and therefore incapable of comprehending our sophisticated, tea-dumping, colonial ways.

That was why the housing official had explained everything about the rent-by-the-month Briars complex to *me* rather than to him, even though he was the one who was going to be living there. I was meant to pass the information on to him in a more digestible form, possibly involving puppet shows and a sing-along. Again, still better than working in the cafeteria.

I'd been nervously babbling at him for a while, going full stream-of-consciousness, so I was relieved when soft snores started emanating from his corner of the car. I could finally stop talking.

Once we reached the apartment complex, I parked in front of the office, ran in to tell them Mr. Demetrio had arrived, then re-parked Camille nearer to the apartment building. I turned toward the snoozing Englishman and tapped him gently on the shoulder.

No dice.

"Mr. Demetrio?"

Nothing but a growly little sigh.

I poked his side, then tried to look innocent as he jerked awake, bumping his head on the roof. After a few milliseconds of panic, he glanced over at me and coughed. "I'm in California."

It wasn't a question and yet somehow demanded an answer.

I nodded helpfully. "Yes, and we've just arrived at your new apartment. Do you need help getting out of the car, Big Guy?"

He shook his head, blinked hard in an apparent attempt to wake up, and tried to extricate his enormous body from Camille. Once he was vertical, Armand shook slightly, then hugged himself, squinting up at the apartment building. I yanked his suitcase out of the trunk and set it down next to him.

"So, anyway, the office finally got back to me," I said airily. "You're paid up until the end of next month. Your roommate's moving in later today, and there's no smoking in the apartment," I added as he fished a crumpled packet out of his back pocket and stuck a bent and crinkly cigarette into his mouth. He glanced at me sideways before lighting it and taking a deep pull. I coughed politely and started lugging the suitcase toward the stairwell.

"Hand that over, Titch." Armand took the suitcase from me and started up the stairs, trailing a cloud of noxious smoke. I hurried ahead of him so I wouldn't be caught downwind.

"You're in 221B," I said, "and the apartment complex is called Bakers."

He froze on the second-to-last step and stared at me, cigarette dangling from his lips.

I grinned. "Heh, just my little joke."

"Hilarious."

"It's number 203 and the complex is called Briars," I told him, "and your roommate's named Lucas Barclay." The roommate I had mentioned several times, but who he had not yet reacted to.

Now, however—

"A roommate," he said incredulously, scowling.

I gave him an apologetic shrug. Personally, I would have expected the school to shill out for a one bedroom, but those decisions were made about a mile above my pay grade.

He nodded in resignation and resumed climbing the steps. I fished the keys out of my pocket and unlocked the door, then stood in the doorway until he had stamped out his cigarette, after which I let him in and gave him his keys. The apartment was lovely, with a big bay window to the east, a high ceiling, and a spacious kitchen.

My dorm-residing-self seethed delicately.

There was a welcome basket on the table; Armand brushed past me without looking around, grabbed it, then made for one of the bedrooms.

"So I'll be back tomorrow to check on you? There's a luncheon you're supposed to be at. I'll just—"

The door to the bedroom slammed.

"—let myself out."

Well. It wasn't like I didn't have more important things to do. The life of a leading man ingénue was full of adventure and challenge. Today, adventure was likely to be found at the gymnastics studio, where I had several routines to practice, and the challenge would be the emotional work—I really had to *internalize* the fact that I was no longer just a sad, bullied, theater kid. Or a disposable extra.

Oh no, I was a lead. A protagonist. The hero, who does not stand around waiting for temperamental artists to acknowledge his existence, but who sallies forth.

I sallied forth in the direction of a boba tea.

3
LUCAS
IN LOVE

July 15th

Serotonin slammed back into my system bite by bite as I munched away on the world's most breathtaking slice of avocado toast. It was *gourmet*: focaccia bread with a playful drizzle of balsamic vinegar and crumbled goat cheese—the kind I could only get here at Casa Maison Domo, or Triple House as it was known by us locals. I was soaking in the much-needed California sunshine on the patio seating as my two best friends not-so-patiently waited for me to regale them about my trip.

"You know," Andie pointed out from where she and Rick had arranged themselves across the table from me, in classic new-couple behavior, "I feel pretty confident that they had avocado toast in Canada."

"You sure?" I responded through my blissful haze. "Because I thought all they had was dismal weather and an excess of cousins."

Rick snorted into his fluffy stack of honey and cinnamon French toast that I was definitely not coveting.

I had suggested to Marla, as had Mom and other choice members of the family, that we would be more than happy to host her wedding here in California, at home, at the Barclay homestead, where there would be perfect weather. But for whatever reason, she had insisted that she and Steven had found a lovely bed and breakfast not far from where they would be moving. In rainy Vancouver.

Well. One's cousin presumably only gets married once, so alas, sacrifices must be made.

I tried, as discreetly as possible, to check my phone under the table—Darren had finally texted back after more than an hour of radio silence: *When are you headed over? I'm still trapped in this meeting*

I responded with one hand, relishing the final bites of avocado heaven with the other. *Ok, don't be trapped too long, I'm gonna finish this brunch and then smooch the life out of you*

Ideally, Darren would've met me at the airport, and we could've had one of those deeply romantic reunions that make everyone else uncomfortable. But my boyfriend was two-hours deep in what sounded like the meeting from hell, and it was a pleasant surprise that he'd been able to discreetly text me anyway.

It's the little things.

As it was, Rick and Andie had ended up on Lucas Pick-Up Duty, and as expected, they'd waited for me amongst the crowd in Arrivals, arms around each other as if I might already have forgotten that they had recently decided *You know what our trio of friends needs? For two of us to start dating and then kick the third-wheel friend out of our shared apartment.*

Which was fine. Really. Because I was happy for them, and yes, I had always kind of expected this to happen, and yes, they had assured me that this didn't mean they were kicking me out of our friend group, but still.

It was the principle of the matter.

I took a deep, cleansing breath, having left nothing but focaccia crumbs on my plate (which was a problem for future me and my personal trainer). "You may engage now," I announced with a satisfied grin.

"You already know what we're gonna ask," said Rick eagerly—we always did this when someone returned from traveling. "Weird airplane stories. Go."

Over the years we'd collected several memorable Incidents, and for a horrifying moment, I couldn't think of anything that had marred an ideal two and a half hours of international travel.

Well. Except.

"Okay, so this wasn't technically from the plane," I began, "but you're going to let me count it on the grounds that I generously lent you my car while I was gone."

"That's fair," Andie agreed. "Hit us."

"Picture, if you will, a hulky, shaggy-haired werewolf still enamored of his goth-punk phase, who sleepwalked into an airport and has no idea how he got there and has even less idea how to leave."

Rick and Andie dissolved into identical wheezy giggles, which was new. "Okay, but did he howl at the fluorescent lights?" Andie managed, asking the real question.

"I need you to understand that he did absolutely nothing. There I was, having a delightful text chat with Darren that I will *not* be sharing with you, and he's just hunched up next to me and fully ignores me when I say hi. I think he may have grunted, but that's it."

"Yep," Rick said, "that's a werewolf."

Andie perched her elbows on the table and grinned. "But, like, a hot werewolf?"

I raised an eyebrow at her. "So . . . a werewolf?"

"Oh my god, Lucas, stop encouraging her," Rick complained. We all laughed, and it was like our old vibe, before the two of them became a closed unit.

We ended our brunch after Rick and Andie had told me all about their week in a series of anecdotes that they tried to keep from seeming romantic.

The three of us chatted all the way back to our—*their*—apartment, where we staged a car-hostage exchange situation. "Thanks for hanging onto my stuff for me," I said as we added a few more moving boxes to my already packed little car. "I would've left the fish with you guys too, but I'd prefer them to live."

Andie gasped in mock offense. "That was *one time*!"

Rick touched her shoulder. "It was multiple times. Lucas, you were right to leave them with Darren. He's many things, but I trust that he's not a fish-killer."

There was an awkward breath between them at the mention of my boyfriend. However, I wasn't particularly in the mood to hear another round of them not-so-subtly voicing their dislike of Darren McKinley, a dislike that had been going strong since we were all in high school together nearly ten years ago.

"I think I'm going to check out the new place," I said brightly, because they were not going to bring their conspiracy theories into my perfectly nice day. "I'll swing by for the rest of my things tomorrow, if that's okay."

Rick and Andie agreed, and after a three-way hug and me thanking them for the pick-up, I slid back into my car, adjusted the seat, and left them waving from their front porch.

My new apartment, the one I'd had to sign a monthly lease for at the very last minute after Rick and Andie had decided that they just couldn't embark on a romantic relationship with another person living with them, was all the way across town. I had, in passing, brought up the possibility to Darren of us moving in together, but he had reasoned that it felt too early in our relationship for that.

Which made sense. A decade of friendship and an on-again-off-again situation notwithstanding, four months of a solid relationship might seem a bit soon to move in.

Rick and Andie would never need to know that I had no intention of heading to my new alone-person apartment until absolutely necessary. Darren should be out of his meeting at this point, and I was itching to see him.

I pulled up to the McKinley estate and shot Darren a text, lamenting yet again that I didn't have a spare key. It had been on his to-do list for a couple of weeks, but the case he was working on kept him busy more hours than was remotely preferable.

My phone buzzed a minute later.

Darren: *so sorry, held up with work*

Darren: *I want to see you but if I don't finish this, they'll kill me :(*

Disappointment lodged in my throat the longer I stared at the message. Deeply suspicious that somehow, cosmically, Rick and Andie had something to do with this particular planet misalignment, I now had no course of action except to drive to the Briars apartment complex and try my best to settle in.

After a quick stop at the housing office to pick up my keys and sign the remaining paperwork, I made my way to apartment 203.

It was . . . well, the only word I could find to describe it was *quaint*. Less LA and more cottage-core chic than I'd been expecting. Nothing that some nice accoutrements wouldn't fix though. Luckily it was fully furnished with a lovely island in the center of the modest kitchen.

My roommate ("Armand Demetrio," according to the lease) must've moved in already—there was a faint but lingering stench of cigarette smoke, and a light trail of dust and dirt that ran directly from the front door to the first bedroom on the right.

A roommate who isn't my best friends or my boyfriend. This is fine— better than fine. It's ideal, even.

I dragged my suitcase to the other bedroom, reminding myself with every step that this was only temporary. On my way back into the living room with a handful of personal effects, my eyes returned to the trail of dirt in the hallway.

My fingers twitched. Quickly, I grabbed the provided cleaning supplies from the hall closet.

What about the counters? Were they sanitized before we got here? I made a beeline to the sink and got to work wiping off all the counters and anything that could possibly be mistaken for an eating surface.

There. I'd done the bare minimum.

After ordering a grocery delivery from the vegan market on 7th, I spent the next few hours unpacking and immaculately arranging the living room into a habitable area. I still needed to get the rest of my things from Rick and Andie's, but the essentials had made it in on the first try. I was going to turn this house (well, apartment) into a home (well, acceptable living space) through the sheer force of my will.

Fleetingly, I considered leaving a note for my mysterious roommate, but resisted the impulse. If I had the choice, I would much rather greet Mr. Demetrio in person tomorrow.

But that didn't mean I couldn't do some internet stalking.

4
SKYLER MIGHT
(POSSIBLY) HAVE MADE
A MISTAKE

July 15th

I knew the second I stumbled off the Greyhound bus that my knees would never be the same again. They creaked and cracked as I tried to stretch, like I was forty instead of eighteen, and my stomach immediately took care to remind me that in the last thirty hours I had eaten nothing that resembled A Food—only mediocre peanuts, gummy worms, and some stale Doritos.

This was my own fault.

Some others that had been traveling on this same bus as long as I had—since Seattle—shuffled around me to grab their bags, while a bunch more remained in their cramped seats, continuing their journeys to who-knows-where. The Norsemen campus bus stop where they unceremoniously dumped us wasn't as busy as I'd expected, but then it was almost 7 p.m. and everyone else had probably moved into their dorms by now.

Sure enough, I lugged my rolling suitcase and my overstuffed backpack toward what I was informed was the registration office and saw a steady swarm of parents puttering away from their kids' dorms after what had likely been a nice afternoon of helping them move. There were some tearful goodbyes, and parents asking if their kid wanted to join them for dinner; that could've been my family. Could have been *me* getting taken out to some local restaurant by *my* parents. They had been so excited to drive me down to California—even if they would have preferred me to stay local, like I'd initially planned. We were going to have a leisurely drive and make frequent stops and they would have brought the rest of my belongings during that one trip instead of needing to mail them to me now . . .

I could've eaten food and showered. I could've hugged them goodbye properly. I could've—

"Hiya! Welcome to campus!" The lanyard-wearing RA with an oversized Norsemen hoodie greeted me in the lobby with more energy than I was prepared for. "You Skyler Evans? I only have a couple students left to check in, so you gotta be one of them."

"Yep."

"Awesome." She held up a binder stuffed to the brim with paperwork. "Anyone helping you move in today?"

I shook my head. It was just me, alone, by *choice*. I had decided to be independent and impulsive for the first time in my life, and now I was standing on a campus I'd never stepped foot on before, in a state I'd never stepped foot in before, overwhelmed with anxiety.

I deserved it.

The RA talked at me for a bit about dorm regulations and stuff as we toured the hall, but I was distracted by thoughts of my mom. She would've listened eagerly to every rule and explanation, ready to break them down for me. She would've loved that. She and Dad could've walked me to my room and helped me set things up, and I wouldn't have felt so desperately alone.

We arrived at my dorm room, which was a single and the most depressing shade of off-white I'd ever seen.

"I know everything kind of looks like prison," the RA continued, shrugging apologetically. "But it spruces right up once you throw some posters on the wall and, like, string fairy lights or whatever."

"Right," I agreed. "To hide the escape route I carve into the wall with a spoon."

"That's the spirit," she said, stepping back into the hall and leaving me alone. Well, alone-er.

I considered sinking onto the bare mattress, but my legs were still stiff from the bus. So instead I dug out my phone and stared at all the missed texts in the family group chat after I'd let Mom and Dad know I was alive and that I made it to campus.

Mom: *Hi sweetie! I'm glad you got there okay! Did you find your dorm? Are the people nice? Have you eaten yet?*

Dad: *Simone stop bombarding the boy*

Dad: *but actually are you good? We love you honey*

Howard and Simone Prescott were nothing if not endlessly supportive. I responded, assuring them that I was good and was sorry I'd left so abruptly, and no, the ride hadn't been too bad, and yes, I definitely ate food.

The group chat texts from Matt and Delia, however, were a bit more mixed.

Delia: *HI SKYLER I miss you! You left in such a hurry, you okay?*

Delia: *pls stop taking so long to respond, Matt's been moping for the last two days, it's very sad*

Matt: *NO I HAVENT SHUT UP*

Matt: *hi skyler im here too, unlike you*

Matt: *bon voyage and sayonara I guess*

And then there were my brother's private texts, sent from earlier today when I'd been deep in crappy wi-fi land. Each one sent an all-too-familiar roll of nausea through me.

Matt: *text me when you get there so I know you're alive*

Matt: *You really didn't need to go out of state if you didn't want to hang out with me for college ok*

Matt: *just say you hate me, rip it off like a band-aid*

My stomach clenched, and I struggled for a reply. Finally, like a coward, I sent a GIF to the group chat to let them know I was alive, but that was it.

The sun had set, and what little of my remaining energy had sunk with it. I decided to pass on a shower and simply lose consciousness. Maybe when I woke up, all my decisions would make sense.

5
LUCAS MEETS A HANDSOME STRANGER

July 16th

The mystery roommate was nowhere to be seen in the morning. It would likely be too presumptuous to text him using the number the leasing office had provided me in our paperwork, so I scribbled a note on a piece of stationery and stuck it to the fridge.

Since this *Armand Demetrio* person was still asleep—at seven o'clock, what, was he going to just waste the day away?—or out of the house, I figured I might as well drive over to work and see Mom. She'd insisted I could take the day off on account of the jetlag—I'd reminded her that Vancouver and California were in the same time zone, but this hadn't seemed to deter her—but Darren hadn't texted back yet, so it was far preferable to keep busy.

And I missed the horses.

The End is Neigh Senior Horse Sanctuary was a sight for sore eyes as I pulled up to the ranch at the edge of my mother's property. Truly amazing how the smell of hay and horse poop took me back to childhood in a hot second. I headed toward the stables, carefully avoiding a fresh pile of said poop. Several of the horses were out and about, likely providing a gentle petting session for a group of summer-camp children, but there was one horse in particular who I wanted to see.

In the stall at the end was Milkshake, the old geezer himself. We had started calling our favorite French Trotter *Grandpa* Milkshake when he turned thirty, and the name had stuck. He was resting, unnervingly still, his sickly body hunched in on itself in the corner.

His once vibrant black coat had long since faded into a softer gray and had thinned considerably: a far cry from the thick gloss of his racing days.

"Hey, buddy," I said, unlatching the stall door and gently stroking his side. "How you holding up? Did they take you for a walk yet?"

It wouldn't hurt for him to take another one—one of the most important things we liked to tell our ranch hands was that for older horses, daily exercise was an essential element of care. I led Grandpa Milkshake at his slow pace outside to a corner of the arena not occupied by the gaggle of visiting children.

We'd just done some longeing when—

"I thought I told you to take the day off."

Cheyenne Barclay, founder of The End is Neigh herself, had made her way down from the family estate in a full face of makeup in order to welcome me home. Her blonde hair glinted in the afternoon sun.

"Yes, and I ignored you," I said with a grin, letting Grandpa Milkshake rest as I pulled her into a hug.

She squeezed me tight around the middle. "How was the wedding? I wish I could've made it. I hope everyone wasn't too disappointed."

"Mother dear, they were positively bereft. You should be ashamed of yourself," I joked. "No, it was gorgeous—Marla looked amazing, Uncle Peter says hi, Sofi and Stefi made a scene at the reception, but what else is new."

Mom cackled. "I hope you got pictures."

"Oh, I certainly did. I'll send them to you. *After* I put them up on FotoBom."

She patted Grandpa Milkshake's nose, surreptitiously checking his breathing. "And you're all set up in your new place? I really hope you're not living with an axe murderer."

It wasn't like I could dispute the idea. The day was still young. "I haven't met him yet—the housing office gave me his name and, like, the *bare* minimum of info. Here—" I pulled out my phone, where the webpage I had found earlier was still open. A quick google search of *Armand Demetrio* had brought up a link to the Drawn & Quartered Comic Convention happening in August. The only photo they'd provided was a low-res, blurry piece of business that told me practically nothing about this guy. There was a mop of dark hair and a vaguely spooked expression, but the rest was pixels. "Look at this." I handed her my phone. "Look at the state of this photo—what did they even shoot this with, a potato? None of the other photos are like this. Can he not be captured on camera or something?"

Mom studied the photo thoughtfully. "Maybe you're rooming with Mothman."

"I wish I didn't *have* to room with Mothman." I sighed. "I'm glad I found a place at the last minute, but . . ."

"But you wanted to move in with Darren," she finished with a tight smile—the kind that, much like Rick and Andie did, she always wore when talking and Having Opinions about my relationship. "Sweetie, listen, you know how I feel about Darren. I'm happy you're happy, but—"

"It's too fast, I know. But he's getting there." It was a good thing my new lease was month-to-month, because the second Darren came to his senses, I was *gone*. "He's got a lot on his mind right now."

"Mm," said my mother, and didn't elaborate. "When I was your age, I wasn't thinking about settling down with anyone; I was wining and dining my way across Europe. I still think a proper vacation would do you some good."

"Darren wouldn't be able to take the time off work," I reminded her.

She held up her hands in temporary surrender.

We guided Grandpa Milkshake back to the stable to rest. My body was tense from the weight of Mom's quiet judgment, which was rolling off her in waves.

"I'm going to take Dakota for a ride," I said, crossing to the other side of the stable where my own horse, Dakota—younger than her retired elders but old enough to have been with me through my entire adolescence of equestrian lessons—nickered excitedly as I approached. Mom and I covered safer topics as I groomed and tacked Dakota, luring me into a false sense of security.

"You know," Mom said as I started leading Dakota out of the stable, "we still need new photos for the website, new models . . ." She flashed me a pointed smile. "If you don't think your pretty face expertly grooming a pretty horse will attract *exponential* amounts of site traffic and encourage people to donate—"

"What? Sorry, can't hear you, you're breaking up," I called back as I rushed to step into Dakota's saddle and trotted her to the arena.

It wasn't Mom's first attempt to convince me to pose for pictures for the sake of our fundraising website, and it wouldn't be her last. I'd given up explaining to her that I wasn't about to plaster my face all over the internet for people to pick apart my numerous flaws: my shirt wasn't even fitted, I was still bloated from a week of vacation, and cameras added ten pounds—

No, thank you.

I urged Dakota into a canter, focusing instead on the burst of adrenaline from the running high.

I stayed at the sanctuary until lunch and helped around the ranch. Mom was clearly thinking about catching her second wind by then, either about Darren or about modeling, so I made my goodbye quick as I hopped in my car smelling decidedly of horse.

I should've gone straight home—or rather, to my temporary apartment—but I really wanted to swing by my usual café-bakery to pick up my custom coffee blend for tomorrow morning. Vegan bakeries were a dime a dozen for miles in any direction, but Latte for Work was always open, mostly for the college crowd.

As expected, the place was packed with students spending their afternoon engulfed in the delicious aroma of French roast and baked goods. That wasn't unusual. What *was* unusual was a young man in the corner.

He looked about the age of the average patron, maybe just out of high school or early college. He was holed up in the corner booth—a coveted position especially during the busy hours—a laptop open in front of him that he very much wasn't using. I paid for my coffee beans and turned back to the booth, and the boy hadn't moved a single inch. His eyes were unfocused, staring off into the middle distance. Was he even breathing?

I was familiar enough with silent panic attacks that I had to check.

"Hey," I said, as gently as I could, stepping next to the booth. "Are you okay?"

For a split second the boy didn't react, which was concerning. But then he seemed to snap out of his reverie, his eyes—wide and blue but bloodshot, had he been crying?—focused up at me.

"What?" he asked, in a voice that suggested he'd temporarily forgotten where he was.

I gestured to his neglected computer and the untouched drink beside him. "I didn't mean to bother you, but I saw you sitting over here looking a little out of it, and I wanted to see if you're okay?"

"Oh, um." He glanced down at the computer. "Yeah, I'm fine, I'm good. I was . . . you know, having an existential crisis. Figured I may as well eat a donut while I'm at it."

There was only a drink on the table, not even a plate or napkin to suggest there'd been any food present. "You . . . don't *have* a donut?"

He stared at the table and sighed, his head falling to his chest. "Knew I forgot something."

I didn't normally sit with strangers at a cafe, especially when I needed to get home and shower, but I couldn't leave this poor kid— up close it was clear that he was pale, probably sleep-deprived, and judging from the intended donut, maybe starving?

"I know all about the good ol' existential crisis," I said cheerfully as I sank down across from him. "The good news is you're still young—once you're over here at the ripe old age of twenty-five, you start feeling like maybe life is getting away from you a bit."

He blinked. "The getting-away-from-me part worked well enough," he said, rolling his neck and resting his head against the back of the booth. "Thought I could do the whole adulting thing, and yet. Here we are."

"Here we are. So you're, what, going to school around here?" I nearly slapped myself. "Sorry, I'm Lucas, by the way; should've led with that."

He gave me a serious little nod, shocks of wavy black hair cresting his forehead. "Skyler. Evans. Yeah, I signed up for summer classes at Norsemen."

Ah, the old alma mater. "Okay, moved to California for school, classic." I shot him another friendly grin. "You have family here?"

Skyler shook his head slowly, giving me a thin, close-lipped smile. "Nope. My family's back in Washington. Where I could be right now instead of sitting in the corner of a vegan bakery in California wondering if I've completely lost my mind."

Intuition sparked in my brain. College wasn't so long ago that I couldn't remember how hard it had been at that age. How overwhelming everything was. "Family can be complicated."

He gave a soft but slightly edged laugh. "Yeah, my brother's really mad at me for leaving." He shrugged helplessly. "And now I'm here, oversharing, and I'm kinda freaking out—"

No friends, no family around . . . and he just looked *so sad*.

You know what helps sad people? Petting horses. And you know what helps me get my mother off my back?

I slid my phone over to him, displaying our website. "My mom and I run a sanctuary for old and retired horses. We do tours, educational visits. Kids come to pet horses who won't snap at them . . ."

Skyler's eyebrows shot up as he scrolled. "The End is Neigh?"

"Yeah, it's morbid, but that's Mom for you. But my *point* is that I have access to very cute animals who like being petted if you wanted to pet some cute animals. Unrelated, but we've been needing to update the website with shots of people working with the horses. I took the photos you see there, which turned out great, but we need someone to be the go-to model. Everyone wants to give good-looking people money. And I'm not especially photogenic."

Skyler's perfectly symmetrical face furrowed in confusion. "Sorry, what does this have to do with me?"

"It has to do with you because you said you were sad and freaking out about being lonely, and horses help people not be sad. And honestly I need someone with a pretty face who can pose with horses." I grinned at him. "Tell me you wouldn't love to hang around with old horses."

"Oh, absolutely, it's the dream," Skyler said in a perfect deadpan.

"How about you think it over?" I handed him my business card. "Have a sleep on it, and let me know. I'm in here all the time, but I'm also embarrassingly accessible on my phone, so. Options."

Skyler was still staring down at the card. "So, just making sure this conversation is actually happening and that you exist and you're here and offering me a horse-related modeling job? Because I'm working on maybe three hours of sleep and I may have started stress-hallucinating about an hour ago."

"I mean, who's to say if any of us really exist?" I joked. "But yes, I'm extremely serious." I reclaimed my phone and stood up. "You'd be saving my ass from a well-meaning but slightly misguided maternal figure here."

Skyler nodded, then as I turned to leave— "Lucas?"

"Yeah?"

He swallowed. He was still pale, but some color had returned to his cheeks, making those cheekbones pop. "Thank you. For offering me horses, and for . . . checking in on me."

"I couldn't very well not. Your entire vibe is extremely concerning, I could sense it a mile away."

His shoulders slumped in despair. "That's not good."

"Hey"—I pointed down at him playfully—"horses. But even if you decide not to, no worries. Though I wouldn't be mad if you, like, wanted to text tomorrow to reassure me that you're alive and that the void hasn't swallowed you."

And Skyler smiled—still soft but more open and unguarded this time. "If the void has cell service, I'll let you know. Thanks."

There was something so achingly genuine about Skyler Evans that, as I left him in the café to return to my car, it made me feel like a mama bird who had abandoned her child. Right as I fought the urge to go back and check on him one more time, my phone buzzed in my pocket. Had Skyler texted me already?

Darren: *hey you, come over, I have a surprise ;)*

I couldn't help a grin, my stomach erupting with butterflies. Maybe Darren was coming to his senses after all.

6
ARMAND NOTICES HIS SURROUNDINGS

July 16th - Thirty days until the convention

I woke slowly, my eyelids unsticking in sections and my body lying numb and inaccessible. Eventually, feeling returned to my extremities, beginning, unfortunately, with a cramp in my left calf. I surged to my feet and tried walking it out, cursing and whimpering under my breath.

The muscles finally eased into a nonexcruciating position, and I stood leaning against the door of the cupboard and shaking my leg angrily. I'd kicked off my shoes and jeans the night before. Or, come to think of it, the early afternoon before . . .

I glanced hazily at my watch: only 2 p.m.—that was quite early for me, most days. I dug the heels of my hands into my eye sockets in an attempt to force my brain to wake up. There was work to be done. Pages that needed to be penciled cried out from the depth of my carry-on. After all, Deconstructionist Monochrome Blah Blah Something Comics didn't draw themselves.

I was meant to have sent in these pages before fleeing the commonwealth, but I wasn't yet used to deadlines being handed down from on-high.

Surrogate Goose had been a passion project for so long that the idea that an international publisher like Drake House had picked up the bloody mindless drivel that was my brainchild felt like an elaborate prank. There were times, usually between two and six in the morning, when I convinced myself that I had fabricated the entire success of my comic. That I was still working my old soul-sucking dancing job to finance the self-publishing, and this was all a sad, drug-fueled dream.

As if she could sense the aquifers of my self-pity threatening to swell, Lakshmi chose that moment to send me a series of vaguely threatening emojis: an airplane, a small fire, and a question mark.

I answered with a voice message: "I live. Unfortunately."

Lakshmi: *Yes you do*

This was immediately followed by a sleepy voice message, the murmur of late-night television in the background. "Are you ready to take America by storm, pet?"

That was an easy question. "No."

Her response was just as fast: "Do it anyway, you wonk. Night."

That was her answer to everything: *Do it anyway.* And the worst part was that it often worked. Lakshmi was the one who'd somehow reorganized the known universe into a place where *Surrogate Goose* was something I could live on. She'd sent me to indie publishers at first, then booked me for conventions and comic shop signings. I'd even appeared briefly on a morning program and been recognized in a pub once. It had been three grueling years before Drake House noticed us, and like the anonymous, newly vehicular gourd plucked from obscurity that I was, Lakshmi had every intention of riding me to the ball.

This was our chance. *My* chance.

I was already hobbling myself by refusing to sell the rights to *Surrogate Goose*, to let some team of wankers turn it into a film or breakfast cereal or whatever.

"We've got to prove you're worth the investment," Lakshmi'd told me. *"Not me, not the comic, you."*

"But Lakshmi, what if this goes the way of Leeds?"

Early during our Drake House run, I'd been interviewed for some nerdy radio segment. I'd been my terrified, monosyllabic self and had spent the whole time fighting the urge to hang up or pretend I was going through a tunnel.

"It won't," she'd said with entirely unearned confidence.

The House had signed us for a year, and it was nearly up. Contract renegotiations and all manner of things which I would not, *could* not understand, were making Lakshmi nervous. As she'd explained it to me, Drake House was ready to make a larger commitment to the comic and myself. But they needed me to prove I was worth it. The big test was going to be the Drawn & Quartered Comic Convention at the end of the summer. They wanted me to *speak*, show my face, be . . . marketable on a global scale. I needed to be a brand: not just the creator of *Surrogate Goose*, but its avatar.

Being somewhat known in Great Britain or even Europe was uncomfortable and I was wholly unsuited to it.

The concept of American Celebrity all but caused me to lose control of my bowels.

But if I didn't show Drake House that I was capable of human interaction, of being *a personality*, they'd drop us. They wouldn't renew my contract, Lakshmi would lose the biggest deal of her career, and for me it would be back to the indie cons, soul-sucking day jobs, and life as a pumpkin.

A shower would help. A shower was necessary and probably mandatory for inclusion in the species at this point.

I yanked my shirt over my head, remembering to check the coast for flatmates before wandering out in my pants. Confident that I was indeed alone, I padded down the hall and into the toilet, and only once I was standing under the warm torrent of water did I realize that I'd forgotten the tiny bottle of shampoo in my travel bag.

Across from me, however, appeared to be an impressive selection of hair products, all nestled in a wire holder that adhered to the shower wall through the ingenious use of suction cups. There were three shampoos, two conditioners, and a variety of other things far surpassing my comprehension.

I wrestled with my conscience for a moment, then stole a small dollop of the most generic shampoo I could identify. As I kneaded it into my scalp, my brain informed me that the bathroom products were not the only additions to the décor I had missed. I tried to visualize the walk from my bedroom, and sure enough, the memory was suffused with a sense of . . . *pink*. Nothing had actually *been* pink, I was quite certain, but there had been enough pink-like things to produce the effect. And a smell . . . *lilac*?

I rinsed the soap out of my hair and off my body with the intent to dry off and investigate, when it turned out that along with my shampoo, I'd forgotten to grab a towel. I stifled a groan and then checked to see if the disturbingly well-prepared flatmate had provided, which indeed they had. There were two hand towels hanging in their little plastic rings by the sink.

With some difficulty, I dried myself off and even managed to wrap the larger of the two slightly more than three quarters of the way around my waist. Clutching it in place with one hand, hair still dripping, I set out to explore the transformation the flat had undergone while I slept.

There were pictures on the walls and flowers in the windows. Surfaces gleamed, and there was a small *tree* growing out of a wicker basket by the door. The pictures were mainly of horses: grazing, rearing, leaping, or simply posing in the sunlight.

Waking up inside a *House & Garden* was doing a number on my head. I was troubled by the terrible accoutrements of bourgeoisie that surrounded me, but I was more troubled by their source. Although the temperature was quite comfortable, I shivered, trying to imagine the sort of person who would be quite so fond of horses and feel the need for this many flower vases.

I made my way over to the fridge—it was already adorned with a whiteboard, what appeared to be several postcards from Paris, and three different magnets in the shapes of, yes, horses. One of them was a unicorn. I shook my head to try to clear it and opened the fridge.

It was even scarier in there.

Nothing but green leaves, fruit, and what I could only call *ingredients*. As opposed to food.

Whoever they were, they didn't just clean—they cooked as well. I was rooming with the ghost of Martha Stewart. A health-conscious Martha Stewart. A terrifyingly domestic creature of unknown origin. My mind was immediately filled with the image of a large white rabbit in an apron. Without being fully aware of what I was doing, I began sketching that image onto the whiteboard.

Somewhere in the kilo or so of paperwork I'd been handed there was surely information to be had regarding this person, but I'd barely reconciled with the idea of having a flatmate, let alone allowing them to transcend the abstract and become an individual.

It had been one thing to *travel*. One thing to carry my personal bubble of solitude across an ocean, brushing up with the personal *bulles de solitude* of others in a public space. However, it had been some time since I'd had to share a *living* space with anyone. There'd been a period when circumstances had me sleeping on my mates' couch, but then Lakshmi and success had happened, and with the exception of *events*, I'd spent the past couple of years holed up in my little burrow of a flat, allowing the refuse of my own existence to slowly pile around me—like the low, mysterious, and load-bearing walls of an ancient civilization—in a warm, inevitable smother of an embrace.

I was in no state to be living in close proximity with another human being.

Especially one so invested in an *intentional* living space.

There wasn't a single thing about me that was intentional. There was never a more passive bit of flotsam in the grand river of fate than Yours Truly. The thought of meeting this conscientious person thrummed across my shoulders as a swath of gooseflesh and rose in my throat as a burgeoning lump.

An unfavorable chemical reaction would likely take place should our intensely different lifestyles collide. I wasn't fit for human consumption and I hadn't been for nearly a year now, since my newfound teetotaling existence. I'd set some specific sobriety-related lines for myself, at the start of my torrid romance with Drake House, and so far had managed to abide by them. I was much healthier now, allegedly, but also much less pleasant to be around.

Participating in the outside world without a hearty dose of social lubricant was not exactly my forte. A few get-togethers a month with my couch-owning mates Sam and Craig, and the occasional check-in from my agent Lakshmi, my sponsor Karim, or my father The Arsehole—this had been the extent of my human interaction over the past year. The world had been nicely split in two: *inside* my bubble of solitude and *outside* of it. How was I supposed to adapt to an entire person *inside* my—

"Knock knock!"

I jumped. "What!"

"It's me, Robin, out on the porch! Luncheon, remember?"

What sort of person said *knock knock* instead of knocking? I smoothed damp strands of hair back and out of my face, then barked at the door, "A mo, Titch!"

"A what, *who*?"

I ignored him and hurried into the other room to dress. Potentially judgmental flatmate or no, there was still *outside* to worry about.

7
ROBIN MEETS
AN OLD ENEMY

July 16th

Armand opened the door and made it down the stairs to Camille, where I had to make it clear that there would be no smoking in my car, thank you very much.

I'd thought his strikingly scruffy appearance the other day had been a result of the long flight, but apparently this was just . . . him. Even though he was clearly clean and well-rested, his hair was damp and hanging in shiny un-styled clumps, his clothes were still faded and scuffed, and it appeared that shaving had not been on the agenda this morning.

Once he'd put his cigarette out, I let him in Camille and rolled the windows all the way down. We'd left the parking lot and started toward the Norse-U campus when I turned to grin at him. "Excited?"

He glanced at me sideways, seemed to contemplate the question for a few seconds, then shrugged.

I revised my approach: "Nervous?"

This time it was a glare.

But instead of a shrug, I got a soft and grumbly "Yes," only about five minutes after the question had been asked.

"Well, you shouldn't be." I patted his knee. "You're gonna do great!"

After that, he stopped responding to me, until I'd parked in front of the arts building and walked him toward the lobby. He stopped by the main entrance.

"That'll do, Titch," he rumbled.

I blinked up at him. "You don't want me to come in with you?" God only knew if he could find his way to the right room.

"I'll be all right. You go do . . . whatever it is you do." He clenched a hand in his hair and looked up at the building, squinting in the sunlight. I was very aware of the fact that he was almost a foot taller than me, about a decade older, and obviously much more worldly and experienced than I was, but he looked so lost and alone I wanted to hug him. "Are you sure? I can—"

"I'll see you in class." He fidgeted for a moment. "Later this evening?"

I nodded. "And I'm supposed to drive you home."

"See you then, Titch." He smiled at me, actually smiled, and headed inside.

What the hell did *Titch* even mean?

I took a deep breath and looked out over campus, trying to figure out what to do with the hours I hadn't expected to have free. Eventually, I decided to cut toward the theater building, see if there was anyone there and if they wanted to hang out. I needed to start doing more to maintain relationships now that I was officially a prima donna, lest I lose all my friends to the green-eyed monster.

After spending my entire freshman year in the chorus, I'd finally won out over sixteen other hopeful and starry-eyed auditionees. I'd proved myself the starry-eyed-est! I was going to play Peter Pan in *The Shadow of Never*—a *Peter Pan* retelling penned by Visiting Scholar Someone Or Other in Norsemen's very own English Department. It was a dark, raw, *whimsical* reimagining of Neverland where Captain Hook was a disillusioned, thirties-something barista with a failed startup; Wendy Darling was a beautiful young Zumba instructor; and Peter Pan was *actually* Hook's younger self who'd traveled through time to try to convince himself to never grow up. Or something. I'd read the script a bunch of times now, and I still wasn't entirely sure what was going on.

But that didn't matter. What *mattered* was that I'd earned the right to be a diva, so now was the time, more than ever, to remind the Little People that I still remembered what it was like to be among them.

I cut through the quad, then around the corner of the music school to the front plaza of the theater—

And froze.

Terri Bishop was lounging across the steps.

Terri Bishop, who I hadn't seen in over a year.

Terri Bishop, who was supposed to be three thousand miles away, going to an elite East Coast school and hobnobbing with other like-minded psychopaths.

But no, here he was. And so were Mason Harris, Glenn Olson, and two other young bucks I didn't know and who would henceforth be referred to as Frat Boys Beta and Gamma. They all appeared to be engaged in filming something—Terri was talking into the phone held by Mason. But he stopped when he caught sight of me, and his eyes widened.

The entire contents of my torso slithered into my kneecaps. I was frozen to the spot.

I should run; I should just turn around and ru—

"FLINCH!!" Terri roared and sprang to his feet, moving toward me like the inevitability of death. I'd never understood how someone so big and so muscular could also be so *fast*; before I managed to move, he had an arm wrapped around my shoulders and a good grip on my collar. He twisted and pulled back, tightening the fabric against my throat in a subtle but extremely effective way.

"Guys, do you realize who this is?" said the voice from my nightmares. Terri was grinning, and Mason was still holding the phone up.

"Who?" asked one of the unnamed frat boys. "Clifford the Little Red Bitch?"

Terri's laugh was loud enough to draw the attention of the other groups hanging around the theater plaza—it had good shade and seating, so people camped out here between classes.

"No, man, this is *Flinch*, my *boy*!" Terri shook me, untwisting my collar slightly so I could gulp in air.

The smell of Terri's aftershave washed over me, and for a second it felt like I was going to throw up so hard my head would explode, but then the dissociation wrapped me back up in its sweet, gentle embrace.

I seemed to float out of my body, watching what happened next from behind a protective film. I could feel the pain and the fear but the same way you can still feel a headache after painkillers. Everything that was happening was happening to a version of myself who was empty.

I was somewhere else. Somewhere safe.

From that place of safety, I heard Terri explaining to the others who I was, that I was hilarious, that you could get me to do *anything*.

"Yeah," Mason, who had gone to high school with us, added, "Terri's made Flinch do stuff you wouldn't *believe*!"

This was not entirely true. It was all believable, and straight out of the handy-dandy high-school bully handbook. Like the time he'd made me chug mustard, or lick a bathroom floor, or shaved my eyebrows. To be fair, Mason had needed to hold me down for that one.

Terri and I had been in school together since our freshman year, and he'd made a career out of making my life hell.

But that was supposed to have ended when we graduated. We'd gone our separate ways: me to the local theater department to be a bright, young star, and him to the cutthroat world of pre-law with the other sociopaths. I hadn't had to think about him for more than a year.

What was he doing *here*?

"Check it out."

I hadn't even realized that Glenn had taken my messenger bag, and now he was riffling through it, pulling out—

My script.

Terri hissed deep in his throat, "Damn, still at it, huh?"

There was a moment of reprieve in which Terri handed me over to Frat Boy Gamma and stepped forward to take my script from Glenn. It had already been removed from its plastic page guard, and he leafed through it in evident disbelief. Frat Boy Gamma's chokehold technique left something to be desired compared to Terri's, so I managed to suck in enough air to keep from passing out. People around us were still watching, but no one was intervening— presumably it looked like horseplay between friends. Terri had become a freaking *artist* when it came to making a beat-down look like clowning.

"Once a diva, always a diva, eh Flinch?"

Flinch was the ingenious nickname Terri had invented for me the first week of high school, and *diva* meant something very different when he said it as opposed to when I called myself that out of pride.

Because I had a lead part.

Terri tore the cover page off my script book and crushed it into a ball. He smiled at me. "Open your mouth, Flinch."

It never helped to fight back—my best bet was to stay quiet and small and hope he got bored of me soon. Shove the pain and humiliation as deep into the corners of my mind as they would go and focus on, despite everything, continuing to exist. I could hear the onlookers laughing, some of them even goading me on like I was in on it—letting Terri see how many pages I could fit into my mouth before I choked.

This part of my life was supposed to be over. Terri Bishop wasn't supposed to be *here*.

This didn't happen to leading man ingénue heroes. This happened to the kind of person I didn't want to *be* anymore—a sad, bullied theater kid and disposable extra.

I kept my eyes closed, letting the laughter wash over me like waves. I was safe at the bottom of a deep, dark ocean.

8

ARMAND IS CAPABLE OF HUMAN INTERACTION

July 16th - (Still) Thirty days until the convention

I stepped away from the glass entryway, found a secluded corner of the lavatories, and attempted to slowly cram my fist into my mouth.

Nervous was to an understatement what Stalin was to the description *bit of a dick.*

I closed my eyes and took deep breaths through my nose, trying to discourage my heart from its current velocity. I did not do well with figures of authority, and I was about to meet with a whole lot of them who planned to temporarily induct me into their ranks.

I should've shaved. Maybe got a haircut . . .

. . . Finished university.

Moment of truth, Demetrio, gird your fucking loins.

I was far too sober for this. That was what it came down to. The world was rushing at me at an unprecedented pace, and I'd been left exposed, unprotected, with nothing between myself and the yawning void. Luckily, there awaited a tastefully sized bottle of Sonoma Bourbon Whiskey among the chocolates and fruits I'd found in the welcome basket the day before, which was, at this stage, the only bright point in my future.

I'd wrestled with my conscience—after all, I'd worked hard this past year to get as clean as I was—but there was only so much that could be expected of a man. It was one thing to face an empty flat while sober, quite another to *perform* without at least the promise of relief down the line. I just had to make it through the luncheon, and then the introductory class later that evening, then I could reward myself with a little numbness.

Once I'd got myself in hand, I found the correct conference room for the luncheon and was given a folder full of papers by a frighteningly blonde woman, who told me to enjoy the buffet. I sat down at the large round table and glanced around, wondering which of the people in it could tell that I still wasn't capable of doing maths without a computer and wasn't entirely confident of the meaning of *Deconstructionist*.

There were eight of them, all over forty and dressed casually but well. Most of them were raiding the aforementioned buffet; one woman, however, was seated across the table, smiling alternately at me and at— Oh bloody hell, last month's issue of *Surrogate Goose*.

My collar grew hot.

Watching people read my work always made me feel as if I were standing naked in the middle of a crowded room; I had to fight the urge to grab it from her hand and bolt out the door. Instead, I managed a grimacey little smile the next time she looked up, and she beamed.

"I love the new storyline." She leaned forward, the beads on her glasses' chain clinking softly against the table. "A bit *racy*, isn't it?"

I swallowed hard, but mercifully wasn't made to answer as the remainder of the board, or panel, faculty . . . whatever they were, finished their grazing and took their seats. After a few introductory statements in which I was warmly welcomed, interspersed with chewing noises, a bearded man wearing a *Tanglewood* sweatshirt told me not to worry about teaching.

"People aren't coming to this workshop to learn how to draw." He gave me a Father Christmas smile, eyes disappearing behind folds of happy cheeks. "They're coming to learn how to draw from *you*! All you have to do is be yourself, and they'll be getting their money's worth."

I nodded brokenly.

"Your agent, Ms. Ranjit, informed us that you may have a few . . . hang-ups"—this was from a much less kind-looking man in matching polo shirt and toupee—"about speaking to the class. Some anxiety issues, I gather?"

If I'd been blushing a minute ago, I was now in danger of permanently bruising my cheeks. It might come as a surprise, but

I *have*, in fact, spoken in public before, and aye, all right, I get a bit nervous, but I wasn't in the habit of pulling an A.J. Rimmer and claiming that I was, in fact, a fish. Well, not yet anyway. Still, Lakshmi had always been conscientious about limiting my performance in front of a microphone to a few well-rehearsed soundbites. Until now. "I th-think I'll b-be fine." I swallowed again. "I've b-been practicing a-and, er . . ." I used both hands to push my hair out of my face, "I've g-gotten better."

Polo-Toupee smiled thinly, but Father-Christmas-*Tanglewood* reached over and thumped me twice on the shoulder. "That's the spirit! You'll be fantastic, kiddo!"

I did my best to smile at him, but then Beaded-Glasses-Chain pointed to the schedule in my folder.

"The first class this evening is just the introductory portion," she said, "so don't feel too pressured to showcase your best work. Take it as easy as you like. You've got a whole month."

"Don't worry, we've worked with plenty of Drake House artists. This is an easy gig: fans pay money, the school *makes* money, *you* make money, everyone's happy!" Father Christmas-*Tanglewood* patted my shoulder again. "Easy as pie."

The rest of the meeting was a lot of talk about "the enterprising culture of Norsemen," which mainly involved, as far as I could gather, an innate understanding of what phrases like *enterprising culture* meant. I was turned loose with an hour or so of free time, and I spent it worrying myself sick.

There was half an hour to go before the introductory class began, and I was back in the men's, trying to avoid my own gaze in the mirror and waiting for a call to go through.

"Did I not say I was going to bed? Do you know what bloody time it is?"

"Yes, I do, I'm still jet-lagged. Lakshmi, did you tell people I have anxiety?"

She'd turned her camera on, but it was dark. There were a few moments of silence on the other line, then, "Armand, pet, you *do* have—"

"I do not! I get a bit nervous—"

"And tetchy."

"—and *tetchy*, but these people seem to think I'm some sort of . . . sort of . . ."

"Artist?"

It was my turn for a few moments of silence. Angry silence. "Lakshmi, I am capable of human interaction," I growled, finally.

"I know, that's why I got you this job. *I* know you can teach a month-long workshop to a load of Californian children. The House thinks so too." I heard the soft *click*s she lit her cigarette with an old Bic lighter, and for a moment her sharp features appeared outlined in gold. "You're the only one with apparent compunctions on the issue. But think of it this way. Teaching will be great practice for the con." Her eyes, glinting in the red cigarette light, narrowed. "Have you eaten anything today? Mind you, whiskey doesn't count."

Lucky guess.

I took a deep breath and then let it out slowly, leaning my head back against the tiles. "Am I going to make an arse of myself?"

"Probably not. You didn't answer my question." I heard her take a long drag of her cigarette, saw the ruby flare, and instantly began to crave one horribly.

I glanced at my watch—plenty of time for a nip outside for a nicotine fix before the execution. "I attended a luncheon. People were nice at me. I got the feeling you told them I might take off all my clothes and run around singing 'Don't Rain on My Parade' at the top of my lungs."

"That was a selling point." She appeared to hear my scowl over the phone, and said in a reconciliatory tone, "I'm aware that you don't like to think of yourself as a diva, Demetrio, but that whole temperamental-artist shtick really sells in America. Remember what the product is."

"Me."

"Achcha. Just remember to breathe."

After about half a pack and a cold drink of water, I made my way to the classroom; it was already half-full, and Robin was sat in one of the upper rows. He looked somewhat disheveled and a little pale, which was concerning, but he waved at me enthusiastically. I gave him a brief nod and busied myself setting up my slides—which were just the text of the syllabus blown up. By the time I'd won my battle with the computer, the rest of the class had come in and taken their seats, their whispering making a soft and terrifying sound reminiscent of the ocean.

I looked up, and silence fell.

Clearing my throat, I stepped out from behind the podium, managing to do so without falling or knocking anything over.

"Hullo, er, my name is Armand Demetrio. I—" I had to battle a blush for a few moments while they applauded. "I, er, thank you, that's—that's sweet. Erm, what I'm here to say, er, is you don't actually need to know how to draw to make comics. It's not a strict requirement, you know, for your message, whatever it is, but we're gonna learn that, because it's nice to have under your belt—that is, it's better to have . . . that tool. Erm. Than to *not* have it."

I was suddenly confronted with the complete certainty that my zipper was down.

My hand flew to my waist but found all was fully zipped. I breathed a sigh of relief and tried to remember what I'd been talking about.

"I'm not going to teach you how to draw; there are much better places to learn that and p-people to learn from. What I *can* teach you, I *hope*, is quite hard to put into words. Evidently. I-I know this workshop has a bloody complicated name and all, but essentially, I think I'm supposed to show you . . . how I do what I do. Er. Part of that *is* drawing, aye, and we'll do that, but some of it is storytelling and layout and things, so—" It was down, my zipper was down.

I checked, and once again nearly slumped in relief.

"I'm also not going to teach you how to make my comic because, heh, that would be daft, wouldn't it? And pointless. I-I'm meant to— I'm going to try to teach you how to recognize those things which— which might *make* a comic, yeah? The bits that make it more than another *Archie Fun Home* rip-off."

The class laughed, and for a moment I thought it was because I'd managed to make a joke, but then I realized it was because my zipper was, indeed, down.

No, it wasn't.

"Erm. So, aye, th-that is what we'll try and figure out, together, in this workshop. It—it shan't be easy—" MY ZIPPER WAS DOWN.

No, it *bloody wasn't*.

"But eventually we'll, you know, separate the sheep from the goats and maybe some of you lot will be, er, *clearer* on what you want to say and how you want to say it." I checked my zipper one more time. And then realized that I'd just touched myself in front of a room full of people at least five times in as many minutes.

I couldn't move.

What had Lakshmi said? *"Breathe, just breathe, Armand."* Oh god, they all must think I'm a pervert.

My vision went blurry for a moment, but I clutched the podium and once again succeeded in not falling over. *Get a grip*, said Lakshmi's voice in my head, *you are capable of human interaction*.

"Errm, so that's, er ... Any questions?"

9

SKYLER FINDS
HIS FOOTING

July 17ᵗʰ

Lucas Barclay had seemed excited to get the text I sent him this morning confirming that yes, I would love to visit his weird dying-horses farm and also could he possibly come pick me up? I didn't start my summer classes until later that day, and Matt's lack of response to my GIF was hanging over my head. I needed something to distract me.

Which, for the moment, was the gigantic black eyes of an arthritic horse who could probably see into my soul.

"So, to be clear," I said, glancing over to Lucas, "you actually get up on one of these guys? Like on their backs? Ten feet in the air?"

He laughed. "Well, most of them not so much—with a few exceptions, like Dakota and Jupiter and Nala over there." He pointed to each horse in their assigned stall. "Our mission here is education for the kiddos and end-of-life care for the horses. A lot of these guys were brought to us from people who couldn't take care of them anymore." He rubbed the enormous side of the horse I'd been introduced to. "They don't have anyone else."

Just like the Prescotts had adopted me. *Didn't think I'd be identifying with a dying horse today, but I guess that's where life has taken me.*

"If you're comfortable . . ." Lucas said, holding up an expensive-looking camera, "a short photo op?" He shot me a bright grin. "I promise I won't make you get on a horse yet."

"In that case, I'm down."

He instructed me where to stand and how to hold the lead. The nice thing about all these horses being as . . . vintage as they were, was that I didn't have to worry about trying to keep them still. This particular elder—Lillybud?—seemed content to chill out here in the pasture, her head gently bumping against mine.

I'd thought I'd be distracted by Lucas circling us and snapping away, but my attention drifted to the acres of grass rippling in the breeze. We were still in the city limits, but somehow this ranch felt isolated and calm. It made sense that Lucas and his mom would open a horse retirement home here. There was such a stillness that didn't exist back home.

I wasn't sure how long I stood there next to Lillybud, both of us just vibing while Lucas did his thing, but finally he walked closer, grinning and holding out his camera.

"You're a natural," he said, angling the screen so I could see the shots he'd taken. "Your face'll make fantastic press."

The photos were really good. There was even a lens flare situation happening that I had no idea how he'd accomplished. "Ah yes, me, the enviable young face of horsepice care."

Lucas gaped at me. "Oh my god. *Horsepice care.* I love it, but do *not* let my mother hear you say that or she'll threaten to rename this place, and we'll have to completely rebrand."

A voice chimed in from behind us. "Don't let your mother hear what?"

We turned to see a petite woman who shockingly resembled Lucas holding out a tray with lemonade glasses on it. She gave me a friendly and intimidatingly immaculate smile. "Are you Skyler? You look like a Skyler."

Lucas handled the introductions. "Mom, this is, in fact, Skyler Evans, whose talent I discovered at a bakery, let it be known. Skyler, my mother, Cheyenne Barclay, matriarch of the ranch. But don't worry, she's harmless."

I'd done some hasty research after meeting with Lucas at the cafe. The Barclay family had been wealthy for generations, dating back to a great-grandparent who had apparently patented a popular brand of canned beef that was still mass produced and sold almost exclusively to poor college kids.

Barclay Beef. Like all the best food, it was disgusting but also *delicious*.

"Nice to meet you, Mrs. Barclay," I said, extending my hand to her. "It's been a really rough last few days, and Lucas has been so nice."

"Nice? *My* Lucas? Can't be, he's a bitch."

Lucas, clearly not offended in the slightest, grinned brightly. "Like my mummy."

Cheyenne ignored her son and grasped my hand. Hard. "A pleasure, Skyler Evans. But call me Cheyenne, because I'm a young, fun mom."

Beside me, Lucas snort-coughed.

"So Skyler," Cheyenne continued, as chipper and friendly as Lucas, "have you had much experience with horses before?"

I glanced at Lillybud, who was still snuffling around my hair. "If by experience you mean that technically I knew they existed in places nowhere near me, then yes, I'm an expert."

Cheyenne stroked Lillybud's neck thoughtfully, surveying me with a critical eye. "Well, Miss Lilly seems like she's a fan. You like 'em?"

"They're sweet," I said, barely able to answer before another elderly horse moseyed my way and nuzzled my shoulder. "Oh. Hi. Who's this?"

Cheyenne and Lucas exchanged a look. "That's Major Bananas," she said. "He's actually one of our more skittish customers. Seems you have a vibe they really respect. Getting a horse to trust you isn't always as easy as it seems." She had another silent conversation with her son about my apparent horse-whisperer superpower, then said: "You're welcome to come hang out after your classes; we could always use an extra hand. Especially when that hand's connected to a young horse prodigy such as yourself."

I didn't realize I was staring in surprise until Major Bananas gently drenched my shoulder in drool. I'd just be sitting in my dorm room when not in class, which wouldn't be conducive to avoiding a guilty, existential crisis. This would give me something to do, and people—and horses—to do it with. "Oh my god, yes, thank you? What would you need from me?"

Lucas jumped in, face alight with excitement. "Petting, which you already have down. But there'd be a bit of heavy lifting occasionally, keeping up with their feedings and you know. Scooping some poop. I can walk you through it—if I can do it, you can certainly do it."

"I find *that* hard to believe, but sure." I hurried to add. "I know Lucas finding me dissociating in a coffee shop doesn't make me seem super stable, but I promise you can count on me. I'm a fast learner and I like trying new things."

New things, like moving to a new state by myself for reasons that I'd never explain. I was a lying liar who lies.

"Heh. *Stable*." Cheyenne grinned. "That's all I'm ever hoping for. Welcome to the family." She brushed a strand of blonde hair off her forehead with her pinkie. "Horse puns are currency in these parts, and laughing your way through a tough time is an important life skill. You know why we take in horses here, Skyler?"

My eyes fell back to the stable of old, discarded horses sadly withering away. "Because you feel sorry for them?"

"Because," Lucas said, unleashing another warm smile that should've been unnerving but was actually incredibly comforting, "whether it's people or horses, everyone goes through rough patches sometimes. And we want to help."

I refused to cry in front of people (and horses) I'd only just met, but a wave of homesickness rolled over me so hard it hurt. I focused on continuing to cuddle Lillybud and Major Bananas, who had won me over. "Thank you. I promise I'll work really hard here for as long as you let me."

"That's great to hear. Be sure to look after yourself and stay in school, though." Cheyenne winked, and after Lucas declined an invitation to stay for dinner later at the gigantic estate up the hill that was apparently their *house*, he offered to drive me back to campus.

"If it's okay with you," Lucas said as he effortlessly weaved through traffic, "I need to make a stop on the way. I'll make sure you aren't late to class."

"Yeah, of course."

He drove us to another gigantic estate, one that was flanked on either side with elaborate hedges. I blinked to make sure we hadn't time-traveled back to the 1800s.

"Don't tell me this is your weekend house," I managed weakly, mid-gape.

"Oh, god, no, this is my boyfriend Darren's house. I got back from out of town yesterday, and he was holding some things for me that I'm picking up." Lucas twirled a set of keys and grinned. "He finally gave me the key to his place!" He wiggled excitedly in his seat for a moment before popping the doors so we could step outside. "I *told* Mom he'd come around."

"That's cool," I said, bobbing my head in a supportive nod and not sure how else I was meant to respond. "Congrats."

I followed Lucas as we made our way up the front walk. I wanted to ask if Darren lived in this enormous mansion by himself, but I was afraid that Lucas would say yes. We stepped into an entirely monochrome foyer and then into an equally monochrome kitchen. Atop a gray counter was a fish tank.

"Hey, guys," Lucas addressed the two fish circling the underwater castle. "Did you miss me? Did Darren take good care of you?"

I examined the little guys swimming leisurely. "Now *this* is the appropriate pet size—I don't have to worry that these guys can kill me."

Lucas sniffed. "Our horses are not pets. Also we've already established that you're Horse Jesus, so don't even pretend like you don't have The Gift. But *also* also, if you were worried about being murdered by tiny fish, I think you'd have bigger problems." He grinned. "This betta," he pointed to the more colorful fish, "is Gaston. Very fitting, as he's flashy and flamboyant. Which means that this little guppy"—indicating the other, duller-colored fish—"of course, is LeFou."

"*Nice.*" It certainly looked like a LeFou. I waved a finger at the little guys, hoping Lucas wouldn't need me to feed them.

After I'd been given advice on how to lift the tank in a way that wouldn't murder the unsuspecting fish, Lucas and I carefully maneuvered Gaston and LeFou outside to the car. We successfully transported them in one (two) pieces to Lucas's new apartment, and after making sure the fish were settled, Lucas drove me back to campus. It was an hour later, once I was heading to class and away from the safety of Lucas's mother-hen energy, that Matt finally texted me back.

Matt: *glad you're not dead*

Matt: *but just know that I'm writing a think-piece as we speak about why Washington is better than California, expect it in your inbox*

Matt: *not that you'd read that EITHER while you're out shopping for a new brother*

My breath hitched the longer I stared at his texts, trying to figure out his tone. Dread crept under my skin. Deciding to play along, I changed the subject:

Skyler: *I can't speak much for California as a state, but I met a photographer who's also kind of a cowboy who offered me a part-time job, so that was nice*

Another text popped in, but in the group chat this time. And it was Delia.

Delia: *um exqueeze me hello matt just said you were a cowboy now so pls spill*

Skyler: *Matthew has misinterpreted the situation, I am not a cowboy*

Skyler: *I am a model. Who has a proximity to horses. But also doing ranch work. It's a whole thing*

It was the most I'd spoken to her since . . . since I'd left. It was so easy to fall back into our rapport; I could see her perched on the corner of the couch, stroking Matt's hair as we watched a film to make fun of—

I wanted to ask how she was doing, how her latest painting was shaping up. But my throat burned, and my fingers were frozen.

Delia: *EXPLAIN RIGHT NOW*

Skyler: *I would but I gotta get to class, first day, ttyl*

Matt: *wow less than a week there and you're already snatching jobs and nabbing friends, sooo happy for you*

Matt: *do good school with whatever it is you decided to study over there*

He was furious.

I was contemplating how to respond when Delia private-messaged me.

Delia: *hey I know he was kind of bitchy a minute ago but I wanted to make sure you know we are both really proud of you for doing what you want to do, okay? Even if it's in California. We just miss you and I haven't forgotten that you owe me $20 from our last poker match, ignore at your own risk*

Delia: *go to class, I love you!*

I stared at her message long enough that the screen went fuzzy, before:

Skyler: *love you too.*

10
ROBIN AVOIDS HIS PROBLEMS

July 17th

Getting out of bed was hard, but I did it, and even made it all the way to rehearsal. Fortunately, it was a wire-work day, which was mostly for the benefit of the tech-crew and didn't actually require much from me. At least, intellectually.

"Loosen up!" Maggie, our set designer, assistant manager, jack-of-all-trades and also my friend, yelled at me from down below. "We're trying to make this look *fluid*!"

I tried. But I couldn't. My entire body was clenched around the idea that Terri was back, and the nightmare of high school was happening again.

Less than an hour spent on social media last night had produced the factual pearl that Terri had officially transferred to Norse-U. He'd been straight-up kicked out of his prestigious East Coast pre-law program, but luckily, our no-standards garbage program had been more than happy to have him.

He was back in town to stay.

Which was a thought that I absolutely could *not* maintain inside my body.

So I tried to make my body *not* my body. It was a tool, and I forced it to relax, to let itself swing from side to side like the carefree Peter Pan I was meant to be—as far from that sad helpless little bastard who'd got a face full of paper as possible.

"Better," I heard Maggie mutter. "Now, less wet rag being shaken, more leaf fleeting on the wind?"

I closed my eyes and let the wires rock me, leaning into the swing and trying to keep each one from ending. Letting every swing be its own endless moment. *Fuck endings. Endings aren't real.*

Like how the nightmare hadn't ended.

Over the years at school, I'd learned to avoid Terri; I'd memorized his schedule every term and had done my best not to call attention to myself: his or anyone else's. But despite my efforts, it had become an established fact that Terri Bishop bullied Robin Finch—even teachers accepted it with a helpless shrug. The school colors were red and yellow, the mascot was a hedgehog, and Terri Bishop bullied Robin Finch.

I'd spent years hiding my light under a bushel, when all I'd wanted was to set the fucking bushel on fire. But now I was supposed to be able to be my fully authentic, loud, extroverted, and sparkling self.

So much for that.

Whatever, I could do this.

All I had to do was avoid him for another two to three years and everything would be fine. I'd done this before. I'd *survived* this before.

It was like paying taxes, only I paid in dignity and bodily autonomy.

After a while, the crew lowered me and unhooked the harness, finally freeing my limbs. While I struggled to regain my land legs, my mind desperately searched for something to focus on other than Terri.

Like, for example, how fantastically awkward Armand had been yesterday teaching his first class. Even now, I full-body cringed just thinking about it. It had been a little adorable, in a really neurotic way . . . like when you watched a video about a diabetic, two-legged pig learning to walk again.

Hopefully tonight would go better; according to the syllabus, we'd be talking about gutter lines and how they could be used as narrating Greek choruses. Okay, sure.

I was being mean. He'd actually been pretty informative, and if I hadn't still been shaken up from my run in with Terri, I would have been geeking out with the rest of the class. Especially since he'd reiterated that at the end of the workshop, we'd be displaying our final projects gallery-style at the Drawn & Quartered Comic Convention.

It was going to be so cool; three full pages of *my* art (a tasteful meet-cute between a vampire and a wizard, in a coffee shop, no less) on a gallery wall. And other peoples' too, but whatever.

It was disconcerting how Armand had just assumed that our work would be worth displaying. As if we were as cool as him. Armand Demetrio, still dark, alternative, and indie to the core. Perhaps he could be forgiven a certain *complete* lack of elegance.

That's what *I* was for. That and bureaucracy. Which reminded me, I still needed to write up that job posting for the workshop—Armand had asked if I could find him a live model for next week's classes.

"You want me to find you a naked guy?" I'd asked him.

He'd blushed and sputtered, *"I need a life model, gender hardly matters, just— We need a body, someone with a presence—"* He'd gone on to explain a bunch of technical things that made it clear he wanted to make the selection himself, but we both knew he'd struggle to figure out the campus job site. The key to a happy life was reasonable expectations, so I'd set it up so applications were sent directly to his email.

I chugged some strawberry-flavored vitamin water and stretched. I still had time for a good long shower and maybe a few hours studying my script before I had to go pick him up. Maggie had disappeared somewhere into the bowels of the theater, but I was hoping to pull her away from whatever important work she was doing and get her to run lines with me later on.

I started back toward my dorm, letting the sunshine dry my sweat and already reaching for my phone to text Maggie.

I was about to turn the corner when—

My hair stood up and my blood ran cold.

Hide. A deep, animal part of my brain yanked me into a crouch behind a hedge. *He's coming.*

"—so that sets precedent. *Obviously.* Professor Yang couldn't be more wrong."

Terri. I shut my eyes tight and tried as hard as I could to not exist.

It worked. Terri and the gaggle of pre-law students disappeared behind the museum, and I finally let myself breathe.

I could feel my pulse in every single part of my body. Even the tips of my fingers.

See? All the old instincts were coming back. I could do this.
I could *survive* this.

11
ARMAND DRUNKENLY
CONVERSES WITH FISH

July 17ᵗʰ - Twenty-nine days until the convention

I woke in the late afternoon, prickling with unease. The more I thought about it, the more troubled I was by Finch's lack of chatter on the drive home the night before. At the time, I had appreciated the reprieve, but now I couldn't help noting its strangeness. The boy hadn't looked too healthy either.

Oh well, chalk it up to . . . something. God knew I'd been a mess during my brief stint at uni. Finch appeared rather more sheltered than I'd been at that age, but that hardly seemed likely to inoculate him from stupidity. In my time, the poison du jour had been a toxic relationship with an older man who aided access to binge-drinking and a variety of exciting new party drugs. What did American teenagers use to harm themselves these days? And why was my head now filled with scenes from *American Graffiti* and *Footloose*? Harrison Ford in a cowboy hat dancing arthritically with Kevin Bacon in Small-Town America—

Time for coffee.

I levered myself up and out of bed, found a pair of crumpled yet clean pants, and officially rejoined the ranks of humanity. I had temporarily exiled myself the night before on account of my first teaching experience, with the aid of Californian Whiskey and a bath. Evidently, I'd grown and evolved, and now *planned* my binge-drinking ahead of time. My friend and old colleague Sam had always had a thing or two to say about my choice to combine alcohol and slippery wet surfaces such as porcelain tubs, but they were an ocean away now, and my current flatmate appeared to be completely nonexistent, so they hadn't a say in the matter either.

The hangover hadn't kicked in yet, so I must have still maintained an inoffensive amount of blood in my alcohol system, but pre-emptive measures never hurt anyone, as far as hair of the dog was concerned. Coffee was necessary, yes, and if it was a little Irish, none would be the wiser.

I made it to the living room and glared at the bright bloody sunlight streaming in through the huge curtain-bare window at the front of the room. I stumbled toward it blindly and managed to wrench the curtains closed with only the minor injuries of a banged shin and a stubbed toe. Once the apartment was habitable again, I opened my eyes and tried to blink away some of the hangover headache . . . and bite back the hangover nausea awakened by the light.

Right, yes, yes, there you are, Consequences. I was expecting you.

It had been a while since I'd indulged to this extent. After all, I'd been so very good this year. However, I'd been correct in my surmise that I could either exist in the outside world or maintain my sobriety, but not both. I sat down heavily on the couch for a moment, waiting for my body to start working with me again. Once its anger subsided somewhat, I pulled myself to my feet and headed toward the kitchen and caffeine. I boiled water in the kettle and was rewarded in my search by a substance resembling instant coffee.

However, once I turned toward the fridge for cream, I came up against something square and yellow. I squinted at it for a few moments before realizing it was, in fact, a note.

Written in a sprawling cursive a bit too loopy for its own good was a block of text that took me several read-throughs to fully comprehend:

Hello, Armand!

I would've preferred to meet in person, but it's pretty clear our schedules don't overlap, to say the least. So I decided I might as well introduce myself! I'm truly looking forward to getting to know you, and I believe this will be a beneficial and educational experience for us both. Have a wonderful day! Hope to meet you soon.

P.S. Help yourself to any of the fruits and veggies I put in the fridge. Oh. Except the avocados, I want to make dip. And leave the spinach leaves too—for salads.

P.S.S. Say hi to Gaston and LeFou! They're in the living room.

"'Beneficial and educational experience'?"

Who *was* this person? And how did they know my name?! I eventually managed to decipher the enormous scrawl as: *Lucas Anthony Barclay.*

Wait a minute—*Lucas*?

I blinked at the name again. Perhaps Finch had mentioned him? *This is what you get for giving the paperwork nary the briefest of glances, Demetrio.*

Lucas, eh?

Lucas with enough hair and skin products to serve multiple pre-bachelorette spa outings, Lucas with floral-print furniture coverings and unicorn magnets, Lucas who was going to make avocado dip and was apparently *not* a woman in her roaring forties. Served me right for making assumptions—the aforementioned Sam (and honestly Lakshmi, Craig, or any of my other friends) would have hit me, called me a tosser, and reminded me once again that "patriarchy is a chronic condition."

I leaned one arm against the refrigerator and clenched a hand in my hair, staring down at the note in consternation. I would have been perfectly all right never encountering my obviously somewhat pedantic and finicky flatmate, but it seemed *Lucas* was not going to let that happen.

Something was nagging at me though; I squinted down at the second postscript . . . Gaston and LeFou? I looked up—I'd just come from the living room; there hadn't been anyone in there . . .

Right?

I peeked around the corner tentatively. Should I perhaps have put on some more clothes before venturing forth from the bedroom? For all I knew, there were two traumatized Frenchmen sitting in my living room at this very moment.

But the living room was empty.

Who the hell were Gaston and LeFou? Was Lucas the type of person to name the furniture?

. . . Bet he was.

But then I noticed something in the corner. Something that glittered in the few rays of sunlight that were still making it past the curtains. Something made of glass . . . I stepped closer and realized there was movement behind that glass—*fish*.

There were fish in a fish tank.

With a little sticky note against the side that said: *Hi, we're Gaston and LeFou!*

I stared at them for a few moments, and they stared back.

This felt exactly like being introduced by someone like Lucas to someone like the fish: we were all—sans Lucas—rather embarrassed by the whole affair. Despite myself, I felt an immediate kinship with Gaston and LeFou.

"Hello, lads." I waved at them. "I'm Armand, but I'm sure you'll come to know me as 'the one who doesn't feed you.'"

They made tiny silent *O*s.

I finished making the coffee, spiked it, and settled down with my lapdesk on the floor across from Gaston and LeFou, finally set to ink the pages I'd drunkenly penciled the day before. Lakshmi had begged and borrowed me an extra week on this month's deadline, and there were only so many threatening emails the editors could send me. Despite holding the contract renewal over my head, they'd approved the anniversary-issue story and layout weeks ago; I'd finished penciling last night, so my work was all ink and sable brushes for the foreseeable future.

This was the part of the comic that demanded the most of my skill, and the least of my brain.

I tucked my hair behind my ears, settled my reading glasses firmly on my nose, and loosened my shoulders, getting ready for a good couple of hours of drudgery until I had to head back to the university and . . . I swallowed back a shudder. A lot of grade-A whiskey had gone into blocking out my last teaching experience. It'd be a damn waste to dredge it all back up again.

I glanced up at Gaston and LeFou over the rims of my glasses. "Take it from me, lads, if your agent ever tells you something is a good idea, swim for the hills."

It hurt to admit, but even while in the throes of resentment, I knew Lakshmi had been right about this. The workshop wasn't only going to be good for the comic, it was going to be good for *me*. I'd isolated myself for so long that being forced to perform daily pedagogical acts of coherence in front of artistically inclined teenagers in a foreign land was almost a crash course in relearning how to person.

Perhaps I'd relearn how to person in time for *Lucas* not to detest me on sight.

I'd been working steadily for several hours when I realized my indulgence wasn't so much hair of the dog as an entire dog at this point. My Irish coffee was becoming increasingly Irish while its coffee-ness inevitably was becoming depleted. It was honestly quite depressing how predictable I was—but that was yet another topic I'd rather drown.

I would make sure I had time to shower and sober up before Finch came to collect me, but for the time being I had to finish these pages and explain certain realities to Gaston and LeFou.

"'S not that I don't like yer Lucas, lads—I'll bet he's an all-round upstanding citizen and pillar o' the community an' all—but I *find* . . . you see, I find people like me more when th' haven't *met* me, y'know?" I took a deep breath and laid out another page to dry on the coffee table. The fish apprehended it without comment. I was nearly done—I'd spread five pages across the couch, floor, and table—and was honestly quite pleased with how quickly I'd managed to turn them out. Yes, I was drunk, but I'd always been a *productive* drunk. I wondered if the fish were at all impressed.

"I bet . . . I bet if me and this Lucas never meet we'd end up *best* o' friends, but iffee . . . if he *meets* me, he'll try to . . . *wisely* try to pretend we never did. Meet. Y'follow?"

It appeared that they did.

"What's he like, anyway?" I directed this question at Gaston, who I'd assumed to be the larger one. "I mean, 'sides the clean-freakiness avocado-dip horses-horses-horses bit? Where *is* he all day?"

The fish didn't give much up, but I glanced around the room, trying to find some clue as to what my mysterious flatmate did for a living. I didn't know what I'd expected to find, but there was a tripod in the corner, leaning against a bookcase. The kind of tripod you mounted highly expensive cameras on. I glanced again at the many, many photographs of horses; he was pretty good too.

I also realized that I was bloody stupid. I found my phone, and a quick google of *lucas barclay horses* led me to a FotoBom account featuring, voilà, more pictures of horses. His socials included a few aesthetic photos of family and friends, and one or two which were allegedly of the man himself, but those were so heavily edited and filtered that he just looked like a catalog item. I could make out something in the eyes; they could hardly be *that* green, could they? But everything else reeked of airbrushing and carefully posed soullessness. They were all about a year out of date, as well. His professional photos were more recent; it seemed like he ran the account for an "equine retirement facility" that was—*ah*, there it was—owned by his family.

So *money*. Or at least middle class.

Frustratingly, there didn't seem to be any pictures of Lucas himself on the account, Vaseline-lensed or otherwise, but I couldn't help noting the photos really were *quite* good.

"So he's an *artist*, eh lads?" I muttered at the fish.

Gaston and LeFou turned their tails on me, seemingly to discourage this line of thought. I nodded at them. "I see, no, I see. He's rich and he makes art for *fun*. Aye, that's the type of person I'd *definitely* get on with . . ." I sighed. "I dunno if y'lads can detect sarcasm, but that was it, right there. He's gonna think I'm a slob 'f a sellout . . . which I *am* . . ."

It had only been a year since I'd been doing the comic professionally. I hadn't even thought making comics like mine was something people *did* professionally—famous comics, aye, fancy graphic novels, I suppose, but not weird little indie comics like *Surrogate Goose*. You couldn't *live* on that . . . but somehow, for the past year, I had. And the imposter syndrome was *cumulative*. I'd never felt this way when I was dancing—I didn't have to be *myself* on stage; I could lose myself in a character or an aesthetic.

That didn't work with *Surrogate Goose*. My *self* was required for use as raw material.

I glanced at the clock that hung on the wall just above the fish. "All right, time to sober up and go teach a generation of young hopefuls t' be *me*, eh?"

The fish appeared somewhat relieved as I left the room.

12
LUCAS IS NEARLY MURDERED BY AN INKWELL

July 18th

I had barely opened the door to the apartment when I had to violently twist to keep from stepping on a mysterious dark object in the doorway. I hung off the doorknob, swinging my foot over the object to land on the carpet safely, then hit the light.

What the actual fuck?

Was that an inkwell?

That settled it. My housemate was probably, *definitely* an alien.

While catching my breath, I stared at the offending inkwell in distaste. What was this even doing on the floor? Carefully, I picked it up—it was filled to the brim with ink. *Oh my god*—I searched for other landmines—this was brand-new carpeting! If this had spilled . . . just think of the amount of baking soda and bleach that would have been needed to clean it up . . .

Not to mention the fact that I could've stepped on the damn thing and *died*.

I followed the inkwells, which did in fact continue (*they multiply like bunnies!*) like a trail of breadcrumbs into the living room, where—

Papers were scattered everywhere, covering the carpet, where they seemed to have been flung every which way—even the couch was unrecognizable under a messy pile of paper and brushes. Three inkwells and two bowls of inky water, every single one resting precariously on the floor.

Keep calm, don't freak out. Keep calm, don't freak out. It's just a landmine of ink sitting on carpet. No big deal—

VERY BIG DEAL.

I plucked each inkwell off the floor and placed them in a secure and upright position on the coffee table. Now that impending doom was no longer upon me, I could figure out what to do with all the loose papers on the floor. They didn't appear to be in any order, so I knelt to scoop them up, intent on tossing them all (in an organized pile, of course) onto the table.

Then I caught a glimpse of the page in my hand, and paused.

Everything was black and white, and for a moment it felt like I was staring at a horror-genre optical illusion. The pages seemed to be panels of a comic, but I couldn't quite make out a coherent narrative, if there was one. There was barely any dialogue, only some weird, globby, Eldritch monster-type figures drawn in increasingly obscure environments.

There was also . . . a penguin?

It was all very well done, clearly drawn by someone with a vision of whatever it was supposed to look like. I had no idea what was going on—I just knew it shouldn't be spread out across the living room floor. How had he even managed to make this much of a mess in twelve hours? I stay over at Darren's for *one night* and *this* happens.

I made sure all the papers were facing the same direction before placing the pile inside the first drawer of the coffee table, then the inkwells inside the second drawer. Grabbing a pen and Post-it from the kitchen, I labeled one "ink" and the other "drawing pages." I stuck each note on their respective drawer, then walked to the kitchen.

There was something on the fridge.

The whiteboard that I had purchased now bore a drawing of a fluffy bunny wearing an apron. There was a word balloon hovering over the bunny's head which read, *Hello, I'm Martha Stewart!* It wasn't quite clear what a Martha Stewart bunny was doing on the fridge, but perhaps there was a note left to explain it.

The note I had left for Armand was still hanging from the clip on the fridge, but now there was a small scribble at the bottom, in a scrawl vastly different from my cursive:

hi

Huh. I turned the paper over to see if I'd missed anything. Nope, that was the extent of the note. I'd written him a *whole page.*

... *"Hi"*?!

The fridge was still stocked with the avocados and spinach leaves, so at least Armand had in fact read the note. Good to know. I turned to wash up in the sink and stopped short. A half-filled mug of some murky liquid was placed on the counter, and I had a nagging suspicion that it wasn't tea.

I sniffed the contents cautiously and instantly reeled backward. Nope. Definitely whiskey.

Suddenly, the inkwell warzone made a lot more sense.

I dumped the contents, sighed, and walked to the bathroom. At this point, all I wanted was a nice hot shower before I had to make myself presentable.

In the bathroom was an appalling lack of Armand-owned hygiene products. The only items I could identify as my housemate's were a bar of soap, a toothbrush, and a lonely razor sitting abandoned on the side of the sink.

He was a caveman. An unshaven, non-ocean breeze-scented caveman. Who probably didn't use conditioner, either. God help me.

I turned to the mirror and— *Oh no. What.* There was, drawn *onto* the mirror, in *marker*, a mustache.

A this-only-needs-a-cigar-to-complete-the-image-of-a-stuffy-billionaire mustache.

I should've been panicking that I lived with someone who actually drew on a mirror, but I was struck by an impulse. I lined up my face with the mustache and, upon having to stand up on my toes, realized that Armand was several inches taller than me.

Stop being amused by this! He drew on the mirror! He'd better hope this isn't permanent marker!

A little soap, water, and elbow grease later proved the ink to be temporary. So after a nice long shower, I shuffled back to the living room and scrolled through my playlists. Normally I would pop on some classic Taylor Swift, but now I was stressed, so I reached for Lizzo instead.

"Hey, guys." I sighed, tossing a pinch of food into Gaston and LeFou's tank. "Apparently I'm rooming with a monosyllabic alcoholic named Armand who refuses to use hair products and sits around drawing cartoons on the floor." My fish were peering judgmentally from behind the coral reef, so I hurried to explain. "Okay, I know that sounded mean. His drawings are actually really good." I watched Gaston nibble at the food and then chase LeFou around the castle. "I haven't even met the guy yet, so if you two could keep an eye out and just, you know, take notes. Let me know what he's like."

LeFou seemed to mouth at the coral in an agreeable manner. Gaston was aloof as usual and could not be trusted to go along with my plan.

Time to get dressed—I was not about to leave Darren and his friends waiting. This was the first time he'd ever offered to introduce me to the people in his life. I walked back to my room and stood staring at the contents of my closet for the better part of ten minutes, struggling to make a decision.

Do I wear the light-green, patterned button-down to match my eyes and that screams fun and personality, or the solid peach that says "take me seriously as an adult person who could definitely fit in with a group of young and fancy lawyers"?

Since I was meeting Darren at one thirty rather than in ten years from now, I chose the peach and called it good.

A fifteen-minute drive later and I blinked up at the gratuitous awning in front of Cresson Cher, which seemed a bit excessive for a lunch. But any excuse to get all dressed up was a good one, so I took a deep breath and headed inside.

The intoxicating aroma of high-end food I wouldn't be able to eat wafted over me as I stepped inside. I basked instead in the warm, dim glow of the pretentious chandeliers as I checked in with the hostess. She indicated that the McKinley party was already seated, and I was escorted to a corner booth where Darren was waiting.

His chestnut hair was immaculately gelled, the way it always was when he was being Professional. It didn't matter that I had been with him earlier—my heart was making up for lost time after our week apart by flipping over in my chest and sending shivers down my arms as he stood, pulling me in for a sweet, chaste kiss.

"Thanks for inviting me to meet your friends," I said, leaning into his touch.

He pulled me back and surveyed my ensemble. "Good shirt choice. I was worried we wouldn't be able to hear the conversation over the stuff you usually wear."

I touched my fingertips to the bland peach I'd picked. Boring and soulless. But mature. "Har har. You assume lawyer conversation is worth listening to."

I scooted over in the leather booth to make room for Darren to slide in. The rest of Darren's posse arrived shortly after as one—was it customary for lawyers to travel in packs? Darren rolled through the introductions, and I was met with a firm handshake from each of them in turn.

After several minutes of what appeared to be chummy work banter, they all got to ordering, and I was pleased with my own resolve in ordering a garden salad.

"So, lovebirds," Teresa Lombardo—one of the few names I remembered—addressed me and Darren during a brief break in the nonstop conversation, "I think we're all dying to hear the sweeping love story that is how you both met. We've only ever heard bits and pieces."

I reached for Darren's hand, giving it a squeeze. "Yeah, Darren, how *did* we meet?"

He glanced out at the table at large. "We were friends in high school," he explained in what I had come to recognize as his lawyer voice. "I was class president and he was a horse nerd. Bit of a chubby duckling the first four years, but then . . ."

"He turned into a swan," Marcia Lopez finished with a sigh. "He *did*, look at him."

I flushed, waving away the compliment. Less a swan, more of a crested mallard.

"We danced around each other for a few years after that, slowly discovering that there was something else between us," Darren said with a dazzling smile. "And now here we are. I realized a few months ago that it was time to grow up and settle down."

The lawyers present all but swooned at his tale, and I swatted his arm. "I'd tell you to quit lying, but this version is flattering, so I'll allow it."

He painted such a pretty story; his friends couldn't have any idea how we really happened. And how he told it was almost—mostly—true. Except the suggestion that Darren had waited until I lost weight and had a growth spurt near the end of college. He'd had my virginity by the time I'd turned sixteen.

But even that hadn't made it official between us—Darren would come to me when he wanted, and I would hold out hope that maybe this time he'd want to make our arrangement more permanent. It had taken years before I finally won.

One of the other lawyers whose name had escaped me in the flurry of introductions addressed me directly. "So Lucas, what have you been up to lately? How's work?"

I grinned at them across the table. "Well, I just got back from my cousin's wedding in Vancouver, which was great, but I missed it here. I took some great photos to add to my portfolio, though—"

"They want to know about your work, Lucas, not your hobby." Darren's arm snaked around my shoulders as he smiled at me.

I gave them the tried-and-true The End is Neigh spiel, figuring that brevity was probably the move here. There were polite *oohs* of interest, but no follow-up questions.

The food arrived shortly after that, and I did my best to keep up with the conversation that Darren had re-launched, but was subsequently lost in a sea of legal jargon as they discussed whatever it was that copyright lawyers usually discussed.

The waiter returned to our table to collect our plates. "Can I interest anyone in dessert today?"

I bit my lip as everyone else ordered chocolate cake, or crème brûlée, or tiramisu. Cresson Cher was infamous for its rich desserts, but ordering one would be an absolute nail in the coffin of progress I'd made this month. "A plate of fruit please," I requested when the waiter turned to me. "Raspberries and grapes, if you have them."

"We just got some fresh ones in today," he said, scribbling in his notepad. He flashed me a grin. "Are you sure you don't want to go with something more indulgent, sir? I could tempt you with a sinful chocolate pots de crème? It's one of our standards."

God, that sounded delicious. But the final button on my peach shirt was hanging on by a thread, which meant that I already owed myself another two-hour session at the gym if I had any hope of Darren—

"Honestly, as much as I'd love to be tempted, I'm good with the fruit, or my personal trainer'll kill me." I lent the waiter a bright smile, because it wasn't his fault I had little to no self-control. "Thank you, though. I'll let you tempt me next time."

The waiter shrugged, smiled, then returned to the kitchen.

"Wow." Darren was staring at me, his wineglass halfway to his mouth.

"What?"

He shook his head, swallowed the rest of his drink, and rejoined his coworkers' conversation.

After the meal, everyone began shuffling toward the door, each person shaking my hand again before they left as a group.

Darren walked me to my car, and I grinned widely at him, unable to keep the note of smugness from my voice as I said, "I think they liked me."

"Well, not as much as that waiter." Darren's hands flexed at his sides. "When'd you get so flirty?"

"Flirty?" It took me a moment to think back on our interaction, and my cheeks warmed. "I was just being friendly. You think he thought I was flirting?"

"'I'll let you tempt me next time'? Is that a thing *non*-flirty people say to service workers?"

It was always weird when Darren got like this, but I couldn't pretend it wasn't sweet to see him jealous. Even if he was being ridiculous. There was still a shadow on his face, so I gently tempered my reply. "I was trying to be friendly and likeable for your friends . . . I guess I must've overcorrected and the waiter got caught in the crossfire. I'm sorry."

"Never mind. Of course everyone liked you." Darren softened, running his hands down my arms and kissing my forehead. "That actually reminds me. The boss is doing a cocktail party at the end of the month for the partners' anniversary. Today was a trial run, but you did good. Maybe if things keep up this way, I could bring you as my plus-one, what do you think?"

I flushed with excitement. Going to one of Darren's big work parties would be huge—it would mean that he was officially introducing me as his boyfriend to the rest of his cohort. We would be indisputably out together, like he was showing me off—"That sounds great! You don't have to worry, I'll knock 'em dead."

"I certainly hope so." Darren smiled, then pursed his lips. I held my breath, wondering if he'd invite me back to his place. But instead, he checked his watch and sighed, leaning back to adjust his perfectly knotted tie. "I should probably get home. I still have work to get done on the Jameson case before Monday. It's making me want to literally *die*."

I laughed but reluctantly agreed that we should both head home. "And I still haven't met my weird roommate yet, so maybe I can catch him at home today."

I stole one more kiss, savoring the tingle of Darren's lips before sliding into my car and pulling away, waving to Darren in the rearview mirror until I turned the corner back onto the highway.

It was only late afternoon and not the middle of the night, when it seemed that the cryptid known as Armand did most of his cryptid-ing, but already my body was locked and ready for whatever nonsense he had planned for the apartment. More drawings on the mirror? More near-death experiences walking through the door? *Where will it end?*

13
(TEXTINGINTERLUDE 1)

July 18th

Lucas: *hi! it's me, Lucas, your housemate! We really have mismatched schedules! I guess you work nights? I leave for work super early so I guess that's why we haven't met*
Lucas: *Just wondering if you usually do your drawing out in the living room?*
Lucas: *That's fine, I just thought maybe we could arrange like a cleaning schedule/house ground rules as we will be co-inhabiting for a while?*

Lucas: *Is this the right number?*

July 19th

Lucas: *Hope to hear from you soon, can't believe we haven't met yet lol :)*

Armand: *Roger. Sorry.*

14
SKYLER PUTS HIMSELF OUT THERE

July 19th

My phone had been buzzing periodically over the past hour, but despite my anxiety, I couldn't break to check my messages until I'd finished brushing Hot Sauce McJones. Eventually, the old gentlehorse booped my temple to show he was done, and I made sure he was properly corralled before stepping away. The thought of reading Matt's texts made my stomach clench, but I took a deep breath and braved a glance at my screen.

It was a series of photos that I recognized as the local Target Matt and I would always shop at. He'd sent pics of himself, with two carts (one full and one empty), posing in front of the home décor aisles as he wrapped his arm around the air next to him.

Matt: *just school shopping with ma bestie*

Matt: *here's where I would put a Skyler . . . IF I HAD ONE lol*

Matt: *just kidding it's much easier without you*

Matt: *I'll pick up a really ugly rug in your honor*

Matt: *seriously you're missing out, do they even have Targets out there*

Matt: *nvm I don't care about California*

The passive-aggressive punch of the last line made my stomach churn. I would have to explain myself eventually if we were going to resolve this. But for now, if Matt wanted to act like everything was fine, then so could I.

Skyler: *Of course there's targets out here, I'm not in the boonies*

Skyler: *get one of those fuzzy blue rugs that look like a dead muppet, love those*

I didn't realize Lucas had snuck up next to me until he asked, in what was clearly mock seriousness, "Are you texting on the job?"

"Sorry. It's my brother." I slid my phone back into my pocket. "He's just checking in. I think he's worried about me."

"Well, did you explain that you're absolutely *thriving* working as a new, minimum-wage ranch hand *and* the fresh young face of horsepice care?" Lucas's grin was contagious as he held up his own phone for me to see. "The website pops now; see what the power of a good camera can do?"

I recognized the photos he'd ended up posting—me brushing Nala's mane, doing manual labor in the stalls, and a particularly memorable day where Lucas had brought me along to assist with an orientation for a summer-camp field trip. He'd been off-camera, obviously, but he'd managed to catch a moment where I—with the permission of the kid and adult guardian—had perched an adorable four-year-old named Daisy on my hip so she could pet Grandpa Milkshake's nose.

"Amazing," I praised. "You really captured my spirit of ennui."

Lucas rolled his eyes, but he still flushed with pride. "Spirit of ennui . . . Please, you're what, eighteen? Less ennui and more *joie de vivre*." Then he sighed, a bit theatrically, as he looked back at his phone. "Doing your shoots has been a good distraction. I'm doing everything I can not to lose my entire mind at home right now."

Lucas had brought up in passing the other day that he had yet to meet the guy he was living with, reiterating that if Darren had just agreed for them to live together then he wouldn't have to deal with any of these shenanigans. He seemed like he was ramping up for a rant, so I indulged him. "What'd he do this time?"

"Oh my god, what *hasn't* he done? Actually, no, never mind, that's a longer list." Lucas listed off on his fingers. "He leaves garbage everywhere in the apartment, he manspreads his workspace across the entire living room, he doodles on the bathroom mirror—yes, the entire mirror—I nearly died stepping on an honest-to-god inkwell he left sitting by the front door, and oh yeah, he barely responds to any of my texts when I try and engage with him." Lucas stopped to catch his breath. "He's like the most chaotic, uncommunicative cryptid who doesn't exist during daylight hours except to undo all of my immaculate cleaning work. Like Depressed, Mildly Destructive Mothman."

Lucas's impassioned speech felt all too familiar. Matt and I had had separate bedrooms, but the memory of cramped living quarters in the earlier foster homes with nothing resembling personal space was as vivid now as it was ten years ago.

"I think you both are just in an adjustment period," I ventured. "It's not easy getting used to living in a house with people you don't know yet. You said you'd rather be living with your boyfriend; well, maybe Mothman has somewhere else he'd rather be too."

Lucas looked thoughtful, then shot me an amused smile. "Aren't you a philosopher today. Yeah, I'll keep at it. I leave him all these notes, but I guess he doesn't *do* note-writing."

I didn't mention how hard it was to respond to someone's message when you were hiding something agonizing.

"Oh! I almost forgot! Darren invited me to this super fancy important work party as his plus-one!" Lucas was nearly vibrating out of his skin as he grinned at me. "He's finally coming around; I *knew* I just had to be patient."

"That's great, congrats!" Lucas's optimism was contagious. Maybe if I was patient with Matt, everything would work out. Eventually.

At the end of the work day, Lucas drove me back to campus. I took a much-needed shower and sat at my desk, staring at my computer.

I should do homework, but I couldn't get my brain to focus. I kept coming back to Matt's texts, dissecting every single one to determine tone. Was there anything I could say to let him know that this wasn't his fault?

My email notifications chirped. I had almost forgotten I'd set up alerts for additional part-time work in the area. Working at The End is Neigh had been rewarding so far, and it was a relief to be making my own money, but it was only part-time, which was not going to be enough. So I would work side hustles and go to school and *not* dissolve into a self-hating, co-dependent puddle. That was what independent adults did, right?

A surprising number of campus job postings popped up, and I scrolled until my eyes caught on a modeling call.

Not photography this time, but something for an art class.

The job description seemed basic enough, especially after what I was already doing for Lucas, though I did catch the detail about how this modeling would involve being stationary for long periods of time. And being nude.

I sat with this information for a bit. I'd never been particularly self-conscious about my body before, but maybe that was because there had been an element of safety in Matt's shadow. And wasn't the whole point of coming out here to try new things, figure myself out? Maybe the idea of being naked in front of a classroom of people sketching me should've been a lot weirder, but it felt like a natural enough progression.

I'd already done a fair amount of modeling for Lucas, and from what he'd shown me, I seemed to be pretty good at it. And it was enjoyable; there was something oddly peaceful about having someone else direct me, to decide how I was perceived, to relinquish me of the responsibility of choosing how my body should perform for a short while. And it was for art, right?

The application barely needed anything more than a short résumé, and after double-checking the pay information and contact details for the professor of the course, I applied.

I couldn't stop rereading my earlier text conversation with Delia. Especially the message she'd sent on my first day of school: *Go to class, I love you!*

I had to stop looking at it. I already had confusion and guilt rolling around; I didn't need to torture myself as well. She didn't mean it—not that way.

It was only eight o'clock and the sun hadn't fully set yet, so I grabbed my keys and walked out onto the quiet campus, my body thrumming with tension.

15

ROBIN IS RESCUED BY BATMAN

July 19th

Norsemen University had a mascot called Varr the Viking. In the abandoned little courtyard behind Machsted Hall, there was a hyper-realistic statue of Varr, and the Nordic icon held his axe at a slight tilt, so the handle stuck out at an upward angle.

This was the protrusion over which Terri Bishop & Co. had hooked the back of my Peter Pan leggings and then hurried off, leaving me to dangle.

They'd just *left* me.

I'd spent the last twenty minutes since they'd left trying to get down, twisting and grabbing, but the axe handle stuck out just far enough that there wasn't anything for me *to* grab. I kept expecting to fall, to collapse onto the ground—which was a good six feet away— but the fabric was holding up surprisingly well. I'd yelled for help, but it was late on a weekday. It had been almost half an hour and no one, not even campus security, appeared to have heard me or walked by.

And I was starting to lose feeling in my thighs.

Apparently I *deserved* this. At some point I'd pissed the universe so very *off* that it had created Terri Bishop to punish me. Though this time he hadn't even stuck around to laugh at my suffering. He'd just *left*.

This wasn't like high school all over again.

This was worse.

Tonight had started out like any basic bullying experience—they'd found me on my way home and Terri had made some jokes about my outfit, going all *MythBusters* about how far my leggings would stretch. But once he'd gotten me up here . . .

Terri's little posse and their girlfriends had laughed and jeered, the sounds loud enough to echo down my spine. But Terri had only stared. Smiling, silent. And when one of the girls had tried to take a selfie with my legs, he'd said: *"Don't be stupid, this never happened. Did it, Flinch?"*

And they'd left.

It was almost like Terri wasn't using me to entertain and impress other people.

It was like hurting me was the *point*.

I whimpered softly and stared despondently at the ground so far below my pointed little shoes.

"Whoa, is someone there?"

I froze. Well, to be honest, the upper half of my body froze. Everything else dangled as uselessly as before.

"Over here!" I called, my voice breaking with enough pathos to serve the needs of every rescue dog in LA County.

"What— Oh my god." Whoever seemed to be addressing my situation rather than myself hadn't stepped into the vague circle of light shed by a nearby streetlamp. All I could make out from the silhouette was that the lifeform addressing me was a Dorito-shaped human. "Are you okay?"

"No, not really," I managed, stifling a moan as speech illogically caused my body weight to shift again, bringing forth pain from exciting new areas.

Mystery Man stepped into the light, handsome and clearly concerned. On second glance, *handsome* did not do him justice; *gorgeous* barely started to cover it.

His wavy black hair and the way it fell around his face reminded me of classical Greek statuary, but *hotter*. Much of him was hot: his large soulful eyes, strong yet cherubic features that when arranged into such a look of apprehension on one's behalf, would inevitably cause one's knees to react liquidly whether one had feeling in them or not. I could hear mine sloshing around somewhere below.

"What happened?" His voice was warm, sexy.

Danger, Will Robinson, Danger!

"Upbringing, mostly," I said hoarsely. "The translation of fear into hate on one side, and overcompensation for self-consciousness on the other. Whom do I have the pleasure of addressing?"

"Skyler Evans." He smiled at me a little thinly. "And you?"

"Robin Finch." I waited for the cringe of sympathy and answered it with an appreciative smile. "That's nothing, my middle name is Peregrine. Any chance you could help me down from here? I didn't exactly have a vasectomy planned for this evening . . ."

"Oh, right! Sorry!" He moved forward immediately and held me by the waist, which would have been a lot more exciting if I'd actually been able to feel his hands. I'm a pretty small person, and I am aware of and resigned to this fact, but I still felt the display of effortlessness with which he lifted me up and off the Viking axe-handle that held me captive was bordering on tasteless.

Worst was that as blood rushed back to the rest of my body, the pins and needles stage set in with a vengeance, and I gripped his arms desperately. Those lovely large blue eyes gave me a questioning look as he continued to hold me aloft. "How long were you up there?"

"A while . . ." My voice broke spectacularly as I waited for fifty percent of my body to return from the ethereal plains of Numb.

I heard a sympathetic hiss—my eyes were shut tight—and Skyler gently set my feet on the grass. He kept a hesitant hold on my waist, making sure I stayed upright.

"Who did this?"

"I'd say—" I coughed. "—two future lawyers and one future senator." Between the physical crisis my body was dealing with and my brain's attempts to comprehend that I had apparently been rescued by Batman, I was about to fall over. "You don't mind if I lean on you, do you?"

And with that, I plummeted headfirst against Skyler's chest.

He laughed, but anger rang under it. Oh, be still my moronic little heart.

"Of course not. How's your . . ." And then he shut up, apparently realizing that gauging injury in these particular circumstances could lend itself to the Awkward.

It was my turn to laugh, though it was more of a squeak, like a guinea pig was dying somewhere in my throat. "Operational,

I believe . . . eventually, anyway." I levered myself up, allowing some weight to rest on my feet. I gave Skyler a resigned and apologetic grimace. "Thank you. I can honestly say I've rarely met a man of your restraint."

He raised his eyebrows adorably. "Restraint?"

"You've only laughed once."

He tried to smile, but there was obvious outrage pulsing behind his eyes.

I didn't quite manage to hold back a shudder. He must have felt it, because the outrage immediately subsided into concern as he gripped a little tighter, holding me steady. I could feel that now—his hands on my waist—because feeling was finally returning to my legs.

And, to be real, at this point *all* I could feel were his hands on my waist—no pain, no pins and needles, nothing but Skyler Evans's strong grip.

Ah Rob, yes, a perfect time to blush, you moron, bravo. And sweat, of course. Why don't you just swallow hard and look up at him with big, anxious puppy dog eyes?

Sweet Lord, you did it. You actually did *it, you fruity little bastard!*

Skyler's face softened slightly, making it obvious to the world that he was fond of kittens and considered me to be among their ranks.

"Can you walk at all?" he asked gently.

"I could probably limp, yes." I nodded.

He grimaced and moved one hand up under my shoulders. The other slid down behind my knees, and before I knew it, I was in the air again.

I couldn't help myself. I squeaked and wrapped my arms around his neck; he must have been trying to kill me.

"Warn a guy, would ya?"

Skyler smiled at me, soft curls falling over sad blue eyes and causing what felt like a temporary abdominal displacement.

"Sorry, I didn't think . . . Where do you live?" He glanced at the deceased waistband hanging limply around my hips. "I could take you straight home."

I clutched at the fabric, holding it in place. I had to swallow twice before attempting to speak. "That . . . is very . . . very kind of you. I'm in Fisher Hall." I gave a weak laugh. "I'm not used to kindness from masculine strangers."

He started walking toward my dorm, shaking his head. "Because of the theater thing?"

I blinked up at him. "H-how did you know I do theater?"

This time it was a real smile, and I was almost blinded. "Are you telling me you walk around campus dressed as Robin Hood for no reason? No judgment, just wondering."

I smiled back, and I never *had* managed to stop blushing. "Heh, I'm actually Peter Pan. And yes, it's for theater. I was wearing it home to do some alterations." To shorten the leggings, ironically.

Skyler shook his head and shrugged, inadvertently bouncing me. "I still don't know why people would do this."

I wanted to *Aww* and run my hand through his hair. And people said *I* was naive. I also had to fight the urge to snuggle up against his chest and close my eyes, a tiny thespian in distress breathing in the imaginary scent of leather padding beneath Skyler's shiny armor.

In reality, he smelled like rosemary-and-mint soap, which was better. The scent suffused my body with warmth and a lightness that didn't seem real—this *couldn't* be real, could it? Terri must have finally killed me. I was dead. Dead and *happy*. I was falling so hard they'd probably end up naming a crater after me.

"Are you going to report this to campus police?"

"Huh?" In the warm, pink, fantasy dream-state brought on by Skyler, I'd actually forgotten about Skyler. "Oh. I . . . I don't know. Maybe."

"I don't want to tell you what to do," said the beautiful man carrying me across the nighttime campus, "but I really think you should. I can go with you, if you want."

So much fluttering was happening inside of me I was in danger of floating away. "How about you let me buy you a cup of coffee instead?"

He looked surprised. "Right now?"

I shook my head and forced the words out before I lost my nerve or passed out from how very *a lot* this all was. "No, um, later. Friday?"

He gave a bemused smile, glancing at me, then back at the path in front of us. I was a little devastated that we'd already arrived at the front steps of Fisher Hall and he was going to put me down any minute now. Sure enough— "Yeah, I'd love to. Can you stand?"

It took me a moment to understand that he wasn't just evicting me from the safety of his arms, he'd also said *yes*! That he'd *love* to!

Once he'd carefully set me on my feet, two things became very clear: one, there was nearly a foot of height difference between us, and two, I'd been a bit cavalier about standing.

I leaned back against the front door, using one hand to keep myself decent, and the other to fish for my phone and keycard, easing my legs back into the role of holding my weight. Skyler was watching me in concern.

"You okay?"

"Oh yeah, I'm feeling better. Yeah—*yup*, much better." I needed to stop talking. "Not better than when you carried me, because obviously that was, well, nice . . . I just didn't mean that I preferred it when you— I guess I just wanted to say *thanks*."

He smiled, then pulled out his phone. "Wanna give me your number?"

Right. Because he'd said *yes, he'd love to*. Whose life even *was* this? I rattled off my number, my voice rising in pitch by the digit, and then watched as my phone screen lit up with a text that said, somewhat adorably: *hi it's me Skyler.*

I held it up to show him I'd received it and then, riding the cresting wave of panic inside me, I said, "So, um. See you Friday. I'll text you. Bye, thanks again for saving me." I fumbled with the key card and darted into the building, up to my room, and into my bed, where I could curl up and gently scream into my pillow.

Maybe I hadn't pissed the universe off quite as much as I'd thought.

16
(TEXTING INTERLUDE 2)

July 20th

Lucas: *hi armand it's me lucas again, how are you?*
Lucas: *I just wanted to maybe ask a favor? You're such a good artist and the wizard hat was so pretty but maybe could you not draw on the mirror please, thank you*
Lucas: *it's just I work so hard so there won't be streaks and I'm always so sad to erase your drawing, but like I need to use the mirror*
Lucas: *helllllooo anybody there?*

17
SKYLER TAKES CONTROL, KIND OF

July 20ᵗʰ

D on't chicken out. Just call him.
I dialed— Shit, should I have texted first?

"Thank you for calling Paolo's Pizza Parlor, home of the famous Pineapple Supreme, where we put a full pound of pineapple on whatever pizza you order whether you like it or not, then stare at you while you eat it—"

I sighed. "You can turn your camera on, Matt, I know it's you."

A brief lag, and my brother's face and infamous bedhead came into focus. His lips pulled into a smirk. "Are you sure? You sure you haven't forgotten what I look like after skipping town like an absolute tool?"

I took a shaky breath, hoping this hadn't been a mistake. "I'm sorry—I . . . I was trying to find the right time to tell you, I swear."

"When? When I died of natural causes at the tender old age of barely-nineteen?" Matt's phone shook as he slumped onto the couch. "I'm just mad me and Delia never got a chance to see you off like onlookers waving their handkerchiefs at the *Titanic*."

I cracked a smile, missing him so much my throat hurt. "You're right. I formally apologize for not giving you an opportunity to break out your trusty handkerchief collection."

Matt laughed, the sound warm and familiar, before catching himself and sobering. "But you're okay, though? This isn't some sort of quarter-life crisis I need to stage an intervention for? Because we agreed we would schedule our quarter-life crises for the same time."

"I've . . . had some stuff to work out." Ugh, that was possibly the most enigmatic thing I could've gone with. "Everything happened really fast, and I'm sorry I threw off our plan. I think I just needed to try and be independent. Do, you know, adult stuff. On my own."

"Like pay bills, do taxes, and weep at the tragedy of lost youth?" His smile was tight, never quite reaching his eyes.

"Something like that." Matt's mention of a tragedy brought the memory of Robin Finch dangling helplessly from a statue back into vivid focus. I let out a heavy breath, tugging a hand through my hair. "Okay, I have to tell you what just happened, though."

Matt perched his chin on his knuckles. "You already have gossip? Who are you and what have you done with my brother?"

"No, it's—" I swallowed.

Robin Finch had looked so helpless, hanging like an abandoned doll. The thought still filled me with a prickling heat—that there was someone, maybe multiple someones, wandering this campus who were willing and able to assault another student and leave them in a dangerous, painful position.

Torturing them.

I did my best to explain, though there was so much I didn't grasp about the situation, and Matt—understandably—gaped at me.

"What the fuck, dude."

"It was awful. I keep thinking about how long he must've been up there, and what would've happened if I hadn't found him." I really needed to talk to my brother about this, even if things were weird with us right now. He was always so good at helping me understand myself. Luckily, Delia's weekly pottery class still met at the same time so I knew I'd get him alone.

I propped my phone up on the bench I'd commandeered so that I could run my hands down my face. Out of the corner of my eye was the same statue, thankfully now devoid of a person. "You should've seen his face, Matt. I've never seen anyone look like that before."

Matt was chewing his lip, eyebrows pursed as he processed the information I'd been sitting with all night. "So this is a hate crime situation?"

"It seems like it could be, but he said he didn't want to go to campus police about it. He did offer to meet up again to talk on

Friday, though, and I have his number now, so." I shrugged awkwardly. "Maybe he just needs someone to talk to."

And it wasn't like I had many people to talk to around here either.

Matt was quiet for a long moment, a conversation's worth of unspoken things hanging in the silence. "That's really cool of you, you know? Making sure he's okay."

It was a kinder sentiment than I deserved, but something in his tone sounded off. "Thanks. I learned that from you, the way you always took care of me."

"Well. At least I'm good for something." His jaw worked for a minute. "Nice to see that you're making new friends out there."

My throat closed. "Matt, I—"

"I, um, actually have to go, but I'll text you later." He barely waited for me to nod before he ended the call.

Leaving me sitting on the bench, muscles locked from our conversation as well as a prickle of insistent protectiveness for Robin Finch.

I still hadn't heard from him since he promised he'd text and then darted into his dorm without a single look back. The way he'd trembled so badly in my arms, I wasn't convinced he'd be able to walk back on his own . . .

Before I could overthink it, I tapped out a quick text, asking if he still wanted to get together for coffee.

To my surprise, the response was immediate, almost frantic.

Robin: *OMG HIIIIIII*

Robin: *yes yes love to but I can only do the evening so maybe not coffee??? Cuz coffee keeps you up and we need our beauty sleep*

Robin: *not you but some of us uggos*

Robin: *should we do dinner instead??*

Robin: *is dinner too early in our relationship? Not that we have a relationship, you know what I mean though*

Robin: *was the dinner thing weird? We don't have to do dinner, I don't even eat*

Robin: *I don't know why I said that*

I'd never seen anyone text that fast in my life.

I responded: *it's all good, what if we drank tea?*

Robin: *omg you're a genius*

Robin: *I love tea. Pip pip*

Robin: *was the pip pip a bit much? I feel like it was a bit much. I'm not British. Which you know because we've met. Last night. I was the guy hanging from a statue.*

Robin: *Just in case you like forgot or something*

I snorted at my phone, then typed back: *Thanks for clarifying. I meet a lot of guys hanging from statues.*

There was a solid minute of triple-dot purgatory after that, and when Robin finally responded, it was with approximately twenty laughing emojis. Then he told me which coffee shop to meet him at, and a quick google showed it was a little place just off campus.

And that was that. I was still tense, but as I read back over Robin's last couple of messages, a small ripple of affection unfurled in me. It was a horrible way to have met someone, but there was something about Robin Finch; underneath the terror of whatever he was going through, he sounded as willing to meet up as I was. He clearly wanted, even needed, a friend. Like I did.

I told Robin I would be there, and I made sure the number for campus police was in my contacts.

Just in case he changed his mind.

18

LUCAS TAKES WHAT HE CAN GET

July 20th

I t was a perfect lazy morning. I was curled up on Darren's luxurious couch, using my day off to putter away on Photoshop while my boyfriend did boring lawyer work beside me.

I checked my phone for the tenth time since breakfast. No word yet from Mothman with regards to whether I would ever receive visual proof of his existence.

At least some things were going well—the End is Neigh website looked stunning, thanks to Skyler having an absurdly charismatic face and an even more charismatic way with our horse babies. It was such a relief to edit photos of someone else, someone with strong features and clear skin and an objectively lean torso. I didn't have to use any of my usual filters to bring out Skyler's shine.

I'd finished adding a picture of Skyler communing with Grandpa Milkshake to the site banner when Darren's hair tickled my neck.

"Who's that?" he asked.

I took a moment to boop his forehead with my own before angling my computer screen toward him eagerly. "Didn't those photos turn out great? I actually just splurged on a 200-mm lens and you can really tell the difference in quality, especially if you scroll down to this one here, see—"

"Lucas." Darren's voice was even but oddly clipped. "Who is the *guy*?"

"Oh!" I'd forgotten that Skyler's name wasn't listed on the website—sure, his face was on the internet, but we still valued privacy when it came to the personal information of our workers. "That's Skyler Evans; we hired him on to help out at the ranch. My mom's been wanting updated photos for the website, and I had to explain to her *again* that I wasn't going to pose for any myself—"

"Because you're insecure in front of a camera, I know," Darren said. Something stiffened in the shoulder I was leaning against. "So you've been taking pictures of this guy instead?"

He was getting jealous again—I took a breath, contemplating what response would stop whatever fight Darren was working up to. "Well, yeah, he's saved my ass. And the kid's got a photogenic vibe, doesn't he? Look at that profile—" I clicked through the gallery. "And it worked out, because our other ranch hands aren't comfortable in front of a camera, but Skyler's got such a childlike innocence about him . . ." Any interaction with Skyler Evans inevitably tugged at my heartstrings—he was a total sweetheart. "I don't know the whole story, I don't think he likes to talk about it, but I know he's going through a rough time, and he doesn't have any friends or family in town, and he's starting college and needed a helping hand . . ."

"And you couldn't say no," Darren jumped in, avoiding my eyes. "That's generous of you." He didn't wait for me to respond before he got off the couch, grabbed his computer, and padded instead to the kitchen island.

I sighed. He needed some time to pout, but he'd get over whatever silly thing he'd got into his head; he always did.

"I want to visit the ranch." He'd set himself up at the counter to work, but now he was staring at me.

I couldn't hide my surprise. "You want to come see the horses?" Darren had never taken much interest in The End is Neigh—he didn't know all that much about horses or photography unless I foisted information upon him. "I thought you were super busy with work."

Darren pressed his lips together before returning his attention to his laptop. "I want to see what you do all day."

"Okay," I agreed, walking to the kitchen to place a kiss on the top of his head, "but it has to be Nice Darren, not Bitchy Darren. We can't spook the horses."

Or the sweet young people who worked there.

Once he had deemed his case notes as done as they could be for now, we headed to the ranch. It was more bizarre than I'd originally expected, having my be-suited lawyer boyfriend strolling through a senior horse sanctuary, nose delicately wrinkling at the smell of horse and outdoors-ness, complaining under his breath that his Italian loafers were probably ruined. Which was fair, considering that the only bit of outdoors that Darren usually subjected himself to was the quarterly brunch his firm hosted at the local country club.

But his gaze was attentive as he scanned every inch of the grounds we strolled through, staying quiet and allowing me to ramble as I led us on a full tour. Until his eyes locked on something that stopped him in his tracks.

Skyler was out in the pasture, holding Major Banana's lead rope as he slowly and carefully guided the old horse to step backward in the way I'd showed him, working those joints and muscles to keep the old fellow as limber as was reasonable for a horse his age. The mama-bird feelings came rushing back in—he was such a fast learner, a hard worker, and always eager to please. I hoped that whatever was going on with his parents back in Washington that they were proud of him.

"Okay, come on, you gotta meet this kid," I said, tugging at Darren's arm and dragging him over to Skyler. "Behave yourself."

Skyler saw us approaching and led Major Bananas to a gentle stand-still, giving us a little wave. "Hey, I thought you had the day off! I forget how long he needs to be on a walk? We've done twenty minutes, but I didn't know if we should go for thirty," he said, shyly gesturing to Major Bananas, who seemed content to be standing still now.

"What you've done is perfect. He just needs to get out and stretch for a bit so his muscles don't atrophy," I assured him. I looked up at Darren, who hadn't glanced away from Skyler since we'd walked over. "And now, why I came in today—Skyler, this is my boyfriend Darren McKinley, who you're finally meeting and who definitely exists and who wanted to come hang out with us and the horses today."

Skyler, as warm and polite as ever, held out his hand to Darren. "Pleased to meet you, Mr. McKinley."

Darren's left arm snaked around my waist before he shook Skyler's hand. "Charmed. So glad Lucas was able to help you out."

Skyler pulled his lips together and nodded sheepishly. "Yeah, I'm really grateful Lucas and Cheyenne decided to become my fairy godbosses." He blinked at me with those wide blue puppy eyes. "I hope your mom also knows how much I appreciate it."

"Oh my god, of course. She talks about you all the time; you're practically her second son." I patted Darren's hand that still gripped my waist. "Skyler's been so good with the horses and the kids. The kids *love* him—"

Darren was still only addressing Skyler. "Yeah, Lucas has always been one to pick up strays. Obviously." He used his free arm to gesture to the ranch at large. "This place is all about charity."

His tone was calm and polite, but the words pricked my skin as they hung in the air. "Darren—" Embarrassment warmed my cheeks as I looked back at Skyler, who had gone rigid and quiet. Clearly whatever imaginary beef Darren had been cultivating hadn't run its course yet. But I'd assumed whatever it was he'd have it out with me—not a kid. "I'm so sorry, he didn't mean it like that—"

"Oh, no, I meant no offense," Darren said, though there was still ice in his eyes, which were fixed on Skyler. "I simply wanted to make sure he understands how nonprofits work before he goes on to join the real world. You'd think someone as affluent and influential as Cheyenne Barclay would find a way to turn this place profitable, but I get it. I know that's not what it's about." He brushed his finger across my cheek. "My Lucas has always been *soft*."

My breath caught, something raw ripping through my throat. "We should go," I managed, glancing apologetically back at Skyler. "I'm sorry, I'll see you later."

He nodded, his eyebrows furrowed in concern as he stared at me, then at Darren, and back again. "Okay. Um. Nice meeting you, Darren."

Darren didn't respond, turning the both of us around and leading us out to where I'd parked my car. We were quiet on the drive back to Darren's house, right up until we made our way inside.

"What was that about?" I asked the moment we stepped through the door. "He's a kid; why were you talking to him like that?"

Darren shrugged nonchalantly, removing his crusty shoes and leaving them in the doorway. "I wanted to make sure he knew where he stood."

"Where he stood *where*? At the *ranch*, where he *works*? Because I *hired* him?" I crossed my arms over my chest. My face had scrunched into a pout without my consent. "What about you? Why'd you decide to come by now all of a sudden? You're not jealous of a teenager, are you?"

"What if I am?" Something had sparked in Darren's eyes, filling them with a blistering heat that stole the air from my lungs. He stepped closer, tension rolling off him in waves as his hands clasped on either side of my waist. "What would you have to say about that?"

There was plenty to say—the thought that I'd be tempted to cheat on Darren with a teenager was not only massively wrong, it was also a little insulting. We'd have to talk about it, but right now the sinful curl of his lip was distracting.

My arms immediately uncrossed and, like a Pavlovian response, I gripped his shoulders. "I'd say you're being very silly," I said, my breath shaky. "You don't need to worry about him, I promise."

And then his lips were at my ear, a slight growl sending excited shivers down my back. "Prove it."

We stumbled to his bedroom, mouths bruising, clothes flying. I wanted to reassure him, make sure he knew he didn't need to feel threatened, but every time I reached for him, he moved my hands away.

"Please," I breathed, daring to arch up from my usual position on the mattress, "I can take care of you—"

Darren's palm, burning hot, pressed my chest back down, playfully but firmly. "Let's not mess with a good thing. I got it." Then he turned off the lights.

Of course—why would this time be any different? I tried not to think too hard, just relished what he was willing to give me. And took what I could get.

19

ARMAND HIDES LIKE A COWARDLY SOD

July 20th - Twenty-six days until the convention

I was sat staring at a potted fern, wondering with increasing horror whether I was meant to care for it. I did this for nearly twenty minutes before realizing with bone-shuddering relief that it was, in fact, made of plastic.

They'd given me an office. Apparently.

This was information that I'd only become aware of nearly a week into teaching the workshop. A student had come up to me after class and asked about office hours; I'd panicked. I joked that I couldn't hold office hours, I'd need an *office* for office hours! And both the student and Finch had looked at me like I was the village idiot. Which I clearly was.

"I *showed* it to you," Finch had muttered, then shook his head. "Jesus *Christ.*"

Then he had taken my hand, walked me out of the classroom, and physically led me a few feet down the corridor. To my *office*.

It was little more than a windowless cubby in a corner of the arts building, but importantly, it provided a space that was neither the classroom nor the flat in which to exist, and meet students who had specific concerns; like the young be-mulleted person (Ashley? Ashton? I had it written down somewhere) who'd felt the need to express their frustration, in person, regarding how long we'd spent on layout so far.

And then there had been the student who appeared to have stepped directly out of a cornfield with the intent of haunting some late nineteenth-century American architecture (Benson? Benjamin? . . . Beelzebub?), who'd wanted to talk about color theory—a strange choice, given my work was strictly monochrome. The students were nice, or at least harmless, and there was something oddly comforting about the realization that they were individuals rather than a faceless mob intent on devouring me whole.

My office was also providing a safe, secluded place in which to interview a young person who might be interested in displaying their naked body for the pedagogical benefit of the aforementioned not-a-mob.

I'd broken down the workshop into four parts by week, and the third involved figure drawing—the study of movement, expressions, body language—and unfortunately the best way to learn these things was through observation and practice. The students could study stock images for as long as they wanted, but nothing had taught me how to capture movement and presence and emotion like the sketches I'd been forever doodling of my fellow dancers. And to do that here, I needed a body. Or rather, a life model.

I'd received a total of three applications and blocked out an hour or so this afternoon in which to make my selection.

The first applicant was clearly titillated by the idea—*nope*—the second couldn't stop fidgeting or meet my eyes, and the third . . .

He came in, gave me a little smile, and sat down.

And he was perfect.

Well, not *perfect*—he was a bit too good looking for that— but he exuded a calm stillness that settled on myself and the dingy little office, surrounding us like a delicate layer of warmth. His very presence was *comforting*, quieting. Like a human cup of tea.

"Brilliant," I breathed. "Do you catch cold easily?"

He appeared a bit puzzled, but the smile remained. "Not really. Um, I'm Skyler, by the way. Skyler Evans."

Right. I knew that. Still, I jotted his name down on the piece of paper I held on my knee, for something to do. "I'm A-Armand. Demetrio. Er." But he must be aware of that already, having received my message and come to my office . . .

"Thanks for meeting with me, Professor Demetrio."

"Aye, but please, just call me Armand." *Bloody hell.* "Professor sounds so . . . so bloody *turgid.*"

"Okay." Skyler laughed softly. He leaned back, one hand on his knee, but even this movement was smooth, fluid, contained—the subtle bulge of muscle in his biceps, the sharp crease of his trousers, the long taper and clearly demarcated phalanxes of his fingers; honestly everything about him cried out, demanded, *begged* to be drawn.

I'd never met anyone who was so blatantly a collection of shapes and shadows.

"Any joint stiffness? Are you comfortable holding the same position for more than twenty minutes at a time?" He clearly was; he radiated whatever the opposite of restlessness was. *Peace.* Like he could remain immobile for hours if necessary, in the center of a fountain or a square, benevolently guarding the local pigeons.

Still, the considerate young man seemed to think about it. "Yeah. I don't get stiff very often, except during the thirty-hour bus ride I took when I moved out here, but I don't think that's necessarily relevant."

"No, this should be considerably less than thirty hours." I nodded. "So"—now for the biggie—"have you considered . . . the nudity?"

His eyebrows—both fascinatingly angled and shapely, the boy had *shapely* eyebrows for goodness' sake—furrowed slightly. "What about it?"

An incredulous smile pulled at the side of my mouth. "It's the type of thing that might give most people pause. They might be self-conscious, for example."

Skyler considered this with the same gravity that apparently suffused every part of his existence. "I guess. But it's not like it's inappropriate in an art class, right? I've never been particularly self-conscious about my body, and if the setting isn't . . . *weird*, I kind of feel like I'd be fine?"

"It isn't weird," I confirmed, then was overcome by my detestable honest streak. "It's a *bit* weird, honestly. It— Look"—I reached up to scratch at my stubbly cheek—"it's as weird as you make it, aye? I used to do something similar, and if you come to it with a firm idea of your role, a certain confidence, untouchability . . . people pick up on that. They accept the situation on *your* terms."

Skyler was nodding, as if this all made sense to him. The problem was, now that I'd started, I couldn't bring myself to stop.

"The only danger is losing sight of your own subjectivity," I continued helplessly. "Don't forget to exist outside their eyes. You can convince them you're an object, but you mustn't convince yourself." I tapped my pen against the paper and shook my head. "Sorry. I just . . . I want to make sure you know what you're signing up for. And you should also know some of the work will be displayed later on at a convention. Sorry."

"I'll keep that in mind." The boy's features were drawn up in introspection. "Don't objectify myself. Got it." He smiled. "I've actually done a little modeling before. Not *naked*, but I think I get what you're talking about."

"You have?" I asked in surprise.

"I put it in my application." Skyler reached into a pocket and retrieved his mobile, tapped at it for a few moments, then handed it to me. "Here."

It was open to a FotoBom page featuring Skyler in a variety of attitudes, accompanied by . . . *horses*.

My stomach turned cold and solid and *dropped*.

They were Lucas's bloody horses.

My Lucas. The one I'd been living with for over a week and hadn't even met yet. Lucas, who, this very morning, had sent me a litany of texts regarding proper shower etiquette—apparently, I was meant to rinse the tub after I showered to *avoid the buildup of soap scum and other nasty things, it just saves so much work in the long run and I wouldn't want you to slip and die because then I'll never find out what happens to that penguin :)*

He was being so very patient with me, despite the rise of deeply understandable frustration with my minging existence.

"Are you okay, Profe— Armand?" the cherubic creature before me asked in concern.

"Aye." I coughed and hurriedly handed him back his mobile. "Quite. Er. Those are lovely. Aye. You've got the job, mate."

Skyler's face broke into a sunny grin. "Wow, thank you!"

"Don't mention it." I coughed again. "So—so I'll see you early next week so we can do a dress rehearsal, or heh, an *un*dress rehearsal."

I gave him a pained smile. "Feel free to bring along a chaperone, er, a friend or parent or someone. *Ehrm*. I believe there's someone in the front office who'll have you fill out the proper forms?" Surely there were forms? No clue what kind or how many, but there were always forms, weren't there?

Skyler stood, still grinning, and held out a hand for me to shake. "Thanks again, sir."

"God, please, *sir* is worse than *professor*."

"Okay, Armand." He laughed. "See you next week." And then he left.

And I sat quietly in my horrible little office and let the water close in over my head. He knew Lucas. He worked with him.

It really was only a matter of time—I was delaying the inevitable, trying to hold back the tide of the world with nothing but my bare hands.

I still hadn't responded to the increasingly nerve-racking texts he'd sent me. To his request for a meeting. Instead, I'd taken to carefully listening at the door before I left my room, and only venturing forth once I was certain he'd left—somehow the thought of meeting him, which had been intimidating before, now caused my heart to pound in my throat.

It was irrational. It was *ridiculous*.

I couldn't put off meeting my flatmate indefinitely, especially considering how small the world appeared to be, and I knew he could be neither as punctilious nor as parochial as he seemed over text—after all, I'd found a TARDIS mug in the cupboard, and Pratchett on his bookshelf. But I'd become somewhat enamored with the idea of Lucas as an unseen presence who flitted about the flat while I slept, cleaning up messes and leaving snide little notes. Commentating on the out-of-context single pages of an already quite abstract comic I left out to dry.

I didn't want to meet this person who so clearly found me both obnoxious and amusing—especially since however negative his current impression of me, the real article could only bring his opinion lower.

It was mad, but part of me truly believed that if I could continue avoiding him until I fled the country (twenty-six days until the convention, twenty-eight until my flight home), I could get away with never meeting Lucas face-to-face. How hard could it be?

"Armand?"

I jumped, instinctively crumpling the paper I held—the one with Skyler's name on it and a surreptitious sketch I'd done of his sitting stance without even realizing—and inhaled sharply through my nose. "*Titch!*"

"Sorry." The little ginger stood in my office doorway and held up both his hands, smirking impishly. "I didn't realize how deep that reverie was. I thought you were just buffering or something."

I glared at him, then actively loosened my shoulders. It had become clear over the past week or so that Robin Finch, who initially appeared to hold me in some semblance of esteem, had become fully convinced of my ineptitude. Which, unfortunately, was fair. "Come to take me back to my kennel?"

He nodded. "Yeah, did you pick out a life model for us to ogle next week? Are they hot?"

This was exactly what I'd been worried about. "That is not the purpose of this exercise," I growled. "The whole point is to learn how to take in the aesthetic space of a person, capture their *energy*, their movement, not—"

"Okay, okay, calm down, Grandpa." He walked over and picked up my bag, shouldering it with an air of wardenship. "So did you find someone?"

I nodded resignedly and unfolded to my feet, stretching. "Aye, and you will treat him with respect and compassion."

"Obviously." Finch rolled his eyes and stood aside, motioning for me to move past him and out of the tiny office. "Can we get a move on? I've got a hot date on Friday, and I need to start my 24-hour skin care routine!"

He clearly wanted me to ask him about this, which was one of the many reasons I did not.

Finch dropped me off back at the flat, then headed right back to campus to prepare for his date. I climbed the stairs, swallowed the nerves I experienced every time I came home—*Is Lucas here? Is today the day? Please let it not be the day*—but as usual, the flat was empty.

I'd been especially concerned because this was a bit earlier than I tended to come home, considerably closer to late afternoon than evening.

As far as I could piece it together, my and Lucas's days went something like this:

Lucas rose obscenely early in the morning and fucked off to work with old horses and small children.

Many hours later, I would rise from my eldritch slumber and work on the comic until Finch came to collect me in the afternoon.

While I was at the university "teaching" my evening "class," Lucas arrived back at the flat and cooked and cleaned and puttered and did whatever domestic tasks functioning humans did to maintain their living environment. After class, Finch would return me to the flat. *This* time—the no-man's land of late evening—was by far the most dangerous, the most likely time we would run into each other. But luckily for me, Lucas tended to be out most nights and every weekend so far. One assumed he had that unthinkable condition known as a social life.

I'd had one, once upon a time. The kind normal people have. Even after I'd got clean, I'd still gone out with Sam and some of the other dancers after work—my sponsor, Karim, had said it was good for me, that there was nothing like a drinks do with friends. The danger was when I isolated myself and started drinking alone.

I thought this as I unpacked the bottle of Wild Turkey I'd ordered, grabbed a mug from the cupboard, and headed into my bedroom to work for a few hours before supper.

Just as I shut the door and started kicking off my shoes and unbuttoning my trousers, there was the jingle of keys, the creak of the front door—

Oh *god*!

I immediately dropped into a crouch and held my breath. He was home. Lucas was *home* and I was home as well. We were both home! He was out there doing things, and I was in here making an utter arsehole of myself.

I could hear him humming, puttering around the kitchen, tutting at the wrapping materials I'd left on the counter, and there must have been something about this mess that seemed recent, because then—

"Armand, are you here?" He sounded almost nervous. I heard him take a step, then another, drawing dangerously close to the door of my room. "Mr. Demetrio? Armand?"

Oh bloody hell. I was a grown man curled into a ball on the floor of his bedroom, hiding from a flatmate who merely wanted to . . . what? Say hello? Talk to me? At the very worst, admonish me for not tidying up after myself?

I could see his shadow moving under the door. No. *No*. Go *away*! I clenched a hand in my hair, bit down on a knuckle, and squeezed my eyes shut.

Knock, knock . . . knock.

Breathe, Demetrio, just breathe. And stop being so bloody dramatic! I should have responded. I should have stood to my feet and opened the door like an adult capable of human interaction—I'd talked to so many people today already, why was the idea of talking to Lucas so much more bowel-liquefying than that had been?

Why had this one man, this one demonstrably friendly albeit passive-aggressive man, become my social kryptonite?

Lucas heaved a softly disappointed sigh and padded back down the hall toward the kitchen.

I only allowed my body to relax once the door to his room shut. Then I collapsed onto the floor like the ridiculous creature I was and took a few deep breaths before doing my absolute best to lose myself in work and whiskey. I had to answer his texts, I absolutely had to. This couldn't continue.

But deferred pain was still an absence of pain, and sometimes that was the best one could hope for.

20
ROBIN GOES
ON A DATE

I sat in the coffee shop and gnawed at my fingernails. I was looking back and forth between the door and the chair across from me. The empty one. The one that Skyler would sit in when he got here.

This was everything I'd ever dreamed of, wasn't it?

A *date*.

My first ever, with a gorgeous knight in shining armor who had already seen me at my most ridiculous and had still said *yes. He'd. Love. To.*

And yet, ricocheting through my body was a loud and high-pitched *Help!*

I was *terrified*. All my life, all I'd wanted was a cute boy to like me and go on a date with me. But now that it was happening, I was almost too scared to breathe.

I swear to god that when the question had left my lips, the only response I'd expected from him was laughter. But he'd said yes. He'd even seemed happy about it, as if . . . as if he was interested in me.

What the hell do I do now?

I closed my eyes and took a few deep calming breaths through my nose, fanning myself with the menu.

"Are you okay?"

I opened my eyes and nearly swallowed my tongue. Skyler was standing over the table, with a concerned, amused smile. He was wearing a plain T-shirt and jeans, but forever looked as if he'd just stepped out of the pages of a magazine. Especially backlit by the very last rays of a classic late July sunset.

Swallowing my nervous scream, I tried to grin up at him in a nonmaniacal manner. "I'm fine! Hi!" I sprang to my feet and grabbed the back of the chair across from me, holding it out and waving my other arm toward the seat like I was presenting a car on a gameshow. "This is for you! I mean, this seat, sh-should you choose to accept it, is yours. You can sit down here. If you want. Please."

At the last minute, I managed to clap a hand over my mouth, hoping it seemed like I was simply doing something normal rather than physically forcing myself to shut up. Then I sat my freakish little ass down and set my hands flat on the table so they'd stop *embarrassing* me.

Skyler appeared to accept the deeply confusing gesture and sat down, biting his lip in understandable awkwardness. "Thank you. Um."

"Eheh." I managed to spark the ignition in my brain. "Um, so how have you been? What do you do? What do you like? Where are you from?" I cut myself off with a pinch.

Skyler froze for a minute, then managed to smile. "Should I answer all of those at once or one at a time?"

"Sorry, how about the first one? How are you?"

"I'm okay. Better than I've been. How about you?"

How did he expect me to think while he kept smiling at me like that? "B'gah . . . Oh, um fine. You know. Better. Than the other night. Heh." Was it just me or was it a million degrees in here? "I'm glad you agreed to this. To meet up with me."

His smile turned a little shy, and it was all I could do to keep from melting. "Yeah, I don't exactly know how to make friends, never been good at it . . ."

Friends?

Oh.

I swallowed hard, gripping the table to keep from keeling over dead on the spot. "Really? Y-you don't have many friends?"

He seemed thoughtful for a moment. "I've only ever had *three*— two back home and one here, and"—I swore his cheeks went a little pink—"I guess you'd make four."

I smiled as warmly as I could and nodded. "I'd very much like to make four."

He laughed softly and started perusing the menu, while I had an internal all-out hissy fit.

Friends.

Yes. I was mad about that, but you know what made me even madder? The fact that the moment he'd said that, I'd been flooded with *relief.*

How much of a coward could I *be*?

Still, it had become infinitely easier to think and speak.

Skyler got himself a cup of tea, and I got a raspberry cheese pastry, and we both munched and sipped for a while. I kept swinging between desperation and despair—one minute I was trying to find a way to re-ask Skyler out on this date, make it clear to him what my intentions were, and the next I was trying to keep myself from doing exactly that by stuffing larger and larger bits of pastry into my mouth.

"Hey, slow down." Skyler chuckled and patted my hand, causing me to almost swallow my own tongue. "It won't run away."

I swallowed painfully and coughed. "S-so two back home?"

"Excuse me?"

"Two back home. Friends. You said you have them."

He still seemed confused, but then his face cleared. "Oh, yes, um, Matt and . . . Matt and Delia."

Delia? His voice had hitched a bit when he said her name, did— Oh my god.

Oh my *god*, was I *that* off base? Dear sweet lordy loo, Robin Finch's faulty gaydar strikes again—disaster ensues! "Delia, huh?" I choked.

Skyler nodded, quietly staring into his tea with the tragic Byronic brow I'd been dreading.

I swallowed even harder. "And she was just a friend?" I was a glutton for punishment.

Skyler's cheeks colored, which was quickly replaced by a delicately masked hurt, some pain he'd already become adept at papering over. "I, uh . . . it was complicated."

I waited silently, trying as ever to *not* start screaming and tearing my hair out.

Finally, he broke into a sad and self-deprecating smile. "I guess it's pretty classic . . . my brother's girl and all."

Oh you would *lead a life lifted out of a country song.* "That's too bad," I managed.

He shrugged, staring down into his mug.

I got the distinct feeling there was more to this story. "Did something happen?"

Skyler looked up quickly, clearly horrified. "No. *No.* It's just . . ." He took a deep breath. "It's complicated because I thought I didn't feel that way about people. Like, I'd never experienced that before. Ever. With anyone."

"No other girls?" Where did I get off asking him stuff like this? Why not just straight up ask: *Have you only ever been attracted to girls or have you ever considered dating non-girls? A boy maybe? Specifically a short, skinny, red-haired boy who may or may not be sitting across from you right this moment? Please?*

Amazingly, Skyler didn't appear embarrassed by the question and seemed to be seriously considering it. "Nope."

That right there? That was a cruel and enduring little ray of hope. "So she's really the only *girl* you've ever liked?"

He nodded, then gave a sad laugh. "She's the only *person* I've ever liked, in that way."

Yes, that did mean what I thought it meant—Skyler could very well be bisexual or pan. *Oh dear god, why am I doing this to myself?*

Just as I was about to start hyperventilating, Skyler gave a gentle cough. "Wow. I've never actually told anyone that before. Obviously I can't tell Matt, that's my brother. It used to be that anything I couldn't tell Matt, I could tell Delia, but they're so happy together and I just needed to get *out*—" He wet his lips, clearly forcing a smile. "What about you?"

"W-what about me what?"

"I don't know, who was *your* first crush?" He was trying to seem playful, which combined with the silky locks and twinkling blue eyes might well have been illegal in certain states.

"Benny Horrowitz, kindergarten. I watched him swallow a slug, and it was the greatest feat of bravery I'd ever seen." This was getting stupidly uncomfortable. "Let's not talk about me. It's boring. Where are you from?"

"I'm from Seattle, where we have slugs but don't usually eat them. As far as I know." He shook his head at me, smiling. "And for the record, anyone who admits to being into slug-eating is automatically the opposite of boring. Where are you from?"

"Ah, Seattle. Rain. Space Needle."

"Are you telling me you are *also* from Seattle or are you avoiding the question?"

"What, do I not look like I could be from Seattle? Not good enough for the Pacific North Wet?"

"Robin."

He said. My name.

I swallowed hard and forced a laugh. "Okay, yeah, I'm from here. Like, *here* here." I nervously crumpled the edge of the wax paper my pastry had come with. "My whole life. Same town. Same people, same . . . *issues*." Oh no.

He watched me carefully for a moment, then, "Issues? Like that guy? The one who . . . assaulted you the other night?" He said it in a gentle voice, like I was an animal he was trying to keep calm.

My body tried to shudder at the memory, but I was holding myself as stiffly as possible now. "Yeah, Terri Bishop. He's been doing stuff like that for years." There was no point in lying; Skyler had already seen the worst of it.

Skyler was frowning, and his hand twitched like it might take mine, which it couldn't because I'd *die*. "Years?" he asked. "You haven't told anybody?"

I shrugged, surreptitiously taking my hands off the table and clasping them over my knees. "Yeah. Um, I actually *have*, but you know how it is. This isn't the kind of thing people care about. Even though he usually does this stuff in public, he makes it look . . . Like, he makes it seem funny, mostly, so they don't see it as a problem, I guess? He was supposed to have moved away, but—" My breath hitched, and I forced a grin. "Well, at least I got to meet you because of it."

Skyler didn't smile back. "What do you mean people don't care?"

I took a deep breath. "He's good at making it seem like we're friends. Like it's a game, and I'm in on it. A-and when I've tried to fight, it gets worse, so—so I just *don't*."

Skyler was straight up scowling now; the simmering rage behind his eyes almost made me faint. "That's horrible. I'm so sorry. Someone should do something. You can't live your life in fear."

All I'd wanted was a date, and all I *got* was *Dateline*. Typical. I tried to keep grinning. "Watch me."

"Robin, that's not funny." He looked so *sad*, and he'd said my name again. *Ugh*. "I'm sorry, I know it's not my place, we just met, but—"

"No, no, you're right." I sat up, frowning. "And actually, on that note, I'm going to head home before it gets too dark." I got to my feet, crumpling up the rest of my pastry into its waxy paper bag.

Skyler's eyes widened. "Wha—? Do you want me to walk with you?"

Oh no, I couldn't possibly handle that. Mercy. *Uncle*. "No." Then despite myself, I immediately added, "Can we meet again, though? Soon?"

He nodded, brows furrowed. "Sure, just let me know when you have time." His concern was causing my legs to liquefy again.

"I will. Um, nice seeing you." And I shot out the door as quickly as my liquidy legs could carry me.

This was so beyond typical. He wanted to save me—the thought made my cheeks burn and my head try to float away—but not in the way I wanted to be saved.

Friends. No, not even friends. He thought of me as a kitten he'd saved from a tree. I didn't want to be his kitten. *Or* his friend, I wanted . . .

What I couldn't have. As usual.

21
(TEXTING INTERLUDE 3)

July 21ˢᵗ

Armand: *Sorry about the shower.*
Lucas: *omg hi, didn't think I'd hear from you! No worries about the shower but also maybe kind of worry about the shower?* :)
Armand: *I shall do my best.*
Lucas: *so I guess now that we've connected, did you want to try and meet up? I swore I almost ran into you the other day*
Armand: *Unlikely. I'm very busy.*
Armand: *Making messes. I'm sure we'll bump into each other eventually.*
Lucas: *I don't know, it hasn't happened yet—sure you don't wanna schedule something?*

22
LUCAS LOSES EVERYTHING

July 22nd

D arren's fancy-schmancy work party was on the horizon, which meant that I'd spent the last two hours in the fitting room of his favorite boutique, making sure that whatever I wore would be absolutely perfect.

"Hm. No," he said in regards to a sleek, powder blue suit I came out modeling. "I told you, a black suit is classic. Mature."

"Yeah, and boring."

"Boring like me?" Darren leaned forward on the chaise he'd been lounging on. "We have to match, Lucas. My plus-one is a reflection on me, I told you that."

"I know, but—" I arched around to check the mirror, admiring the tastefully subtle little sparkles across the jacket lapels. "Gray is blah, and black washes me out."

Darren got to his feet with a soft sigh. "Black is slimming, Lucas."

My heart sank, and my fingers crept protectively to my stomach.

"So sorry to interrupt," interrupted the fitting-room attendant, holding out several more options. "But may I perhaps offer a compromise? A rich, midnight blue for instance? Or this—" he presented me with a lovely suit with a satin trim "—a sea-glass green, would really bring out your eyes."

It *was* a marvelous color. "I love that," I said, deliberating between it and the blue I was wearing. "I'm torn. I love the sparkles, though . . . What do you think, in your professional opinion?"

The attendant's eyes flickered from Darren to me. He cleared his throat. "Well. It is true that black is timeless, and a very dapper choice for a formal event—"

"See?" Darren angled his chin at the fitting room before turning to the attendant. "He'll do the black."

We drove back to his house in tense silence, my fingers clenching together in my lap. The atmosphere was stifling, and I braved a glance over at Darren gripping the steering wheel. "I think that poor attendant thought we were gonna start fighting or something. Make a whole spectacle slap-fighting in front of the customers . . ." I shot him a careful smile, "destroy the fitting room in the throes of passion?"

"Oh," Darren said coolly, "was that why you were flirting with him?"

I'd been avoiding this conversation since the Skyler incident. I steadied myself. "Okay, why do you always think I'm flirting with service people? It's their job to be nice and friendly. I *am* nice and friendly—"

"It's not about being nice and friendly," Darren snapped, pulling smoothly up to the house. "It's about being embarrassing." He stepped out of the car, slamming the door shut.

"Embarrassing?" I followed him into the house, mouth agape. I had braced myself for another few hours of soothing Darren's ego, reassuring him of my fidelity—not whatever this was. "You're embarrassed by me?"

Darren tossed his keys onto the kitchen counter with a loud *crack* against the granite. "That's not the point. I thought we were past this."

"Past *what*?" I stood in the kitchen doorway staring at him, my pulse racing. "What are you talking about?"

Darren scrubbed the roots of his hair, gazing up at the ceiling for a long moment. "Maybe you shouldn't come to the dinner."

I inched closer, his words buzzing in my ears. "Darren, what? Why? I—" I gently reached for him and he allowed me to hold his arm. "Maybe I'm stupid, but just explain it to me, okay? I don't know what you're talking about—"

"Lucas." His voice was colder this time. "You're always looking for validation. From me, from random servers, from the goddamn *teenager* you pay to fawn over you all day. It's exhausting. And childish."

I was frozen, still gripping Darren's arm like a lifeline. I couldn't breathe.

"I need to be taken seriously at work, Lucas—" he shifted, taking hold of my shoulders "—and I can't have you sashaying around this party asking people if they like your *sparkles*."

"I-I wouldn't do that; I know how important this dinner is for you, I won't say anything. We bought the black suit, we'll match, just like you wanted." I spread my arms helplessly. "I won't talk to any servers or smile at any waiters, I promise."

Darren groaned. "I told you, that's not the point."

"Then what *is* the point?"

"The point is this was a mistake." It came out of him in a rush, like he was out of breath. He dropped his eyes, fiddling with the corner of the counter. He looked . . . unsteady.

Darren was never unsteady.

"What's a mistake?" I asked, barely above a whisper.

He swallowed, still avoiding my gaze. "Us. This. I don't know if it makes sense anymore. I don't know if it ever did."

My chest hollowed out, and I was shaking. "What do you mean? *This* has been working since high school—"

High school, where he'd been there for me through the death of my dad, through the bouts of bullying, through my first kiss, my first time, my first—

"As a *hookup*, Lucas," Darren said, and my rib cage shattered. "I need to settle down and think of my future. We're almost thirty and you're just fucking around with horses all day at a job you got from your *mom*, pretending you're going to be a real photographer."

My feet seemed to sink into the floor. "Why are you talking to me like this? I-I don't understand, Darren, you were the one who wanted to make this official—"

Darren scoffed, stepping backward. He held up his hands defensively. "Don't act like you weren't desperate for this to happen. Like you haven't been planning our wedding since sophomore year."

"I haven't! I—" Now I was the one short of breath. "Is . . . is this why you didn't want me to move in?" I was going to be sick. "You want commitment and to settle down? I'm giving you that! How can I be pressuring you to move too fast but also not be serious enough?"

Darren stared back, quietly deflating. My heart hung in my throat, watching as he rubbed the back of his neck. "I didn't see it going this far, that's why." He slid his hands into his pockets and hung his head, peering up at me from below his hair. "I think we should take a break."

And there it was.

I grasped for something, anything to reason with him, to convince him he was wrong about us, wrong about me, but all that came out was: "But I don't know what I did wrong!"

"Lucas," and how dare he sound so tired, so done, "you're not right for me. At least not now."

All my fears, all my insecurities that had accumulated since high school came crashing down around me. My head buzzed, my hands went numb. "Then when? It's been ten years, what more can I do—"

Darren shrugged, like he wasn't breaking my heart into pieces. "I don't know that there's anything to do. I need someone serious, someone with discipline, and I don't think it's fair to push you anymore. You are who you are."

"Darren, please, I'll do whatever you want, I can be that person, I can—" I was crying, sniveling like a child, but I couldn't stop, couldn't breathe; I would get on my knees and beg, *Please don't do this.* "I love you, and I know you care about me. I-I can be whatever you want me to be. Just don't—"

"Lucas, I can't be whatever you want *me* to be. I'm trying to become somebody, and you . . . you're holding me back. I thought we could evolve together, but I don't think you *can*." He was standing straight again, immune to my tears, the way I reached for him. "Don't make this harder." Darren held out his palm.

I didn't understand, nothing was making sense, and I could barely see through the haze that was hovering at the edges of my vision.

"My key, Lucas."

Somehow my fingers found my key ring, fumbling over the shape of his house key, the one I'd waited so long to be given, which he *had* given me. I let it tremble into his hand. "Please—"

And Darren smiled, and I knew that smile—it was the one he always wore when listening to me talk about my photos, or about the future, or when, for some brief, gleaming moment, I was proud of myself.

It wasn't sweet—it was pitying.

"Take care of yourself, Lucas." He slipped his hands into his pockets, then jerked his chin toward the door. And stared at me.

I couldn't breathe, but I forced my feet to move, to push me back outside into hateful sunlight, down the front walk to my car.

23
ARMAND LETS
THE SIDE DOWN

July 22ⁿᵈ - Twenty-four days until the convention

"All right." I threw up the slide I'd made of several pages side by side: a classic Kirby dynamic spread, a Satrapi progression, a Tezuka action sequence. "You lot can see this, aye?"

There was a general murmur of assent from the class.

"You see the movement? It's not always about fancy panels, action lines, and all that. Look at the *breaths* here, the negative space. The bits you show, the framing, the perspective, they're important, aye? But it's also the bits you *skip*, where you *linger*— Er, yes?"

I should have known all their names by now, but the girl with her hand in the air was unfortunately known to me only as "the one with blue glasses and afro puffs who needed to work on her word-to-picture ratio."

She beamed at me. "Like pages twenty-two and twenty-three in Issue Two?"

I tried not to visibly cringe, but I did audibly gulp. The only thing worse than people reading or discussing my current work was people reading or discussing my *past* work. The spread she was referring to depicted a truly *loony* sequence, involving a drop of water and a moth, that, to be fair, I'd drawn while coked out of my mind four years ago.

She had a point, however.

"Oh, aye, right." I tried to smile at her. "Exactly. It's about the choices you make. You get to . . . to *curate*. To make good choices. Encapsulation, see?" I switched the slide to a page from Keum Suk Gendry-Kim's *Grass*.

There was another murmur of understanding that made its way through the classroom. People made notes or nodded, as if what I'd said had made perfect sense to them.

"Young artists tend to throw all their energy into characters and micro-expressions," I heard myself continue to ramble against all odds, "becoming slaves to the close-up and allowing the rest of the world to hang off them like scenery, but—but it's always struck me as a flawed approach, you know? I want you lot to at least have the tools you might need to create story-scaffolding through form decisions—a stage for your characters to perform on that's more than just a bland vehicle for content. Is that so wrong?"

The students stared at me wide-eyed, almost somber. After a moment, one of them said, "No, we get it." And the others nodded along as if I'd just given them a rousing speech outside the gates of Syracuse.

This was never going to stop being *bizarre*.

But it *had* got a bit ... fun.

My rapport with the classroom had been improving steadily, to the point where I no longer vomited before class. However, they still left me drained at the end of every evening; I felt I'd come off eight hours of manual labor rather than two hours of talking.

The students, strangely enough, seemed to be enjoying themselves. More strangely, their work was *improving*. Some were hopeless, aye, but a few seemed to be picking up what I was trying to teach them and applying it to their artwork. Nearly everyone's pacing had gotten better.

Even Finch had refined his *odd* vampire romance cartoon. Though he'd seemed rather distracted lately.

"Hey, Armand." He approached me awkwardly after class, worrying his hands. "Um, sorry, I messed up the schedule. I've got rehearsal tonight; is there any chance you could take a rideshare home?"

Something was clearly wrong. Finch usually exuded joy like cartoon stink lines, but now he was gray and sketchy around the edges—it was abundantly clear that his "hot date" had not gone to plan. He still carried the same amount of nervous energy, but he was framed by a blight of sheepishness rather than his usual crackle of mischief.

I felt bad now for having been annoyed by his chirpiness. "Not a problem, Titch. Er. Are you all right?"

"Huh? What? No, I'm great." He gave me a brittle grin. "Sorry again. Gotta run. Have a good weekend!" And darted out of the hall.

Right.

I was more than capable of finding my own way back to the flat. I gathered my things and started out of the classroom, finding myself unwilling to go home directly. I had no desire to sit in my office for any length of time, but the longer I took getting home, the less likely I was to run into Lucas.

I wandered across the campus, thinking about the next day's lesson—we were still on layout and gutterlines but preparing to move onto foreground. I was less concerned now with my students being tempted into all-consuming detail work; we'd established a strong baseline, and they were unlikely to lose sight of the bigger picture.

At this point, I looked up to find I'd wandered so far from the arts building and was quite lost. Chagrin burned in my chest. Also heartburn. I hated the idea that without Finch's gentle guidance I was not quite capable of getting myself home.

I got handled. I knew this, but nowhere in my soon-to-be-dropped contract did it say I had to *like* it.

I channeled enough brain power into analyzing my surroundings to realize I was nearly off campus, faced with a row of pubs and shops that were doing a lively evening trade. A small world of soft lamps and the clink of glasses and dull roar of conversation. This allowed me to discover something new about myself.

It turned out, I was now a codger who hated university pubs.

They were full of light and laughter and youth. These aspects had not always been repulsive to me, but I supposed we grew and changed as people. I had not previously known that I had grown and changed to *this* extent, and I wasn't particularly grateful for the opportunity to find out. But I wasn't ready to head back to the flat, and it couldn't hurt to have a few drinks at a shitty pub before a rideshare took me home and I'd have to ink more pages.

I'd been having miniature heart attacks whenever the pages I'd left out to dry in the living room suddenly vanished, but I always found them again in a neat pile, accompanied by a snarky note. Though I hadn't heard from Lucas since yesterday.

It was possible that Martha was not pleased with me. Perhaps I'd done something especially heinous, though as certainly had become quite evident, I was a veritable joy to live with. One mirror drawing too many, perchance.

Even Gaston and LeFou had begun giving me reproachful looks lately. All the more reason to do my drinking out of the house.

I chose a little place called Valhalla, the outward appearance of which was deceptive in regards to the amount of noise one encountered upon entering. Noxious pop music filled the air, large screens displayed the physical achievements of various athletes, and the population was largely juvenile, drunk, and sloppy.

They all looked so happy it made my gorge rise.

Codger.

Still, I found a spot at the bar and squinted up at the drink prices scribbled in chalk. I couldn't help softly whistling through my teeth.

The bartender headed over, looking not quite as happy as the clientele. She apparently took her job seriously, however, as she leaned past the beer tap and shot me a white, perfectly symmetrical, American smile. "What can I get you, stranger?"

I sighed. "I don't suppose you have discounts for faculty?"

She laughed, which was not a good sign.

"The prices here are aimed at the trust-fund crowd." Someone chuckled over my shoulder, and I turned to see a young man seated next to me, smiling and cleaning his glasses with an honest-to-gods handkerchief.

Perhaps *young* was a bit generous, especially considering the average age in the room was barely out of its teens; he had to be in his midforties, going very distinguished at the temples and sporting the kind of laugh lines and crow's feet that made me think of strong Western men in blue jeans and plaid.

I swallowed heavily. "E-excuse me?"

He replaced his glasses and immediately went from roguish to sophisticated, smiling at the pretty bartender with only half his mouth.

"Two gin and tonics, honey." He glanced over at me as an apparent afterthought. "You a gin man?"

"W-whiskey," I managed.

"All right then, one gin and tonic, one whiskey sour for my young English friend here." He slapped a card on the bar, then glanced over at me, still smiling. "Discount for faculty, huh? You giving a class on how to perfect an East London accent?"

A smile pulled at the edges of my mouth. "How long?"

"Three years." He grinned. "Got my MA at Oxford." He paused for a moment as our drinks arrived, and took an appreciative sip of his gin and tonic, while I downed about half of mine out of sheer nerves. He chuckled at me again for no apparent reason and leaned in a little closer. "So what brings you to our shores?"

I cleared my throat. Surely it hadn't been *that* many decades since I'd flirted with anyone . . . Except it had. I was learning how to person again, I really was, but this felt like a sudden jump in difficulty level. A surprise exam. "I'm teaching a comics workshop," I said finally. "Extremely prestigious."

"Dr. Ken Lazlo." He presented me with a hand to shake, which I did. "I'm a postdoc in the English Lit department. Visiting Scholar, technically."

"Of course you are." I couldn't help myself.

Luckily for me, he chuckled and raised an elbow to show me the leather patch. "I keep my pipe in my other tweed. So what's your name, *lad*? Don't force me to start calling you Laughing Boy."

I smiled despite myself. "Armand. I'm just tired."

Laughing Boy was an ironic term for someone looking miserable—very English and sardonic. And dated.

I know it made me trash, but I really couldn't help it: I found it charming.

Ken could tell. He placed a hand on my arm. The hairs there tried to stand to attention as gooseflesh pervaded up and down my skin. I swallowed again and looked over at him fully.

The glint in his eyes told me he had a bit of a head start on me as far as gin was concerned, but the sudden subtlety of his touch on my arm and the discreet angling of his legs told me a lot more. The area between my jawline and my ears grew hot, color rising to my cheeks. How long *had* it been?

Over a year. Even before Drake House had signed me and I'd quit my old job, I'd somehow managed to keep myself to myself. I still went out with friends on occasion, but they tended to keep me close, like I was a precious, somewhat addled elderly relative being shown a night on the town. When I did the rare signing or promotion event (where I was merely expected to sign things or stand places), there was always Lakshmi or some liaison or other; Robin Finches in their various guises and incarnations tasked with keeping me on track.

I hadn't been out to a pub on my own in ages, and I was starting to remember why.

Ken ordered and bought me half a dozen more drinks, telling me all about his novel, screenplay, and the stage play he'd written. He told me about his research and travels. About how he'd spent a month stranded in Glasgow with pneumonia. About how the policemen in Venice could be easily bribed with pirated DVDs of *Space Trip*. About a certain little eatery in New Delhi, etc., and once I couldn't help laughing or smiling at practically everything he said, Ken called us a car and next thing I knew ...

I leaned my forehead against the cool metal wall of the lift that was taking us up to Ken's flat. His mouth was against my neck and his index finger was snug in one of my belt loops, his large square hand secure and solid over my hip. Once the doors slid shut, Ken pressed my back into the wall, fingers already fiddling.

I responded in kind, letting an entire year of missed opportunities tremble their way through my fingers as I loosened his tie.

July 23rd - Twenty-three days until the convention

I woke to the sound of the shower running, and my first thought was to wonder what Lucas was doing home so late on a Saturday morning.

Then I opened my eyes and realized that while Lucas might have been home, *I* was not.

I was at Ken's flat, in Ken's bed, and I could see, from where I lay, my underpants flung over a lampshade.

Before I could stop myself, I'd curled into a ball and was trying to stuff my fist into my mouth.

Why did I do this!

I actually *liked* Ken. I wanted him to think of me as something more than an easy pub pull, and naturally, I'd chosen to demonstrate this by *being an easy pub pull!* This was why I wasn't allowed out on my own.

I straightened out again, covering my face with both hands, and then peeked through my fingers at the flat. I'd been a bit busy the night before and had yet to fully take in the surroundings. It was small and overstuffed with books and oversized antique furniture, but it was clean, and there were no immediate indications that I'd gone home with an axe murderer. I sat up in the large, tousled bed, and glanced over at the door that—by the sound of it—led to the bathroom. Should I join Ken in there or wait, pretending to be asleep when he came out?

I really had enjoyed myself last night; he was funny and sophisticated, and I couldn't help liking the way his nostrils flared whenever he was being overly descriptive in that delicious, self-indulgent, patronizing way of untenured men. Also, needless to say, we had enjoyed quite a lot of nonverbal fun, and he had excelled at that as well.

In the back of my mind, my friends judged me: Sam rolled their eyes and Craig tutted. I was notorious for my taste—they would have seen Dr. Ken Lazlo coming and hastily herded me away from his tweedy arse—especially when it came to intellectually superior men in middle age whose pomposity could and would not be curtailed. Men who would, without the slightest provocation or note of apology, correct my pronunciation or patiently explain that the Hegelian Dialectic *wasn't* simplistic and dichotomous, *actually*, for the following reasons.

I'm not proud of this, but there was a special little glow I felt when men like that deigned to take time out of their day—or night—to try to educate me.

I was about to get out of bed and go join Ken when the sound of the tap shut off. After a few moments, he came out of the bathroom wrapped in a thick robe, his salt-and-pepper hair slicked down and glinting.

When he saw me, his eyes widened and his mouth quirked off to the side in a surprised smile. "Hey, you're still here . . ."

My stomach dropped.

I tried to smile as well. "Yes, er, good morning."

"Good morning." He made his way over and cupped the back of my head with one hand, gently kissing my forehead. "I think I saw your pants over by the bookcase."

I nodded a little brokenly and got up to start hunting for my clothes, wrapping the sheet from the bed tightly around my waist.

I'd already collected everything but my shirt, when Ken's arms suddenly snaked in from behind and fastened over my chest and stomach, his head resting on my shoulder as he nuzzled my temple. His stubble tickled, and I had to fight down a shiver.

"I'm sorry I'm practically throwing you out, but Charlene's plane gets in this afternoon," he murmured, as the hand on my stomach began to both travel and misbehave itself.

I drew a hissing breath and gripped his wrist, stalling the hand's nefarious designs. "Charlene?"

"My wife, remember? I told you last night. She went to Michigan for a job talk and she's coming home today."

I tried to ignore the bitter lump rising in my throat. "Oh, aye, right."

Ken chuckled and nipped at my ear. "Could you be any more adorably English? 'Oh, aye, right,'" he mocked. "You're a better man than I am, Gunga Din."

"Aye. Wow," I muttered hoarsely. "Have you seen my shirt?"

Less than ten minutes later, I was fully dressed in a rideshare, and twenty minutes after that I was standing in the Briars lot.

He might have mentioned a Charlene last night. I didn't remember.

Maybe.

Damn.

I didn't know why I ever expected things to go differently . . . I truly had no one to blame but myself and my warped proclivity for rejection. Who the hell was I to lecture anyone about making good choices? Even in the intensely specific context of bloody comics layout.

Deep down, I clearly *hadn't* expected things to go differently. I'd actually been relying on the fact that Dr. Lazlo would toss me out on my ear come morning.

I stood staring up at the stairs of the Briars complex that led to my flat and tried not to think of them as unsurmountable. My body felt heavy but hollow, and also very far away. I was safe, though, in the knowledge that Lucas was almost certainly out—it was nearly noon on a Saturday, and he was likely somewhere doing something supremely Californian and aesthetic which might involve horses. It was a small mercy that while he was unfortunately witness to many other shameful aspects of my life—such as everything about me—this particular walk would go unseen.

Eventually, I made it up the steps and got my keys in the door, preparing for an hour or more spent in the shower, but then . . .

I stepped off the welcome mat into a disaster area.

There were messily balled-up tissue papers covering practically every surface, so that for a split second I thought I was faced with the results of an indoor snowstorm. Interspersed among the tissues were bits of ripped-up photographs and wispy stuffing—the kind you might pull out of a stuffed toy. There had been a few spills in the kitchen—Kahlua and cocoa, as well as several patches of melted ice cream and an uneaten frozen burrito in the microwave.

A glint drew my eyes back to the living room and I watched the sunlight wink over a messy pile of CDs next to the hi-fi. I sifted through a few of the albums: Tchaikovsky, Mendelssohn, Mozart . . . *ABBA?* And here was Queen's *Night at the Opera* and some Celine Dion . . .

Out of curiosity, I pressed Play on the stereo.

The sound of synths pulsated under Steve Perry's voice telling me that one day, I would be found by love.

Oh my god.

Before I could stop myself, I pressed Skip. And Eric Carmen was telling me about his long-gone, misspent youth. That now, against his wishes, he was all by himself.

Oh my *god*.

I shut the player off and before I could think better of it, I turned toward the hallway and called out, "Lucas?"

Silence.

I tried again, louder. "Lucas, are you there? Are you *all right*?" I stepped into the hallway and knocked on his door, then pressed my ear against it to listen—*nothing*. I knocked once more, and this time the door cracked open enough for me to peek in and confirm the room was empty. I shut the door, checked the bathroom—nope—and that was it, that was the entire flat.

He wasn't here.

I sat down heavily on the couch, surveying the devastation spread so eloquently before me.

It was safe to say that whatever degree crap I was feeling, Lucas was out there feeling much, much worse.

24
(TEXTING INTERLUDE 4)

*July 23*rd

Armand: *Lucas are you already?*
Armand: **alright*
Armand: *Lucas?*
Armand: *What happened?*
Armand: *Lucas, I'm sorry, I hope you're airtight*
Armand: **alright*

25
SKYLER SHEDS HIS LAYERS

July 24th

I hadn't heard from Lucas or Robin in several days, which presumably meant I no longer had any friends. Bianca, one of the ranch hands whose daughter lived near campus, drove me to and from The End Is Neigh, but ever since Darren had showed up at the ranch, I hadn't seen Lucas or Cheyenne at all.

This morning I was doing fence maintenance—some of the horses loved scratching themselves on the posts, which slowly collapsed, becoming increasingly horizontal and stretching out the wires. It was my job to walk along the fence and do the little repairs I could by hand, and mark where we might need new postholes. I'd stopped to rub the nose of Hortense—one of the sillier but sweeter senior horses—when I heard the puttering of a golf cart.

I turned to see Cheyenne Barclay pull up in the "feed wagon," and she hopped out to set a bucket in front of Hortense, who no longer cared even a little bit about me.

"Hey, Skyler." She grinned. Her blonde hair was in a tiny ponytail and a plaid shirt was knotted at her waist over high-rise jeans. It was weird—she looked like a stereotype of her job. "You doing okay?"

I smiled. I'd been hoping to run into her to ask about Lucas, but she'd been away from the ranch on non-horse-related business. "Yeah, thanks. Um. How's Lucas?"

She sighed. "He's okay, poor baby. Just a bad breakup with Darren, which I can't say I didn't see coming. He's staying with some friends right now, but he'll be back soon. I'm sure."

No wonder I hadn't heard from him. For some reason I couldn't figure out, Lucas had really loved his boyfriend, and I was positive that, whatever had happened, it wasn't his fault. "That's awful," I said, trying not to think about Lucas "Eternal Positivity and Sunshine" Barclay being emotionally devastated. "I mean, I did meet Darren once and he was . . ." Was talking about this with Cheyenne unprofessional? *Screw it.* "Kind of a dick to Lucas."

But Cheyenne didn't chide me. She leaned in closer, eyes wide. "He was always a dick! That boy's been toxic for years, and I know why Lucas never listened to *me* about him, but I kept hoping maybe he'd realize it and break things off. Just . . ." Her face fell. "I hate that it ended like this."

I nodded, pulling off one of my work gloves so I could scratch my nose. "I hope he's not being too hard on himself." I hadn't known Lucas that long, only a couple of weeks, but that had been long enough to notice that as nice as he was to other people, he could be pretty mean to himself.

"I hope so too." Cheyenne came over and thoughtfully considered the work I'd done on the fence. "This is looking good! Hand me those pliers, would you?"

I kept working until midafternoon, when Bianca drove me back to campus, then I took a quick shower and headed to the arts building, where Professor Demetrio had asked me to meet him.

I checked my phone as I walked, but there were no new messages. It was understandable why Lucas wasn't responding to my texts. But I still had no idea why Robin was doing the same thing. I hadn't heard from him all weekend, since we'd had tea and I'd told him about . . . her.

I hadn't told anyone about her before.

It was a little unsettling to think about how easily it had come out of me, after months and months of keeping my feelings for Delia locked down, knowing they would ruin everything for her and Matt if either of them ever suspected. And for some reason Robin had seemed so eager to know about me . . .

He'd wanted to divert the conversation away from his assault.

God, I was stupid.

I still believed that Robin should report Terri—it seemed like the best way to try to ensure his own safety on campus—but had I forced that issue too strongly? We had only just met, and the both of us wanted a friend, and maybe I'd already scared him off. I should've been gentler, should've used that time to make sure he felt comfortable, to talk about something other than that traumatic evening . . .

Robin must've been hesitant to text me back. Still, I sent him a quick message to see how he was doing.

The message stayed on read.

Nothing to do but wait. Wait and see a man about a job.

Armand had wanted me to bring someone with me for the run-through, but the only person I would've asked was Lucas, and even if I *had* heard from him, it didn't seem like he'd be up for naked-model chaperoning.

I reached the art classroom and knocked; a muffled voice called, "Aye, come on in."

The lecture hall was currently abandoned save for the man stooped over the desk at the front. The last time I'd met Professor Demetrio— no, wait, he wanted me to call him *Armand*—we'd been in his tiny office, where he'd been hunched into a seat. He was slouching now, but was still absurdly tall and broad.

He looked up past scraggly, dark curls, raised his eyebrows, and muttered in that gravelly English accent, "Ah, Skyler, you made it. On your own, then?"

"Yes, sir." I gave him a smile that turned apologetic when he winced. "Right, I forgot you don't like being called 'sir.'"

"It's fine. Er, shall we get started?" He seemed distracted, but maybe he was nervous. He'd been awkward last time we'd met, though not for any apparent reason. Just, baseline awkward.

He waved me toward a raised platform in the middle of the room. There were a few yoga mats lying on it, side by side. I glanced over at him. "What are those for?"

Armand gave a lopsided smile. "Your knees and hips, mate. You stand that long with no cushion, you'll feel it in your joints."

Immediate flashbacks to the thirty-hour bus ride. "Good to know."

Armand took a deep breath, then launched into it. "I want to start them off with some gesture drawing, so quick poses, no more than a minute and a half each." He clambered onto the platform and struck a pose, feet flat on the mat, knees bent and arms held out in front of him—his bottom half moved like he was doing tai chi, but the arms made him look like he was hugging a barrel. "You can do whatever you like with these, as long as it's dynamic." He turned smoothly, one knee coming down to the mat and his arms rising as if to block a blow from above.

It was weird. His movements had been so nervous and jerky before, but now he seemed natural. Almost graceful.

Armand kept switching the poses, and I realized I should be paying attention so I could get an idea of what he wanted. Like he'd said, it was mostly poses that caught him in the middle of a movement. I was pretty sure I couldn't make the transitions between them that elegant, though. It was like he was dancing.

He stood up straight again. "For the longer poses, we'll do one standing, if that's all right, one sitting on that thing"—he pointed at a foam block—"and one on the floor." He sat down on the mats and leaned back on his arms, one leg folded in front of him and the other lying straight out. "Twenty, twenty-five minutes each if that's all hunky-dory?"

I nodded; there was a lot more to this job than I'd expected. When I posed for Lucas, he usually preferred to capture me in a natural stance before quickly moving to another. Belatedly, I started taking notes on my phone.

"If you get pins and needles, just make a muscle, little contractions." He showed me on his leg, where I could see his quad stiffening and then releasing. "And don't forget to warm up beforehand. Have a good stretch." Then he was quiet for a bit. "Er, Skyler?"

"Yeah?" I was still typing the notes about stretching, and when I glanced up, he'd stood and was awkward and hunched again.

"At the—your other modeling gig . . ." He swallowed. "The photographer . . ."

"Lucas Barclay," I supplied.

He nodded and bit his bottom lip, hands in his pockets. "Do you know if he's . . . all right?"

It took me a moment, but then: "Wait, do you know Lucas?"

"I, er," Armand hedged, "I think I live with him."

No. Way. "Oh my god." I stared at him, eyes widening. "*You're* Lucas's mystery roommate? You're Mothman!"

Armand's hands flew out of his pockets, and he folded his arms over his chest, rocking on his feet. "He told you about me? And he calls me *Mothman*?" His eyes widened in horror before he shook himself. "Er, never mind. Do—do you happen to know if—"

"He went through a breakup." I wasn't sure if Lucas wanted me to be telling people his business, but Armand looked so worried. "He's been staying with friends for a couple days. He's not dead, but that's all I know." I couldn't help grinning at him. "Wow, I can't wait to tell him I actually *met* you."

His face flushed, and he climbed down off the platform. "Aye. Right. Um. Take your clothes off."

I laughed in surprise. "Okay? Buy me dinner first?"

"No! That's not—" He blushed darker and used both hands to push the hair out of his face. "Bugger it, I meant the first time you stand up there starkers, *best* if it's not in front of a classload of students, eh?"

"Good point," I agreed, and started kicking off my shoes.

"Er, I know you didn't bring anyone along, but shall I grab another member of staff or—"

"I don't think a stranger would make this less awkward," I cut him off with a grin, "and besides, if I can't trust Mothman, who *can* I trust?"

Armand sighed and turned away to grab something from his bag, which turned out to be a plain white sheet. "This is yours going forward. Things can get minging without your own sheet."

No idea what *minging* meant, but I finished getting undressed and took the sheet from him, spreading it over the yoga mats. Then I climbed onto the platform and looked out over the empty classroom.

"Brilliant, you're a natural. Make sure not to rest all your weight on one foot during the longer poses." It was weird to see him swing between awkwardness and businesslike instruction. "And if you start having a reaction, let me know immediately."

I frowned down at him. "A reaction?"

He'd gone back to baseline awkward, but it didn't seem to be because of my lack of clothes. "Er, yes. If you start getting shy. Or hives. Or an erection."

Somehow it hadn't even *occurred* to me that that would be a concern. I tried out some of the poses Armand had done, contemplating how to respond. "Okay. Um. That doesn't happen to me very often, but I'll let you know."

He nodded, as if making a note for himself, then went back to demonstrating the best ways to stand without messing up my joints. It was strangely moving how casual he was acting.

"Is that something that happens with a lot of models?" I asked. "The ... erection thing."

He shrugged. "Sometimes. It's natural." He smiled at me. "Sounds like you've nothing to worry about. Are you cold at all?"

"Nah, I'm good."

Once he indicated I should, I climbed off the platform and got dressed. Even though this was only the second time we'd met, I felt weirdly comfortable with him—maybe it was because I'd just been naked, or because he was so clearly worried about Lucas.

"I know I sound like a broken record—" Armand clasped his hands, suddenly making strong eye contact "—but if you ever feel out of sorts, or want to back out ... believe me when I say I know how vulnerable this experience is. You're, well, literally and figuratively naked. It can be rough ..."

His earnestness was appreciated, and as he spoke, I remembered something he'd said to me before, about having done something like this in the past. "Can I get your advice? It's related but, um, personal I guess?"

Armand broke off, eyebrows high with surprise, but he nodded.

"So ... I know you said it was important to set the tone, or boundaries or whatever, and how this isn't sexual." I leaned back against the desk, letting my arms cross against my chest. Was it weird to be asking him this? I checked in with Armand, hoping I hadn't overstepped our professional relationship, but he simply inclined his head in encouragement. "But I'm worried I won't be able to tell if things become sexual, because I don't usually feel that kind of thing. Attraction or, um, drive. What if ... what if I give off the wrong vibe?"

Armand's shoulders unclenched. "You're not responsible for how other people react to you. I'll boot their arse if they don't follow your lead."

And he would too, I could tell. I let myself smile a little, even though I still prickled with nerves.

"And I don't know if I need to tell you this," he continued, "but there's no wrong way to have emotions."

He left me the opening; I had to push through. "Okay, but, um, what if you can be wrong? Or like, hypothetically, you had accepted that you don't feel romantic or sexual things, but then one day you do, and it's really weird and unexpected, but it hasn't happened again so it must be a fluke, right? Or I just never knew myself in the first place, or I'm lying or—"

"Do you know why I hired a life model?" He dropped his hands to his hips, still making more eye contact with me than he'd managed the entire afternoon. "Rather than having the kids trace stock images?"

I shook my head.

"Because nothing stands still, not really. And that's life, innit? Changing, fluid, never static? Good art captures that. In the same way, you don't always have to stay in one pose, in one *shape.*"

Only someone like Armand could successfully equate my sexuality crisis to his art class. "I guess. Still feels jarring, though. You sure that not being sure doesn't make me strange?"

Armand looked confused for a moment, then his dark eyes cleared. He smiled at me. "No more than anyone else, mate." For a moment he hesitated, as if he were contemplating the pros and cons of patting me on the shoulder before deciding against it. "But if you wanted to talk . . ." he continued, his large hands spread to either side.

"Thanks." Somehow, I'd relaxed having verbalized all this: labels, identities, or whatever. My vulnerability felt safe here with him. He'd seen me naked, after all. "This was really helpful. Sorry if I made things weird."

"I think we already established that being weird is not weird." Armand loosened a little, giving that sad, lopsided smile and scratching at his scruff. "All right. Er. See you tomorrow. Don't forget your sheet."

I was almost to the door when Armand said, "Hey, Skyler?"

"Yeah?"

He was looking tortured again. "If you see Lucas—" He shook his head. "Never mind. Forget it."

I raised a friendly eyebrow but didn't push. "It was an honor doing business with you, Mothman. I'm a big fan."

"Get out."

26
ROBIN IS RIDICULOUS

July 24th

My phone gave an obnoxious little chime, and I grabbed for it, careful to read the text preview so I wouldn't have to open it.

I cringed and put my phone away.

When I looked up, Maggie was glaring at me. We were supposed to be running lines . . . That was, she'd generously agreed to help me practice my part, but I'd been acting like a distracted jerk all day.

"Okay, who are you texting?" she asked, folding her arms and leaning back against her book bag. We were sitting on the grass outside the Volcanology building, annoying the occasional graduate student by giving them the Vulcan Salute. It was one of the few prime locations that was also as far as humanely possible from the law school. Terri had no reason to be anywhere near rock nerds.

"Nobody."

"Mm-hmm, who are you *not* texting, then?"

". . . Nobody."

"Why do you lie to me, Finch?"

I shrugged and ducked my head. "Because the truth is mind-numbingly stupid?"

Maggie gave a dramatic sigh—honestly, she was wasted on set design—and lay on her side, head supported on an arm and braids spilling casually over one shoulder. She looked like the centerfold for *Done With Your Crap* Magazine.

"So"—she examined the nails of her other hand—"is he straight or taken?"

"Neither!" I said defensively, then gazed up to the heavens, spread my arms wide, and fell backward onto the grass. "*Both*."

"Wow."

"I mean, *kinda*. Not really, though. He could be queer. Also he's single."

"Wow."

"It's a long story. I asked him out, but he couldn't tell. And now he wants to be my *friend*." I watched a few clouds go by and did my very best to sink to the center of the earth. After a while, when I still hadn't succeeded, I said, "Maggie?"

"Yeah?"

I sat up and started beheading individual blades of grass. "What's wrong with me?"

She rolled her eyes. "You want it alphabetically or by category?"

"Category. Specifically, matters of the heart."

"Well," she said slowly, "you're a *little* dramatic." Then she turned over and reached into her bag, pulling out the PB&J her girlfriend had made her this morning.

No one was ever going to make *me* a PB&J.

Maggie saw the way I was eyeing her sandwich and bit into it, maintaining steady eye contact. "Alfo," she said through a mouth full of bread, "you ne'er faw faw ree peepoh."

I looked over the arm I'd used to shield myself from the spray of crumbs. "I what?"

She just offered me her crusts. I accepted them like the garbage can I am.

"So you're saying I should text him back?"

"No, keep ghosting him. I bet it's making him feel *awesome*." Then she frowned, a rare show of interest. "I thought you said *you* asked *him* out."

I gave a guilty shrug. "I'm a bad person." My natural defensiveness kicked in. "But it's only been a couple days. I could be busy. I *am* busy."

"Ugh." She grabbed my script and hit me over the head with it. "Can we get back to work? There's no point in you distracting people from my beautiful sets with your bad acting."

"No. I'm still sad." I finished the last of her sandwich crusts and just looked as pathetic as I knew I was. "Be nice to me?"

Maggie groaned. "Fine. I bet if you text him back, he'll text *you* back. And then you'll be friends. And then he'll realize he's loved you all along."

I started to smile at her shyly. "Really? You think so?"

"Oh my god, *yes*. Now can we work?"

"What should I text him?"

Maggie almost got up to leave, so I started working again, but I was definitely going to text Skyler back. I'd text something funny that'd make him think I was cool and smart and nothing I actually was.

Though I had no idea how to explain my radio silence.

I let it percolate in the back of my mind while I focused on other things, like dropping off some of Armand's paperwork, getting groceries, dodging behind a dumpster to wait till Terri and Co. headed into a frozen yogurt shop, browsing the student store for new paperbacks . . .

Oh no.

Oh *no*.

Skyler was in the checkout line.

I dropped like a kingfisher and flattened myself against the paranormal romance shelf.

Don't breathe. Don't even breathe. Breathe and you're dead.

"You know you can rent this textbook instead of buying it, right?" the checkout guy was saying. "It's only fifty bucks a month."

Nooo, I wanted to stand up and declare, *it's a trap!* This was it, this was my chance to repay him, to save him like he'd saved me. My extra year of experience as a college student could serve him here, my wisdom could be bestowed with grace and magnanimousness.

"Oh, really? I don't know . . ." Skyler sounded uncertain.

"It would still save you money, dude."

No, it won't! You'll end up spending more and then you'll lose all your notes! I shut my eyes tight, willing my legs to straighten and my throat to make sounds. This horrible man was taking advantage of Skyler, and I was letting it happen. I was complicit.

"Nah," Skyler said, "I'm good."

He didn't need me.

I was no good to him.

I listened as Skyler finished the transaction and left, taking with him what was probably my last chance not to be the worst person in the world. What could I even say to him? *Hey, still in love with someone else?*

My phone chimed and I jumped, looking down to see a new text from Skyler. I read the preview: he still thought I was busy rather than awful. He wanted to know if I could recommend any good local pizza. Also, was I okay?

I put my phone back into my pocket and resumed my efforts to sink to the center of the earth.

I was going to have to answer him at some point, but until then, I was going to keep being absolute garbage.

But not where people could see. I straightened up and plastered a grin on my face, just in case anyone was watching. My world might have been burning, and maybe I was still holding the match, but the show must go on.

27
LUCAS IS NOT OKAY
(HE PROMISES)

July 25th

I t was taking every bit of strength to keep breathing.
During the flashes of time I was present in my body, Rick and Andie had—separately and then finally together—attempted to get me to eat. It was like I was being crushed under the weight of disappointment and lifelong insecurity. I was unable to move or do anything that wasn't thinking about texting Darren and telling him whatever he wanted to hear so that he'd take me back.

Rick had confiscated my phone after I'd made the mistake of mentioning this.

It was good of them to let me stay here, it really was, even though I was on the couch in the living room instead of in my old room, which apparently they'd already converted into Andie's office. It was like I had never been here to begin with.

And through the cloud, desperate as I was to block it out, Darren's voice played on repeat.

"This was a mistake."

"You're not right for me."

Exhausting. Childish.

Delusional. Desperate.

I didn't realize I had moved until I returned to my body in front of Rick and Andie's open fridge, staring at the contents. Would drinking ketchup straight out of the bottle count as eating something?

I shouldn't. Too high in sugar.

"Lucas?"

I turned, in slow motion, to see Rick and Andie standing in the doorway. They were staring at me in concern, and more distressingly, were holding hands. Because apparently that was what couples did, even when it was insensitive in the presence of their romantically deficient friend.

Me, who was so unlovable that his boyfriend dropped him without a second thought; me, whose *best friends* would rather kick him out so they could fuck. Me, who, despite all his efforts, no one wanted to meet or keep or love.

"I've decided," I announced, "that I hate love. Whoever invented love sucks."

"That's the spirit," said Rick, the hypocrite, while still grasping his girlfriend's hand.

Andie, for what it was worth, smacked his chest. "Babe, that's *not helping*." She returned to frowning at me in concern. "Do you want to talk about it?" she asked. "It's just that, it's really shitty, and I want to go over there and kill him, but we're worried. We haven't seen you like this since . . ."

"Since Dad," I finished for her, letting the fridge door smack closed. "Yeah, I haven't felt this bad since Dad." It shouldn't have been, shouldn't have felt like a family member dying—but it did.

They looked like they wanted to group-hug me, which ordinarily would be more than welcome, but I couldn't handle it right now—my skin was too tight, and my chest still wasn't working properly.

Best to remove the temptation. "I'm going to the gym," I said, marching back into the living room as they stepped aside. I didn't want to leave the house, or even the couch, for approximately ever, but the gym at this apartment complex was hardly used. Thank god, because if I had to interact with another human who was not in this room, I would die.

"I'm glad you're up and want to get out of the house, bud," Rick began, maneuvering himself in a way that suggested he was trying to block my path to the front door, "but maybe the gym can wait a bit; it'll still be there when this all isn't so fresh—"

"It's either the gym or the couch," I pointed out. *Why isn't he being reasonable about this?* "Only one of those options gets me closer to human again." Besides, they hadn't been at Briars in the aftermath. I'd been weak, clawing in a grief-stupor for anything in the fridge that was within reach. My memory was hazy about specifics, but my stomach remembered.

Rick still looked uncertain, but after I promised to text them later, he returned my phone and I walked the short distance to the gym.

A couple of rigorous hours on the elliptical. That was what I needed.

I focused my breathing and concentrated on the burn of my muscles as I cranked the setting higher, then higher—it wasn't enough; he was still under my skin, his bright hazel eyes, the warmth of his hands—

I continued until I was lightheaded, at which point I finally switched off the machine, my body buzzing with endorphins. I was briefly ill in the gym restroom, but then I felt stronger, more energized, and most importantly, free of whatever garbage I had put in my body before.

A few hours later, after a quick shower at Rick and Andie's apartment, I informed them that I was going to head on home. I didn't want to burden them more than I already had, and sitting in the same room with two people in a healthy, stable relationship felt like the universe rubbing it in. Like *yes, thank you, I get it, no one will ever love me.*

Not waiting until my workout high dissipated, I said goodbye to Rick and Andie, allowed them to gently hug me, and drove back to Briars.

To no one's surprise, Armand wasn't there. The apartment was as quiet as a ghost town. The living room was in proper order, the kitchen was clean—

Wait.

I might've been half out of my mind the last time I was here, but something pulled at my memory. Something that resembled a mountain of crumpled-up tissues in the living room, which was now gone.

Weird.

I walked into the kitchen where I distinctly remembered drowning myself in a boatload of junk food after having decided to poison my body past its ability to recognize pain.

I stared at the microwave, remembering the frozen burrito.

That was a whole new low for me. Even though I hadn't eaten it like I had apparently everything else, my stomach still churned. *The vegetarian nearly eats highly processed beef as a result of being heartlessly dumped.* Could I be more pathetic?

Angrily scribbling myself a reminder note and sticking it to the fridge, I prepared to lock myself in my bedroom and wait for the inevitable adrenaline crash, when something on the counter caught my eye.

A plate of muffins sat next to the stove, accompanied by a small Post-it stuck to the side of the plate.

feel better

He'd made me pity muffins. Even a total stranger, who had blatantly refused to meet me in person, could see that I was pathetic.

I should've been grateful, but it was a bitter reminder of why I needed to be pitied in the first place. The wallowing could wait. I grabbed my camera from the bookshelf and stormed right past the muffins and back out the door again.

With any luck, I might encounter some roadkill to photograph.

28
ARMAND IS PERPLEXED BY A MUFFIN

July 26th - Twenty days until the convention

Monday afternoon I lay in bed, in the center of my own little mandala of foreboding, surrounded by echoing, geometric ripples of *ugh*. Figure-drawing week had finally arrived, and I was a nervous wreck.

The good news was that whenever I found myself obsessing over Lucas's welfare, I could easily distract myself by worrying about Skyler. I'd worked with life models before, of course, even ones as young as him, but there was something about him that made me . . . protective. It wasn't just that this was his first life-modeling gig; it was what he'd said about himself and his disposition. I worried I'd been too quick to dismiss him, to shut down the conversation.

I turned over in bed, still loath to officially join the waking world, and ran through the conversation for the umpteenth time.

He'd spoken of his gray-aceness in uncertain terms, and that made sense. He was young and far from beholden to prescriptive labels; it was only natural that he'd think and speak of his inclinations in *investigative* language. For all I knew, he didn't even consider himself asexual.

But there was nothing wrong with the boy thinking of himself as a mystery worth exploring, so long as he didn't transform into a problem in need of solving.

I was likely making a mountain out of a molehill, and Skyler was fine, progressing through what passed for a natural, normal adolescence in this country and in his generation. To *me*, however,

Skyler seemed particularly vulnerable. There was a strange sort of openness that thrummed with his every movement and which reminded me so disturbingly of an ethereal version of my younger self, to be perfectly and narcissistically honest.

There was nothing shameful about this line of physical work, being a professional object and whatnot, but I'd be lying if I didn't say it had its dangers. Life modeling, like the dancing I used to do, required a certain negation of self—a *tool*ifying, if you will. Which you probably shouldn't.

I flung off the covers with the intent to finally, really this time, roll out of bed and begin this dreaded day, but didn't get much farther.

Damn it, I was worried that Skyler would be tempted to romanticize his own body and its effect on others (combined with his own perceived "coldness") and be led down a road paved by Pygmalion's ivory wife. *There, I've said it.*

Or at least, done my best to.

That thought spurred me out of bed and into the shower.

Once clean and cleansed, I made it to the kitchen, where I stopped in my tracks, faced with something I hadn't seen in *days*.

A note. A little yellow sticky note on the refrigerator, most likely a bollocking, a passive-aggressive request regarding washing up, an arrow pointing at a mess I'd left followed by a question mark.

He was *home*.

"Lucas?" I called out, my voice breaking. I swallowed and tried again. "Lucas, are you here?"

No answer. I slumped in a muddled mix of relief and defeat, taking the time to read the note itself.

This one was short and pointed, Lucas's usual fare, yet insanely more obtuse:

I am a vegetarian.

What could that possibly mean?

I squinted at the kitchen at large; the muffins I'd baked the day before in a moment of weakness still stood in their place on the counter, untouched. For a millisecond, my feelings were mildly bruised, but the wonderment at Lucas's response cast them in shadow.

I am a *vegetarian*?

I blinked at the note a few more times before turning it over and scribbling my own rejoinder. Feeling a little better, I reappropriated one of the now-rather-stale muffins and bit into it in a confused act of defiance.

I almost choked when Finch knocked on the front door.

He chattered aimlessly at me as we drove, which I had come to perceive as a good thing; I had begun to think of Finch's prattling as one does the crying of a sick child—the time to worry was when it stopped. He still seemed a bit pale and wan but clearly at least invested in the semblance of excitement about "the show" drawing nearer— right, he meant the play he was performing in.

"Wait till you see me wire-flying! I'm telling you, I was *born* to exist in a zero-g environment."

"That's nice, Titch, can't wait." I sighed.

He glanced at me out of the corner of his eye. "You know it's the day before the con? I already got your ticket."

Oh bugger everything, the *con*.

For a moment I was worried I might vomit, here in a tiny yellow car in America, but instead I shut my eyes tight and breathed deep through my nose, trying to focus on the feel of my hands gripping the seat, the breeze from the window, the rumble of the engine traveling up my legs—

I'd actually let my brain shove the convention and the fact that I was meant to speak at it into a dark little corner of my mind and forget about it. But Finch was right. There were twenty days left before the workshop was over and I was expected to speak before a large crowd and answer questions and account for myself and my comic—

"Armand, are you okay?"

"Mm-hmm. Aye." I groaned, opening my eyes and unclenching my hands. *Breathe, pet.* "Sorry. I'm a bit . . . I'm fine."

Finch gave a concerned little nod, no mockery, for once. "Okay, just let me know if you want me to pull over."

"I'm *fine*, Titch."

Now he rolled his eyes, but mercifully changed the subject. "Why did you want me to pick you up so early today? I mean, early for *you*."

"I'm meeting with the life model before class," I said, choosing to interpret his teasing as a good sign. It was how he expressed affection for me, it seemed. We parked, and as usual Finch walked me to the arts building, as if he were still uncertain of my abilities to find it on my own. He didn't seem offended, however, when I told him it would be best if he wasn't present for my meeting with the model. In fact, he seemed to be in full agreement.

"Are you kidding? It's not gonna be awkward enough when it's me and a billion other people? No, let's get up close and personal with *you* in the room. Because, you know, you're so *good* at defusing uncomfortable social situations." He winked.

Yep. Definitely affection.

I glared at him half-heartedly. "I can't fire you, can I?"

"You can talk to the university about replacing me." He shrugged, then lowered his head and grinned up at me past his messy ginger fringe. "But you won't, because I'm adorable and you think of me as your snarky younger brother. Besides, you're British, so verbal abuse is a bit like Vitamin D for you, *innit*?"

I gave him a reluctant smile. "Aye. Now run along and do something useful."

"Will do." He waggled his eyebrows at me. "Want me to pick up a card for Martha Stewart?"

I never should have told him about Lucas. "No, he seems to be . . . doing better."

"Still, you should let him know you care." He struck a pose. "Maybe write him an epic love soliloquy. I'll declaim it for you. Oh, Lucas Barclay, would you be *bae*—"

"*Titch*."

He chuckled impishly, turned on his heel, and scampered off— every inch an overly enthusiastic and dimwitted Pekinese. A ginger one.

I would spiral about the con later; today was more than game to offer up its own extravaganza of challenges. I took yet another deep breath and headed into the classroom.

Skyler was already there, reclining against the desk and staring up at the rows of seats and easels; his back was curved ever so slightly, highlighting the muscle of the shoulders. The thighs filling out the line of his trousers as they supported his weight, knee bent and sole pressed to the side of the desk—the very picture of an urban

Olympian, carved by the hands of a sad, stupidly talented and wishing old man.

The thought gave me pause in the worst way—I was falling for the Pre-Raphaelite trap *myself*.

I was thinking of Skyler as nothing more than an outlet for my own expression, his beauty and vitality reduced to a reflective surface for my skill and bloody artistry—whatever statement I might potentially make, using his body. He wasn't an ethereal muse or creature of the night, a spirit of indomitable youth and effortless beauty . . .

He was a boy.

I cleared my throat and Skyler looked over at me, and for a second I could see the apprehension before it was hurriedly covered. Before we'd even had time to exchange hellos, I set my bag down on the table and said very clearly, "There's no need to carry on with this if you're uncomfortable, mate. I'll make sure there'll be no consequences if you change your mind."

The students who'd been groaning their way through panel design would be disappointed, but I could figure something out. I'd split them up and have them sketch each other perhaps, fully clothed obviously, but—

"I'm not nervous. Who's nervous?" Skyler grinned at me, stuffing his hands into the pockets of his jeans and leaning his head back, taking a deep breath through his teeth. "I'm good, really. I want to do this."

I watched him for a few moments, trying not to empathize hard enough to hurt. I knew what he was looking for, and that he'd find it. There was so much freedom in surrendering yourself to another's interpretation—to present yourself as the vehicle of a stranger's passion and accept whatever utterance was the result. No need to define yourself when others were more than happy to do it for you.

"Right, then." I opened the bag and drew forth the long, thick robe I'd stolen from a hotel somewhere, probably Manchester, and handed it over to Skyler. "You get undressed while I go play silly buggers with the thermostat, aye?"

"Aye-aye," Skyler muttered and took the robe from me, already kicking off his shoes.

The custodian had shown me how to do this the other day, as well as how to mess with the lights so I could make sure the students practiced some proper chiaroscuro. Once Skyler gave the okay on the temperature, I asked him to stand on the dais, and tried the different lighting arrangements combined with the various poses—the plan for today was a quick round of gesture poses followed by two or three undraped contrapposto, so nothing too difficult.

Skyler was remarkably skilled at keeping still, especially for someone who had never worked as a life model before. I complimented him on it again and he shrugged. "I never knew it was a skill to just do nothing," he joked. "I can be without doing."

To be without doing. The idea sent a chill down my spine, especially since I'd spent so many nights trying to accomplish the opposite.

All I *was* was doing, having convinced myself it was the only proof of my existence and here was a young boy shooting holes in my dogma by simply standing still. I couldn't help smiling up at him in admiration, which, when you remember the scenario, might strike some as a very stupid thing to do.

Skyler's eyes narrowed as he caught me staring, but something in my gaze must have put him at ease, as his face immediately softened and turned carefree once again. He broke the pose to put his hands on his hips and grin down at me. "Don't worry, I won't forget to exist outside their eyes."

Heat rose to my cheeks despite myself. "Pardon?"

"What you said to me in your office." He scratched the bridge of his nose. Then he smiled mischievously and put on a truly *horrible* mock-cockney accent. "I know I *mostn't convince me-self I'm an object*."

Before I could open my mouth to answer, I caught sight of the clock on the wall. "Put your robe on, mate, and take a seat. The horde's coming."

The students filed in, whispering excitedly at the sight of the raised dais in the middle of the room. Some of them had spotted Skyler sat in the corner, wrapped in his robe, but more of them hadn't. Once they had all taken their seats and prepared their materials, I climbed up onto the modeling dais and gave them all a good glare.

"All right, listen up, you lot. We're done with paneling, rah rah, bless, yippee." I scowled around at the openly guilty and relieved faces. "Now. You are about to be given a privilege, an opportunity, a bloody *gift* in the way of learning musculature and movement—how to capture a *presence* on the page—and it's my job to make sure you don't squander it, so listen carefully. There will be no phones, no recording devices of any kind. There will be no whistling, no snickering, no comments, and no rude gestures. I want to make this crystal clear, you do *anything* I judge to be even remotely inappropriate and you will never set foot in my classroom again, understood? Think of it as an absolute zero tolerance policy on being a pervy little wanker. If you make this young lad at all uncomfortable, I. Will. End. You."

A brief moment of clarity followed, and I amended: "—r participation in this class. I will end your participation in this class."

I waited for the class's silent confirmation and stepped off the dais, indicating that Skyler could take my place. He nodded and climbed up, then removed the robe and handed it to me. "All right, we'll begin with a series of gesture poses, a minute and a half each. Skyler, if you please."

I watched the students carefully for a long time, and while there were definitely a few flushed faces and trembling charcoal pencils, they all seemed to be intent on behaving themselves.

All but one.

I squinted up at Finch, seated as he was in one of the upper rows, his face striving to match the redness of his hair and his pencil lying limp and unused in his faltering grip.

What was wrong with that boy?

29
ROBIN DIES

July 26th

He was oh-oh-my-*god* he was *him* and he was *all of him* and Jesus *Christ* there was more of him than I'd expected.

I gulped and tried desperately to force oxygen to my brain, maybe get the reasoning process restarted, some sort of motor function, the ability to *blink*—I'd take anything at this point.

Skyler was standing center stage, buck-ass nekkid, as if he couldn't care less.

I tried to shut my eyes but I couldn't; it was a bit like staring into the sun, though I guess, considering, the moon would be a more appropriate metaphor.

I tried to shake myself, but there was no getting around the fact that what stood before me was the vision I'd been conjuring up every night for days now. Only *better*. No way had I imagined skin that flawless, or a frame that spare, to say nothing of other portions of anatomy I had never dared to exaggerate in my mind. My god, I couldn't look *away*. Someone was going to notice! I wasn't even drawing anything! Was I still holding a pencil?

My fingers tightened around the graphite—

CRACK.

There was a dry shuffling as dozens of heads turned toward me, and Skyler's beautiful eyes flicked up to find me in the sea of faces—then widened in recognition.

It was all I could do to keep from stabbing myself in the neck with the pencil stub and thereby bringing an end to this torture.

A lightning bolt from god would have been particularly welcome, tearing through the ceiling and incinerating me where I sat in my conductive little puddle of humiliation.

If only Skyler would put some clothes on, my higher brain functions would return . . .

As it was, Armand requested a change of pose, and I all but attempted to garrote myself with my shoelaces as light and shadow dripped in and out of crevices on Skyler's body, outlining so much more than a human structure.

He really was the most beautiful thing I'd ever seen in my entire life. And he *maintained eye contact*, shifting into the new position, and then he—

He *smiled*.

At *me*.

And I reacted with all the dignified poise that you'd expect and fell out of my chair.

30
LUCAS VS CHEYENNE

July 26ᵗʰ

Mom met me at the ranch with a hug and two pints of Ben & Jerry's ice cream.

"I told myself I wasn't going to indulge until my cheat day," she said, her hair brushing my chin as she squeezed me, smelling like her hibiscus shampoo, "but my baby is sad, so screw it."

She'd been messaging me periodically to see how I was doing ever since I had, in a stupor, incoherently texted that Darren had dumped me and then had failed to articulate anything more. But I'd been to the gym twice since leaving Rick and Andie's, and I was dressed and outside the house, so even though the world still looked like a gray-filtered apocalyptic hellscape, that was an objective improvement.

"What am I supposed to do?" I asked after I'd given her all the details I hadn't been able to manage before. I stabbed half-heartedly at my pint of Phish Food. "Like, how is anyone supposed to move on after finding out that the last ten years of their life was a lie?"

"Well, first off, you could consider my offer to move back in with me here, at least until you find your footing again," she said, gently running her fingers through my hair like she used to do when I was a kid, "or go see the world like I suggested. And keep reminding yourself of what I've always told you: you're a kind, brilliant, loveable man, and that one day someone will come along who will appreciate you for all you are."

My heart ached with the desire to believe her—Mom was always so confident and persuasive, but . . . "Right, a kind and brilliant man who was just *proved* to be unlovable—and who also apparently is the world's worst judge of character."

She sighed, setting down her cookies and cream on the end table, and perched her chin in her hands. "See, I knew something like this was bound to happen at some point."

I blinked incredulously. "You knew that Darren would dump me out of nowhere in his kitchen?"

"Of course not, but I've had a bad feeling about that boy, ever since you both became joined at the hip in high school. He was far too self-involved to ever be a good partner for you."

My chest knotted. "So, what, this is 'I told you so'?"

"Not 'I told you so,' more . . . maybe this is the universe's way of finally taking out the trash."

I tasted bile in the back of my throat. "Okay but if Darren is trash, then what does it make the person who fell in love with that trash?"

"Human, baby, not trash." Mom pulled up her legs to sit crisscrossed on the porch swing. We'd done this so many times over the years, the patio serving as a confessional where we could gossip or rant or cry. I immediately felt fifteen again—depressed and insecure and bitter at the world.

The setting sun cast a pink and purple glow over our backyard down the hill toward the ranch, where the horses were grazing. It was too pretty for the situation, and a prick of irritation rose up. "At the very least it makes me stupid. Because only stupid people stay with trash for that long, right?"

"You were a teenager, Lucas. That doesn't make you stupid. You were in a vulnerable place, so it only makes sense that you—"

"I don't *want* to be vulnerable!" It burst out of me before I could stop it. "I shouldn't need to be with someone to be strong. I mean, *you're* not like that. You raised a child alone, you run a business alone, but I'm—" Repulsive. Unloveable. Pathetic.

Mom's face was pinched with lines that she had worked so hard to be rid of. "I had hoped," she said slowly, "that I had raised you to know that you were never alone."

"Right, because my *mom* being the only one who loves me is supposed to make me feel better."

Mom's face fell. "Lucas—" She reached for me, but my whole body tensed. If she hugged me right now, I would shatter. "Baby, there are other people out there who'll love you. You don't only get one love. If you just put yourself out there again—"

"What, like you?"

She pulled in a sharp breath.

My chest was too tight, and every molecule of my body was bloated from the quarter pint of ice cream I'd eaten. It didn't matter that she was trying to help—everything sucked and I was so tired of her being a hypocrite. "How many years did you spend telling me how Dad was your one and only and you would never love again? And it's not like I don't know that you sometimes go out on dates, but no one's ever serious enough for me to meet them. So which is it, Mom? Because how come when it's you, you claim you'll only ever love once, but when it's me, when it's *Darren*, suddenly it's 'there's other fish in the sea'?"

Her mouth dropped open, but I wasn't about to wait around and let her try to talk her way out of this one. I stood, letting the porch swing fall backward behind me. "I'm going to go down and see the horses."

I considered taking Dakota out for a ride—work off the calories—but didn't want to put her through that. That horse had already been with me during the darkest years of my life—she didn't deserve to be dragged into this too. Instead, I stopped at Grandpa Milkshake's stall, because hanging out with a sick and dying horse felt far more appropriate right now.

He was hanging in there like the fighter he was, but it was only a matter of time. He was resting in the corner, his rib cage visible past his struggling breaths. I stroked his neck. "Hey, boy," I whispered, and something unspooled in my throat. Here was this horse, alone in the world, deteriorating in a cell while the others—the younger, healthier geldings—were the ones most beloved of the children and visitors. No one ever asked to see the dying horse in the corner of the corral.

Would I also die in a corner somewhere, alone and unloved?

Probably.

I did my best to make him eat what he could before leaving him to rest. Every muscle in my body seemed to have evaporated, leaving me weak and heavy. I desperately wanted to return to my childhood home and curl up in the room that Mom had preserved, snuggling in bed while she made me soup. But I didn't want to deal with her right now.

So I drove back to the Briars apartment. It wasn't quite home, but at least I wouldn't be surrounded by reminders of my shortcomings as well as mementoes from my earlier years when I'd somehow been exactly as stupid as I was now.

The front door closed solemnly behind me as I entered the kitchen, and I was hit with the warm and unmistakable smell of baked goods. I scoured the room for evidence that Armand had been baking again.

On the counter, staring me in the face, was another plate of muffins.

These ones were bigger than the last batch, and appeared to be stuffed full of chocolate chips. *Thousand-calorie death traps.* A note accompanied these muffins as well: *didn't realize I'd made meat muffins.*

Meat muffins?

My note was still hanging on the fridge—the one I had hastily scribbled to remind myself never to contemplate eating frozen beef burritos again. *Is that why he thought I didn't eat his muffins before?*

I stared down guiltily at the miniature heart attacks.

He'd bothered to bake muffins for me, and I'd just blown it off. I really was a terrible person.

Waving goodbye to all my future diet plans, I reached for the nearest chocolate chip muffin and took a generous bite. It was *delicious*, better than it had any right to be. My hips still remembered the ice cream from earlier, but what was the point of keeping healthy? What was I if not a lonely dying horse in a world that had tossed me aside?

I grabbed the plate of muffins and started out of the kitchen. In the living room, Gaston and LeFou were swimming slower than usual. "I get it, guys. Life sucks and there's nothing you can do about it. But you two have no excuse. So snap to it, okay? You're making me depressed."

Leaving Gaston and LeFou to clean up their act, I turned back around, plate of muffins in hand, and locked myself in the bedroom. I was going to eat every single one of these deliciously deadly sugar grenades, and I would hate myself, but I couldn't possibly hate myself more than I already did, so what the hell.

Armand's gesture was sweet but misguided. Hopefully he'd never know that his muffins were wasted on a miserable, undeserving piece of shit like me.

31
ARMAND MOURNS A LOSS

July 26th - (Still) Twenty days until the convention

The first figure-drawing class was going far better than I'd had any right to expect. Skyler was brilliant, of course, but the students had a hand in it as well— having a body to draw really seemed to be igniting something in them. Everyone who'd grown listless was suddenly bright-eyed again, drawing like they were consumed with the fiery passions of creation.

I wandered the room, trying not to burst with pride at the general air of busyness that had settled over the students. I paused beside Ashley/Ashton The Mulleted; they were excitedly scribbling character-study after character-study, finally allowed to indulge in micro-expressions and outfit design.

"Watch the feet," I muttered despite myself, and they nodded.

"I will not go the way of Rob Liefeld," they responded, with the air of a soldier on the eve of battle mouthing their commander's words of wisdom under their breath.

She of the blue glasses and adorable afro-puffs (another A name, for sure), was doing an excellent job crafting a story told entirely through body-language, not a word bubble in sight. "Nice," I said softly as I passed by her easel, and she paused to beam up at me.

The renewed energy among the students was fantastic, and it was just in time for them to begin preliminary work on their final projects.

I almost felt bad calling time and couldn't help smiling when the class groaned as one. "Buck up, lads, we get to do this all again tomorrow!" I handed Skyler his robe. "Shall we thank our model?"

A brief round of applause turned Skyler a bit pink, but then he stepped up to the edge of the dais, now clad in the thick, stolen Manchurian robe, and gave a regal bow—winning every last heart in the room.

The students filed out, and after Skyler had dressed behind the privacy screen I'd set up, he said goodbye, glancing sadly at the upper rows. I followed his gaze: there was still a figure sitting slumped in one of the chairs, head in his hands.

Skyler hesitated, but after a few seconds, when Finch continued to ignore him, he made his way out.

I waited till Skyler was gone, then made my way up between the seats and finally sat down across from Finch, leaning over the back of a seat.

I tried to make eye contact, but he kept shrinking further and further into himself until he appeared to be nothing but a small, fuzzy, orange creature hiding in a pile of clothes.

"Titch . . ." I cajoled, "what happened?"

He peeked up at me, looking so pathetic and miserable I had to physically fight the urge to yank him forward into a hug. As it was, he made hugging impossible by raising both his arms and wrapping them around his head, face hidden in the crooks of both elbows.

He then, naturally, attempted to communicate.

"ArnmfuuuWAA . . ."

"Right," I tried, gently poking one of his forearms, "care to try that again?"

He lowered his arms, revealing a damp face. He took a deep breath and leaned his head back so all that was visible was his Adam's apple. "I am such a *freak*!"

I waited for him to elaborate, but when he didn't, I sighed and sat up, rubbing my temple. "Look, Titch, I love adolescent meltdowns as much as the next bloke, but I'm going to need a bit more to go on."

He straightened and finally met my eyes. "What the hell does *Titch* even mean?" he squeaked. There were actual tears now.

Oh, lovely.

I shut my eyes tight for a few seconds, then forced myself to reopen them and deal with the sniffling child in front of me. "*Titch* is like . . . *squirt* or *pipsqueak*," I admitted. This did not seem to rally his spirits. "It's affectionate," I added, a little desperately.

He sniffled and wiped at his cheeks with the heel of his hand. "Okay. Fine. I'm sorry I'm literally the worst person in the world."

"I get it." I laughed awkwardly. "If I were your age, I'd be distracted by Skyler too. And we've all embarrassed ourselves before. I've fallen out of plenty of chairs." I patted one of his delicate knees. "I know it seems like the end of the world—"

"Shut up." He flicked my hand away and crossed his arms. "I've met him before, okay? It's more complicated than that."

"Aye?"

"Yeah. He . . . he rescued me last week." Finch hunched in on himself defensively, once again avoiding my gaze. "And then I asked him out, and he said yes, only *apparently* he thought I was asking him out as a *friend*, and then he spent half the time talking about this girl he left back home . . ."

Oh.

Dear.

"I'm sorry." I reached out again, then stopped myself. I wanted to ask if being Skyler's friend really was such a letdown, but I stopped myself.

Finch managed an unhappy little smile. "Yeah, me too. I kinda ran away after that. And I've been ghosting him. For four days."

"And *this* is the first time you've seen him since?" I would've done a lot more than fall out of a chair. Poor Finch. Poor *Skyler* . . .

Finch nodded, still sniffling a little, but starting to laugh as well. "I *told* you, I'm *literally* the worst person in the world."

I shrugged. "But now you've seen him and made a fool of yourself. That's the worst of it, innit?"

He snorted down at his lap. "I guess . . ."

I could only hope Finch's delusions wouldn't ruin his and Skyler's chances at a deeper connection. "This *is* what we do, y'know."

He looked up at me. "'We'?"

"The *piners*." I grinned winsomely. "We're born without dignity and we die without love. But you mustn't let the . . . the *fantasy* kill the future."

"Wow. That was corny."

"I know. I am also the worst person in the world."

"Thanks."

"Aye."

We sat in silence for a few minutes longer, then I coughed. "Well."

"Yes."

"Would you like me to drive?"

"Is there any chance you'd stay on the right side of the road?"

"It is unlikely."

He sat up straight and smoothed his hair out of his face, which still shone with tears. "Guess I'd better get a grip on myself." He smiled at me tiredly. "I don't suppose I could be excused from the rest of the figure-drawing classes?"

I shrugged. "If that's what you want. Or you could, perhaps, talk to him? Salvage your chance at friendship?"

He got to his feet and stretched, all 170 centimeters of him. "Sure, right. I'll definitely do that. You know—" he gave me a paternalistic smile "—you're really getting a lot better at this whole . . . *talking* gig."

Color rose to my face, but I did my best to ignore it. "Titch," I began warningly.

"I mean it." He placed a hand on my shoulder and leaned in, eyebrows climbing. "I think teaching has been really good for you. It's been a while since you tried to commit verbal suicide in front of the class."

"Damn it, I *am* capable of human interaction!"

"Yeah, *now* you are. Seriously, you're going to do great at the con." He scampered down the rows toward the exit. "Race you to Camille."

"I withdraw from said race," I muttered and started down as well.

Finch chattered animatedly all the way back to the flat, as if those moments of vulnerability back in the classroom had never happened. Though as he did, there was something fragile about his smile and how he skipped from one topic to another.

I let him ramble on. Had it even been my place to engage him as much as I had? Thwarted love was a natural part of growing up, as was the realization that Skyler's friendship had greater value than whatever romantic fantasy Finch was concocting in that head of his. Who was I to stand in the way of his bloody *bildung*?

My trainer briefly caught on the welcome mat, and I realized I'd climbed the stairs without noticing and already had my key in the door. My heart expanded to fill my throat, remembering the note I'd found earlier in the day—Lucas had come home; he could very well be just past this door—

He wasn't.

I considered calling out again but was overcome with a new bout of shyness. Especially once I saw that my second batch of muffins had vanished. Best leave him to his own devices. He'd surely come out once he was good and ready. Like a badger.

There were messages from Lakshmi reminding me of the latest deadline and that I should be working on my convention speech. Lest the cushy bubble we'd been living in, courtesy of Drake House, pop and splatter us with sudsy failure and sticky obscurity.

I got to work, slowly pickling myself in whiskey and inking like a madman, occasionally muttering to Gaston and LeFou, trying to explain the intricacies and contradictions of teenage angst when contrasted with mature, well-aged malaise. They didn't seem to be paying as much attention as usual—LeFou especially seemed lethargic and uncommunicative.

I worked till four, realizing when I stood to make my way to bed that, as usual, or as was *becoming* usual, I'd drunk a bit more than I'd meant to. It stood to reason—I was nervous about the con, sad about Lucas, and concerned for Robin and Skyler. I just needed to start paying better attention. Setting limits for myself.

Using the wall as support, I made it to the toilet and performed all the voiding and ablutions required to once again become a person. I was considerably grateful that Lucas had remained in his bedroom.

Despite whatever progress I'd allegedly made over the past week and a half or so, I still wasn't fit for human consumption.

July 27th - Nineteen days until the convention

When I woke the next afternoon, Lucas still hadn't emerged, and Gaston and LeFou were both floating at the top of their tank, already starting to smell like the underside of a pier.

I came upon them while brushing my teeth, and the brush hit the carpet with a hollow *thud*, spattering my legs with paste.

I'm not proud of this, but I reached into the rancid tank and tried to animate them, as if part of me thought they were just asleep. It was possible that I might have been speaking to them as well, whimpering and begging them like a child to *Wake up, please*. When there was no response, I retrieved my phone with slimy fingers and desperately googled: *reviving dead fish*.

Retrospectively, it seemed like there shouldn't have been as many hits as there were.

There wasn't, however, anything useful.

I ended up standing over the tank and, aye, weeping—softly and with what was hopefully a certain amount of manly dignity.

I had been talking with—*at* these fish for weeks now, and I felt we'd had . . . How could they just . . .?

A second realization dawned on me. I'd thought the disappearance of the second batch of muffins had been a positive sign.

How badly was Lucas doing? What had *happened*?

He still hadn't responded to any of my texts. My eyes wandered toward the hallway, to the door of his bedroom. I could, I could always just, but that—

That didn't . . . No.

Just no.

Even in these, the gravest of circumstances, I couldn't handle the idea of knocking on his bedroom door. Not hungover, with a tear-stained face, dead fish in my hands.

Instead, I retreated into the numbness of my own mind. I wrapped Gaston and LeFou in a plastic bag and set them gingerly in a corner of the freezer. Then I took on the impossible task of notifying Lucas. I couldn't bear the thought of giving him the news over text, so I grabbed a page from the pad on the counter.

The fish are dead, I wrote. Then: *They're in the freezer.*

Oh fuck. *They were dead before I put them in the freezer.*

This was a disaster. I crossed everything out, crumpled the note, and began again on a new page.

It's not my fault.

No, *my condolences*, bloody hell, *something's happened.* How was this getting worse?

In a desperate attempt to be done with this task, I scribbled something nonsensical onto a fresh note and slapped it on the side of the empty tank.

I focused on getting dressed and presentable in time for Finch to collect me. Then ignored his concerned inquiries about my welfare and his comments on the fact that I was, once again, visibly hungover.

"Are you *sure* you don't want to go to the doctor? The campus clinic does walk-ins, and you're looking *really* pale—"

"Titch." I groaned helplessly. "Just *drive.*"

Finch was unrelenting in his attempts to get me talking right up until the moment he realized that if he followed me to the classroom, he'd likely have to face Skyler again.

"I. Um. I can't make it to class today, emergency rehearsal," he said, in a deeply unconvincing manner, before abandoning me at the entrance to the arts building, just as I was having a realization of my own:

Skyler!

Perhaps Skyler had heard from Lucas. Perhaps he knew what had happened—I hurried to the classroom, then sat on my desk and tapped one of my heels against its side until Skyler finally showed up.

The moment he walked through the door, I stood, nearly toppling over in my eagerness. "What's happened!"

Skyler froze on the spot. "W-what?"

"What's happened to Lucas?" I squawked. "Gaston and LeFou are dead, man, *dead!*"

It was at this point that I heard myself and sat down heavily, putting my face in my hands and trying to pretend the last few seconds had not happened.

"The fish?" Skyler muttered sadly. "Really?"

I peered up at him over my fingertips, hoping against hope that he had somehow missed my ridiculous outburst. "Aye, they were floating belly-up this afternoon. Have you heard anything from him these past few days? Anything at all?"

Skyler worried his lip and fidgeted before pulling out his mobile. "No, but I can call Cheyenne and ask if there's been any news." He held it to his ear, and I could hear the ringing mocking my anxiety.

"Who's Cheyenne?"

Skyler mouthed, *His mom.*

His *mum*?

"Oh, hey, Cheyenne." Skyler stepped away. "Have you heard from Lucas lately? Oh." His eyes widened, then, as I watched, his entire face slowly softened. "Wow. And that's . . . good? That's *good*. Okay, thanks. No, no, that's— Thank you. Heh. Yeah, I'll see you tomorrow." Then he hung up, slipped his mobile back into his pocket, and gave me an uncertain smile. "She says they had a fight, but that it's a good thing. She says he's fine."

I gaped at him. "*You know his mum?*"

Skyler shrugged. "She runs The End Is Neigh. Lucas and his mom are really close, so I think if she says he's good, she's probably right. She says they finally talked about Darren."

I was gnawing on my knuckles. "Who's Darren?"

"He's— Well, he *was* Lucas's boyfriend." Skyler shrugged again. "He was not a nice person, if you ask me." He scratched the back of his neck, then glanced up at me, a smile pulling at the corners of his mouth. "So have you guys run into each other yet?"

I shook my head, still partially stuffing my fist into my mouth.

"Then he doesn't know you're this worried about him?"

I accidentally bit down and all but broke the skin of my thumb. "Gwha? What? No! That is, aye, yes, I *am* worried, w-wouldn't you be? A-aren't you?" I tried to shove my hands into my pockets but my jeans were too tight to achieve this while seated. I abandoned the attempt and crossed my arms, trying to ignore the softly amused smile Skyler was giving me.

"Not *too* worried. I mean"—Skyler thoughtfully ran a hand through his hair—"if Cheyenne says he's doing better . . . But I think I'll call him tomorrow morning, just to make sure. Are *you* okay?"

"Aye, quite, ehrm, yes."

"Are you sure?"

"Oh just shut up and take your clothes off." I stood and started preparing the dais. "Just, er, let me know if you hear from him, will you?"

"I will."

I could practically *hear* the grin in his voice.

I turned my efforts to the imminent lesson, doing my best to take Skyler at his word and keep my worry in check.

32
LUCAS EMERGES
FROM THE FOG

July 28th

I sat on the couch in the living room, staring at the now-clean but also very now-empty fish tank.

I was a killer.

Through no fault of their own, Gaston and LeFou had left me for the great big fish tank in the sky. They had deserved better than me, someone who hadn't even noticed the malfunction in their water filter until it had been too late.

After saying a few words and, as gently as I could, laying them to rest in the toilet before flushing them to oblivion, I ordered a new filter and scrubbed the grimy tank until it was good as new. As if the two fish I'd murdered had never lived there.

At least Armand had been here, which was a thought as guilt-inducing as it was perplexing. Because why had I found out that my fish had shuffled off this mortal coil via a Post-it note with three hand-scribbled emojis: a skull and crossbones, a crying face, and a freezer. The most enigmatic eulogy I've ever come across, but it was unnervingly kind of him to have preserved their little bodies until I could give them a proper send-off.

My phone buzzed. *Not now, Mom*—but it was Skyler.

"Hey."

"Lucas? Hi, I didn't know if you'd pick up." His voice was hesitant but gentle. "How are you doing? I heard your fish died. I'm so sorry."

I blinked at my phone and then at the empty tank. "How'd you know that?"

"Oh!" Skyler paused. "Right, I've been meaning to tell you. I kind of . . . met Armand? Your roommate? Mothman?"

I nearly dropped my phone. "You *what?*"

"Yeah, I got a part-time gig doing life modeling for the workshop he's running at Norsemen. I guess he found Gaston and LeFou yesterday before class? He sounded super worried about you."

This was far too much information all at once. I stood up from the couch and began pacing the living room. "Okay, okay, okay, back up. So you work with Armand . . . What—" There were so many questions I wanted to bombard Skyler with. "What's he like? Give me as much detail as you can because you know what I've been working with here."

Skyler huffed a soft laugh. "Well, I think he's a bit shy talking in front of people, but once you get him talking about something he's comfortable with, like art, he's actually really knowledgeable. Like, *I* don't understand a lot of the techniques that he's teaching, but that's why I get to just stand there while everyone else does the work."

For a moment I became sixty years old, lamenting that modern technology had left me without a phone cord to twirl as I paced the room. My eyes fell on the stack of comic pages I'd picked up from the floor a few hours ago. "And what are the chances he explained what his comic is about?"

"Oh, none. He doesn't seem to like talking about his own work that much. But he's extremely patient with the class. And he made me feel more comfortable than I ever expected about being naked in front of fifty people."

"That's . . . good." Skyler was eighteen and legal and I knew plenty of people in college who'd done life modeling with no issues. But the public nudity made Skyler more vulnerable than usual, and a wave of protectiveness washed over me. "So he's not a creepy old man, then?"

"He's definitely not creepy, unless you consider general awkwardness creepy. But yeah, no, he's like, *maybe* thirty? If I had to guess?"

I didn't know if I'd made any assumptions about how old my roommate was—his apparent aversion to texting had made me think *boomer*, but the snacking habits and doodles had felt like those of a floundering undergrad.

Before I could decide what to ask next about the enigma that was Armand Demetrio, Skyler continued, voice going a bit softer. "I also talked to your mom. She said you guys had a fight but she thinks you're okay." A pause. "*Are* you okay?"

That certainly was the question, wasn't it? In my excitement and burning curiosity to learn about Armand, I'd forgotten about the travesty that was my life currently. I took a break from pacing and flopped down onto the couch, staring up at the atrocious popcorn ceiling. "Let's see, my boyfriend dumped me, I yelled at my mom, and I accidentally murdered two sweet fish, so we could be better."

"Yeah, I'm sorry about that too. Darren seemed, um . . ."

"Like an asshole, you can say it. Sorry you were there to see that." I was feeling stupider by the second. Hindsight really was 20/20. "You ever feel like it's so unfair that you weren't good enough for someone even when you did everything you possibly could?"

"Yes."

"Yeah, it sucks." I traced the fabric lines on the couch cushion. Maybe it wasn't appropriate to commiserate with Skyler since he was an employee—though technically Mom was his boss, not me—but there was something comforting in his silence. There wasn't judgment or preconceived biases, there was just . . . compassion.

The kind of compassion that involved seeing a wrecked apartment and knowing that the person who had made that mess was broken and sad and unable to be a human. That they might feel better after some homemade muffins. There was something so genuine and open about that kind of compassion, and it made me want to curl up in a ball and hide.

Armand hadn't seen me that night, but he had *seen* me—raw and unfiltered and ugly.

"Lucas?"

I was still on the phone with Skyler. Thank god it wasn't a video call so he didn't have to watch me silently stare off into the middle distance. "Yeah, hi, sorry."

"Gotta make sure the void didn't eat you." Someone spoke in the background, and Skyler's voice was muffled and distant as he responded, before he returned to the phone. "So my break's over, but could you text me later? And maybe let Armand know you're alive so he doesn't ambush me the second I walk into class again?"

"Is that . . . a thing he's done before?"

"Oh, yeah. I think he thought he was being subtle about it, but he really has been asking about you almost every day. A bit dramatically, even. I think he took Gaston and LeFou personally."

My cheeks warmed, and there was a weird pinch in my chest. "I'll text him. Um. Thanks, Skyler. Sorry I haven't been around recently."

"Take care of yourself, okay? And come back to work when you can. The horses miss you. Especially Grandpa Milkshake, he's been neighing about taking you out of his will."

"Oh, he's said that, has he?"

"Of course. I would know. I'm Horse Jesus."

I snorted into the phone and after we ended the call, I stayed on the couch for a time, contemplating what on earth to text Armand after days of ignoring his check-ins. The idea that he'd been asking about me, that he'd seemed genuinely concerned . . .

As far as I knew, I was alone in the apartment, but I felt a twinge of nervousness anyway. Like I was swimming out of my depth.

Maybe I could decide what to say while I scrubbed the bathtub. Hadn't done *that* in a while. I padded down the hall to the bathroom, switched on the light, and froze. There was something on the mirror.

It was a detailed sketch of a horse—an almost perfect, lifelike negative of my horse Dakota, whose photo was framed and hanging on the living room wall. My eyes flickered to the scribble in a word balloon next to the horse's head: *Why the long face?*

I burst out laughing.

The picture wasn't that funny, and the pun was *terrible*. But I couldn't stop. I laughed until it turned into a raspy cough.

I rubbed my throat, sore from its sudden workout, and stared in awe at the mirror horse.

It was the first time I'd laughed in days.

Once again, there was that warm tightening in my chest that forced me to swallow hard. Armand's doodles, while often inconvenient and sometimes obnoxious, were always funny, allowing me moments of reluctant amusement even as I proceeded to wipe them from our communal mirror. But this drawing wasn't just funny. It was elegant, and time consuming, and . . . sweet.

Going out on a limb, I tiptoed out in front of Armand's room. I leaned my ear against the door, listening for any sign of life. After a moment—

Snores. Loud ones, emanating from the room like a bear's cave.

He was here.

All it would take would be for me to knock on the door . . .

I took a deep breath and raised my hand.

33
(TEXTING INTERLUDE 5)

July 29th

Lucas: *thanks for the mirror horse. you suck at puns though lol :p was gonna knock on your door earlier but didn't want to wake you from your coma*

Armand: *wish you had*

Armand: *You feeling better I hope?*

Lucas: *if by better you mean still wanting to die then yes*

Lucas: *I'm sorry I ghosted you for a while btw*

Armand: *Yes, that is unforgivable. Who would do that*

Lucas: *A monster, clearly. ;p*

Armand: *Sorry I monstrously didn't respond for a while. Had to go to bed.*

Lucas: *You WENT TO BED at 9am?!!!*

Armand: *Early night.*

Lucas: *party animal huh?*

Armand: *If by animal you mean I curl up in my den and hibernate then yes.*

July 30th

Armand: *Still want to die?*

Armand: *I mean do you feel butter*

Armand: **better*

Lucas: *yes I feel butter. In fact I can't believe I'm not butter*

Armand: *Glad to hear it. Sorry about your fish.*

Lucas: *that one's on me. they deserved better*

Armand: *Seems like you do too.*

Lucas: *maybe*

Lucas: *thanks for cleaning up after me. you shouldn't have had to see that*

Armand: *Right, how embarrassing to leave a mess for your flatmate to tidy*

Lucas: *:)*

34
ROBIN HAS NOTHING TO LOSE

July 31ˢᵗ

Okay. So. It had officially been a week of me ghosting Skyler. Four days since I'd seen him in Armand's class, which I'd stopped going to, obviously, and I had somehow miraculously managed not to run into him anywhere else on campus. It was safe to say he hated me at this point.

"Or he's completely forgotten about you," Maggie added. "That's always an option."

We'd finished a tech run-through a few minutes ago, and I was trying to convince her to get lunch with me. She was resisting because she had "work" or whatever.

"You don't mean that." I sulked. "I'm a lot of things, but 'forgettable' isn't one." I was perched on top of a speaker, and two different sound-techs had already yelled at me about it, but I'd simply hugged my knees and pouted.

"You are definitely a lot of things." Maggie raised an eyebrow at me, shrugging on her backpack. "So if he hates you now, why not just text him?"

"What?"

She started out of the theater, and I scurried after her.

"No, seriously, what do you mean?"

"Like, what do you have to lose at this point? Either he hates you and doesn't text you back, or he does answer and we know he's got zero self-respect."

She was right. Not about Skyler having zero self-respect (I could only be so lucky), but about the stakes being at an all-time low.

So I said goodbye to Maggie and tucked myself into a shady corner of the theater plaza, trying to text faster than I could change my mind.

Robin: *hey so I'm a piece of shit do you still want to hang out*

Then I flung my phone onto the bench I was occupying and breathed into my cupped hands.

The sound of the notification all but stopped my heart.

Skyler: *where are you*

I stared at my phone. Was he serious? I told him I was in front of the theater and barely managed to stop myself from reminding him what a total asshole I'd been for the past week. In detail.

Skyler: *I'm outta class, see you in 5*

I stood up from the bench and started pacing the plaza.

There was no way he was coming here to like, kill me, right? Though it seemed more likely than the idea that he was absolutely *fine*. That didn't make any sense.

I widened my circle of pacing slightly, which brought me to the edge of the plaza steps, able to peer out over the quad, see if I could pick out Skyler coming toward me—

Or.

Conversely.

Terri Bishop, discretely vaping behind a tall magnolia, could glance up at that exact moment and lock eyes with me.

I was frozen to the spot. He was alone, there was barely anyone else around, just a few sunbathers who might as well be lawn ornaments—no real witnesses, no attentive audience, and yet Terri had tucked his vape-pen into his pocket and was starting toward me. Deliberately.

In my worry about Skyler, I'd dropped all vigilance. I'd gotten so good at avoiding Terri, anticipating where he'd be, steering clear of highly visible places on campus, but now I'd gone ahead and offered myself up like chum to a shark.

He was getting closer. I needed to *move*.

My feet barely came unstuck and I stumbled down the stairs, my legs weak and nightmare-watery, ready to buckle under me at any mome—

"Robin?"

Strong hands gripped my shoulders and kept me from falling facefirst onto the path. Without meaning to, I clenched my fingers in the stretch of T-shirt across his chest and stared up into Skyler's painfully blue eyes.

"*Fuck*," I managed. And glanced over at Terri in time to see him casually change direction—as if he'd never been headed toward me. Skyler followed my gaze, and the two of them actually made eye contact for a moment.

"Is that the guy?" Skyler asked, the hands on my shoulders growing the slightest bit tighter. He was watching Terri with a frown that would have made the gods bow down and beg for forgiveness. "That's him, isn't it?"

"I'm sorry I didn't text you back!" It burst out of me, practically a screech. "And I'm sorry I was so weird in class, and that I ignored you and—"

"Robin." His face was full of concern, though he couldn't quite hide the hurt. "We can talk about that in a minute. Is that the guy who as—"

"I want to talk about it now." I took a deep breath. "I—" *Think of a lie, think of any lie* "—I was embarrassed about what happened with Terri, and then I freaked out in class 'cause—'cause—'cause I wasn't *expecting* you!"

Skyler's beautiful shoulders slumped. "You were avoiding me because of what I said at the café, weren't you? About reporting Terri." His perfect brows converged. "I'm sorry, I didn't mean to pressure you into talking about it."

"Yes." I was going directly to hell. How was *he* apologizing to *me*? "It's a work in progress." God, he looked unreal. "I'm just sorry my ... my *drama* got in the way of becoming your friend. Can we try again?"

Directly to hell. Do not pass Go.

He smiled back at me, though the muscles around his mouth were still tight and his eyes were sad. "Yeah. Um. I'd like that. But maybe this time, don't vanish off the face of the earth?"

"I won't," I promised. This could work. As long as he never found out what a horrible, manipulative liar I was. "So, a little bird told me you were on the hunt for good local pizza?"

"A little bird, huh?" He laughed. "Was this little bird perhaps one of the many texts I sent you that you didn't even *read*?"

I grinned at him winsomely. "Nope. Definitely a bird." It might take him a minute to stop being mad at me, but it already made zero sense that he was even talking to me right now.

Maybe Maggie was right and Skyler's standards were low enough for me to clear. I was certainly going to try.

35

(TEXTING INTERLUDE 6)

*July 31*st

Armand: *Need more venezuelan munchkins?*
Armand: **vegetarian muffins*
Lucas: *a guy cannot have too many venezuelan munchkins :)*
Lucas: *ok but do I want to know why that was your autofill option for vegetarian muffins*
Lucas: *thanks for those btw, I had no idea you could bake!*
Armand: *I bake when I'm upset.*
Armand: *Your Better Homes and Gardens came*
Armand: *I put it in the loo*
Lucas: *HOW DARE YOU*
*August 1*st
Lucas: *Skyler says hi. He says he misses being naked in your class lol jk he says he misses you and that you're a "cool chap"*
Armand: *He's a sweet kid.*
Lucas: *HE IS THOUGH*
Lucas: *It's really funny that he knew the both of us before we've even met*
Armand: *It is suspicious. Are we entirely sure Skyler isn't with the CIA?*
Lucas: *I thought skyler said you're british? Shouldn't he be interpol? Or MI6?*
Lucas: *Do u even know what the cia is?*
Armand: *I am from England.*
Armand: *Where are you from?*
Lucas: *born and raised in the golden state :)*
Armand: *So . . . where?*

Lucas: *Here. California.*

Lucas: *Also you are weirdly formal over text. Sir.*

Armand: *First time in US. Didn't know states come in colours.*

Lucas: *wow, first time? have we americans impressed you yet?*

Armand: *You all seem very happy. And smell like powdered sugar.*

Armand: *And bacon.*

Lucas: *I'm vegetarian, remember? no bacon smells here lol*

Armand: *I didn't mean to offend you.*

Armand: *You're not very happy either.*

Armand: *Sorry. That came out wren.*

Armand: **wrench*

Armand: **ranch*

Armand: **WRONG*

Armand: *god.*

Lucas: *XD lol goodnight*

August 2ⁿᵈ

Lucas: *So I've been all over the internet and I can't figure out what your comic is about???*

Armand: *Ah yes. Everything is going to plan.*

Lucas: *what. plan.*

Armand: *Remember The Emperor's New Clothes?*

Lucas: *hell yeah, I love Panic! At The Disco*

Armand: *Sorry?*

Armand: *I meant the story by Hans Christian Andersen*

Armand: *That's me, but with knowing what the bloody hell I'm doing.*

Lucas: *u tease*

Lucas: *I gotta know!*

Lucas: *Don't keep your readers in suspense!!*

Lucas: *What is the penguin doing there!!!*

Lucas: *What is the meaning of the frog with the shot glass!!!*

Armand: *Whatever you want him to be doing. Whatever you want it to mean. Death of the author.*

Lucas: *uh huh yep sure uh huh*

Lucas: *I'm thinking about the death of a certain author alright*

Lucas: *look I don't even go here, but I just like Knowing Things*

Armand: *So does the frog.*

August 4ᵗʰ

Lucas: *where's my bottle of tarragon?*

Armand: *I don't know what tarragon is.*

Armand: *There was a bottle that smelled weird.*

Armand: *I may have put it on the front step.*

Lucas: *THAT WAS GOING TO GET USED IN A VERY DELICIOUS BATCH OF SOUP YOU SWINE*

Armand: *You seem upset.*

Armand: *Sorry about your soup.*

Lucas: *alas somehow I shall persevere*

Lucas: *seriously though, is ramen all you eat? bc I'm pretty sure there are some nutritional guidelines against that*

Armand: *The modern world was built by ramen eaters.*

Armand: *I also partake of the occasional canned meat delicacy. Any relation to Barclay Beef? I believe it makes up more than seventy-eight percent of my DNA at this point.*

Lucas: *funny you should say that*

Lucas: *little did you know that you are, in fact, speaking to Mr. Beef himself*

Armand: *Wait are you serious*

Armand: *?*

Armand: *Oh my god. I feel like I'm meeting royalty. Except you're not a complete waste of space and public funds. Wow. Heir to the Beef.*

Lucas: *I've been a vegetarian for more than a decade so I don't really have anything to do with the Beef Family Legacy except to use that money to help our horses*

Lucas: *oh my god I hate that so much, you are not making heir to the beef happen*

Armand: *Too late. It's already happened.*

Armand: *Wait, is that where the meat comes from? The horses?*

Lucas: *BITE YOUR TONGUE WHATS WRONG WITH YOU*

36
SKYLER CONSIDERS THE HUMAN CONDITION

August 5ᵗʰ

Robin had been true to his word. He wasn't ghosting me anymore; in fact, we were texting fairly regularly now. Though he'd explained himself for his silence and apologized, it was a bit of a struggle to move past my hurt and disappointment. I should've tried talking to him after Armand's class, while the other students were leaving. But Armand had still been there, and I'd figured I could snag Robin after the following class. I hadn't anticipated that he wouldn't show up then.

A lot of our new routine was him sharing a bunch of theater gossip that I was not remotely in on and yet strangely invested in. And I would hit him back with the fascinating ins-and-outs of my beginning psychology course. He liked to respond by pretending he knew how to psychoanalyze the subjects of his theater gossip, which was wildly nonsensical but always amusing.

It was much better than him ignoring me for a week. But, to be fair, I had come dangerously close to ghosting Matt and Delia as well, so. Fair.

And I'd decided not to bring up Terri again. Robin should be able to talk about him on his own terms, in his own time.

Today we sat in the rickety theater seats, nibbling on the sugary snacks Robin had brought us as I helped him run lines. It was about a week out from his opening night, which I'd thought meant that he would have everything memorized by now. Apparently he did, but he'd explained that practicing alongside another person was necessary for his craft.

"Are you sure I'm actually helping here?" I asked, after about an hour of watching Robin bring these words to life. "You can tell me if you only wanted an excuse to hang out. You don't need to pretend I'm a good scene partner because I know the truth."

Robin rolled his eyes, his cheeks still flushed from the energetic portrayal of Peter Pan he'd just given from the comfort of his chair. His face pulled up in a performatively haughty expression. "Don't sell yourself short. I can honestly say that you're doing better than the senior they cast as Hook. You should see him in rehearsals. I'm up there giving the performance of a lifetime and he's giving me *nothing*."

I laughed. "I'm sure you're right. I'm no expert, but it seems like you're doing great—I can't wait to see it all come together."

Robin shifted from where he'd perched on his chair, flopping down into a proper sitting position. "So you—" he cleared his throat "—you're gonna be there?"

"Of course." I grinned, gesturing down at Robin's script for *The Shadow of Never*, officially the oddest Peter Pan retelling I'd ever read. "Really, though, you're kicking this play's ass."

"Psh. Shut up."

"I'm serious." I gently swatted him with the script, and grinned wider when he swatted me back with his empty box of cookie dough bites. "It's so cool that you do this. What made you want to be an actor? Did you always know, or did you figure it out later?"

It was like Robin had been waiting for me to ask—he lit up, rolling into a passionate speech about storytelling and wanting to reach people emotionally and make them feel things . . . It was as captivating to listen to as it was familiar.

Somehow, right on cue, my phone buzzed with a text from Delia.

Delia: *breaking news, new painting just dropped*

Delia: *working title is: that feel when you're stuck in an elevator and the speakers are only playing terrible electronic remixes and you really have to pee: by delia leigh*

The photo she attached showed a beautiful but completely incomprehensible collection of colorful shapes and smudges.

"Is that Matt?" Robin asked, eyeballing my phone even as he popped open a bag of sour gummy worms.

I shook my head. "It's Delia. She finished the painting she'd been working on. Look—" I handed him my phone, a soft smile pulling at my lips as I watched his face; he was scrunching his freckled nose in puzzlement. "She's an artist too."

"Cool. Cool, cool, cool." Robin's face continued working for a second before he grinned, handing my phone back. "Well. It's really good. You certainly have taste when it comes to . . . um. Unrequited crushes." He froze for a second. "Is it . . . unrequited?"

The old familiar ache returned to my chest. "Oh, definitely." I slumped in my chair. "It's weird, though. She doesn't have any idea how I feel, but sometimes she'll say something that I'll keep coming back to, and I know it doesn't mean what I want it to . . ." I rolled my hands down my face. "I just want to be able to move past this so I can go back to being her friend."

Robin was quiet for a long moment, biting his lip. "I'm sure it's possible to maintain a friendship with someone you have feelings for," he finally said. "Like, I bet she doesn't want to lose you either. And she'd be stupid to let you drift away."

I swallowed. The gentle sincerity on his face simultaneously comforted and made me feel painfully exposed. "I'll make it past this eventually. But it's my fault things shifted."

Robin picked at the crinkling old leather of the theater seat, avoiding my eyes. "Hard to believe anything's your fault. How . . ." He swallowed, then followed through, "How'd it shift? What changed?"

"I did," I admitted, before I could chicken out. "Or my feelings did. The three of us were friends, even after she and Matt started dating, and everything was fine, and then—" My breath trembled. "Before I knew what was happening, I realized I felt something different for her. Obviously I never said anything, to either of them. I didn't want to make things weird just because I suddenly didn't understand myself, and I would never want to hurt my brother." I looked to Robin—for support, for reassurance, for . . . I didn't know what. To my surprise, he was staring back at me, eyes wide. "I thought if I ignored my new feelings for Delia, they would go away, and everything could go back to normal. But they didn't go away. So . . . I left."

I was out of breath, almost disoriented from the explanation that had tumbled out of me. "And now Matt's upset that I left without explaining why, but he won't admit it. How can I explain me needing space from them without hurting him worse? Hurting both of them?"

It wasn't on Robin to have the answers—there was no easy fix for this—but I found myself holding my breath, stiff with nerves, waiting for his advice.

"Maybe . . ." he began slowly, thoughtfully, "you should ask him. Like, get it all out in the open. Not that you have to tell him the truth," he hurried to add when he saw that I'd gone a bit rigid, "but you're nothing if not caring and kind. You didn't want to hurt him, so maybe he should know that, at least. And if he stays mad at you after that, then he's a dick. No offense."

The knot in my chest, while not fully unraveled, loosened. "You know—" I nudged Robin's shoulder with mine, giving him a grateful smile "—you're kind of smart about these things. Maybe you should be the one doing psychology."

He flushed bright red and dramatically shuddered. "Over my dead body. But yes, as a soon-to-be-famous actor, it's my job to understand the human condition, to use the brilliance of my craft to bring people together, to achieve world peace, to—" He broke off with a laughing squeak as I threw a chip at him.

Robin was probably right. Not about the Matt-being-a-dick part, but I had spent a while now allowing the both of us to avoid the elephant in the room, to continue our usual banter as if everything could just quietly get back to normal without us ever having to talk about it. But Matt deserved better than that. Delia deserved better.

And maybe I did too.

37
(TEXTING INTERLUDE 7)

August 6th

Armand: *Have you seen the inkwell I left by the door?*
Lucas: *I put it in the coffee table drawer where it will not attempt to KILL me when I walk in the front door. pick up your crap omg*
Armand: *Sorry.*
Armand: *Where did you put the one by the bookshelf?*
Lucas: *OH MY GOD how about the same place I put the other one!! why don't you keep them all together?! IT MAKES NO SENSE*
Armand: *They are all together. On the floor. Where I like to work.*
Lucas: *I cannot even comprehend your weirdness. they do make desks, you know. nice ones, made of mahogany*
Armand: *Floors are cheaper.*
Lucas: *not if you get ink spilled on the carpet and have to get them replaced. capiche?*
Armand: *Then don't spill ink :)*
Armand: *I do have a desk back home, but it wouldn't fit in my carry-on.*
Lucas: *har har*
Lucas: *so do you miss London?*
Armand: *Yes. But I'll be on my way in a fortnight.*
Armand: *My flight leaves two days after the con*
Lucas: *what con? Don't tell me you planned a heist without me*
Armand: *[link to Surrogate Goose Panel at Drawn & Quartered Comic Convention]*
Lucas: *OMG if I come to this will I finally find out what your comic is about?!?!*

Armand: *Unlikely.*

Armand: *but I'd love it if you came*

Armand: *What about you? Planning to renew the lease here?*

Lucas: *FUCK IF I KNOW DUDE*

Lucas: *sorry yeah but no seriously I have no clue, I've never lived on my own before. Lived with my mom all through high school then moved in with roommates, ALMOST moved in with darren and now this.*

Lucas: *kind of hoping this all hasn't been foreshadowing for me not knowing how to be alone*

Armand: *Are you home?*

Lucas: *No I'm finally back at work and trying to remember what a horse is*

Lucas: *just kidding I know they're food*

Lucas: *also accepted a photography gig for the school so trying to Be Normal*

Armand: *So you're not alone.*

Armand: *That is, you seem to have a solid support network. More than that, you're a man of many connections and impressive influence. Almost intimidating.*

Lucas: *intimidating lol sure*

Armand: *Who wouldn't be intimidated by King Beef*

Lucas: *you are absolutely NOT DOING "KING BEEF"*

Lucas: *also how dare you make me giggle while I'm busy being sad*

Armand: *mwaha*

Armand: *But seriously, I know you must be feeling shitty but sometimes it's better to be alone than with the wrong person.*

August 7th

Armand: *Lucas?*

38
ARMAND HAS AN EPISTOLARY EXPERIENCE

August 8ᵗʰ - One week until the convention

My alarm went off at three in the afternoon, and I pawed at it angrily. It was the weekend, no need to scramble out of bed, shock my body into well-feigned sobriety, and rush to the university. I could lie here if I so wished, for hours, in a state of utter gormlessness.

Waking up was starting to feel a bit too familiar: the ashy mouth, the chlorine burn in my sinuses, the pounding headache and shriveled insides. I could tell before I'd even opened my eyes that too much light was leaking through the blinds. That the moment I *did* open them, my eyes would begin to melt, the world would tilt away and pulse in an unstoppable flicker vertigo. Full Bucha effect.

I dug the heels of my hands into the hollows of my eyes, intensifying the pain briefly to the point of ecstasy, and then reached for the water bottle a kinder—if inebriated—version of myself had left on the floor near the bed. I downed it, breath whistling through my nose, then started the slow, precarious undertaking of sitting up.

I'd fully buggered my sleep schedule, staying up too late—or too early, rather—texting with Lucas. I was glad to hear he'd talked to Skyler, and that he was generally feeling better. The same acerbic wit that had made his little notes and naggy texts such a weirdly guilty pleasure had begun to suffuse his tone again. Back were the unexpected bits of dark humor, the flashes of self-deprecation, and streak of pure meanness. The mix of sweet heat and bite was what first kept me from dismissing him as nothing more than a fussy, bothersome flatmate. The same reluctant respect I'd developed for him early on had grown, despite the fact that he hid my ink and whined about all the ways I cocked up and the rubbish I left behind; respect which had then been transformed by concern and had bloomed into a full-blown affection.

Bollocks, Finch was right. I *did* only ever take to people who offered me verbal abuse.

Speaking of abuse . . . I slowly stood up out of bed, still shielding my eyes from the light that trickled through the window. My body was re-adjusting to consciousness, but it could use some help. I stumbled out of the bedroom and down the hall to the toilet, where I washed and engaged in a brief spell of glowering at myself in the mirror.

I'd barely done any work last night. I was nearing the manky end of my Yerkes-Dodson curve.

And I was drinking too much.

The admission felt like the tear of a muscle, the crack of a bone, a bloody moment of emotional incontinence . . . or an emotional moment of bloody incontinence.

I glared down at the mobile I'd brought with me to the loo. At the next step I absolutely had to take.

"*Sabah el khir, habibi.* Good morning, America!"

I winced at Karim's cheerful, deeply obnoxious voice. "It's afternoon here, I think."

"Well, it's just after midnight in Southall, technically morning, so . . . four in the afternoon in California?" He chuckled, both of us painfully aware how typical it was for him to be versed in time zones, while I struggled to locate myself in the known universe. "Getting dicey over there, is it?"

There was no point in sanitizing any of it. "I'm on a bender. It started with just a few nips to get my nerves in check, but then . . ."

As expected, Karim commended me for making the call, and when I started dragging him into my spiral of shame, reminded me that lingering on blame and self-loathing was its own kind of indulgence.

"You know you have to find a meeting, *hayati*, I can google—"

"So can I, Karim. Thank you."

"You must. What would your Lakshmi say?"

She'd tell me to find a meeting. Rather, she'd threaten me into it. So would Sam, and Craig, forever the peacemaker, would offer to cook me supper or go see a film and then, over the length of an evening, slowly manipulate me into going to a ruddy, rotten, *wretched* meeting.

A mere three weeks away from my friends, from my carefully controlled environment, and all the work I'd done, all the progress I'd made over the past year, was effing and blinding at me from the bin. This trip was supposed to be the catalyst through which I would redeem myself. Prove that I was, against all expectations, a real person. Not merely a person, but a person that a corporation like Drake House might consider as a long-term investment.

And instead my head pounded, and I bent to drink more water from the tap, letting it run over my face as well. I couldn't stop all at once. The convention was right around the corner, only a week away—*shit*—and if I showed up shaking with the sweats and the trots ... The thought did not bear contemplation. I had to be smart about this, control myself like a rational adult with the barest hint of moral fiber.

"You still there?" Karim's voice echoed off the tile surrounding, and I fought the urge to simply hang up.

"Aye, Karim, thank you. I'll find a meeting. Good night, *Sidi*."

"Good afternoon, Armand."

I hung up and returned to staring at myself in the mirror and making promises. There was a solution: not temperance, but moderation. Prudence. Calm, rational, good choices that I made for my own benefit.

For example, coffee.

Once I was back in my bedroom with a mug of sanity and a leftover muffin, I settled on the floor against the side of my bed and took stock of last night's failure to produce. I'd inked a page and a half, and then at least had the presence of mind to notice that my crosshatching had turned somewhat less than precise. I held my hand out over the floor—just the slightest of tremors. A quick nip would take care of that, and I could make up the work. Of course I could.

I settled down to work, trying to find comfort in the familiar world of ink and sable brushes and nib pens. I missed the contained little bubble I had at my drafting table back home, but the lap desk I'd brought with me had served me well. Though, I *did* need more light.

I steeled myself before standing and reaching for the blinds, but just as I did, my phone chirped from its place by the bed. I reached for it instead—almost leapt. I hadn't heard from Lucas since the day before, so I was surprised—relieved, even—to see a block of texts coming in one after the other:

Lucas: *But how do you know if someone is right or wrong for you*

Lucas: *people wear all kinds of faces in public vs in private, how are you supposed to know who to trust?*

Lucas: *and if someone shows you who they really are but you don't believe them, and don't believe everyone else who tells you for years that this person is no good, then does that mean you deserve what you get? Asking for a friend*

Lucas: *sorry if this is tmi, it's just*

Lucas: *this is what I don't understand about skyler getting up naked in front of people because like I never realized how much more naked you feel when someone who knows you, knows every part of you, decides that those parts are broken*

I sat back down on the bed, staring at my phone, heart in my mouth. I tapped out a reply before I could think on it for too long, *I know how that is.*

That wasn't enough. I didn't want Lucas to think I was placating him or offering empty cliches. I swallowed.

Armand: *I've been there. It's such a bloody mindfuck.*

Armand: *Like who can I blame for my own stupidity? And how can I ever trust myself again?*

And then I panicked.

Armand: *not that you're stupid, I just mean this sounds similar to something I went through with an ex*

Lucas: *yeah*

Lucas: *Did you ever recover?*

I put my phone down and scrubbed at my hair with both hands. Why was this so *hard*? I took a deep breath and picked it up again, carefully texting.

Armand: *Yes and no.*

Armand: *My friends helped, so I wasn't alone. I tried to isolate myself but they wouldn't let me.*

Armand: *One person can break you down but when so many people are trying to build you up, it's only fair to try and stand.*

Oh god. Shut up. What *tripe.*

Lucas: *damn that's deep, you a poet now? ;)*

Lucas: *#dropthatpoetryanthology*

I groaned to myself softly.

Lucas: *but seriously though, thank you. I've never really talked about this with anyone before. Like my mom kind of gets it, but . . .*

Lucas: *also I'm the third wheel in my friend group and skyler is a teenager, so*

I floundered, trying to find a way to say *no please keep talking to me I love it* without sounding utterly deviant or deranged.

Armand: *I like talking to you.*

Armand: *I hope that doesn't sound weird.*

I was holding my phone so stiffly my fingers had started to ache. I shook out each hand in turn, realized that I was making a horrible, sad little whine in the back of my throat, and that I'd been doing it for quite some time. Why wasn't Lucas responding? Had I ruined it? What, exactly, *was* it that I had potentially ruined?

I was about to start typing out apologies when my phone nearly buzzed out of my hands.

Lucas: *It's not weird. You're sweet.*

Oh god. Why was my body reacting to this simple conversation like it was a thrill park ride? I stopped, took a deep breath, and tried to regain even the slightest, barest shadow of chill.

Armand: *Speaking of sweets, any requests?*

Armand: *I was thinking raspberry sticky buns? I could have them ready by the time you get home from work today?*

Too much? It was likely too much. Why didn't I have the ability to operate in middle gears? Why couldn't I *person*? And to make things worse, I was agonizing over every line like a bloody teenager.

Lucas: *I'm supposed to be dieting damn it, I haven't earned my treats this week*

Lucas: *but yes those sound amazing*

Lucas: *also no work today*

Lucas: *just a depressing lonely day at home*

I blinked down at the screen, the hangover still pulsing dully behind my eyes and my mouth going very, very dry.

Lucas: *also didn't you say you bake when you're upset? Did I bum you out?*

I swallowed thickly, heart thumping in my chest, palms sweating. I knew I should type slowly and carefully but my hands were hardly listening to me.

Armand: *I'm not upstart are you hammer?*

Armand: *upset home*

Armand: *Are you currently at the flat?*

A moment, then:

Lucas: *yeah*

Lucas: *wait, are you?*

I stood up. I couldn't help it—my body was suddenly brimming with nervous energy and I circled the room twice before realizing I hadn't responded yet.

Armand: *Yes.*

I stopped in front of the closed door of my bedroom, every inch of my skin prickling. Beyond this door was a hallway, and at its end was another door, and behind that door was . . .

Lucas.

Lucas, who was in pain. Lucas, who was lonely. Lucas, who wouldn't even accept a bloody bun without passively commenting on whether he was deserving of it. I held my phone in both hands, all but pressing it into my chest like a pastor with their bible. Like a child with her doll. Like a monumental idiot with his phone.

Lucas: *what are the odds lol*

Armand: *Considerably better than what's been happening so far.*

Lucas: *fair*

I fisted a hand in my hair and made two more rounds of the bedroom, my thumb trembling over the screen as I carefully tapped out the words: *Do*

you

Don't be such a damn coward, Demetrio!

want

I had to stop and gnaw at my knuckles for a time before I could continue, *to step out into the living room?*

I sent it. Then dropped into a crouch and hugged myself, realizing in horror that I still hadn't gotten dressed today—I was in my pants and a T-shirt. But just as I was starting to scramble for a pair of jeans, Lucas's response came.

Lucas: *I'm sorry if this is selfish but I kinda don't want to be seen right now? I know you're leaving soon and it's dumb that we haven't met but I'm still feeling raw.*

Lucas: *is that ok do you hate me*

I stood to my feet again and collapsed onto the bed, my body gone all but liquid in relief. There was a hoarse echo of disappointment as well, but mostly I felt strangely proud of Lucas that he was willing to make that admission. I was even more strangely proud of myself for having apparently made him feel comfortable enough to make that admission.

Armand: *Not in the slightest.*

Armand: *That is I don't hate you in the slightest. It is very OJ.*

Armand: **ok bollocks*

Lucas: *can we keep talking though?*

I grinned at my phone despite myself and sent a quick *yes*. Then followed that up with a *please*. And then, in a moment of outright audacity, I asked if he might see his way to sending me a picture of himself.

Lucas: *I look better in person. Or I will eventually FML*

Armand: *FML?*

Lucas: *oh god you ARE an old man! or do we blame this on brits not understanding american slang? bc that happens too*

My body locked up in horror. I had spent this entire time assuming Lucas and I were close in age, but I had no reason to believe that—didn't Americans move out on their own at absurdly young ages? Like Skyler? Like Skyler, *who was Lucas's friend.* But Lucas had referred to him as a teenager, which meant he was likely older, but how *much* older? Was he joking about the "old man" or was this where it all went to utter shite?

Armand: *I am 28 as of last September.*

Armand: *Please tell me you are beagle.*

Armand: **ladle*

Armand: **lacerated*

Armand: *L E G A L I'm so sorry*
Lucas: *WHAT IS YOUR AUTOCORRECT*
Lucas: *I'M DYING*
Lucas: *but yes I'm legal beagle lol I'll be 26 in nov.*

Once again my muscles dramatically relaxed and a groan bucked at the back of my throat. I tapped out, *thank god*, sent it, then realized that perhaps I was showing my hand a bit too freely.

Lucas, however, did not seem at all bothered, because he sent me a winking emoji followed by a cheeky question as to what I was wearing. Without missing a beat I replied, *a three-piece suit. Dior.* And something incredible happened.

I heard him laugh through the wall.

The timbre of his voice was somehow *golden*, bright, like the rich tone of distant music. He sounded like the human embodiment of warm sunlight against the side of my face. I was filled with a happy prickle at the thought that I'd made him laugh, the idea that he was just a few meters away, smiling down at my words.

In less pain, if only for a few moments.

39

ROBIN MEETS A CULINARY LEGEND

August 9ᵗʰ

"Where am I supposed to be right now?" I asked Maggie, fully committing myself to the role of clueless celebrity talent. We were doing last-minute promo shoots for the play, and the pre-show buzz was now an event that lasted days.

I was filled with a wonderful, horrible tension that thrummed like rubber bands and was successfully distracting me from the dread of opening night. I was Peter Pan, lighter than air, and I'd barely even considered a certain Skyler Evans in a certain capacity for almost a week. Well, a couple of days.

An hour.

Except that was a total lie.

I kept thinking back to the conversation we'd had about Delia and how to remain friends with someone you wanted to kiss the ever-loving shit out of. That wasn't the exact wording, but it had been heavily implied. What was I supposed to do about the fact that he was too wonderful and it was physically impossible for me not to be in love with him and that I was also Robin Finch, prima donna.

Maggie finally looked up from her clipboard and acknowledged me by rolling her eyes. "We're done with the ensemble shots, so yeah"—she waved me back toward the stage—"it's time for your favorite part of the day."

I forced a grin. "Glamour shots?"

Sure enough, the moment the words left my mouth, I was pounced on by Kita and Lawrence, who insisted on redoing my makeup and hair before the shoot. I was trying to get lost in the pre-show euphoria again, I really was, but I'd fully jinxed myself by letting my brain whisper his name.

This had become my new normal—I'd be doing something else, *anything* else, and out of nowhere the thought of Skyler would drift closer in the back of my mind like a megalodon rising silently from the depths.

Once Lawrence had made my face one giant cheekbone and Kita had gotten my hair fluffy beyond comprehension, I headed out onto the stage. The set remained hung from the last dress rehearsal; it was the matte painting of Neverland, but with elements of barista-ing hidden in the details, and of course the prop coffee counter stood off stage right. There were a few people milling about in the orchestra pit, mostly crew and some cast members who were sticking around to watch how the lead (that would be me) was fawned over by the media (the one guy hired by the theater department). There was a blond leaning against the stage, a fancy-looking camera hanging around his neck.

When he saw me, he hopped lightly onto the stage, extending a well-manicured hand.

"Hey, I'm Lucas Barclay, I'll be your photographer today." He had a goofy smile, and it didn't matter how messed up I was feeling, I couldn't help but *like* Lucas Barclay.

I grasped his hand and pumped it twice, grinning up at him. "I'm Robin Peregrine Finch. Pleased to meet you, Lucas Barclay!"

Lucas Barclay . . .

"This looks like it's going to be amazing," he was saying, but it sounded like it was coming from a long way off. "Amazing and weird. Like, why is there an espresso machine in Neverland, right?"

"Why indeed," I managed, frowning up at him. Why did that name sound so familiar? Lucas Barclay, *Lucas* Barclay, who the hell was Lucas *Barclay*? Why did I know that name? *Lucas Bar—*

"Oh my god, you're Martha Stewart!" I shrieked. "You're *Lucas Barclay*!"

"Y-yes . . .?" He coughed, clearly startled, but still keeping that sweet smile. "Um . . . have we met?"

I shook my head, ruining whatever effect Kita had been going for. "I work for Armand! Your roommate? The guy you *never* see?"

Lucas's eyes widened and his jaw dropped a little, but before he could say anything, I grabbed his upper arms and pushed him back.

"Oh wow, let me *look* at you!" I took a few steps back, then scanned him up and down.

He was tall, though not as tall as Armand, and built like a fitness model, with the kind of face that put you in mind of the boy next door. The *handsome* boy next door. The handsome and stylish boy next door.

I grinned at him. "You are so much hotter than I expected." Ooh, was Armand in for a happy, sexy surprise!

Lucas, who had moved elegantly from shock to friendly amusement, waved the compliment away and put his hands on his hips. "Wow, so you know Armand, huh?" he shook his head in disbelief. "This is ridiculous. Everyone's met this man but me."

"You guys still texting?" I'd left my prima-donna persona behind because intrigue always took precedence—especially with Armand and his soul/roommate crap.

Lucas's tan cheeks flushed, but he seemed amused. "He told you that? What do you do for him, exactly?"

I shrugged, laughing. "Everything? You've seen how he lives. My job is to make sure he gets places and does things, you know? All of the things."

Lucas nodded, gently biting his lower lip in a smile that made it clear he knew exactly what I meant. How could he not? He had a front row seat. "He does seem kind of . . . eccentric? But nice," he quickly amended. "With the muffins and everything." Lucas glanced down and fidgeted with his camera.

"Muffins?" I blinked at him.

"The ones he baked for me." Were Lucas's cheeks going a little pink, there?

Oh my *god*, they were going to be so cute together!

Then I processed what he'd said and had to keep from outright punching him. "*He baked you muffins!*" I gasped. The idea was absolutely mind-boggling.

Lucas nodded, smiling through his blush. "It was sweet . . ." Then he gave me a conspiratorial eyebrow pop. "What can you tell me about him?"

I rubbed my hands together like a cheap movie villain and chuckled. "Ooh, anything you want to know! I can tell you straight out that he wouldn't bake muffins for just *anyone*." I had to stifle a snort at the image. "And he's a bit of a grumpy bear."

"I *have* noticed he's a man of few words, even over text."

I nodded. "True, but those words he *does* say are spoken in a sexy-as-all-hell English accent, so it's kinda worth it."

Lucas's smile pulled off to the side. "Yeah, I know he's British."

"*Sexy* British," I clarified. "Like, he has this sort of early nineties Marc Jacobs British grunge thing going on, like if Dev Patel did a Kurt Cobain biopic . . . but I don't think it's intentional. *And* I can also tell you he's got to be one of the most socially awkward people I've ever met. *Ever.*"

"I kinda picked up on that." He grinned. And there was so much affection in it my heart nearly died inside my chest. "It's been hard to miss."

Was *anyone* ever going to smile about *me* that way? Bake *me* any damn muffins?

No, no, they were not.

And just like that I was thinking about Skyler again.

I shook myself slightly. "How the hell have you guys not met yet? Be honest, you've been hiding from each other." It immediately became clear that I'd said something wrong, because Lucas paled and his mouth twisted into a pained grimace.

"It's been a rough couple of weeks," he said, avoiding my eyes.

I was overwhelmed with remorse. "I'm sorry, I didn't mean to imply anything, I'm sure you'll run into each other eventually. Even though there's only, like, a week left? Before he leaves?"

He gave a sad smile. "I hope so." He cleared his throat, holding up his camera. "Shall we get down to business, then?"

I nodded and adjusted my costume. "Where do you want me?"

Once we wrapped up the photoshoot, and exchanged numbers because the Armand back-channeling had to keep going for the good of humanity, I made it home and into bed and did some very belated googling. I found Lucas's photography portfolio and—

Pictures of Skyler. With horses.

I immediately pasted one of them into mine and Skyler's chat with an accompanying: *this you?*

Skyler: *oh no you discovered my secret*

Skyler: *I've told you that I work with horses at least five times :D*

He had. And every single time I'd spent the next ten minutes imagining him in a billowy white shirt.

I was about to respond with something snarky and not at all defensive, when another notification popped up on my screen. Not a text from Skyler, a random DM to my FotoBom account.

It wasn't from anyone I knew, and the profile was blank. But the message was a picture of the *Shadow of Never* poster. Holy frigging *crap*, did I have my first fan? I clicked on the picture and—

My heart clenched.

It was the poster. Opening night's date was circled. And someone had added an L to my last name.

Flinch.

40
SKYLER AND LUCAS HAVE A BREAKDOWN

August 10th

I had thought that on our drive back from work Lucas would want to talk about his photography gig for the opening night of *The Shadow of Never*. But he and Armand had made plans to meet in person, which was definitely more important.

"But is it too soon though?" Lucas said, his grip on the steering wheel concerningly tight. "A few days ago I said I wasn't brave enough to step out into the living room when he was already there in the house."

He looked genuinely worried, so I carefully bit back a laugh. "Too soon? Lucas you've been living with him for *weeks*. And he's flying home in like five days."

Lucas tutted. "Yes, but—"

"But I think it's really cool that you both agreed to meet." My time being a model for Armand's class was over, but it was hard to forget about a giant British man awkwardly pining for your oblivious friend. "I'm sure Armand is as nervous as you."

"I guess. It's just that I . . . I don't know, should I be this concerned about what some guy thinks about me?" Lucas rattled a shaky sigh. "Maybe I *should* just go travel the world and find myself or whatever."

"Kind of thought you'd already done a bunch of traveling," I said, able to clearly imagine Lucas gallivanting around Europe with a flowy scarf and a baguette. "Why are you even rich if you haven't done an Eat Pray Love?"

He snorted. "That's a fair point. I always meant to, but I've only been as far as Canada, which, yikes. God knows I eat, but I don't pray, and as for love—" he gestured to the road ahead of us "—well you see what I've been dealing with—"

The car jolted, lurching us off-balance. I braced myself against the door, and Lucas's arm shot across my chest.

He navigated us to the shoulder of the road before turning to me, eyes wide. "You okay?"

"Yeah, I'm good." I glanced down at Lucas's fancy car that had betrayed us. "Is the car good?"

Lucas exhaled, finally dropping his arm. "I guess we hit a nail or something . . ." He shot me an apologetic glance. "Sorry for soccer-momming you."

"It's okay," I assured him. "Thanks for saving my life."

Lucas rolled his eyes, then stepped out of the car. I followed, and—

Whatever we'd driven over, the front left tire was *history*.

"I don't suppose you have a spare?" I tentatively asked.

"I'm like eighty-nine percent sure I do, but this is one of the newer models, and it's not in the trunk like a normal car, it's somewhere . . . maybe *under* the car?" Lucas ran both hands over his face and groaned. "I know my mom tried to teach me how to change a tire at some point, but I was thirteen, and you remember how you don't care about anything when you're thirteen?"

"Like it was yesterday," I said, "or at least, barely five years ago."

Lucas turned to me, one arm across his middle and the other crossing up over his shoulder. "And I don't suppose you know about cars and flat tires?"

"Who, me? I'm but a wee infant baby."

Lucas snorted sardonically. "Damn, we're a walking stereotype. The boomers were right about us."

Luckily he had AAA, though after calling there was nothing to do but lean against the side of the car and wait to be rescued.

"So . . ." I began, watching Lucas's leg bounce anxiously, "want to talk more about how excited you are to meet Armand?"

His face went pale as he let out a little gasp. "*Shit*—" He fumbled with his phone, presumably sending Armand a text that he'd be late.

Then his arm flew back up across his chest like it lived there now. "Skyler, I think I manifested this."

"You gave yourself a flat tire?"

"I've been so nervous about this meeting that maybe the universe channeled all that energy into my car breaking down."

"What are you nervous about? He clearly wants to meet you, what's the worst that can happen?"

Lucas's eyes dropped back down to his phone, which he'd been absently tapping on. "That he's disappointed," he finally said. "And that's the issue. I don't even know why I care so much about what he thinks of me. He already saw how messed up I was after Darren, but . . ." he trailed off, shrugging one shoulder in a weirdly awkward move. "I just . . . I have no idea what I'm doing."

Now if *that* wasn't the most relatable thing I'd heard all day. I continued gently, carefully, "Well, instead of wondering what he expects of you, maybe it would be easier to think about what you expect of him."

Lucas looked lost, like he was years younger than he was, closer to my age. "I don't even know that," he said softly, a tinge of red coloring his cheeks. "I *do* know that he's easy to talk to. We haven't been texting for very long, but it's kind of wonderful. Now that he, you know, texts *back*. And everything I told him, about Darren or whatever . . . it just seemed like he was actually listening. Like he understands what I'm going through." He bit his lip, staring down at the ground. "It's weird. It's like I know him already."

It seemed too soon after Darren, but judging from Lucas's body language and the way he never did stop blushing, I had to ask. "Do you think you like him?"

"I—" Lucas began to hunch in on himself, which reminded me so much of Armand that it caught me off-guard "—I really like talking with him. And you're going to think I'm so stupid and immature, but I'd never considered having anyone else but Darren in my life. In like. A romantic capacity."

I couldn't speak for Armand Demetrio and didn't know what his intentions were toward Lucas, but I did know that he was a sweet man who seemed to care about Lucas's well-being. That, much like Lucas, he was a man who made people feel safe in his presence. "I wouldn't say

I'm an expert in this area," I said, as the understatement of the decade, "but perhaps you don't need to go into this with certain expectations. It's just a meeting—maybe see where things take you. You don't have to define yourself by the relationships you do or don't have."

Lucas blinked at me, then shook his head in amusement. "One of these days I'll remember that apparently you were a philosopher in another life." There was a buzz, and he checked his phone again. His face fell. "He says he has to leave soon for class. I blew it."

"Well, technically, the *universe* blew it," I pointed out.

Lucas laughed. "Yes, good, you're right. Avoid accountability at all costs."

We were saved by AAA soon after that, and Lucas was able to drop me off at my dorm without further incident. He seemed to be in better spirits, so hopefully my advice had helped a little. It was always simpler to lend advice to someone else for their problems—which were usually pretty easy to decipher—than to solve my own.

The irony wasn't lost on me.

There was still a problem I had left to solve. I dug out my phone, hesitating for an impossible moment before texting Matt.

Skyler: *hey can we talk*

It took Matt several minutes—the dreaded three dots showed him typing, then stopping, then typing again—but he finally responded.

Matt: *yeah*

I set up the video call, and this was it. No going back now.

"What's up?" Matt asked, his demeanor calm and collected, though the edges of his mouth were tight and the smile didn't reach his eyes. "You see Delia's painting? I told her it looks absolutely sick, though I have no idea what's going on there, not even a little bit."

"Yeah, it turned out great." I forced myself to take a deep breath, to face the consequences of my actions once and for all. "Um. I needed to talk to you, though."

"Oh? What about?"

"Matt," I said quietly, "I know you're mad at me. Let's just get all this out in the open, okay? Just tell me what you want to tell me."

He scoffed. His eye started twitching. "What? I'm not mad, dude, I'm fine—"

"I can practically see the ulcer you've given yourself from the stress of being upset." I didn't want him to be mad, Matt never got mad, but if that was what it would take for us to go back to normal, for him to forgive me, then so be it. "Talk to me."

Matt blinked back, and I wondered if he would make an excuse to hang up again. Then a weird whimper snuck out of him. "I . . . I'm . . ." he propped up his phone and hugged himself. I hadn't seen him use such closed body language since middle school. "Okay. Yeah. I'm mad. It's so fucking weird, dude. I thought I could be cool about this whole thing, because I love you and want to support your decisions and stuff, right, but . . ." He rolled his hands over the top of his head. "We had a plan, Skyler. I— You never said you were considering anything else. I thought we told each other everything."

"We do," I agreed, weakly, desperately wishing this could continue to be true. "I didn't plan it. I'm sorry."

"I just don't *understand*! I don't understand why you left and I don't understand why you won't tell me, and I—" Matt's voice cracked, and his eyes shone with tears. "I feel shitty, Skyler. Like you abandoned me and I don't know why. And I hate it, I hate being upset with you, and I haven't been sleeping and Delia's worried but she doesn't want to say anything and please can you just fucking tell me what's going on?"

I hadn't fully crafted my apology like I should have. "I'm sorry I hurt you, Matt," I managed, my own throat growing tight the longer I stared at the pain on my brother's face. "That was never my intention, and I promise, I swear, you didn't do anything wrong. This is—" Half truths. Half truths I could tell him. "You and Delia mean so much to me, and I saw how well things were going for you guys. So I . . . I guess I wanted to give you an opportunity to figure out where that was going. You've always taken care of me, Matt," I pressed on before he could protest, "always made me feel welcome in your family, and comfortable with your friends, and all you do is look out for me. You never focus on yourself and what *you* want."

"You're saying I can't want to go to college and hang out with my best friend—"

"Of course not, but." I swallowed down the lump in my throat. "You'll always have me, Matt. I promise I'm not going anywhere. But between you looking out for me and me never being independent, it felt like a moment where just a little bit of space may have done us both some good. I'm so sorry I made you think I didn't want to be near you."

Matt sniffed again, and everything in him seemed to relax in the span of one inhale. "So . . . what you're saying . . . is that I'm a big sad whiny baby."

"That is not at all what I said, but to be fair only one of us is covered in snot right now."

He choked out a laugh. "Being mad is so exhausting; you may not have been kidding about that ulcer."

I smiled. "I really am sorry. Are we okay?"

"Fuck you. Yeah, we're good, but I miss my brother. When can you get back here to visit?"

"Soon," I promised. "Thanks for talking to me."

"Guess I have to retract what I said about that psychology major. I am not easily emotionally cracked like a gourd."

"That is an absolute lie, and Delia will agree with me."

We both reassured each other that we were sorry and we were okay and nothing would change that, and afterward, I sat on my bed, buzzing with overwhelmed relief.

I shot off a text to Robin, telling him that he was right, that it all worked out, but I didn't hear anything in response. I fought the urge to double-text to see if he was okay. He was probably just doing last-minute play cramming—I couldn't imagine how busy the cast must be this close to opening night.

Worst-case scenario I would see him at the show.

41

LUCAS ISN'T WAITING BY THE PHONE

August 12th

Operation *Try Meeting Again Because for Some Reason It Hasn't Worked so Far and We're Running Out of Time Oh My God* was a go, and I resolved to not sit on the living room couch like I was waiting for my prom date. Armand wouldn't be headed home until after his class, which meant that I had about three hours to kill.

We had agreed to meet around dinner, and the likelihood that he'd eaten anything of substance during the day was approximately zero, so in a burst of inspiration I rummaged through the fridge and decided to make eggplant lasagna.

It was always a lengthy endeavor, but well worth the effort. There was no better comfort food, and it would certainly be better than hot pockets or whatever Armand would otherwise eat for dinner. I was anxious, my nerves alight at the prospect of seeing Armand in person, of having him see *me*, but I took comfort in the process of chopping vegetables and administering seasonings and, huh, we could actually do with a cute little spring salad as an appetizer. I could whip up a vinaigrette—

It was approaching seven—our designated meeting time— and the lasagna was nearing perfection. In my cooking haze, I had failed to properly set the table. I threw on one of the tablecloths I'd purchased the moment we'd rescheduled post my car breaking down. Elegant embroidered napkins? Check. A solid first two courses with the understanding that Armand had volunteered the dessert? Check. Should there be candles?

Nope, too much, Barclay. Walk it back.

In putting the finishing touches on everything, I glanced at the clock, which showed that it was now seven fifteen. No cause for concern yet, but as a pre-emptive measure, I shot Armand a quick text.

Lucas: *hey, where are you*

For the next almost-twenty minutes I paced between the kitchen and living room in a nervous purgatory. A terrible thought occurred to me, which was that he'd forgotten. A split second later an even *more* terrible thought occurred, which was that he'd remembered but had decided to stand me up. Leave me pacing a kitchen full of food like an absolute idiot.

I ventured another text: *you okay?*

My stomach was twisting, and some of it was from the delicious smell of freshly baked lasagna that was mocking me from the glass serving tray. But mostly it was the growing certainty that I was the butt of a joke, that Armand and Robin were laughing right now, talking about how Armand had only agreed to meet me out of pity—

It was eight o'clock.

Lucas: *OH MY GOD ARE YOU DEAD*

This time I only needed to pace for ten minutes before my phone buzzed. I opened the text so fast I nearly dropped it.

Armand: *God I'm so sorry*

Armand: *Should have texted sooner. Sorry. Got ambushed by nerds.*

Armand: *People who read the comic. I hate them.*

Armand: *I mean I don't like them.*

Armand: *I mean I wasn't happy about being approached. And made to talk.*

Armand: *I'm sorry I missed you.*

Armand: *Sorry*

I tried to breathe a sigh of relief that he didn't seem to have stood me up, but I was met with such a wave of disappointment that I had to sink onto the couch.

Lucas: *its ok, just glad you're not dead*

Lucas: *and you didn't stand me up, that would've sucked*

I shouldn't have typed that last bit. It was too vulnerable.

But he wrote back immediately this time—

Armand: *I honestly was looking forward to seeing you, it was going to be the highlight of my rubbish day*

Armand: *& I really mean that, not just being biscuit*

Armand: **British kill me*

I let out a soft laugh despite myself.

Lucas: *hey don't talk about your fans that way, you're talented and they're appreciating you! :)*

Lucas: *but speaking of biscuits, if you're on your way you shall have food waiting for you, I can wait up*

Armand: *I swear I'm trying to leave but this one young person keeps crying*

Another half hour passed, though, and no sign of Armand. It was getting late, and knowing the schedule Armand kept, it was likely he wouldn't make it in until double-digit hours. I stared forlornly at the lasagna.

Lucas: *hey look I'm sorry but I have work in the morning and I can't stay up much longer*

Armand: *I'm so so so sorry Lucas, do you see why I hate this*

Lucas: *no worries! the food's in tupperware in the fridge so you can help yourself whenever you get in*

Lucas: *drive safe!*

Lucas: *oops just remembered robin would be driving, so I guess he can drive safe and you don't get eaten by fans ok*

Armand: *I'm so sorry again, I promise I'll make it up to you*

Lucas: *maybe I'll see you at robin's play :)*

Armand: *I'll save you a seat.*

I stared at our conversation for entirely too long, chest buzzing. I tossed a modest portion of the lasagna into the microwave for a minute, then chewed absently, barely noticing how sub-par it tasted reheated.

He *had* been planning to show up. He *wanted* to meet me. He wanted to *make it up to me.* The implications of this fluttered around my brain, not making a lot of sense and coming dangerously close to flooding my stomach with butterflies. When was the last time I'd looked forward to something this hard?

I needed something to distract me before I melted into a complete breakdown.

Surely it wasn't too early to start planning my outfit for the play.

It would be nice to go *out*. Somewhere that wasn't work and wasn't the apartment. It turned out that a lot more of my social life than I'd realized had revolved around Darren.

And now I had *two* things I needed to be distracted from.

I ran my hand along the hanging clothes, reaching impulsively toward the back of the closet, where the colors were. I pulled out a robin's egg blue silk top—I'd loved it the moment I'd seen it but vividly remembered Darren calling it "very . . . *Easter* egg." The tag was still on.

The stupid part of me—the part that had so easily convinced me that Armand had stood me up on purpose—still believed what Darren had said. That calling any kind of attention to myself was *childish*, and that I'd make myself look ridiculous if I wore clothes like this.

But the rest of me—the parts that still warmed at the comfort and compassion Armand had shown me over the past few days, at the thought of a night at the theater, at *"I'll make it up to you."*

The rest of me couldn't wait to be the most fabulous damn Easter egg Armand had ever laid eyes on.

42
ARMAND GETS LOVE BOMBED

August 14ᵗʰ - One day until the convention oh god oh god

I stood at the front of the classroom and surveilled my troops, trying not to allow myself to be overcome with emotion. I'd managed to save enough time for this, the last class, to be spent on critique. The students were presenting their work to each other, explaining their processes, making suggestions, and complimenting each other, using the terminology and storytelling locutions I'd taught them.

Ashley (Long-Face-Freckle-Mullet), who had rolled their eyes so decisively during our full week of layout discussion, had done a marvelous job pacing. Aiden (Button-Nose-Sleek-Goatee), who had struggled with drawing bodies in any other stance than standing, had used multiple dynamic poses. Aubrey (Square-Jaw-Cat-Eye-Specs), who could not draw at the start of the workshop, still could not draw, but had developed increasingly creative ways to hide this fact with *stylization*.

Every single one of them had made progress. Myself included.

And I definitely wasn't near tears.

Some backroom deal had been struck early on between the university and the Drawn & Quartered Comic Convention organizers so that the three-page works my students produced would be galleried on the same day of my talk and Q&A panel. It was quite brilliant, when you thought about it—the students had all been awarded free entry to view their own work, but family and friends would have to buy tickets if they wished to dote.

Money would be made and everyone would be happy.

I really was a sellout. With any luck, I'd continue to be one for the foreseeable future.

Please, god, let me be a sellout.

"Well done, lads." I cleared my throat. "You've all done a lovely job . . . er . . ." Now, in the last twenty minutes or so of our final class, I was meant to make a speech. To wrap up the entire workshop to the best of my ability . . . but it was as if I'd never learned to speak to them properly. I'd fully regressed—I couldn't stop swallowing, my palms were damp, the back of my neck was sweating, I could feel my pulse in my molars. What could I even say to these people? Sorry to have wasted a month of your life? But no, they *had* improved, if not thanks to anything *I'd* done—

"Ahem."

I pulled myself back from the brink of despair. Finch had stood up in his seat and the rest of the class was turning back to look at him.

He was grinning his impish, Peter Pan grin, eyes sparkling and cheeks flushed. When he spoke, his voice had a theatrical cruise-conductor quality which seemed to draft everyone in the room into his dastardly machination. "I think we should all go around and take a few minutes to tell Professor Demetrio how much we learned in this class. How much fun we had, and how grateful we are that he came here to teach this workshop. Does that sound good to you guys?"

There was a general, enthusiastic cheer of assent, while I tried my absolute best to evaporate.

That little *bastard*.

"I'll start." He beamed, rocking back on his heels. "When I first heard about this workshop I was *so* excited. *Surrogate Goose* is a *phenomenon*, right? Like, it's so weird, and it came out of nowhere. And now Mr. Nowhere Man is teaching a class? How cool is that?"

The students gave a collective chuckle. I'd leaned back against my desk, legs crossed, hugging myself with one arm and biting my knuckle like a bloody caricature of myself.

"Anyway, I really appreciate how comprehensive this class was," Finch continued. "Like, we covered so much in only a month."

"Yeah." Blue-Glasses-Afro-Puffs (Ashlyn? Adrian . . . Ariadne) stood up. "Me too. I thought maybe we were just going to cover basics or comics history or whatever, but this was like comics *bootcamp!*"

"I don't feel like I only learned about comics." Blond-Apple-Cheeks (Bently) stood up—why were they all standing up? What was happening? "I feel like I learned about *art*."

Nose-Ring-Purple-Hair (Corrine? Corey. No, Cyrus) stood up as well. "I feel like I learned about *life*."

This *kept going*. Until each and every one of these sun-kissed Californian children had stood from their seat and expressed their appreciation for whatever they perceived me to have been doing during these ill-conceived sessions. All I'd done was ramble and rant and try to make sense out of this . . . *thing* I was compelled to make. What had Finch called it? A phenomenon? More like a ridiculous, self-indulgent spectacle.

Finch watched over it all with an evil, beatific grin, and when the last of the Sparticuses had O Captain, My Captain-ed me into oblivion, the horrible little traitor led them in a round of applause.

All but curled into a ball on my desk, I thanked the students, trying to pretend my voice wasn't thick with emotion and my face wasn't burning. Several of them requested hugs, and I was helpless to refuse.

"See you at the con!" said Braids-Sloe-Eyed-Gap-Tooth (Damian) and hugged me around the middle. "I can't believe it's tomorrow!"

I swallowed hard and kept it together until the last of the students had left—except for Finch, of course, who skipped down the auditorium steps like the malicious fae child he was.

I said nothing and glared at him, which he took as an invitation to say, "I'll see you at the play tonight, right? We're seeing *everyone* at the play tonight, right?" He poked my biceps. "*Right*? Everyone who might be about six feet tall? Everyone who might have a dimpled chin?"

Finch had apparently run into Lucas at some point this past week. After smugly informing me of this encounter, he'd waited, as if I might beg him for information. When I'd stood firm, he'd begun peppering me with infuriating little factoids.

Lucas was blond. He had a nice smile. Big hands.

Unfortunately, Finch had also been witness to the last time Lucas and I had tried to move against the will of several gods and forces of the universe by attempting to meet each other. He'd watched as several members of a local Indie Comix Club—an organization I had not heretofore known existed—had embarked upon an uncomfortable ritual in which they praised *Surrogate Goose* and myself to the point of tears. Theirs, not mine.

Well, nearly mine.

Finch had known I was meant to be meeting Lucas that night, and to his credit he'd done his best to help me leave. He seemed concerned that Lucas and I barely had three days left in which to try to see each other, but he was obviously also a bit pleased that his play would have a role in this comedy of errors.

"Lucas *is* coming?" Finch asked, his voice gone slightly hesitant.

I let my shoulders shudder in a heavy sigh. "I certainly hope so, Titch." I tried to smile at him. "I assume *you're* excited for tonight?"

For a moment his wicked smirk almost faltered, something other than mischief and unadulterated joy contracting behind his eyes. Nerves? It almost looked like fear.

He shook it off and ushered a grin back into place. "I'm so excited I could pop." He poked my biceps yet again. "You gonna run around screaming for the next couple hours?"

I shrugged dejectedly. "I think I'll just wait in my office." I'd brought some work with me, as always, though the Indie Comix Club incident had left me gun-shy and reluctant to act predictably.

"Great, see you later!" And he scampered off, forever bursting with endless, cheeky, intolerable energy.

I stepped outside for a quick smoke, then holed up in my office like I'd planned. I had brought work along, but I'd also brought something else. It sat snug at the very bottom of my bag and posed incontrovertible proof that I was turning into my father.

I shut the door and took a few quick nips from the flask, just to steady my nerves. I was simply sad about the workshop ending, nervous about the con tomorrow, rueful about missing Lucas's dinner, and anxious about seeing him tonight.

After all, I was in control. I was the master of my own fate, making conscious adult decisions.

Which was why I nearly jumped out of my skin when a voice message arrived from my agent.

"Did you find a meeting, pet?

This was one of my conscious adult decisions turning on me—I'd told Lakshmi that I'd contacted Karim. She knew what that meant.

"Yes. I sat in a church basement with a load of strangers and now I'm cured," I grumbled, trying not to sound guilty.

Lakshmi clearly tried not to sound skeptical. "Glad to hear it."

I *had* found a meeting, and it *had* helped. But it wasn't pretty.

And neither was drying out. All I had to do to stop drinking so much was *stop bloody drinking so much*.

I could almost *feel* the whack Karim would have aimed at the back of my head and hear his scolding: *"You think it's that simple? You kill me, habibi."* There would be a reckoning when I got home, back to my safe, controlled environment, but for now I had to focus on short-term goals—those things I could realistically change. Goddamn fucking buggering bloody *mindfulness*.

This was far from my first time drying out or even my first time attempting it on my own. I knew what I needed, and while the sobriety tracker app suggested to me at the meeting was a nice thought, old-school sharpie marks on the bottle served just as well.

I resolutely refused to acknowledge the fact that sharpie marks didn't have quite the same effect with a flask.

What I needed was to *work*.

I needed to work and utterly divorce myself from reality, from the many-flavored banquet of anxieties that threatened to fill every last part of me. First and foremost among these was the worry surrounding my and Lucas's potentially disastrous first meeting. Tonight. There were so many, *many* ways I could cock this up.

What if I forgot how to form words or became suddenly and catastrophically incontinent? What if, upon meeting me, he flat-out rejected me because I offended and repelled him so? What if I'd completely misunderstood the tone of his communiqués and what I had perceived as flirting was actually friendly heterosexual banter, and the moment he realized my intentions he tried to kill me in a fit of homophobic passion? Perhaps he thought I was a woman? Or simply far more desirable than I really was? He had mentioned my fame; what if he was under the impression that I was also rich? Perhaps he was expecting Mr. Bond: English, sexy, and debonair, but would instead be met with Mr. Bean: English, neurotic, and humorously tragic.

Even if the worst happened, would it matter? I was leaving the country in three days.

"You still there, pet?"

I looked down at my phone. I could tell Lakshmi, but that would result in some of the most tedious and relentless ribbing known to man, and I did not feel I possessed the necessary resilience to withstand it in my current condition. The damage done would outweigh whatever advice she gave me.

The only thing that could distract me from my anxiety about meeting Lucas was my anxiety about the convention.

"But Lakshmi," I spoke tremulously into my phone, "*Leeds.*"

"You're twice the man you were then. Literally, you've put on at least two stone in the past year."

I laughed despite myself. "Why are you still up, anyway?"

"Who do you know who still sleeps?"

"Go to bed, you harpy." I said goodbye and took a few deep breaths.

She was right. I was a different man.

But while my ability to articulate myself in front of a crowd had demonstrably improved over the course of this bloody workshop, my talk at the convention would require a much greater skillset. Teaching was not so different from dancing—I could lose myself in the form, the ideas, the rhetoric. Teaching required me to discuss the work of *others*, which should not be confused with the bowel-freezing task of discussing my own work. I would need to *account* for myself at the convention, make a case for my and my work's existence, be charming and palatable, and seem passably sane in front of a crowd of *hundreds*.

Thousands, if you include the livestream.

I reached for the flask again, making a conscious, adult, mindful decision.

43

LUCAS BRINGS MILKSHAKE TO THE YARD

August 14ᵗʰ

It was finally happening—tonight I would meet Armand. He was saving me a seat, and we would watch our mutual friend in a play, and no amount of flat tires or rabid fans or cosmic tomfoolery would change The Plan.

I'd finally committed to cutting the tag from the Easter-egg blue button-up and paired it with comfy white chinos. But even after a shower and shave and cologne, I found myself standing in front of the bathroom mirror just a bit too long.

Maybe it was the warmth brought on by the most recent text exchange with Armand, but there was a slight possibility that I didn't look completely terrible. My freshly washed and styled hair was cooperating, and the pastel of the shirt brought out my eyes, which were the better of my assets.

If Armand met me like this, would he like what he saw?

"You're always fishing for validation," Darren had said. *"It's exhausting. And childish."*

And maybe it was—but I couldn't help it. I was who I was. At least Armand hadn't given me any credible reason to think he would be judgmental or cruel. It was more than likely that, should I be repulsive to him, he would simply fly off back to England and I wouldn't have to see him again.

But that wasn't nearly as comforting as I'd thought it'd be.

It was over an hour before curtain, but I couldn't spend another minute pacing the apartment and overthinking. I could overthink on my way to the theater to beat the crowds. Multitasking.

My phone buzzed just before I was about to merge onto the highway. I answered the call on speaker. "Hello?"

"Lucas, honey"—it was Mom, her voice soft and tight—"do you think you can make it over to the ranch tonight?"

I hadn't really talked to her since she'd copped an attitude about Darren. "I'll see what I can do, but I have a lot planned tonight and tomorrow—"

"Baby, it's Milkshake. I've given him some pain medication, but he's going. If you wanted to be with him to say goodbye ... Dr. Sanchez says it'll probably be tonight."

I swerved into a U-turn.

The End is Neigh was quiet when I arrived. I hurried toward the stables but saw that instead of being in his stall, Grandpa Milkshake had been led out into the pasture, lying on the grass. Dr. Sanchez, the family vet who had partnered with us in looking after our horses for years, was crouched beside Mom, her eternally friendly face unmistakably grave.

"I'm glad you came," Mom said as I made it over. Her eyes were red-rimmed already, her face ashen. How long had she been out here with him?

"Of course." I sank onto the grass on the other side of Grandpa Milkshake's head, which rested on Mom's lap. He was still breathing, though each breath was labored. I was immediately grateful that Mom had anticipated and given him pain medication. He deserved to go without struggle.

Mom and I stroked his face, and neck, and side, hoping he was still present enough to hear and recognize our voices. I watched his big, beautiful black eyes blink slowly up at us. He'd been sick for so long, after such a rich, productive life, and if leaving us meant that he wouldn't be in pain anymore, then so be it. But my throat closed up regardless, eyes stinging with tears.

Mom had been there for several horses passing over the years but had never let me be present. She'd figured that after Dad, I'd dealt enough with death in the family at a young age without adding more. I was older now and I knew what to expect, but suddenly the dark inevitability of it knocked the air out of me. My hand, which was stroking Grandpa Milkshake's thin mane, started shaking.

Mom reached out, grasping my hand tightly.

Around us, the sky moved from blue to pink and purple. Distantly I realized that the play would be starting soon, and unless I headed out I would miss it.

I would miss Armand.

But then I glanced over at Mom's face, lined with sadness but staying strong, and knew I couldn't leave. Besides, my pants were already ruined with mud, the shirt that had done me so many favors earlier was sweat-stained and wrinkled to hell.

We grew quiet as Grandpa Milkshake's wheezing breaths began to slow. I'd been sitting long enough for my legs to cramp, the stress of just *waiting for it to happen* wracking me with exhaustion. I stared down at his frail body and wondered if horses could sense death and whether he was scared.

My hand was still clutching Mom's when we felt him breathe one last time and then go still.

"I'm sorry," I whispered, to Milkshake, or Mom.

Or Armand.

44

MR. ARMAND GOES
TO THE THEATER

August 14ᵗʰ - The bloody convention is to-bloody-morrow

I couldn't remember the last time I'd been to a play, so I hadn't been sure if I had to dress up or bring flowers or what.

"Your assistant's lead?" Lakshmi's voice over the phone yesterday had been hoarse and flat and entirely done with me.

"He's not my assistant, he's my . . ." What was his job description again? Something liaison . . .?

"But he's the lead? And he's what, nineteen?"

"Aye."

"Then you bloody well bring him flowers."

"Noted."

"And you wear *whole* clothes—nothing fancy, Armand, just not *shredded*; you understand the distinction?"

"Do I own any clothes that aren't, as you say, shredded?"

"No, but I packed you some anyway. A shirt should have four openings, no more. You don't embarrass this boy on his big day."

I hadn't told her about Lucas, so she had no way of knowing I'd already made a pathetic attempt at appearing human tonight. However, it was fascinating to note that even an ocean away she'd managed to develop maternal feelings for a boy she'd never met. Finch's innate vulnerability was that strong.

"I'll get some flowers."

"Good lad."

And I had. Now, in my office, I changed into the starchy, posh clothes Lakshmi had bought me and which I'd somehow managed to wrinkle over a mere couple of hours. Come to think of it, it might have been a result of shoving them into my messenger bag.

And so, rumpled, a tad drunk, but game for anything at this point, I found the venue, collected the ticket Finch had left for me, and took my seat at the back of the theater. Next to the one I'd saved for Lucas.

Which remained empty.

I'd considered waiting for him at the front, but the idea had made my legs threaten to stop working, so sitting down had probably been in everyone's best interests.

A sad little part of me, that I'd honestly thought had been struck out of commission weeks ago, wished I hadn't drunk so much in anticipation of meeting Lucas, that I'd managed to stay sober and unwrinkled and the slightest bit suave just for tonight.

But I hadn't, and Lucas was about to get a glimpse of reality.

If he ever showed up.

As the theater around me slowly swelled in humanity, and the house lights began to flicker in warning, I checked my phone, which like an obedient fool I'd immediately silenced upon entry, and saw a text from Lucas waiting for me.

Lucas: *I'm so sorry I can't make it tonight :(:(:(:(milkshake's gone*
Lucas: *I know it's last minute but I'll try to be at the con tomorrow*

I stared at this text for a few moments in uncomprehending silence, then responded, *I'm sorry, see you there,* hoping that would suffice or make the slightest bit of sense in these, the oddest of circumstances.

I had no idea how the absence of liquefied ice cream had led to us missing yet another—if not the last—of our chances to meet before I flew away to England. But my flask-related activities earlier in the evening ensured I was somewhat numb to it.

He wasn't coming.

That was fine.

Truly, it was fine. Lucky, honestly, given that I wasn't exactly at my best. I didn't want Lucas to be here. Hadn't spent the entire day silently counting down to this moment. Hadn't used the idea of finally seeing Lucas tonight as the scaffolding for the whole of my universe, which might otherwise collapse in on itself in a splat of self-loathing and flower petals.

The lights went down, and as I sat there, roses wilting in my lap, I tried to focus on literally anything else. Fortunately, I was given the opportunity to notice that Finch, the boy I was here to see, the friend I was meant to support, was actively not sucking on stage. He was, in fact, not sucking to the point of being quite good.

It was *eerie*. He didn't move like himself—none of the jerky bursts of hyperactive energy I'd come to know so well. Even when he wasn't wire-flying like an ethereal creature, he was making lightning switches between the persona of a naïve, fresh-faced, boy-foot bear with teaks of chan, and that of a glint-eyed, grinning, *sinister* hobgoblin that clung to the shadowy corners of the stage. He was simultaneously endearing and terrifying, his voice modulating from the brassy ring of a laugh to the rasp of a barked command—exuding watercolor layers of equally bright joy and rage, all vibrant against the canvas of pure, unblemished, sociopathic boyhood.

I, along with every member of the audience, found myself *enthralled*.

It slowly began to dawn on me why Finch's life had been so fraught with misfortune and why his emotions seemed to get the better of him on a regular basis.

The poor bastard *was* an artist.

A real one. The kind that can't bloody help it. No wonder he was so hopeless socially—every faculty, every ounce of will and every synapse were spoken for, caught up in manufacturing a Peter fucking Pan I fucking *believed*.

There was no growing out of this, either. The boy was doomed; not only was he passionate, he apparently had the talent to back it up. He had no options at all.

I looked down at the roses in my lap and realized that perhaps lilies would have been more appropriate.

I also realized that while Finch's performance was appallingly good, the play itself was simply appalling. It appeared to be a Peter Pan retelling, but with all the whimsy wrung out. Finch's Peter was still the lovely, terrifying, Puckish creature he was meant to be, flying and flitting about the stage, but far too much time was spent on "Jimmy Hook," who wore plaid and a beanie and a beard and lamented his lost youth and artistry. Wendy, who was, I would argue, the most fascinating character in the original work, was relegated to beautiful, mindless prize, and The Lost Boys were a heavy-handed metaphor for a White Supremacist group trying to recruit "Jimmy" into their ranks. Tiger Lily and her people were, unsurprisingly, nowhere to be seen.

At one point, Wendy—dressed in athleisure wear and carrying a yoga mat—tried to explain to Peter that she was in love with him, while Jimmy stood in the background doing some sort of interpretive dance composed mainly of grimaces and stomping.

"Peter, what are your exact feelings for me?" Wendy asked, sitting on a bench center stage, vines and steam valves entwined around her.

Finch, that is Peter, stood balanced on one foot on the back of the bench like an autumn leaf clinging to a dry branch. "Those of a devoted son, Wendy." He giggled.

Jimmy wriggled in the background in an explosion of silent rage.

Wendy gave a heavy sigh. "I thought so."

Peter leaned forward into a handstand, walking back and forth across the bench back, which clearly hid a set of parallettes. I'd had no idea Finch was such an accomplished gymnast. "You're so funny," he told Wendy, but also seemed to be speaking to the incomprehensible Jimmy—who was now miming making multiple espresso shots and downing them one after the other. "It's like there's something you want to *be* that isn't my mother. Something you want *me* to be that isn't your son."

Wendy gave Peter a simpering look. "Don't you have any other type of feelings for me? Nothing in your heart? Nothing in your . . . other places?"

My god, who had *written* this?

Peter righted himself and shook his head, grinning widely. "Nope! I want to be a little boy forever and have fun!"

I reached for the playbill and squinted at it in the dark of the theater—I had to know who was responsible for this—and my heart stopped.

The Shadow of Never, written by Dr. Kenneth Lazlo.

I almost laughed out loud but covered my mouth at the last moment. Of course. He *had* told me he'd written a play, after all.

Distracted as I was, my eye was still drawn to a soft light in the audience a few rows down. Someone was texting during this pretentious middle-aged wank of a play, and I still couldn't help but think: *How rude!*

Yes, I was sitting here in the relative finery purchased by my agent (on account of my apparent inability to dress appropriately), and I still felt that whoever thought being on their phone during a performance was acceptable, was, in point of fact, *damn uncivilized*.

Before I could help myself, I heard Ken's voice: *"Could you be any more adorably English?"*

I swallowed hard and tried to keep my shoulders from seizing up. This was stupid. I tried to concentrate on Finch, on this horrible, *horrible* play, but the damn light was as distracting as ever.

Despite the picture I might have presented so far, feeling lonely was not something I allowed myself to do lightly. It could so easily get out of hand, especially in public, and that was how things like Ken happened.

But somehow the very act of sitting here, surrounded by people and darkness, with one extremely empty seat beside me, was stripping away my carefully constructed buffers.

Ladies and gentlefolk, if you will direct your attention to the third to last row near the aisle. The dark boy with the flowers, yes; here, ladies and gentlefolk, we see Armand Demetrio, a semi-young, semi-successful cartoonist, alone at the theater. Mr. Demetrio will return to his flat later tonight, unaccompanied. He will work, drink, and fall into bed without having spoken to a single person, not even a fish. Armand Demetrio lives, as you can clearly see, ladies and gentlefolk, as he will die: alone and unloved. Thank you for your time.

I was letting it all get to me, or perhaps it was simply the experience of holding a bouquet of roses, the seat beside me pulsing like a black hole of could-have-beens. Feeling trapped and surrounded by strangers. Alone.

Alone and *trapped*.

My throat closed up, my hands and feet became cold, and every single cell in my body informed me that I needed to leave this room right now, right now, *move, Demetrio—*

I moved as quietly as I could and slipped out of my row and toward the back. There, a lovely young lady in an usher's vest accepted the roses and agreed to deliver them, along with a card

I'd hastily scribbled, into the hands of that charming little ginger in tights. Her wide smile suggested she was more than happy to do so on my behalf.

I made it outside the theater and took several big gulps of air, before finding myself a shadow away from the electric lights and leaning against the wall, lighting a cigarette with shaky hands. I took a harsh drag and shut my eyes, pressing the back of my head against the rough brick wall.

"Laughing Boy?"

My whole body locked up.

There was a figure standing in even deeper shadow, but when he stepped forward, I saw the glint of salt-and-pepper curls, the craggy forehead lines of Dr. Ken Lazlo.

My heart was still pounding, my temples and the area behind my eyes throbbing, I couldn't get enough air in or out, my chest was going to *explode*—

"Whoa, whoa there, it's okay, kiddo, shh." Ken placed two large warm hands on my shoulders and pressed down, grounding me, somehow keeping me from running and fraying at the ends. He was smiling, a hand-rolled blunt tucked into the corner of his mouth and glowing a friendly ruby red. One shiny shoe carefully stamped out the cigarette I'd dropped.

I trembled under his hands but eventually began breathing normally. Or at least normally enough to glower at him. "W-what are you doing out here?" I asked, still swallowing in an aching throat. "This is *your* show."

Ken stepped away, gently relinquishing his grip on me and smiling shyly—fuck him for being charming. "I . . . I can't watch my own work. It makes me want to die, you know?"

I did know. *And I'm sure it doesn't help when your work is bloody shite, you bellend.* I didn't say that and just reached over to take a hit off the joint he'd so thoughtfully brought along. Ken handed it over wordlessly and gave me another sweet, patronizing smile. Resting one hand comfortingly on my hip.

"It's good to see you again," he said. "I never really got to apologize about how things ended last time."

I realized belatedly that he was slowly moving further into the shadows—into a dark, secluded corner between the theater wall and a hedge.

My body, giving little thought to the matter, was following a script even more transparent than that travesty being shown on stage. Dr. Ken Lazlo was going to use me to distract himself from the labor pains of creation, to celebrate the glory of his artwork—to make us both feel like we were part of a romantic, doomed, *edgy* affair—

I laughed out loud.

Then handed him back the bifta and stepped away, back toward the light at the front of the theater. "Goodnight, Ken."

He looked stricken, for how long I've no idea, since I'd turned away, shoved my hands into my pockets, and hurried out across the nighttime campus.

45

ROBIN TAKES
A STAND

August 14th

*T*hat was awesome!

I couldn't breathe, but somehow there was still way too much oxygen in my system—I was floating right off my feet. *They gave me three curtain calls! Me! Three! Curtain calls!*

Slumping against a cool pillar backstage and pressing my steaming face against it, I left patches of sweaty makeup all over it and didn't give a fig.

I was a *god*.

"Robin! Hey, Finch!" I glanced up to see nothing but a big mass of red as Maggie shoved an enormous bouquet of roses in my face.

"Look what your *friend* brought you." She smiled at me over the flowers.

Suddenly I wasn't hot anymore; I was cold and shaky and *stressed*.

"S-Skyler brought those?" I gripped the pillar, hoping its solidity would act as a good influence on my spine. I hadn't seen him before the show, but he'd said he would come. Was he still here? Could I catch him?

"Tall, gorgeous brunet?" She shook the roses at me, sending a few petals flying. "He made a run for it, but there's a card, I think."

I took the roses from her and dug through them till I found a folded piece of paper; it was a bit ragged, like it had been torn out of a notebook. I flicked it open with one hand:

bloody incandescent job titch.

A.

P.S. I'll be at the office

I stared at the note for a few moments, then managed a broken smile. "They're not from him."

Maggie's face fell slightly, as if she actually felt bad for me this time. "I'm sorry, I shouldn't have said—"

"Don't worry about it." I grinned at her and took a deep whiff of the roses, trying once again to pretend that it wasn't *despair* flooding my bloodstream.

Why would Skyler bring me roses? That was the kind of thing your millennial employer did, not your totally and completely uber-platonic friend. We obviously weren't meant for each other—he was meant for Jessie's Girl, and I was meant to die alone. To suffer in silence with grace and stoic bravery like Olivia de Havilland or Jennifer Aniston.

I struck a pose. "Roses from a handsome man are roses from a handsome man, right?"

She rolled her eyes. "By any other name . . ."

"Shut up. Here, hold these." I shoved the flowers back at her. "I gotta go find Armand and drive him home. See you at Squeaky's." We always went out to this crappy all-night greasy spoon after opening night, and this would be the first time I'd be attending as part of the *main* cast rather than a lowly chorus person. And that meant I could bring people, didn't it? What if I invited Skyler? And in the residual heat of the performance we—

I shot him a text before I could talk myself out of it.

Backstage, a few minutes later, I changed into my street clothes, trying not to notice how truly *heinous* I smelled, then got my bag and bustled out of the stage door. It had just *click*ed shut behind me—

When someone grabbed the front of my shirt and *yanked*.

My feet all but left the ground, and next thing I knew, my back was against the wall and I could smell the Jager on Terri's breath.

I'd forgotten.

In all the excitement and stage jitters and Skyler jitters, I'd actually forgotten Terri's threat.

"That was quite a performance, Flinch." He was so close to me, but the shadows meant I could barely make out his face, only the glint in his blue eyes. The world had become limited to Terri's hand clenched in my shirt, Terri's shoulders crowding out the light, Terri's forearm pressing me so hard into the wall some of the joints in my back cracked.

But this couldn't be happening.

No one was watching now.

And it wasn't a joke. Terri was going to hurt me, *really* hurt me.

Still, none of this seemed real—I was coming off one of the highest highs I'd ever experienced, and the thought that Terri had been here the whole time, just *waiting*—

I didn't even struggle. I didn't scream. I just stared up at Terri in utter disbelief. "What are you doing?"

He grinned and drew his fist back like a cartoon villain. "What's it look like?"

"It looks like you're stalking me," I said. He blinked, apparently forgetting to throw the punch, so I kept going. "Like you bought a ticket and watched a two-hour play starring *me*, for the sole purpose of jumping me afterward and . . . and what? What's your *plan* here, Ter?"

Terri seemed genuinely lost for a moment, but then he shook it off and laughed. It sounded forced, though. "I don't need a plan, Flinch. I do this shit for fun."

"You *did* plan it." My voice shook, but I kept talking. "You sent me that creepy threat online, and now you've cornered me with no one else around and— This isn't the playground, Terri. We're not kids anymore. This isn't a *prank*. If you hit me, I'm going to the police."

Terri leaned in. "Say that again."

"HEY!"

We both glanced up, and my heart dropped. This time it *was* fear. No, not fear. *Horror.*

Skyler stood haloed by the lone streetlamp that illuminated the stage door. His fists were clenched and so was his jaw, and he was glaring and he was so beautiful and heroic it took my breath away.

"Leave him alone."

The hand pinning me to the wall dropped as Terri stepped away from me. I nearly collapsed onto the ground as Terri directed his full attention at Skyler. "Can I help you?" He gave that charming we're-all-in-on-this-toxic-horseplay-am-I-right grin that shouldn't have ever worked on anyone, but always *always* had.

"Don't touch him," Skyler said, though his eyes were on me, not Terri. I could feel my mouth hanging open.

Terri laughed again. "Dude, we're just kidding around. Calm your shit." The hand that had been clenched in my shirt a moment ago was still tightly fisted at his side. The knuckles were white.

Skyler was bigger than me, but Terri was *enormous*, and Skyler didn't exactly seem like he'd ever been in a fight before, and oh my *god* I was going to get him *killed*—

Skyler fished out his phone and held it up in plain sight. "This isn't kidding around. It's assault. I think you attacking him would be of interest to campus police. You know, as a joke."

Terri laughed again. "You really think the cops are gonna care about a little rough-housing between friends?"

Skyler didn't move or change his expression. "Is that what you think this looks like?"

This couldn't actually *work*, could it? Terri was going to kill us both.

But his eyes lingered on the phone, which Skyler was holding remarkably still.

None of us moved. Or breathed.

Then—

"Catch you later, Flinch," Terri muttered. He straightened up and away from me, and then he was gone, his dark silhouette disappearing into the night.

Unsurprisingly, my knees buckled and I slid down to the ground. It was nice and cool through my jeans, and I shut my eyes because I knew what was coming next. I could feel Skyler kneel next to me— not too close, because of course he wouldn't want to loom over me like Terri just had because he was *so sweet*—

"I can't believe that worked," he breathed. "Are you okay?"

"*No!*" I squeaked before I could stop myself, then buried my face in my hands.

"Robin, I'm so sorry, did he hurt you?" Skyler placed a hand on my arm, and I immediately shrugged it off and started to scramble to my feet.

"I gotta go, thank you for your help, I need to—" At which point I tripped over my own damn self, and Skyler had to catch me and hold me up.

"Hey, hey, slow down." Skyler leaned me against the wall—so differently from the way Terri had shoved me up against it—and smiled at me. "It's okay, take a minute."

I could feel my face burning and his hands where he gently held my arms. "No, I need to go . . ."

"The show was amazing." Skyler's voice was still soft, like I was a frightened animal. Which I *was*. Not a romantic hero, a Disney freakin' sidekick who needed semi-comedic rescuing at every turn. Skyler was still talking. "You were fantastic, really."

This was *torture*. "Let me go," I groaned.

Skyler immediately let go of my shoulders and took a step back, his smile transformed into a horrified frown. "Sorry, I didn't mean—"

"You don't mean *any of it*!" Oh shit, were we doing this? No, no, we were not. I buried my face in my hands. So I wouldn't have to see the confusion on Skyler's face. The *justifiable* confusion.

"Robin"—Skyler didn't only sound confused, he sounded scared "—could you . . . could you look at me, please?"

I let out a shuddering breath and met his eyes, amazed that I didn't instantly melt or burst into flame.

"I'm sorry," Skyler repeated. "I don't want to force my friendship on you. I just . . . I wanted to make sure you're okay."

I couldn't take this anymore. "Force your *friendship*—seriously? You really have no . . .? Okay, so, you're naïve, I get it; it's sweet and sexy but it's also damn infuriating, you know?" Oh shit, we *were* doing this. "I've never been good at this because *I'm* supposed to be naïve too! Only not naïve like you, naïve like I believe in true love and bluebirds and crap. But the point is *one* of us has to be, y'know, *not* naïve, and I guess that's me, so here goes." I took a deep breath. "When I asked you out—when I said I *liked* you—it wasn't as a *friend*, it was because I'm attracted to you and not only because you keep saving my ass, although yeah, that might have something to do with it."

Skyler was staring at me with his mouth open.

But I wasn't done. Nowhere near. "And I know I said it was possible to maintain a friendship with someone you have feelings for, and it is, but not for *me*. Because I'm garbage. Garbage with feelings for you. And it's *your fault* because you're funny and thoughtful and shy *and* brave, and you can stand naked in front of a room full of people but you blush when you mention the girl you love. It's even the fact that you *have a girl you love*—how sick is that, right? But—but that's not the point. The point is . . . the point is I really, *really* like you and every time you show up and save me or simply do something *wonderful*, it makes it so much worse, and I want to hate you but I can't because I . . . because I *can't*. And I know you're just being you and wonderful and well-meaning and all, and I probably shouldn't have said any of this and, you know what, I'm gonna leave now okay?"

I tried to run, but this time his hand came down on my arm—still gentle—but also somehow *pleading*.

I gasped. "I— Sorry, but I need to—"

He held up his other hand. "Give me a second." He looked like his brain was going to overheat. His brows were furrowed and his mouth was all twisted up in pain.

"Robin." He spoke slowly, carefully. He took a deep breath. "I think you're great, you know? You're so fun to hang out with, and I value you a lot as a friend, but, um. When I said that Delia was the only person I'd ever liked, I meant it. I've never felt attraction to anyone else."

His hand on my arm slid off, and I had to fight the urge to grab it up with both of mine. But I let him keep talking. Destroying me with every single word.

"It's always been like that, and I'd come to terms with being asexual, but then that one time with Delia happened, and I don't know, maybe that was a fluke. I-I'm sorry, I don't know if I can feel that again. Not the way that you do."

I tried to laugh, and surprise, surprise, it came out as a sob, wracking through me as a spasm. I covered my mouth, trying to keep it in, to stop being so horrible, so selfish, so completely and totally unlovable—

"No, please don't." Skyler reached for me again. "I'm sorry—I . . . I need to think."

I shied away from him and desperately wiped away tears. "Okay. Yeah. N-n-no worries." And then finally I ran.

Worst. Person. In. The. *World*.

The good news was that by the time I'd made it to Armand's office, I was pretty much all cried out. The bad news was that when I got there, he took one look at my face and barked, "What the hell happened, Titch?"

"You first," I hiccupped. When I'd got there, he'd been curled up in his office chair, head in his hands. "Did things not go well with Lucas?"

"He couldn't make it. We'll try again at the con, don't worry about it." Armand scowled, fully deploying those eyebrows. "Titch, I'm serious. Have you been crying?"

I leaned against the doorframe and considered my options. For about two seconds. "It happened again." I sobbed. So much for being cried out.

"What happened again?"

I told him about Terri, and about Skyler being Batman, but before I could get into what had happened tonight, Armand stopped me and clarified, "This boy's been harassing you?"

I hugged myself and nodded. "Yeah, but this time was different. I . . . I'll report him."

"You'd better." He gave me a wretched but determined smile and pointed to a piece of paper stuck to the corkboard over his desk. "Or I'll have to. I'm a mandatory reporter."

I laughed through my tears. "You wouldn't know where to *begin*!"

He blushed, and it was so endearing I wanted to ruffle his hair. His greasy, greasy hair. "I'd figure it out. Shut it," he growled, then gave me another concerned scowl. "What *else* happened?"

Of course he could tell.

Slowly, painfully, I told him what had gone on with Skyler. As I talked, his posture became more and more rigid and his face paled. When I was done, he just stared at me.

"You ran?" he asked incredulously. "He came out to you and you *ran*?"

I shook my head. "He didn't come out to me; weren't you listening? He did the *opposite*—"

"Bloody *hell*, Titch." Armand used both hands to scrub at his face. "That's exactly what he did. He told you a truth about himself, and you *ran from him*."

I glared, straightening up. "That's not what happened. You weren't there. You don't *know*." I'd thought he would understand. Weren't we the piners? "We could be great together! We could be perfect. My life was so close to being perfect, and I came *so close* to having everything I've ever wanted, and it was just *ripped* away." All I'd wanted was Skyler to see me as a romantic option, as something other than a small, helpless creature he kept having to save, but it turned out that me being pathetic wasn't even the problem. I'd been trying to romance a brick wall this entire time.

Armand sighed, watching me with those dark, hangdog eyes. "Look, Titch, I can't tell you how to feel—" he worked his jaw slightly "—but I think you've hurt Skyler quite badly—"

"*I* hurt *him*?" My voice echoed down the empty halls of the arts building.

Armand shook his head, biting his lower lip. He unfolded himself out of the chair and shrugged on his bag. "This is none of my business," he said. "Shall we?"

There was a coldness in his voice that made me want to start crying again, but I just stood aside so he could step out of his office and lock the door.

I really had thought he would understand.

46
SKYLER IS NOT A CODFISH

August 14th

"**W**hen I said I liked you—it wasn't as a friend, it was because I'm attracted to you—"

I had walked back to my residence hall in a daze but couldn't make it inside. I was on my tenth or twelfth pace of the parking lot, arms crossed tight over my chest and holding my shoulders. As if that could stop the shaking. As if it could change the fact that . . .

He ran away.

I'd told Robin something that only Matt—and I guess, kind of Armand—knew about me, and he ran away.

I'd thought I was going to throw up. And I might have, if my whole body hadn't locked up in distressed shock.

I went over what had happened again and again; I couldn't stop. Replaying how Robin's face had crumbled as he explained through tears that he didn't want my friendship. He never had.

I didn't know how to do this. To look a heartbroken person in the eyes and say *I'm sorry I don't understand what's going on with me or why I feel, or don't feel, the way I do. Sorry if I did something to lead you on, sorry that I might not be able to give you what you're looking for.*

Sorry that's not good enough.

I gripped my phone too hard as I pulled it from my pocket.

Skyler: *you up?*

After a moment:

Matt: *skyler it is barely nine o'clock pm at night, what am I, ninety years old*

Matt: *yes I'm up u doofus, whattya want*

Skyler: *kinda freaking out can we talk*

In seconds he was calling me.

"Sky? You okay?"

"Um. Yeah. I just . . ." I gulped, struggling to take a breath. "Robin—he told me he likes me. That he's attracted to me, and that he wants . . ."

"Did you tell him? That you're ace?"

I kicked my shoe against a parking curb. "Yeah. And I thought I explained it as best I could, but I was just so surprised, and I had no idea that he—" The memory of Robin clattering to the floor during workshop the other day, his face blazing pink, unable to make eye contact with me.

I'm stupid, I'm so stupid.

Matt was quiet. Even over the phone I felt his tone change, his usual jokes slipping into something serious. "Fuck. I'm sorry, Skyler, that must've been really uncomfortable for you."

"Well, yes, but—" I needed to explain this correctly. "I tried to tell him that I, you know, don't feel attraction in that way—" *Don't think about Delia, don't think about Delia.* "I made him cry, Matt. I've never seen someone so upset, and it was my fault."

"Skyler, no," Matt jumped in immediately. "How he reacted is his business. It's not your fault for being honest. You shouldn't try and hide or change yourself to make someone else comfortable."

Easy for Matt to say. It was nothing I begrudged him for, but he had the benefit of having known extremely early on what his preferences were, how he felt about sex, and what he wanted from relationships in general. "But that's the thing—how could it be 'changing myself' if I don't even know for sure what my 'self' is?"

"Sky—"

"Is it fair to shut him down because I think I *might* be ace without experimenting to know for sure?" I paused to breathe, which was just as well because Matt had gone quiet too.

Finally, he said, "I get where you're coming from, I do, but you remember sophomore year?"

"What about—" Then it hit me.

Billi Hinkley from history class. Matt, and several other friends, had informed me that they liked me—something that Billi themself had confirmed not long after. I had liked them well enough; they'd been smart and kind and wittier than anyone else in the class. I'd spent an entire class period staring at the back of their head, willing something to click. I'd known that pretty much everyone in our grade was having sex, that there was supposed to be more than what I'd felt so far—if I could just get my body to react, then maybe something could happen with us . . .

"This is different," I managed. "I do like him, and yes, maybe I thought I was ace, but maybe things could change. Maybe if I wasn't like this, if I was—"

"Stop right there." Matt's voice, while as kind and well-meaning as ever, cut through the phone as sharply as if he were standing in front of me. "Don't you dare finish that sentence. I'll kick your ass." Neither of us had turned on our video, but I knew he was pacing in his room like he always did, running a hand down his face in frustration. "Listen, I can't tell you what to do here—I mean, I could, I'm three months older than you so I have seniority—but you can't force feelings, Skyler. They either happen naturally or they don't. You don't owe anyone reciprocation."

"But we know that sexuality can be fluid," I pointed out, desperately grasping for a way to make sense of this without mentioning Delia, "so that means what we think might be true of ourselves at one point in time might not always be true, right?"

"Yeah, but . . ." The wind went out of Matt's sails. "Listen, I'll support you no matter what, okay? I may not have known you your whole life, but I know you like I know myself. And you don't always prioritize what's best for you. I just want you to be happy, whatever that looks like for you. *You*, though. Not anyone else."

A lump had dangerously formed in my throat, and my whole body ached like I'd run a marathon. "I know, Matt. Thanks. I want you to be happy too."

"Love you, dude. I'm proud of you, okay? Stop thinking wrong things about yourself."

It was so tempting to believe him, to be reassured by his natural confidence. I wanted to trust what I had, for the last few years, felt in my core was my natural state of being. "Thanks. I'll try."

We said goodnight and I ended the call, already missing him. If our relationship could survive me running away, it could survive anything. I knew now that Matt would always be there for me—but in the end this was my responsibility to figure out.

I couldn't tell him about the biggest piece of evidence that my orientation could change: the fact that I'd fallen in love with his girlfriend.

But it wasn't her beauty that had led to the shift in my feelings for Delia. It was her humor, her charm, and her artistry that had drawn me in.

Robin was funny and charming and creative. There was no reason why I shouldn't be able to replicate those feelings with him.

The shock of his confession was slowly dissipating the longer I fidgeted, as well as the sting of rejection, the confirmation that my nature was incompatible with the people I cared about.

There was someone who cared about me, thought I was attractive, and had earnestly delivered an entire speech to tell me how he felt. After Delia, how could I so firmly assert my asexuality? If I'd been attracted to someone before, surely it could happen again.

Maybe Robin *had* run away. But how was what I'd done any different? I hadn't been able to handle my new feelings for Delia, and I'd known I could never talk about it, so I'd left home and hurt those I left behind.

"I know I said it was possible to maintain a friendship with someone you have feelings for, and it is, but not for me."

Matt's voice crept in from the back of my mind. *Or maybe you can't change. Maybe this is who you are, and you can't use someone else to force something you don't feel—*

But it *was* possible for my feelings to change—my love for Delia had proved it—and I cared about Robin enough to want to keep his friendship; if I could just shift my attraction to her over to Robin, if I could allow the version of myself that I'd known for eighteen years to grow and change . . .

Robin would be happy. And I could finally move on.

47
ARMAND IS MURDERED BY AN INKWELL

August 14th - Tomorrow, tomorrow, oh god, tomorrow

As Finch drove away, I wondered if I should have done more. If I'd failed in my role as employer, educator, elder. There was clearly a correct way to have handled the situation with Robin and Skyler, but whatever it might have been lay well beyond my limited capabilities.

At least Lucas hadn't been there to see the mess I'd made of it.

Numb—but not at all pleasantly—I climbed the stairs and let myself into the dark, empty flat.

Of course it was empty. Whatever milkshake-related emergency Lucas was dealing with was obviously an all-nighter type of deal.

The miniscule victory of Ken—or, more specifically, the *lack* of Ken—was quickly drowned out by the screaming despair brought on by literally everything else. I could still feel the rough stranglehold of the panic attack around my throat, its weight on my chest, the hollowness of the flask in my pocket.

The itching void at the back of my throat.

Yes, I'd turned down Ken. But I hadn't made it through the bloody play, or been able to help Robin and Skyler. Had all but *punted* myself off the wagon, and just in time for the biggest event of my career. Just in time for . . .

Lucas.

To not even show up.

And time was exactly what we were running out of. The con was Friday, *tomorrow*, and my flight out of Los Angeles was scheduled for Sunday.

If I didn't conduct myself properly in front of the world tomorrow, Drake House would not renew my contract, and I and my weird little comic would fade into obscurity.

And Lucas and I would have fully missed each other. Missed the chance to even begin to find out what this was between us. If anything. If there had been the slightest chance that it was what I hoped it was—something I couldn't fully articulate and hadn't had the audacity to imagine for myself, to allow myself to fully want—that chance was long gone. We were too late.

How was a man expected to withstand this kind of pressure? Let alone sober?

I reached for the bottle near my bed, then at the last moment grasped my phone instead and did the unthinkable.

I called Lakshmi.

"Demetrio, pet? What is it now?" There were traces of sleep in her voice, but she was clearly trying to rouse herself, narrowing her eyes at me. "How high's the water?"

My initial response was not much more than a whimper, but then I managed, "Well over my head."

She studied my face over the grainy video and sighed. "On the lash?"

I wanted to lie. I failed. "Aye."

My brilliant, endlessly compassionate agent rolled her eyes up at the ceiling in what initially seemed like a bid for divine patience, but then she surprised me. "I'm sorry."

"You're what?"

"I should've believed you when you said you weren't ready." She shook her head, glaring at the floor. She seemed furious, but apparently not with me. "I know you've been under the cosh, but I thought a month was long enough to prepare, and that the workshop would be good practice—"

"It was!" I choked. "The workshop's been lovely! I just…" *Couldn't handle it without a crutch.* The shame and disappointment burned in my throat and chest—I swallowed painfully and wished I could argue. Tell her she'd been right to push me.

"I can call the organizers and tell them you've had an emergency. We'll move up your flight—"

"No." I ran a hand down my face and then left it over my mouth. She was right. I couldn't do this—at least not on my own. "Does . . . does that mean what I think it means? For the comic?"

Her silence—the moment of hesitance—was answer enough. "Forget that. If you're *harming* yourself, pet—"

"I'm not." This lie came easily. "I'm just . . . being a wonk. I—I *am* capable of human interaction. It's not as bad as it looks. I've got it under control, I—"

"What time is it by you?" she cut me off. "How's this for a deal? Take the next few hours to think on it, and if I don't hear from you again by midnight, I'll make the call."

I swallowed again. Three hours. I could already smell the acetone stink of alcohol leaving my body via sweat glands. I couldn't reasonably make the argument that a little nip would steady my nerves—anything more at this point would lead to a good old-fashioned blackout.

Accountability, Demetrio, consequences and bloody mindfulness. It was time to rejoin the land of the living and upwardly mobile, even if it was only as a second-class citizen. I wanted to reassure her that she wouldn't have to make the call, but what left my mouth was: "I'm meeting someone there. At the con."

Lakshmi raised an angular brow. "Hopefully, you'll be meeting *loads* of someones."

"No, I mean—" What *did* I mean? "Never mind." The heat pulsed in my face, and I almost wished we were talking about me being a souse again.

"This is the mystery flatmate, Lucas Barclay, yeah?" She smiled.

I didn't confirm it, but I didn't need to.

"Take the night, Demetrio," she said gently. "I don't want you to feel you've been stitched up with the con. If need be, we can handle the heat from Drake House; there are other ways to survive in this business. Just look after yourself."

I nodded mutely, worrying at my bottom lip. "I'll think about it."

"And take a shower. You probably reek."

I grumbled a goodbye and hung up on her, stripped off, then sat on the edge of the bed as god made me and held my head between my hands.

Three hours. I could make it three hours. And then another ten. And through the convention—through the talk—

My stomach dropped and my gorge rose. Lumbering to my feet, I lost my balance, and stepped directly onto an inkwell that had lain in wait for me on the floor near the bed.

It shattered, and shards of glass buried themselves into my foot.

I shrieked and fell backward onto the bed. The blood and ink beaded and bled together on the carpet in patterns that at any other time would have struck me as beautiful. As it was, I sat up and pulled my foot toward me, intending to yank the glass out of it. Unfortunately, the blood and ink which obscured the wounds made that impossible. Gritting my teeth, I managed to lever myself to my good foot and hopped around the puddle toward the door.

Dripping a red-and-black trail, I limped my way down the corridor to the toilet. My whimpering and swearing echoed off the tile, interrupted by the squeak of my skin meeting the porcelain of the tub. I turned on the tap and shoved my foot under it, leaning backward and gritting my teeth against the cold water and pain.

So caught up was I in my own agony and stupidity that I didn't hear the front door open or footsteps padding down the hall.

"Oh my god, are you okay?"

I glanced up into a pair of startling green eyes and realized several horrific, world-ending things at once.

First: that a man was standing in the doorway. A very dirty man, with mud on his face and bits of hay in his hair.

Second: that man was Lucas.

Third was, of course, that I was sitting on the edge of the tub, cradling a foot which was steadily streaming blood, completely naked.

"Gnnrk!" I made a mad grab for a towel and threw it across my lap, trying to pretend that my whimpers of pain hadn't turned into panicked croaks.

"Here, put pressure on that." Lucas's voice—strong and commanding—briefly snapped me out of myself, and I even caught the second towel he threw my way. I did, however, continue staring at him in shock.

"What are you—"

Lucas didn't even glance up as he hastily washed his hands. "We need to stop the bleeding. Pressure. Now."

I did my best to obey, watching numbly as he shook the water off his hands, and pulled on a pair of latex gloves, then reached into the medicine cabinet for what appeared to be a first-aid kit and a large pair of tweezers.

I gulped despite myself. "What are you doing with that?"

Lucas crouched beside me, set the open kit on the floor beside him, and took hold of my foot. He pressed briefly on the towel and wrapped it into a tourniquet around my ankle. "We'll need to get the glass out."

I tried to remember how to breathe, fidgeting and grinding my teeth as more pressure was applied. "Just forget it, I'll go to a doctor."

"My dad was a pediatrician—he taught me first aid." Lucas's brow remained furrowed, his mouth tight, and eyes fierce.

When the bleeding appeared to have stopped, he examined the wounded area and let out a relieved sigh. "You were lucky. These glass shards are pretty sizeable."

I grasped desperately for balance and anything resembling coherence. "Really," I panted, "you don't have to."

Lucas rolled his eyes as he carefully extracted the first shard of glass with the tweezers. "Don't be a baby," he muttered.

I tried to keep my silence as he worked, with only the occasional squeak of pain as a piece of glass was removed.

Eventually, Lucas leaned back on his heels and inspected my foot again. "There. That's all of it."

I let out a hiss. Sweat prickled over every inch of my skin. "Bloody hell . . ."

Lucas stood and disposed of the glass shards, then grabbed a bottle of antiseptic from the cabinet, along with a handful of gauze bandages.

He looked back at me and smiled, likely amused by the exasperation on my face. "Almost done, I promise. I just need to patch you up." He swabbed and dabbed all around the heel of my foot, shushing me gently as I continued to pathetically keen.

To finish, he wrapped several bandages around the area and gingerly ran his fingers down the edges of the gauze to smooth it down.

"All right, good as new. The cuts weren't deep enough to need stitches, so you'll be fine. You might want to take some anti-inflammatories and be careful not to lean too much weight on that foot for a few days," he instructed and, standing back up, he cleaned the work area, and re-sanitized the tweezers.

I stared at his back wordlessly for a few moments, then managed to clear my throat. "This wasn't . . . urm . . . well, you didn't have to, errngh . . . wasn't necessary . . ."

He glanced back at me, eyes narrowing over a small grin. "Pretty sure that was *extremely* necessary."

I looked away, swallowing thickly. "Urghh . . . *thanks*. For, um, er . . . for kn-knowing what you were doing."

"You're welcome." Lucas walked back over, kneeling to retrieve the discarded bloody towel. "I'm just glad I was here."

The words hung heavily in the air. A thick silence fell, and I watched those stunningly green eyes widen.

I'm here. He's here.

We're both HERE. NOW.

Lucas swallowed and slowly brought his gaze up to meet mine. Everything had happened so fast that he'd clearly barely even registered who I was.

"Hi," he said softly.

I shifted wretchedly on my porcelain perch. "Hullo."

Lucas dropped his gaze, and despite myself, I started fiddling with my towel. The last vestige of my decency. Lucas's eyes followed the movement.

Then he leapt to his feet and cleared his throat, cheeks going visibly pink even under the layer of dirt. "I should go— I mean, things to do . . ."

I shut my eyes tight. "Yeah. I should, uh, find some clothes. Erm."

I kept them closed even as I heard him mumble a goodbye and hurry out of the room, and then the front door slamming shut.

I remained frozen on the edge of the tub for what seemed like an hour.

That did not just happen.

That could not have just happened.

Lucas had not walked in on me injured and in, to put it delicately, a state of dishabille.

He had not tenderly seen to my wounds while I had scrambled to hide both pain and certain bits of my anatomy. I had not whimpered and fidgeted like a child, and he had not shushed me like a benevolent nanny.

I had not been naked, and he had most definitely not been handsome.

And smelling strongly of *horse*.

That would have been very strange, if that had happened.

Which it hadn't.

Because if absolutely any of it had happened, there was absolutely no way for me to avoid ritual suicide at this point.

After an eternity or so, I got up off the side of the tub and arranged the towel properly around my hips. Then I gingerly tested my gauze-wrapped foot. The dressing Lucas had applied held and dulled the pain to a degree I had no reason to expect. I limped over to the sink to wash the blood and ink off my hands.

I happened to glance up at the mirror and immediately thoughts of ritual suicide returned. I was drenched in sweat, hair clumped and standing on end, face unshaven and still a glowing, incandescent red. These were not ingredients that added up to *sexy*.

I looked like a man who had, quite recently, had a mass of glass in his foot.

I washed my face and hands, smoothed back my unruly hair, and was about to consider and choose between the various forms of suicide available to me, when my mobile chimed from the bedroom. I limped sadly back down the corridor, found it in the pocket of a discarded pair of jeans, and then leaned against the door.

I squeezed my eyes shut. I couldn't bring myself to look at the message.

What if it was Lucas?

What if it was Lucas saying he no longer wanted to meet tomorrow? That he'd changed his mind and there was really no reason for us to try to meet since, technically, we already had.

The bottle of Wild Turkey winked at me from its place by the bed.

My lungs felt too large to fit inside my chest. They were trying to climb up my throat. I held up the phone, gritted my teeth, took a deep breath, and opened one eye.

It was a reminder I'd set myself.

One and a half hours. Ninety minutes till midnight. Ninety minutes in which to let Lakshmi know whether I'd decided to do my job and fulfill my obligations at the convention. All of that—the entire horror show complete with blood, nudity, and *Lucas*—hadn't even taken a full two hours.

Careful to keep weight off my injured foot, I placed one hand over my face and took a deep breath through my nose, sliding down to the floor.

One and a half hours to find both my courage and the sticking place. I'd thoroughly bollocksed my chances with Lucas, but I could still make things work with Drake House. I could still show and be something other than a complete and utter waste of funds and long-term investment.

I could *do it anyway, Demetrio.*

48

LUCAS GETS WHAT
HE WANTS

August 15th

"So," Rick began around a mouthful of bagel and a pointed slurp of herbal tea, "you've been extremely mysterious, but now that you've made proper use of our shower and couch, we're gonna need you to cough up the rest of the details right now. Spill."

I groaned and dropped my forehead to the kitchen table. I hadn't been able to explain what had happened last night when I'd driven to their apartment two seconds away from a full-fledged tailspin. And being such good friends, they'd let me clean up and sleep until morning, but now they were getting their revenge.

"Milkshake's gone," I mumbled into the tablecloth.

"Okay, see, you did mention that when you came in covered in dirt," Andie politely pointed out. "And we're very sorry to hear that, but you know perfectly well that's not what this is about."

Damn it.

I tugged Rick's oversized robe tighter around myself. Was it too late to fall into a coma? Or flee the country? "I ran into Armand," I finally managed, the lingering gut punch of being *perceived* resurfacing with a vengeance. "Last night, when I got home from the ranch. I looked . . . Well, you saw me."

I lifted my head just enough to see Andie had dipped her head into a sympathetic nod. Rick, however, was having none of it. He jerked the knife that was still coated in cream cheese my direction. "You have got to give us more than that, buddy boy."

The problem with that was I hadn't stopped replaying every last second of the . . . encounter in my head until I had eventually lost consciousness on the couch. "He—" I cleared my throat, deciding to tackle the easier part of the explanation first. "There was an accident, I guess. He had shards of glass in his foot that I had to take out."

You waltzed right in like you owned the place, manhandled him without permission, then flounced away without an explanation. Nothing about this paints you in a good light, Barclay.

My friends, however, didn't seem to think so. Andie's face lit up. "You mean you played doctor?" she teased with a lift of her eyebrow.

God, I wish, my horrifically traitorous brain thought before I could stop it. "I did the bare minimum," I corrected her, trying to shift out of horny mode in order to think about how much blood there'd been. It was amazing Armand hadn't sliced open an artery. "I can't explain it—it's like I didn't notice that we were both there in person until like ten minutes later when it finally sinks in that he's *naked*—" My flushed forehead found its rightful place back on the table, not showing my face. "He's so gorgeous, you guys."

Which was an understatement. Armand was *breathtaking*.

The grainy photos I'd found of him online hadn't done justice— even sitting on the edge of the tub, he was tall and his chest was wide and his dark hair had been tousled . . .

But his eyes.

Wide, panicked, and full of self-consciousness, but deep and warm and so brown I could sink into them. I'd felt the low, gravelly rumble of his voice (and the accent, oh my god) in my own chest, and he was so awkward and soft and—

And I'd acted like an overbearing, entitled brute.

I could blame it on the blood and the fact that time had been of the essence in getting him patched up, but the reality was that before I could treat this vulnerable man kindly in his state of distress, I had charged directly into problem-solving mode without asking his consent to touch him.

Darren was right about me—when given the chance, I got controlling and bulldozed over people. Which was why he'd always refused me the opportunity to be in charge, ever, of any situation. It made me annoying, overbearing. Bossy.

"Sounds to me like this is the opposite of a problem," Rick offered cheerfully, perhaps assuming that the thesis of this story was that I was covered in mud, which was merely the tip of the iceberg. "Going off your reaction here."

"He's out of my league!" I wanted to maintain this particular narrative in front of Rick and Andie, but I couldn't help admitting, "I steamrolled right in, probably making him super uncomfortable, and he's— Everything about him was aesthetically debauched and there *I* was covered in dirt and smelling like horse and what kind of first impression is that? Why would he even want to look at me?" I covered my face with my hands that thankfully now smelled like honeycomb soap and not sweat and dirt and horse. "I can't show my face at the con. He's seen enough."

"Lucas—" Andie gently patted the top of my head "—I haven't met or even seen the guy, but if you think he isn't at this moment thinking that you're the one out of *his* league . . ."

I coughed incredulously. "Right. A smelly, muddy nag is exactly what you need when you're naked and injured and hoping that maybe your roommate looks and acts like a normal person and not someone who clearly rolled out of a dumpster."

It was becoming clearer by the minute that Rick and Andie were intent on arguing with me, or trying to convince me to still meet Armand at the con in broad daylight. I got to my feet, pinching the robe closed around me. "Andie, can I borrow some clothes?"

She crossed her arms. "So you can go meet this nice man in public like you promised?"

"Absolutely not, you just don't have any caffeine in this house."

She sighed, then waved her arm toward the bedroom.

I found a patterned button-up and black slacks that were a little snug but fit well enough, considering that none of Rick's clothes would fit at all.

Ten minutes later, I was driving to Latte for Work with the windows down and the radio on. *This is a perfectly normal day. I'm getting breakfast. Nothing awkward happened last night, and I'm not thinking about my decision to not meet up with Armand at the convention. The last chance I will ever have with him.*

Rick and Andie would argue that I could still salvage this, could present a different side of myself to him in public and change whatever he already surely thought about me. But my stomach churned at the memory of how I'd acted, of how my body had reacted to Armand's gorgeous everything, of how much stock I had placed in the fantasy, the completely misguided and misplaced idea that someone like him could ever like someone like me—

Maybe it would be easier to let it go. Let him leave the country, and we wouldn't have to talk about it, I wouldn't have to face another devastating rejection.

Stop thinking about it, it's done. You ruined it. Get your sad little coffee and go back to wallowing.

I stepped inside the bakery, basking in the divine scent of organic pastries, ordered a sugar-free blueberry muffin—

Then froze.

Darren.

He was sitting at the corner table, the one I always chose, his hair mussed in a way that didn't seem intentional. The moment our eyes met, he shot to his feet with a small grimace.

"Hey." He strode as elegantly as ever toward me; I was still frozen. He stopped directly in front of the pastry display.

"What are you doing here?" I managed through a tight throat.

Darren's face was gentle now. He seemed nothing like the distant creature he'd been when I'd seen him last. "I saw your post about Milkshake . . . and this is your favorite place to get brunch," he explained, his voice oddly soft.

"I know *that*. But why are *you* here?"

Darren took a deep breath, slowly. "I wanted to apologize, and I couldn't do it over the phone. I—I panicked." He dropped his voice, his eyes following. "I got scared."

I gaped at him. "*Scared*? Of what?"

"This." He gestured between us, like he'd done when he'd said, *"I don't know if it makes sense anymore. I don't know if it ever did."* "I was overwhelmed. I said such awful things to you, and I'm so, so sorry." He reached for me but hesitated, his hand shaking. His beautiful face screwed up with such unfamiliar distress it rendered me speechless. "You were right: you've been trying and I've been the one being an ungrateful asshole. And I didn't really realize what the idea of settling down meant until the moment you walked out of my kitchen."

When you kicked me out, I wanted to correct him, the words bubbling up my throat. *When you made me give you your key back.* But Darren had never apologized like this, had never seemed so genuinely gutted, never would have ever done anything like this in a public setting before.

"You said you were embarrassed of me," I said instead, immediately self-conscious of how bitter the words sounded coming out. "Do you know how badly that messed me up?"

"I know." Darren looked wretched. "I was an idiot, I never should've said that." This time, when he reached out to me, he gently curled his fingers around mine. "Can we start over?" With his other hand he reached into his pocket and pulled out—

His spare house key.

"I love you," Darren whispered. "Move in with me. Please."

My heart jumped to my throat and I couldn't breathe. "I . . . I thought you weren't ready."

"I didn't think I was," Darren admitted. He squeezed my hand, the one holding the key had never been steadier. "Everything was dull without you—I'm making my choice, Lucas. You always wanted me to commit, well here it is. I'm choosing you. If you'll have me."

I could feel myself trembling, and vaguely I was aware of other people milling around us, but everything had faded into the background. Surely this wasn't a real conversation; it sounded so much like what I'd imagined Darren would say, back in my darkest moments.

I pinched the key between my fingers, holding it out between us like a shield. "This isn't a yes," I managed shakily, trying to ignore the way his face lit up, the color returning to his cheeks. "It's an 'I'll think about it.'"

"Of course," he said in a rush, "that's all I could ask for, after what I did. Please—" He gestured shyly to the corner table. "Can . . . can we talk for a bit? Catch up?"

I nodded numbly, grabbed my muffin, and allowed him to guide me to the chair. He left briefly before returning with a coffee for himself.

"It's been weird not talking to you," Darren said after he'd sat and there'd been a long, tense moment of silence. He fiddled with a napkin. "I'd ask how you've been, but I guess I know."

"It hasn't been pretty, I can tell you that." My eyes dropped down to the table. The barely scabbed-over shame and hurt trickled back in. I wanted to scream, to tell him exactly how badly he'd hurt me, but I shoved it down. Instead, I gave him a self-deprecating little huff. "Really dramatic, you know me."

He smiled softly. "Yeah. I do. And to be fair, I was pretty messed up too. I got wasted at the bosses' dinner party."

"The one you uninvited me to?" This was followed quickly by: "Wait, you got *drunk*? At a work party?"

Darren chuckled. "I told you, I was messed up. I needed to call a rideshare to get home. So much for acting like a responsible adult."

The idea of Darren McKinley publicly losing his shit at an event as important as his bosses' anniversary was unfathomable. "Well," I said with a tentative grin, "that makes me feel better about the destruction of my apartment and complete and utter breakdown."

He laughed, an achingly nostalgic sound. His eyes were bright as he appraised me. "I've never seen that shirt before, is it new?"

I'd forgotten about the shirt I'd grabbed from Andie's closet. "No, it's a loan; there was . . . a bit of a situation last night with the roommate. Remember I told you about him? Armand Demetrio?" Just saying his name sent a confusing wave of emotions through me that I hurried to push back down.

"Yeah, the disgusting boomer living in your apartment? Mothman, right? You finally meet or what?"

You could say that. "It . . . wasn't the meeting we'd *planned* on, and there was blood and first aid involved, and anyway I was covered in dirt from being with Milkshake, and honestly he wasn't as old or disgusting as I'd thought he'd be—"

"Hm." There was a smile on Darren's face, but it had gone rigid. "You're blushing."

Was I? I touched my cheek and found it warm. "It was just awkward. He was naked and he'd cut his foot open on something." And now I was thinking about Armand again. *Stop it.*

"Not following why you needed to borrow that shirt, but, yeah, sounds awkward." Darren picked up his mug and gestured toward me. "Maybe grab a bigger size next time."

Cold jolted through my skin.

My body felt tight again, like it didn't fit. I became uncomfortably aware of every pore, of the way I was sitting in the chair, of the snugness of Andie's shirt against my chest. Darren was sipping his coffee, his eyes gleaming at me over the rim.

"I'm so stupid," I finally managed, struggling to keep my voice steady. "I can't believe I never noticed you doing this."

Darren's smile froze on his face. He cocked his head. "Doing what?"

"Criticizing how I look. What I'm wearing, how I'm standing— you said you weren't embarrassed by me!"

"Lucas." Darren was calm, too calm. "Lower your voice, please."

"No." I had never stopped gripping his key, but now it was burning a hole in my palm. My legs were shaking as I stood. "Darren, I can't keep trying to be good enough for you." I smacked the key onto the table, relishing the way his mouth dropped open. My fingers trembled as they grabbed the pastry bag, crushing the muffin I hadn't touched. Unbidden, a different image pushed through the rest: a plate of homemade muffins sitting on the kitchen counter.

I could easily call to mind dozens of times I'd cleaned Darren's house, or cooked, or bought groceries, especially if he'd had a rough week. Even though he had never done the same for me.

But Armand had. And he hadn't needed to know me for ten years to do it.

And Darren was still shushing me. "Let's talk about this, okay? Like adults," he stage-whispered, glancing around to see if anyone was watching. "Please, you're overreacting. Sit down and finish your muffin—"

But his words couldn't reach me now. The curtain had fallen and all I saw was an insecure douchebag who would always choose his own ego over me.

"Stop," I said, straightening my shoulders. "You're embarrassing yourself."

I didn't wait to hear whatever bullshit he responded with.
I left the bakery without looking back.

49

ROBIN BESTOWS HIS WISDOM

August 15th

I knocked loudly on the front door of Apartment 203 of the Briars complex. *Place your bets: How long will I have to do this before Armand wakes up?*

I'd tried calling him several times while I was waiting around to speak to campus police, but with the understanding that he was Armand, and it was *morning*, and there was no way he was going to answer. I was secretly glad he hadn't picked up; we hadn't spoken since the night before, when I'd been crying about Skyler and he'd basically called me a creep. If things were going to be awkward between us—and they definitely were—they might as well be awkward face-to-face rather than over the phone.

I went to knock again, but the door creaked open. Armand was pale and—I'd never even *thought* this word before—wan. He looked *wan.*

I couldn't help it; I immediately stopped being mad at him. This beautiful, giant man was the most pathetic thing I'd ever seen in my entire life. "Armand? Are you okay?"

He nodded stiffly and moved aside so I could head past him into the apartment. I studied his face as I went by—he didn't look mad at me anymore, or mad at anything really. He looked like a man waiting to be pressed into a meat grinder. But the apartment was strangely clean with no lingering smell of booze; if anything, it smelled of coffee and . . .

"Did you make croissants?" I whirled around to stare at him. "From *scratch*?"

Armand had closed the door behind us and was now leaning against it, arms crossed tightly over his chest and brows furrowed, cheeks pink. "I bake when I'm upset," he said, like that made any kind of sense.

"It's going to be fine. You and Lucas are gonna hit it off," I told him, grabbing a warm, golden crescent from the big plate on the kitchen island. It felt like a *cloud*. I took a bite and then leaned against the counter with my eyes closed. "Oh my god, your pain tastes *amazing*."

The silence that followed had a stinging brightness to it, like an overexposed photo. I turned to him again, raising my eyebrows questioningly. "Okay, what."

"Urgh"—his voice was thick and timorous—"it happened. We met."

"What happened? Who did— *Oh my god*, you met Lucas! When did this happen? Oh my god, oh my god, tell me, tell me, tell me!" I stuffed the last of my croissant in my mouth and ran up to him, grabbing his hands. "Wha' *haffened*?"

He gave a full-body cringe but didn't pull his hands away. "It's a long story."

"Then get *started*!" I glanced at my watch. "We don't have to check in at the convention center for a few hours."

Armand was shaking his head and pulling his hands away. "I . . . I'm not sure he'll be there. Er. Or even wants to see me again. At all. Ever."

"*Oh*?" I held on tighter.

He stopped fighting and *wilted*. "I was, well, ehrm, I stepped on an inkwell . . . w-while n-no-not wearing much, and there was blood a-and ink and, well, hurmmpphh never mind."

I let that mess of an explanation hang in the air between us for a few moments, then I said carefully, "You stepped on an inkwell?"

He shut his eyes and didn't respond, so I knelt down and wrenched up the leg of his pajama pants, nearly tipping him over.

"Gnrrchkt?" he said in protest and grabbed the wall for balance.

"This isn't so bad! We can work with it." The bandage on Armand's foot looked like a pretty professional job. "Did you go to urgent care? Wait—" I gasped "—did *Lucas* do this?"

I'd never seen Armand Demetrio so red or so wretched, and in both cases that was saying something.

"He did, didn't he? Oh man, I would have paid *money* to see—"

"Titch, stop it," he groaned, rubbing at his hairline. "I need to get ready."

I stood up and gave him my most pitying pout. "No, what you need is an emergency makeover. Don't get me wrong, first impressions are important, but that doesn't mean you can't drown them out with a really, *really* spectacular second impression!"

His eyes widened in horror "An emer—? Oh *no*, no no *no* no!"

"Yes yes yes *yes* yes. Now go to the kitchen and get me tea bags, lemon juice, olive oil, and—why not?—cucumbers."

He blinked at me. "A-are we making a salad?"

I stared at him. How could one man be so completely and wonderfully ridiculous? "Maybe later, but for now? You, good sir, are going to, dare I say it? *Exfoliate*!"

His shoulders slumped. "I am?"

I nodded, hair bouncing, and headed back into the kitchen, rooting through the drawers by the sink until I found what I needed: a plastic bag and saran wrap. "Now get over here so I can wrap your foot."

"Wh—"

"So you can *shower*, Stinky."

He keened softly like a creaky door or air being let out of a balloon. "This is *so bloody inappropriate*," he muttered.

I rolled my eyes, grabbed another croissant, and crouched down to start waterproofing his injury. He stood there and took it, holding his pajama pant leg up and out of my way. After a few moments, he harrumphed and straightened up, fisting a hand in his hair. "Titch, thank you for, ehrm. This isn't your job."

"Isn't it though?" I asked through a mouthful of heaven. "Do *you* know what 'liaison' means?"

"Truly—" His voice went terrifyingly earnest, so I did us both a favor and cut him off.

"Just go, get in the shower, Mandy, and don't make me come in after you!"

"On one condition." He sighed. "You never, *ever* call me that again."

"No promises. Now get in there!" I used the tube of saran wrap to give him a motivational *fwack*.

He glared at me, then simply gritted his teeth and hobbled into the bathroom.

While he showered, I took the opportunity to run out to the pharmacy on the corner and pick up a few supplies, including a plain black walking cane. The convention center was huge, and the idea of Armand limping along sadly was a bit too much.

I got back just as he was coming out of the bathroom and nearly gave him a heart attack.

"Not yet." I handed him several bottles. "Go back in there and use these."

He stared down at them like they were mysterious potions. I had to quell the urge to start singing "White Rabbit" by Jefferson Airplane. "This one's a pomegranate face peel, and this one's a shea butter firming body lotion. Ooh, and *this* is some under-eye cream. For those dark circles, you know? And the puffiness, and the lines—"

He shut the bathroom door in my face.

But when he ventured forth again, his skin was practically glowing. He looked like someone who occasionally got eight hours of sleep. He was rubbing his smooth cheek a little self-consciously, and there was definitely a lessening of the raccoon effect around his eyes. "I feel *raw*," he grumbled.

"Good. Hopefully it'll make Lucas want to eat you up like cookie dough."

"I told you, Titch, I don't think he's coming."

"You said he's *seen* you, right? Trust me, he's coming."

Armand scowled. "Ti—" But then he unclenched a little, and his grumpy mouth twitched into a brief half smile. After a moment, he seemed to have worked up the nerve to say, "Have you spoken to Skyler at all?"

I froze. "I thought that was none of your business?"

"It isn't," he growled. "This really is *deeply* inappropriate. You both have technically worked for me—"

I rolled my eyes. "We worked for the school, you egomaniac. But no. We haven't talked." I shrugged, hoping it made me appear casual rather than devastated. "I don't think there's anything to talk about. Except—" I pointed at Armand's head "—what the hell we're going to do with your hair."

"My ha—" He sighed heavily.

Smart man.

"*Fine.*"

Sure enough, there wasn't another outburst till the time came to choose an outfit.

"Ooh, you should wear these!" I held up a pair of dark, faded, and very narrow jeans for his inspection.

Armand eyed them warily and shook his head. "No, Lakshmi bought them for me, and they're far too tight in the . . . Eerhm, they don't fit."

"All right, you've just convinced me, you're *definitely* wearing these." I tossed them at his head and turned back to continue burrowing through his suitcase.

"Titch!" There was a strangled bark behind me, and I turned again to see him gripping the jeans with both hands fisted, the color rising clearer than ever in his recently exfoliated face. "*No.* This is— arrgh— *Listen* to me: My goal is not and never has *been* to show off my arse, all right? That is *not* how I want to impress Lucas." He cringed. "I mean *Drake House.* Bloody hell."

I folded my arms over my chest and gave him a long perusal, head to toe and back, just to see if I could make him go any redder. "Forget Drake House. I told you, Lucas will be there, and would you rather he associate you with a *bloody foot* or a *tight keister*?"

He sputtered at me for a few seconds, then hung his head, shoulders sagging.

"Good man."

When I was done with him and he re-emerged from the bedroom, he looked a lot better than he had any right to expect, especially considering how much resistance he'd put up. It was like he had no sense of self-preservation ... which, considering his lifestyle, shouldn't have come as a surprise.

Though I couldn't help noticing he smelled a lot less like whiskey than he usually did.

"Okay, let me see." I grabbed Armand's arms and tried to get him to straighten up, then stepped back.

Oh yeah, I was *good*. I'd found a tight black turtleneck in his suitcase, and I'd gotten his curls to do this swoop thing, and now that he'd *shaved*, he resembled a movie star in their second week of rehab. Seriously, if you didn't know him and he never opened his mouth, you'd think he'd stepped off a runway somewhere.

Speaking of ...

"You got your speech?" I asked, like a mom asking a toddler about their lunch bag.

He glared, but then tellingly patted his pockets. "Aye."

"You're going to do *great*, I promise." I glanced at the kitchen clock. "The organizers wanted you to be there by one, so we've got some time to burn. What do you want to do? Go scream under an overpass?"

He bit his lip and shook his head at me. "We could go to campus," he said, his rumbly voice weirdly soft. "To see the dean."

I blinked at him. "We ... could do that. I don't know *why* we'd do that, but—"

"So you could tell her about that boy. The one who hurt you." His voice was getting stronger even as his face looked more tortured. "I don't want to pressure you into anything, but if you wanted—" Then he broke off into a horrified squeak as I hugged him. "Titch!"

"I know, I know, this is inappropriate." He *definitely* smelled less like booze. "Forget the dean. I filed a report with campus police this morning. I promise. They said they can't do anything after the fact, because the attack was interrupted, but it'll be on record in case ... in case he tries it again."

"Brilliant." I felt him swallow, still stiff as a board. Then he gave a helpless sigh and looked up at the heavens. "Can you let go of me now?"

I stepped back and grinned at him. "Man, poor Lucas has his work cut out for him."

He glared at me and ran a hand through his hair, destroying the careful, purposefully tousled style I'd achieved and sending it straight back to just plain tousled. He was *impossible*.

"S-since we're ignoring the basic tenets of professionalism," he began, and hilariously tried to shove his hands into the pockets of his *very* tight jeans, "may I say something about what happened between you and Skyler?"

"When have I *ever* been professional?" I pointed out. *Be a man about this, Robin.* "Yeah, okay. But don't be mean."

Armand nodded and bit his lip. "I know you think he's . . . meant for you. Or some rubbish like that."

"I said don't be mean!"

"Aye, sorry." He rubbed one of his eyebrows, squeezing his eyes shut for a moment. "Would it really be so horrible to simply be his friend?"

"Would *you* want to 'simply' be *Lucas's* friend?" I snapped.

He widened his eyes at me, eyebrows converging in concern. "*Yes.* I . . . I'd be a bit disappointed, aye, but if that was what he wanted, *absolutely.*"

"Well, okay," I huffed, "I guess you're a better person than I am."

"That's not what it's about," he insisted. "Wanting to be with someone is more than wanting to have *sex* with them, for fuck's sake!" He seemed to catch himself, taking a deep breath and unclenching his hands. "O-or even wanting to romance them. If you like Skyler, the nature of your relationship shouldn't bloody matter. You wouldn't want him to do anything that makes him uncomfortable, would you?"

Armand was right, this was none of his business—and he clearly didn't feel about Lucas the same way I felt about Skyler. No wonder he'd managed to procrastinate meeting him for so long.

I checked the clock again. "We should get going, just in case there's traffic."

Armand kept watching me for a few moments, probably hoping I'd say something like *Oh yeah, pssht, no, it's definitely fine that Skyler—along with the rest of the world—sees me as some kind of sexless, unattractive comic relief*, but eventually he sighed, seeming to give up.

"Aye," he rumbled sadly, and ran his hand through his hair once more, ruining every last bit of my good work.

50
ARMAND RECEIVES UNWARRANTED ATTENTION

August 15th - NOW

F inch parked in the lot of the convention center, and we sat quietly for a time. He'd asked if I wanted to be dropped out front, and then accepted my mute, petrified, shake of the head no. My gratitude for the few moments of silence he was allowing evaporated, however, when he glanced at his watch and clicked his tongue against his teeth.

"Will five more minutes of this tantrum be enough?"

I was going to commit murder in a tiny yellow car in America. *Tantrum*, was it? A bit rich coming from a boy ... who was experiencing the throes of first love and first rejection. Bloody hell.

"Aye," I grumbled, "I'm ready."

There were costumed people milling about the parking lot and on the grass in front of the convention center, and Finch beamed and waved at several groups of people. They waved and smiled back but didn't approach him or show any signs of personal recognition. These all appeared to be friendly strangers who nevertheless shared a deep kinship.

I would likely have appreciated at least some of the costumes and represented fandoms as well, but my blinders of terror were in full effect. I was flashing back to my first day of teaching at the university: the existential nausea, the cold sweat, the sensation that I was watching myself from several meters above and mere seconds away from a bloody blackout.

Finch led me to a small conference room where I met DQ-Con official people who gave me lanyards and water and papers and told me things. I looked over at Finch, and he gave me a small smile.

"Is that okay?" asked the kind-eyed, bespectacled young woman who stood before me. The collar of her shirt was heavily starched and her pencil skirt was slate. Her hair was a fascinating mix of mousy brown and electric blue. I couldn't remember a single damned thing she'd just said to me.

I swallowed. I opened my mouth. And nearly collapsed in relief when Finch stepped forward.

"That's great, Ainsley, thanks. Mr. Demetrio would like to sit somewhere quiet and without a lot of people until it's time for the panel, if that's okay?"

Ainsley smiled at me—and not like I was an elderly, demented pet—and nodded, then gestured to the other end of the conference room. There were a few chairs, separate from the rows that lined the middle of the room, set against the far wall near a table loaded with coffee urns, pamphlets, and free pens. "We've got this room till three thirty, so you guys can hang out here if you want."

"Thank you," I croaked.

Ainsley went pink and grinned at me shyly. "No problem. Um."

"Come on, Grandpa." Finch gently took my arm and began leading me toward the back of the room. Leaning my cane against the wall, I sat and accepted the bottle of water he shoved into my hand. He stripped off his jacket, then dropped the large holdall he was carrying and rooted through it, eventually pulling out a volleyball, and kicking the bag toward the wall. "Okay, I'm gonna go take some pictures and stuff, and I'll come get you in about an hour."

I frowned at him, realizing he was dressed in something not un-reminiscent of a PE kit, with a large number ten on his chest. "There's sports?"

Finch tucked the ball under one arm and shook his head at me, grinning. "Don't worry about it." And he scarpered.

I sat in my quiet corner and gently *disintegrated*.

After a medium-length infinity, I pulled the folded sheet of paper from my back pocket: it was covered in the messy scrawl of my normal handwriting (rather than the painstaking script I used for lettering), but was little more than a series of bullet points for me to hit during my talk. I'd learned the hard way early on in the workshop that when I tried to script my lessons, I quickly got lost. I was a man to whom tangents came quite naturally—at times *aggressively*—and finding my way back to a written paragraph was much harder than working back to an overall concept. Teaching hadn't become *easy* toward the end, but it *had* somehow managed to become . . . fun.

That had a lot to do with the fact that I could natter on about comics generally. Which was very different from having to natter on about my *own* comic specifically.

Oh god, just *imagining* it made me want to vomit—

I shut my eyes and gripped the plastic bottle in my hand so tight it squeaked. I breathed through my nose, bending forward over my knees.

Once again, I felt the emptiness of my pocket where the flask should be.

I couldn't even promise myself a drink when I got back to the flat. I had to get through this on sheer nerve and Christmas crackers.

And the thought of Lucas.

I knew deep in the darkest corner of my soul that there wasn't a single chance in hell he was still coming to the con. Not after what had happened, no matter what Finch said.

We hadn't texted since. I was flying out the day after tomorrow.

This endeavor wasn't happening.

Originally, we'd agreed to meet after my panel in the gallery space set aside for my students. *Lucas, wandering the gallery space considering my students' work . . .* I opened my eyes and sat up, my heart thumping too hard and climbing into my throat, and my brain suddenly too distracted to continue eating itself.

There was no chance he was coming, but it couldn't hurt to wander by the place we'd said we'd meet, could it? I was deluding myself, but I had nothing else to cling to.

I jerkily stood up out of my chair, and Ainsley gave me a little wave. I waved back and marched—hobbled really—directly out of the conference room into the seething mass of humanity. I wandered through the press of people, keeping to the edges of the enormous hall and trying to quell the feeling that I'd found my way into another world, where a large, colorful crowd of people provided the same visual experience as a Hardys sweetshop.

I had been to comic events before, of course, but never on this scale. Drawn & Quartered Comic Convention wasn't some twee little con in Rotherham; there were bloody movie stars somewhere about. And I was an *invited speaker*. An attraction. I was used to spending a grueling day behind a shared desk, feverishly signing old issues while Lakshmi (and Sam and Craig who sometimes came to help) tried to coax people over to the table apportioned to us, a local romance author, and a tarot reader.

There was no *Surrogate Goose* table here—there was a *Surrogate Goose* Corner in the Drake House Complex. In the sea of color and texture, my monochrome artwork stood out like the edgy, *ridiculous* adolescent in a family photo.

Merchandise hung on display, and young people dressed in Drake House apparel were selling it alongside action figures, posters, and collectibles. It felt *bizarre*. Like an elaborate joke or misunderstanding. How could this level of corporatization still qualify as *indie*? How could anyone use that description with a straight face?

Well, I probably wouldn't have to worry about that for much longer. I'd shown up and I was presentable and all, but bet you tuppence I would still make an utter arse of myself on stage and Drake House would drop the comic and Lakshmi would behead me and the world would end—

"Oh my god, Professor Demetrio! Hi!"

Oh *no*. I cringed but then saw Blue-Glasses-Afro-Puffs— (Ariadne)—beaming up at me. There were two people behind her who were unquestionably her parents. "Oh hello," I managed, trying not to panic. Or at least *show* that I was panicking. I hadn't thought to prepare for the uncanny valley of seeing my students in any other context than the classroom.

"I was just taking my folks over to see the workshop gallery," she said, then indicated a direction. "It's this way, if you want to come. I know you hate looking at your own work." She glanced back toward the *Surrogate Goose* Corner, then shrugged, giving me an adorable little half smile.

I felt my face heat up but also a bloom of gratitude in my chest—
it was terrible to think that I was so transparent, but comforting to
know that my students didn't seem to hold it against me. I followed
Ariadne and her parents through the colorful throng and toward a
large auditorium. There was a stage at one end, and a small crowd had
gathered around the speaker. Their distorted voice echoed, as did the
soft rumbling of the audience. It was a Q&A session. I turned away,
shuddering.

At the other end of the hall, there was a gallery space, where my
students' work covered the walls. I stopped in my tracks. I'd seen each
piece individually, of course, but there was something about seeing
them all spread out in one place that caused a fluttering in my chest.

They were *good*. And even better, somehow, they were all *different*.
There'd been a big part of me that feared I was doing little more than
turning out a classful of mini-me's. But while my influence was visible
if you knew where to look, each of these kids' visions was unique and
their styles distinctive. Finch's odd vampire wizard romance had a
great deal of substance to it, with color themes and a dynamic lineup.
Damien's spread showed near flawless technique, with fewer sloppy
motion blurs, Cyrus had truly taken to heart the lessons of cinematic
panels as pacing—I could practically hear the soundtrack—and
Aubrey . . . had done a fantastic job with the available resources.
Which had primarily been gall.

And there they all were, milling about with their friends and
families, sending the odd wave my way but otherwise engrossed in
the experience of seeing their art professionally displayed for the first
time.

I definitely *wasn't* choking up.

"Armand, there you are!"

I turned to see a red-faced Finch running up to me—perhaps he
had found a volleyball game. "I've been looking all over for you! I
thought we were staying in the room with the nice lady!"

"Have you seen Lucas at all?" I asked, twisting my fingers in the
hem of my sweater.

Finch gaped at me and then let his shoulders sag, mouth twisting
in an incredulous smile. "You have no idea the kind of heart attack you
just gave me, do you?"

"Sorry." I took a deep breath. "He's not coming, is he?"

"We don't know that yet," Finch said soothingly. "I'm sure he'll be here." He glanced around and then nodded toward the stage. "I can't believe you found the right auditorium on your own. I'm impressed."

I chose not to divulge the role played by Ariadne and her family. Instead, I focused on the fact that the last speaker was clearly finishing up, and bits of *this* crowd were filing out so that a new crowd could replace them. A few con officials were coming through with brooms, checking the seats for forgotten belongings.

"Do you remember the lineup?" Finch asked, then, when I stared at him mutely, simply continued. "Okay. So the panel moderator makes opening remarks, then you give your talk, then the panelists respond." He searched my face. "You remember who the panelists are?"

As a matter of fact, I did. They were three auteurs of three different indie comics practically indistinguishable from my own, but for some inexplicable reason not remotely as successful. They were all from local publishers—small, boutique, indie publishers that trundled along doing their best with what they had. Not like the behemoth of Drake House that had plucked me from obscurity. The same obscurity whose icy bosom I was soon to return to. My fellow panelists had likely just spent their day the way I'd used to—meet and greets and signings, hawking homemade merch, and accumulating large amounts of con crud.

Not hiding out in a small, quiet room, slowly succumbing to their own stomach acids.

The idea behind the panel was that I was meant to be aspirational. I was the ascended indie kid co-opted by the mainstream as a vehicle for their own performance of authenticity. This panel was me making myself available to the prodding and criticism of my former peers so they, too, could get the best possible odds on their tarnished souls. I had no clue what they might say, but whatever crimes they laid at my feet were likely justified. They were already seated at the table—one had pink hair and the other two were identical in nearly everything but the placement and subjects of their tattoos.

"So the tortured reverie is a yes?" Finch smiled. "Okay, and then there's the audience Q&A."

I nodded, still scanning the incoming crowd for Lucas, because I was delusional. And desperate for a point of light in the tumultuous sea of strangers.

"Don't worry, he'll be here." Finch took my elbow again and gently led me toward the stage. The room was seriously starting to fill up with a much larger crowd than had attended the previous panel. The low roar of the rabble rumbled through me like seismic waves. People were already standing in the back of the room.

I took my seat beside the pink-haired person and they smiled at me. I tried to smile back but my face felt numb. The moderator stood, and just like Finch had said, made a series of opening remarks, during which I continued to scan the crowd as best I could.

Everybody and his brother-in-law had shown up with a camera, it seemed, but I was keeping an eye out for the fancy kind that would match the cases and stands often strewn around the flat. I was looking for a glitzy camera and a flash of green eyes.

Out of the corner of my eye, I noticed Finch being strange in the front row: He was rather pale and rigid, gripping the edge of his seat. He kept glancing over his shoulder surreptitiously as if afraid someone would see. Well, I *did* see, and I followed his gaze to the corner of the room, near the middle row, where . . .

Of course. Skyler.

And standing beside him—

My microphone let out a sharp burst of feedback as I accidentally knocked it over. I scrambled to set it upright again while ignoring the expressions of concern and likely ire directed at me by the other panelists. I was just grateful I hadn't knocked over my water glass, or worse, the jug.

Lucas Barclay looked rather different when not covered in horse. The hair was blond and not naturally spiky, the face was tan and assembled in a series of attractive squares and triangles. I'd observed the wide shoulders the night before, but now in combination with the face of a good-natured cowboy . . .

I crossed my legs under the table and immediately started gnawing my knuckles, trying to stop blushing and hoping against hope that he hadn't caught me staring at him.

But he had—he grinned, showing beautiful white American teeth, and gave me a shy little wave. I smiled in spite of myself and forced my knuckles out of my mouth, using the hand to wave back instead. Miraculously, I didn't knock over anything else.

He'd come. He'd actually come. Did that mean there was still a chance? Even though we only had a couple of days left, did he want to pursue this strange thing we'd begun?

Despite the fact that it should have been cataclysmically awkward to stare at each other for as long as we did, neither of us seemed able to look away.

Lucas wasn't taking pictures, and I was only brought back to myself when the bloke next to me nudged me hard in the ribs.

"W-wha?" I blinked away the daze. Pink-Hair was giving me an amused smile while gesturing toward the moderator.

A dapper and extroverted man suited to his job, the moderator was chuckling at me. "And it appears Mr. Demetrio has allowed his mind to wander. Are you prepared to tell us a bit about your goals for *Surrogate Goose*?"

Oh *right*. I still needed to *speak*.

I swallowed and nodded, heat pulsing in my face. Then I pulled my microphone forward, hunching toward it, and smoothed out my tattered page of notes. Lucas was giving me a quiet, encouraging smile, and I could feel it idiotically reflected on my own face.

"I, urgh, haven't any, errmmm, *goals*." *Oh, brilliant start, Demetrio.* "That is, not—not any that would make sense to anyone who wasn't me." *And that sounds as if you think you're smarter than everyone, well done.* I shut my eyes tight for a moment and tried to start over. "I started making this comic during the darkest period of my life"—my voice had gone reedy and fragile, but I soldiered on—"a-and it helped me *out* of it. I know it's got this reputation for being bleak and . . . and hard to understand, and honestly that's because I'm just faffing about." I worried my hands, trying not to be overcome with relief when a laugh rippled through the crowd.

I ran a hand through my hair and then left it there, leaning forward on my elbow, holding Lucas's gaze like it was a lifeline. His eyes narrowed and his grin widened. He bit his lip. I nearly groaned.

Instead, I glanced down at my notes and kept talking, riding this wave of serotonin as far as it would take me.

"It's always been confusing to me why other people enjoy the comic." At this, there was a murmur of ascent from along the table. They were smiling and nodding in understanding. Marveling along with me that others might find anything of value in our creations.

None of us knew how or why this worked.

"It's confusing," I continued, "but it also makes me incredibly *hopeful*. This thing that I make b-because it helps me make *sense* where there otherwise is none, it actually appeals to the rest of you. Or s-some of you, at least." I swallowed, glancing around the crowd. "I dunno how many of you were dragged here."

Another laugh. *Oh god, this might be going well.* I took a shaky breath.

"I've had time to think this past month, while I was t-teaching at Norsemen." I had to stop as my students howled and hollered in the way of Americans whose hometown, school, or sports team has been casually mentioned, and I couldn't help grinning at the lot of them. "Settle down. Anyway, I realized that while we like to pretend that we make art for, well, *artsy* reasons—you know, mysterious, spiritual, unknowable mid-life crisis reasons—and I know it doesn't sound very edgy, but I think all we're doing is making bids for connection. We just want each other to be happy." I found several faces in the crowd I recognized—Robin, Skyler, the students again—all beaming. "It feels good to make people happy, and that doesn't always mean making happy content, necessarily. It might mean working through some real shite—" I winced "—sorry, er, *crap*, and processing it as best you can using, heh, *penguins*—" several audience members whooped "—or bloody obtuse literary allusions, or intense graphic contrast. There's no inherent meaning to any of that." I ran both hands through my hair again, swallowing and avoiding the eyes of the other panelists. "I know it sounds *trite*, but my intentions don't matter, when you come down to it. There's only as much meaning as *you* put in. Y-you being *you*. Er, not *me*." I looked over at Lucas again, helplessly.

He was grinning at me and had his arms folded over his chest, as if waiting to see what I would do next.

"I must say, the thought that this drivel I make—" I glanced along the table "—that *we* make, out of the mankiest, most cack-handed, *obnoxious* bits of ourselves—"

Pink Hair and the tattoo twins muttered again in agreement.

"—can actually reach you lot, make you less bored or less lonesome . . . It's *overwhelming*. In my case, I'm taking my own darkness—and not a sexy, bloody *sibylline* darkness, mind you, a crusty, *pongy* darkness, full of moldy half-eaten takeaways and ink stains on the carpet—" The crowd gave a mirthful roar, and somehow even in the cacophony, I could pick out Lucas's warm, golden, sunshine laugh.

"And somehow making you smile." I did so myself. "That's the job. You reach out with your tender bits, and if you're lucky, someone reaches back."

The hall hummed with a warm, intimate silence. That increased in cringe by the second.

"A-and that's all," I said weakly. "There's no deep, secret meaning to any of it. J-just a git messing about." I rubbed the back of my neck. "But I *love* that it makes you happy." I grimaced at the moderator and my fellow panelists. "Th-thank you?"

The awkward silence rang on, burning in my throat.

The applause began slowly, then escalated, thundering against my eardrums and somehow *inside* my chest.

I'd done it. I'd managed to speak.

Somehow, despite the endless sea of hungry eyes, despite the forest of phones and bright, excited faces, despite the swallowing void of strangers' attention, I'd managed to speak. And possibly make *sense*.

There was still the rest of the panel to get through, the responses from my peers and the questions from the audience, but the part I was meant to carry on my own was over. The question of whether it had gone well remained—whether I'd just made an utter arse of myself in front of the internet and Drake House publishing overlords— but at the moment I could hardly bring myself to care. The sword of Damocles had snapped the single horsehair by which it hung, but hadn't yet plummeted down to sever my head from my neck.

We were mid-plummet.

And there were much, much worse places to be.

For now, I allowed others to do the talking, listened with half an ear as the other panelists took the garbled mess of a speech I'd made and wrung from it some semblance of deeper meaning and perhaps a shred or two of useful advice. I nodded along and tried to look attentive, though truly I was drowning in the sea-green of Lucas's eyes.

51

ROBIN IS NO
STRANGER TO DRAMA

August 15th

I was so *conflicted*!

On the one hand, there was absolutely no way I wasn't about to watch this drama unfold between Lucas and Armand. They were making such *intense* eye contact. Lucas was standing at the side of the room and, despite the bedroom eyes, seemed hilariously cool about all this. Armand fidgeted, slumped, stuttered, and fiddled obnoxiously with his pencil, but no one could say he looked anything short of sex on a stick. There was *magic* in the air, and somehow everyone could tell. Mine wasn't the only head swiveling back and forth between these two.

But on the other hand, standing next to Lucas was . . . Skyler. Amused smile on his lips. Hands in his pockets. Silky black locks falling gently in front of beautiful blue eyes.

He was watching the mini spectacle that was Armand and Lucas as well, but he was also sneaking glances at me. I gripped the edge of my seat and forced myself not to run.

Again.

The thought of facing Skyler since our last "conversation" was making Armand's crisis croissants threaten to reappear. I was in the front row; I could make a run for the exits by the stage.

But that would mean missing the final act of this stupid, sad, explicitly gay remake of *The Odd Couple*.

Be brave, Robin! Or if that fails, be nosy!

The non-Armand panelists said some stuff, and then the audience Q&A started. Armand was doing a surprisingly good job of fielding questions. Sure, he was sweating a little, but the more questions he took, the more coherent his answers became. He and the other panelists had clearly recognized some deep kinship with each other and had begun discussing the very nature of *Art*, and the audience loved it. Armand was still Armand and reluctant to talk—but when he did, there was a self-deprecating charm that had replaced the miasma of resentful self-loathing. He almost sounded *dignified*. Like he actually wanted to be here and was having fun. He even kept his cool when Lucas asked a question.

I couldn't help thinking back to that first, burningly awkward lecture he'd given at the start of the workshop. The difference was astounding. I felt like a proud mama bird watching their offspring fly confidently toward an invisible jet turbine.

After a while, the moderator took it upon himself to make sure some of the other panelists had an opportunity to answer questions from the audience before the time was up. Armand slumped back in his seat and covered his eyes for a few moments as if to catch his breath. But then he found Lucas's gaze again and those two made sweet, sweet eyeball love for all the world to see.

The panel ended with thunderous applause, and Armand shot to his feet. He started for the stairs that led off the stage, but a whole pack of eager fans barred his path, and even more of them were inadvertently blocking Lucas's. Oh no, I couldn't take this anymore.

I got up, raised both hands and said in a loud voice, "Out of the way, *out of the way*! Ladies and gentlemen, please make way for Mr. Demetrio and his *roommate*, clear the stairs, *now* ladies and gentlemen! Everybody *move*!"

Amazingly, they actually listened to me, and Armand made it down the stairs without impediment. Lucas managed to push to the front of the crowd, and in classic meet-cute fashion, neither of them quelled their momentum in time and they crashed into each other pretty spectacularly.

Luckily, Lucas's camera and Armand's cane were tucked away and they didn't do anything as silly as bonk heads. Armand gripped Lucas's shoulders to steady them both, and they stared into each other's eyes for about twenty seconds longer than was comfortable for the rest of us.

Armand eventually seemed to come to his senses and let go of Lucas, color rising rapidly to his face. "Errmhmm . . . er, hi." He coughed.

Lucas, for his part, had never stopped grinning and didn't so much speak as chuckle in response. "Hi! Finally."

Armand swallowed and tried unsuccessfully to stuff one of his hands into the pockets of his very tight jeans. Again. "Yeah, finally. Eheh." He seemed to have realized they were still surrounded by people, and was looking around anxiously as if hoping they would just disappear. *Ha*, as if they would, when he and Lucas were giving us all such a good show.

Sure enough, the crowd that had initially gathered had maintained its size and a surprising level of silence while watching the star-crossed roommates.

Despite the crowd, Armand couldn't seem to keep the next bit down. "I wasn't sure you were coming. I thought maybe . . . after last night . . ."

"I wasn't sure either." Lucas's eyelashes fluttered shyly, and he bit his lip, likely killing Armand. He added a final nail to the coffin: "How's the foot?"

Armand glanced down and gripped his cane tighter, his face turning a rather impressive shade of burgundy. "Oh, er, fine. Erm." He looked around again at their audience. "Um, would you like to find somewhere more p-private? To . . . to talk?"

"That sounds absolutely— Oh *hey*!" Lucas had caught sight of me. "Robin! You were right about the accent, ooh and the awkward grumpy bear: totally worth it." He reached out a hand toward me and god help me, I high-fived it. At least partially just to see the look on Armand's face, but he was busy giving Skyler a very British hello nod.

Skyler.

Skyler who had said hello to Armand and was now staring at me. I quickly turned my attention back to the other two.

"Would you like to, er, food? I mean, get dinner?" Armand was once again, somehow, without the slightest hint of game, managing to charm Lucas—and the rest of us—directly out of our pants.

"There's a sweet little Japanese place downtown I've been wanting to check out," Lucas said. "I'll buy dinner if you promise to order anything other than Ramen."

Armand laughed at that, and next thing I knew, they were making their way out of the convention hall, the sea of fans parting as if they were a pair of gay Moseses.

Skyler, however, had stayed put.

And so had I.

He was trying to get me to meet his eye, but I was far more interested in the floor. It was a shiny floor. I liked it—I could study it for a good hour.

I couldn't look at Skyler. Not without getting smacked in the face by the same realization over and over again. That Armand had been right.

That what I'd done was unforgivable. And that I'd known it all along.

I'd reduced this beautiful, kind, *sweet*, sweet man to . . . a crush. Well, not so much a crush, more like the love of my life, actually, but still. I'd been so caught up in the idea that he didn't see me the way I wanted him to—as a love interest, not a sidekick—that I'd blown any chance for any relationship we might have had.

Finally, his sneaker came into view and nudged the toe of my Converse. "Robin?"

I looked up at him, one arm wrapped around my middle and the other twisted awkwardly behind me. "Yeah." Then before he could say anything else I blurted, "I'm sorry."

"What?"

I shut my eyes tight. "I'm sorry I ran away after you came out to me. That was an awful, horrible thing to do, like, literally the worst thing in the world. And I don't want you to think that I don't want to be your friend, because I *do* want to be your friend. Problem is, I want to be *more* than a friend but that's *my* problem not *yours* and—"

"Robin."

I opened my eyes. He was almost smiling. "Yeah?"

"Take a walk with me?" He inclined his head to the side.

I chewed on my lip. "'Kay."

He started out of the convention hall, glancing back at me over his shoulder.

After a moment, I followed him out of the hall and into the convention gardens. There were fewer people out here because it was late afternoon in the middle of August and there was air conditioning indoors, but Skyler seemed intent on finding a private, intimate place for this conversation to happen.

Like, oh, I don't know, a stone bench under a pair of flowering Jacaranda trees. Because that wasn't romantic and picturesque and fuck me, right?

Except . . . *not*. Obviously.

Skyler sat down on the bench and patted the seat next to him, giving me a hopeful little smile. God, I was such an asshole.

I shifted uncomfortably for a moment before setting myself on the bench. I clasped my hands in my lap and *didn't look at him.*

Skyler sighed. "Robin, about what happened last night—"

"I'm really so sorry about that," I cut him off. "Really, we— I can leave now and never—"

"*Robin.*"

I forced my mouth shut and stared at him wide-eyed, feeling my face slowly transform into a tomato.

Skyler bit his lip. "Please let me say this." He watched me for a bit, like he was waiting for me to calm down. Which was *not* going to happen. He seemed to realize that and kept going. "Just because I don't feel physical or romantic attraction for you right now doesn't necessarily mean I never will."

"Huh." My heart was pounding in my temples, in my throat, in my everywhere. I gripped the fabric of my kneepads and tried to remember to keep breathing.

He twisted his fingers in his lap. I wanted to take them. I wanted to take his hand, possibly more than anything I'd ever wanted ever. Then he reached over and took mine.

He. Took. My. *Hand.*

My face caught fire and I stopped breathing.

"Are you okay?" Skyler asked.

I nodded vigorously, wishing that I wasn't such a freak. "Yes, of course, why wouldn't I be? You've only ever been honest with me, and you don't owe me anything, and I'm such an idiot—"

"I really do want to be your friend," he said again, crushing every last sliver of my heart, "but I know you want me to be something else. And . . . I'm not sure I *don't* want that too. I like you. I do. I don't want to make any promises that I might not be able to keep. But . . ." His eyes hovered on my lips. "Maybe things can be different. Maybe it would mean I'm growing up."

What was *happening*?

Skyler swallowed. "Would it be okay if I kissed you?"

52
SKYLER LEAVES THE WINDOW OPEN

August 15ᵗʰ

"**W**ould it be okay if you *what*?" Robin squeaked.

"Well," I began, nervousness itching at my skin, "if my feelings changed once with Delia, that means it can happen again, right?" Maybe this was when things would click, when I would finally *know what I was*. "It couldn't hurt to try."

"No." He gulped, eyes wide. "No, it could not."

I inched forward until our foreheads were barely touching. His warm breath brushed against my cheek, which was strange but not totally off-putting. Maybe I was worrying for nothing. I closed my eyes—

"Wait!" A hand pressed against my mouth.

My eyes shot back open to see Robin leaning back, palm firmly between us. His face was scrunched up, like he'd just been punched in the stomach.

"I'm sorry," he groaned. "I'm so sorry. This is wrong."

I blinked back the whiplash of how this conversation had gone. "It . . . is?"

"Yes." Robin dropped his hand, moving it to twist in the hem of his shirt. "You shouldn't have to force yourself to have feelings for me if you don't. I don't want that." His face pulled into a watery smile. "I would *love* to be your friend. A-and you're not Peter Pan, okay? Don't think I didn't catch that. You're not a kid, or stunted, or whatever, ugh, and I'm so sorry I made you feel that way. I mean," he sputtered, seeming to struggle for a moment, "*look*, I-I saw your face, when you thought I was going to kiss you, and—" he swallowed. "You didn't . . . you don't *want* to do this. Not really. And that's *fine*. If your feelings change one day, *cool*. I would like to, um, be there when— *if* that happens, but if it *doesn't happen*, then that doesn't make you a little boy. Or"—he grimaced—"you know, *broken*. And I shouldn't have made you feel that way. I'm sorry. I'm just . . . so sorry."

My throat had gone tight, and I was frozen on the bench. Something like a hysterical laugh bubbled out of my chest before I could stop it, and I pressed my hands to my forehead. "Okay?"

Robin pulled my hands down and held them tight between us. "I would be so incredibly honored to be your friend. Like, obviously you shouldn't *want* to be mine because I'm *literally* the worst person in the world—"

"You're not."

"I am, though! It's sad. And I'm sad. And everything is sad and it's all my fault."

Robin had never been able to hide anything on his expressive face—it was twisted with regret now, like he was so sure I would pay him back by running away from *him* this time, or yelling, or telling him to his face that he was awful.

All I felt was relief, the cloud of expectation lifting from my shoulders. He didn't think I was broken or lying. He still wanted to be my friend.

"It's not your fault," I reassured him—the memory of the despair on his face last night briefly resurfacing before I shoved it back down. "I guess you can't help your feelings any more than I can."

"But I'm so sorry I made you uncomfortable," Robin said softly, biting his lip. "I'm *so sorry*." He took a deep breath. "Um. Actually. C-can I hug you?"

My shoulders relaxed, a smile tugging at my lips. "Yeah. Yeah, I'd like that a lot."

Robin pulled me in, his arms curling around my shoulders. I gripped his waist, and this was so much nicer than cradling him after a traumatic event. His hair brushed my cheek, and it smelled clean, and like strawberries. I let myself nuzzle into the embrace.

My phone buzzed.

"Oh, sorry—" I disengaged from Robin to see that Matt was calling. "I could—"

"Don't worry about it!" Robin said quickly, all but leaping from the bench. "I'll go grab us one of those popcorn balls shaped like the Death Star."

I grinned. "Please do. Ask for extra salt."

Robin flashed me finger-guns with both hands and scurried back toward the convention center. I hit Answer.

"Hey, Matt."

"So for the sake of transparency, I'm still thinking about what we were talking about last night, so I wanted to check in and see if we're good. Plus, Delia hasn't heard from you in a minute and wanted to make sure you weren't dead."

I eased back down onto the bench, nudging my shoe against the metal frame. With all that had been going on, I'd been neglecting the group chat. "I'll text her," I promised guiltily. "And everything's good; it's just . . . we talked about what happened last night. Me and Robin."

"Aaand . . ."

"And I asked if maybe I should kiss him. Like. To make sure."

"You did what now."

"I didn't, though," I said before Matt could do something dumb like freak out. "He said he didn't want me to do anything I didn't want to do and apologized for making me uncomfortable."

There was a loud silence before Matt huffed in my ear. "Well, that was the bare minimum, so good on him for that, I guess. But Skyler, what the fuck, dude? I told you not to try and act the way other people want you to."

"But then wouldn't I just be acting the way *you* want me to?"

"You know, you're being real funny, but you said *you* offered to kiss *him*. So if he hadn't stopped it, you would've done it, right?"

I paused, really thinking about it. About how close it had been to happening. About how I'd been able to feel Robin trembling beside me and how I'd been nervous, but not in a tummy fluttering way—I'd been nervous that it wouldn't work. That I wouldn't be able to give Robin what he wanted. "I guess."

"You guess." Matt was quiet again, which wasn't a good sign. "Okay, so, thought," he finally said. "Don't freak out, okay, but I think you should really come back home for a bit."

"But I've only been here a month," I protested. "I'm set up in a dorm, I have a job here, classes—"

"Skyler Lancelot Evans," Matt barked, even though that was not, and never had been, my middle name, "if you don't come home this instant for this intervention that I've just decided to stage for you, I'm going to take this up with a higher power."

I blinked at the phone. "God?"

"Worse. *Mom*."

"You wouldn't."

"I would and I will and so help me I will bro-nap you straight out of California and the whole family will back me up."

He was still convinced he was right. That at some point I should be content with the fact that I was always going to be different— more different—than everyone around me. That I was doomed to disappoint anyone who dared to like me. But I still hoped that I could change sometime down the line.

"Fine." I sighed. My classes were Pass/Fail anyway. I'd be able to get away with it. "I'll book a ticket." Another thirty-hour bus ride wouldn't kill me.

I swiped over to my private chat with Delia, wanting to make good on my promise before I could change my mind.

Skyler: *sorry I've been quiet but I wanted to beat matt to the news: I'm coming home to visit for a few days*

Her reply came in almost instantly.

Delia: *OH HELL YEAH it's gonna be so good to see you, we're gonna eat so much ice cream and barf <3*

I smiled down at my phone for a long minute, and I sent her a GIF of a sparkle-puking cartoon cat before my eyes could fixate on the heart.

Robin was returning, hands full of what looked like gigantic salty, caramel-y Death Star-y abomination goodness, hair bouncing and a bright smile lighting up his face. We'd only just decided to be friends and I'd have to tell him that I was leaving.

Was I running away again?

"I told them to throw all the salt they owned on here," Robin chirped, shoving one of the giant popcorn balls at me before plopping back down on the bench, "so RIP your blood pressure."

"Thanks." I chewed on my lip for a moment. "Um. So, I think I'm going to pop back home for a little bit to visit. Only for a few days."

Robin froze, Death Star halfway to his mouth. "Oh. Yeah, okay. Everything okay?"

Define okay. "I think so, it's just . . . I have some things to work out with Matt." And Delia would be there. I needed to be able to face her. To get closure. "Like, I'm not looking forward to the bus ride, but it'll be nice to see him again since we've made up."

Robin was nodding a bit jerkily. "Right, right. Um, so buses suck; what if I drove you there? Unless that's weird. Is that weird? I don't want to overstep. I totally get it if you want to do this alone—"

"That would be great, actually," I said, a wave of fondness rolling through me at the delighted surprise on Robin's face. "Thank you."

It hadn't even occurred to me that Robin would offer to drive me all the way back to Seattle. But spending some more time with him sounded nice, and I'd have both him and my family in the same place; everyone who cared about me along for the ride while I tried to figure out who and what I was—

Maybe I didn't have to do it alone this time.

53
LUCAS SETS
THE PACE

August 15th

Thankfully *Takoyummy* wasn't far from the convention center and we beat the dinner rush, because we'd no sooner been seated when the restaurant flooded with teenagers dressed head to toe in costumes, each more cumbersome and vaguely impractical than the next.

Kinda made me wish one of the *Surrogate Goose* penguin cosplayers would show up, just to see the look on Armand's face.

As it was, he visibly relaxed the moment we settled into our corner booth and I'd ordered for the both of us. His hulking frame, which he'd held so rigid during the panel, slumped into the upholstery.

I grinned, reaching for my water glass. "That bad, huh?"

"No, not really. That was barely the eighth worst experience of my life." He gave a rueful grin, settling further into the comfort of the booth. "So . . . 'Tell us about your artistic process,' huh?"

I nearly did a spit take as laughter bubbled out of me. It had been a split-second decision, as dozens of fans had lined up to ask Armand questions about his craft and the enigmatic narrative of his comic (only one of which he attempted to answer), and I couldn't help myself. "I was simply giving the people what they want, Armand—everyone wants the dirty, dirty secrets about what goes on behind the scenes. And it just so happens that I've had a front row seat to the carnage."

Armand blushed prettily, so I continued, "But seriously, though, your talk was so good. I'm a lowly peasant so I didn't understand all the art terms, but the way you held command of the room . . ." I cupped the back of my neck and rested my elbows on the table. "It was *incredibly* impressive."

My god, his face was so red. "Are—" he swallowed "Are you taking the piss?"

"Not even a little bit."

The same shy, crooked smile I'd seen slip when he'd caught sight of me from the stage made a stunning reappearance. "Fingers crossed that Drake House agrees with you. Which—" His face suddenly fell. "I guess I'll find out on Sunday. When I'm back in London."

I'd almost forgotten he was leaving the day after tomorrow. For a moment, the fun, tingly tension that had surrounded us turned into a much more urgent and melancholy tension. "Right."

"You know," he rumbled softly, clearly trying to recover the date-atmosphere. "You're not what I expected."

I knew it. I knew he'd be disappointed. And why wouldn't he be?

I forced a playful tone. "What, were you expecting a slobby, butt-ugly troll?"

"No," Armand said, and his cheeks had never stopped being pink. "I suppose I just never expected you'd be a sexy cowboy." He then tried to adorably cover his eyes with his hand and disappear into the booth.

I coughed in shock, and this time my face joined Armand's in the fiery color palette. "You're not exactly what I expected either."

"I-I'm not?"

"Well no, I hardly recognized you—what with clothes and all. Let alone a turtleneck in *August*."

Armand bit his lip. "Would you believe I didn't choose this ensemble?"

I smirked at him over the rim of my water glass. "I was wondering what the ghost of Steve Jobs was up to these days."

"I had ground to make up," Armand insisted, "what with the blood and the ink, a-and the *naked* . . ."

"I wasn't that much better." I grimaced—if only I could purge that night from my mind forever. "I'm sorry I was so bossy. I mean, I just started ordering you around; I can't imagine what you think of me—" And this was it, this was when he would tell me it had been too much, that I'd already showed too much of my ugly side and it had ruined everything.

Armand had gone very still and was staring at me wide-eyed. "Right." He coughed. "How dare you be competent and comfortingly assertive in your care." He smiled. "It was *lovely*—er, as much as anything involving that much blood can be lovely, that is. I felt safe with you, Lucas. You weren't *bossy*, you were—" His face was practically glowing. "Thank you. For ordering me around and taking care of me. E-especially since you seemed to have been having a rather rough night to begin with?"

I'd nearly slumped in relief at, *"I felt safe with you, Lucas."* No one had ever said that to me before. "Yeah, I'd just come from Milkshake's deathbed."

Armand blinked at me. "Pardon?"

Oh god, way to kill the mood, Barclay. "Grandpa Milkshake, one of our senior horses . . . he passed. Old age, nothing traumatic. And that's where I was right before—" I offered him a gentle, sympathetic smile "—you impaled yourself on an inkwell, like I kept *saying* you would if you keep leaving them on the floor—"

Armand's hand had snuck across the table and rested over mine. Warm and smooth and beautiful.

"I'm sorry." He withdrew it immediately and fisted it in his lap. "That must have been terrible for you, I've seen how much you love your horses."

His face scrunched up, as if he thought he'd crossed a line. But all I wanted was that hand back. I snuck mine closer, letting our fingertips graze. "That's okay. It was his time, and he went quietly without pain or fear . . ." *Oh god, don't think about a dead horse right now. Talk about something, anything else!*

Armand beat me to it.

"I have to say, though," he said thoughtfully, "you do look familiar, from somewhere other than that humiliating little episode last night."

My eyes snapped back to him in amusement. "You mean you think you might've seen me before, *not* covered in hay and mud?"

Armand nodded and squinted at me. "Aye, I'm quite sure of it, especially when you smile. I've seen you somewhere before . . . *happy*."

He paused for only a second, then his lips pulled up in a grin. "The airport. When I arrived at the baggage claim. I think you were texting."

No way. "*You* were the werewol—" I cut off with a choked laugh as I gaped at him. "I *do* remember you! You didn't respond when I talked to you. Kinda looked like you were in your own little angsty world."

Armand chuckled awkwardly. "That does sound like me. I remember you looking disgustingly full of joy. Who were you talking to? Was it Skyler?"

The other shoe on the subject change came crashing down. My throat went cold as I swallowed. "Darren."

"Oh, aye, right. The ex." He fiddled with his chopsticks. "Sorry."

I forced a shrug, hoping it was nonchalant. "No worries. It wasn't a big deal."

"Oh?" Armand asked, a little pointedly. Okay, maybe a lot pointedly.

I picked at a loose thread in my rolled-up napkin. "Right, I forget you were actually *there* to witness the dramatic aftermath . . ." I gathered from the strength I'd pulled out of my ass this morning. *Please don't think worse of me after hearing this.*

"He, uh—" God it was really going to suck having to say this out loud. "He's a piece of shit, and the fact that I didn't see it for like ten years makes me extremely stupid and pathetic . . ." My gaze drifted down to the table instead of staying on Armand's distracting face. "He was always jealous, he wanted to be in charge of how I acted and how I dressed, but I think I always kind of knew he was embarrassed by me. He never even publicly admitted our relationship—whatever it was— until, well." Until I'd lost weight, until he'd deemed me acceptable. I shrugged again, braving a glance back up. "I was the only one that ever called us boyfriends. And then he has the absolute audacity to ambush me at my favorite bakery this morning to convince me to take him back. Obviously I didn't," I added at the look that flittered across Armand's face. "But, yeah. That's the highlights for you. Feel free to run out of here in disgust should the impulse strike you."

But there was nothing on Armand's face but kindness—not pity, not judgment—that stole the breath from my lungs. "That's not an entirely unfamiliar story," he said quietly, gently.

Okay now there was a definite lump in my throat. "I know I've already mentioned it," I said, and it wasn't enough, "but thank you. Again. For everything. The muffins. The notes. For, um, caring."

Armand hunched further in on himself. "Oh, er. It was nothing. I just . . . I'm glad you're feeling better."

"I am." Which was so startlingly true that my skin buzzed. I raised a playful eyebrow at him. "Nothing snaps you out of your funk like finding a large, naked man bleeding in your bathroom. And you're blushing again."

"I am?" Armand reached up, like he had to touch the warmth of his cheek to believe me. His jaw was lightly stubbled and defined, and I knew I was staring but I couldn't stop. He smiled crookedly. "I am."

"It's weird though; I thought for sure I was going to run into you the night of my breakup. Aren't you normally home around that time?"

Armand's Adam's apple jumped. "Oh, heh, I was busy being thrown out of someone's bed." Then his eyes shot wide open in a visible panic. "No! Not because— Rrrg, his wife was coming home, n-not that I *knew* he had a wife before. I-I was *drunk*, which, not that I do that often! G-go home with people, at least, not anymore. It—" He put his face in his hand and pinched the bridge of his nose between his thumb and forefinger. "Just . . . let's just say it wasn't a good night for either of us."

There was such awkward vulnerability in the way he stuttered through the explanation. Did he think I was going to judge *him*? And the idea that anyone would throw this man out of bed, or out of anywhere, made me absolutely indignant on his behalf. "Well, clearly it was his loss, and he sounds like a raging asshole."

Armand's lips pulled into an embarrassed smile past the hair hanging in his face, and then he smoothed it back. "Actually, it's even worse than that. He's the utter toss-pot who wrote Finch's play."

"I read the reviews." I shook my head at him in disbelief. *This* was the drama I missed out on by staying at the ranch with a dying Milkshake? "You *slept* with 'Neverland-is-a-metaphor-for-middle-aged-mediocrity' guy? Gross."

"I only saw half the play myself. And then I went outside and Neverland-is-a-metaphor-for-middle-aged-mediocrity guy tried to pull me *again*."

"Oh my god—did it work?"

"I am pathetically proud to say that it did not."

So we both shot down our exes to be here today. This tidbit quickly turned into a mass of warm nerves the longer we smiled at each other. I struggled for breath and for a coherent sentence. "You know, even though you're not what I expected, I'm pleasantly surprised. Turtleneck and all."

Armand sighed helplessly. "You do enjoy making me blush."

"Well," I teased with a quirk of my lips, "you make it pretty easy."

He leaned forward a little, and now our entire forearms were brushing. "I know."

Despite the restaurant's air conditioning, my skin felt flushed. I took a sip of water and didn't realize until after I'd set the glass down that Armand's eyes had moved from mine and had fixated instead on where—without knowing I'd been doing it—my finger was tracing the rim of the glass.

The opportunity was too good to pass up. With extreme slowness, I dipped the finger into the water and brought it to my lips to linger there.

Armand looked like he would spontaneously combust. Which was when I returned my finger to the water and flicked it at his face.

He had no sooner squeaked in surprise when our waiter approached with our platters of food.

We continued to sneak glances at each other throughout the meal. I had loosened my tie, unbuttoned my collar, and rolled up my sleeves ages ago. Which meant that Armand had also rolled up the sleeves of his ridiculous turtleneck, putting me entirely—despite my best efforts—at risk of a premature heart attack.

We chatted between bites and discovered that we both loved *Space Trip*, and Discworld, and it was so easy. Every time I made him laugh or blush, or said something that made him cock his head thoughtfully and bite his lip, his eyes bright and interested and with an intensity that lit my skin on fire, my heart flipped over. The way the hanging lights caught in his endless dark eyes . . .

I'm going too fast.
But he's leaving. Is it now or never?

My heart pounded. I swallowed and cleared my throat. "Hey, so. I guess it's best to get this out in the open sooner rather than later, but . . ." I took a deep breath, cursing the fact that outside of Darren—*because* of him—I had no idea how to do any of this. "If it's not too presumptuous, I feel like I'm not the only one feeling like there's . . . chemistry here?"

Armand coughed in a way that sounded like maybe he'd swallowed his tongue. "Er. Um. Yes. You're . . . you're . . . nope. Not the only one."

"Right." I forced the words out while I still had the nerve. "I like you a lot. And you're really fun to talk to, and I'll be real, I haven't felt this relaxed in a long time. But we barely have any time left, and I know part of it's because neither of us got our shit together sooner, but if you're leaving on Sunday—" I swallowed, terrified to try and put this into words. "I want to see where this goes. I'm just not sure what I'm ready for, and I don't want this to be something rushed, or a one-night thing, or . . ." My nerves got the best of me.

"Me neither!" Armand's voice was a squeak. He rubbed the back of his neck. "The last thing I want is a one-night stand."

"So you understand why I want to wait?"

He cleared his throat and sat back, his body hunching in on itself. "Of course. I understand. Of *course* I understand. Obviously. Naturally. Er. Yes. Quite. I understand completely."

He was so flustered that I couldn't help my smile widening into a grin, barely containing a laugh. "So you understand, then?"

Armand bit his lip and nodded. "Not to be glib, but it won't be the end of the world if we don't . . . ehrrm. And I know I'm rubbish at writing, or texting, but . . . we could still talk."

Awkwardness aside, talking about this so directly—to be able to discuss what I wanted with clear boundaries and intentions—was unfamiliar but more comfortable than I'd any right to expect. "Right—I'm sure it'll be just as hard to get ahold of you on a regular schedule in England as it was here," I teased, fighting the urge to reach out for him again while he was here, in front of me, within touching distance.

Armand chuckled, sending a warm ripple through me. "I'll just need to figure out how to draw on your mirror from a continent away."

I laughed, and he was so charming and devastating, I wondered how the hell I was supposed to make it out of this alive.

54

ARMAND GETS CARRIED AWAY

August 15th - Six hours after the convention and one day until the end of the world

"**Y**ou don't really believe that!" I laughed, unlocking the front door and stepping aside so Lucas could slide past me, still spewing his ridiculous notions.

"All I'm saying is Craig Charles is aging like a fine wine." Lucas put his camera down on the coffee table and tossed his bag onto the couch. "And Chris Barrie is aging like a tomato, you know?" He further loosened his tie, a gesture which I should not have found a tenth as distracting as I did.

I closed the door behind me and leaned against it, grinning at him past the hair in my face, then pushed as much of it as I could behind my ears. "A *cute* tomato. And I think we can both agree that Danny John-Jules isn't aging at *all*."

Lucas paused, one hand still holding his tie off to the side, and let a languid, sultry smile find its way to his lips. "You are not wrong." He finished pulling the tie off and draped it over the back of a chair. His collar fell open slightly, and I watched his Adam's apple bob, then felt mine rise and fall in answer.

Before I'd got a handle on myself, I'd moved away from the door and taken a few steps toward him—luckily, I caught myself in time, half a meter of safety between us. I wished for at least the twelfth time tonight that I could fit my hands into the pockets of my abominably tight trousers.

More than anything, I wished I wasn't quite so sober right now.

Lucas was still giving me a playful smile, and his eyes traveled from mine to the rest of my face. Then the rest of me—shoulders down to knees and back upward.

The heat didn't keep to my face.

I swallowed hard, almost painful in a dry throat, and took one step closer.

His smile widened, and then he bit his lip, lowering his eyes. A hand reached up to rest gently on my biceps. I kept my hands resolutely at my sides, until he took one of them in his.

I just hoped he didn't mind the sweat and slight trembling.

"I . . ." My mouth was talking again without my permission. "I'm really . . ."

"Yeah?" He leaned in, looking up and trying to catch my eye.

"I'm really, really glad we finally met," I managed, in a low whisper that was a bit too guttural for my own comfort. "*Really* glad."

"So you're glad, then?" Lucas's mouth worked for a moment, like he was keeping down a laugh or a grin. "Me too." His hand moved up from my shoulder to trace my jaw, his finger rustling softly against the bristles that had already started to appear there. "Really, *really* glad."

"Hehhneh . . ."

Lucas's eyes were centered on my lips, and I bit down yet another rather embarrassing moan trying to claw its way up my throat. I shut my eyes and moved in, stopping when I could feel his breath on my lips, and waited.

But not for long.

Lucas's lips met mine, and within a millisecond I had an arm around his waist and he had a hand in my hair and the turtleneck had never seemed like a worse idea.

I slipped one of my knees between his and pressed as close as I dared. His fingers clenched in the hair above my ear while my hand fisted in the back of his shirt. My other hand slipped around the front and began untucking his shirt both as quickly and as gently as I could, starting for the buttons.

Lucas broke the kiss and buried his face in the corner of my throat, hands dropping from my hair and chest. They rested on mine, quelling their search for entry into his shirt.

I wanted to die. "I'm sorry!" I wheezed. "I got carried away. You *just* said— We *just* agreed—"

"Shh . . ." Lucas whispered into my neck, and I tried to suppress the shiver. "I got carried away too."

"Unn-hnn." God help me it was a whimper, but Lucas had the kindness not to notice, and stepped away from me slowly, hands lingering on mine.

"I'm not trying to torture you, I swear." He chuckled. "Or myself. I just . . . don't want to mess this up."

I swallowed and nodded. "That's, yes. Me too. Thank you." I wanted to *die*.

He smiled up at me, eyelids drooping down and lips still glistening, cheeks flushed. He raised my fingers slowly to his mouth and kissed them so softly I nearly moaned. He kept my fingers against his lips. "I'd better see you in the morning."

"You will. G'night." I groaned, then watched him make his way to his bedroom and listened for the *click* of the door shutting.

Then I spent a few minutes actively *not* slamming my head into the wall as hard as I could.

I paced the living room, hands gripping my hair, then grabbed my bag where it hung by the door and fled the flat, taking huge lungfuls of the cool evening air before lighting a cigarette and leaning against the wall of the building.

Bloody hell, that man was going to kill me.

And I was going to love every second of it.

I stared down at my hands, feeling the urge to draw, since other forms of expression were not readily available. I needed to do something to make up for that disgusting display upstairs. It couldn't be that hard to prove I was more than a pair of hands and a bucket of hormones.

And just like that, I had an idea.

55

ROBIN IS A WORK IN PROGRESS

August 15th

S o the plan was to leave directly after the Sunday matinee of *The Shadow of Never*, and then make it back before next weekend's run.

Because I'd offered to drive Skyler to Seattle. A thirteen-hour drive alone in my car with the boy I liked and had refused to kiss.

After dropping Skyler off back at his dorm hours ago, I had driven around for a while, until I was ready to get myself a large double-fudge strawberry blast milkshake with sprinkles, sit in my car in an abandoned parking lot, and cry my eyes out.

I'd wanted so badly for things not to end this way, to turn the tide of the universe away from the inevitable tragi-comic conclusion in which I, sad, lovesick nerd, learned my place like the Duckie I was. Accepted my fate. Grew up and got over and made do.

But Skyler deserved better than my desperate, selfish infatuation. In the same way that I didn't deserve to be terrorized by Terri Bishop.

I wasn't Terri's punching bag, and Skyler wasn't Batman.

So this was *good*. This was a chance for me to prove what a good friend I could be.

This time I'd be friendly and charming and cool, and my heart wouldn't climb up into my throat if he looked at me for a little too long with those *eyes*, and his smile wouldn't make me *melt*. We'd be friends. I'd be such a good friend.

I was just starting to slide down the other end of the sugar high when my phone buzzed. I squinted at it through my tears and answered, sniffling. "What? Why aren't you sexing Lucas right now?"

"Titch—" Armand's voice broke "—that's . . . Rrg." I heard him swallow. "C-can you come get me?"

I sat up from my slump and rubbed my hand across my nose. "Sure, I'll be right there."

"Wait, Titch, why are you crying?"

I hung up on him and started Camille, coaxing her out of the drive-through parking lot and toward the Briars complex. Ten minutes later, I found Armand pacing at the base of the stairs; his sleeves were rolled up and his hair was mussed, and his face was shining in the light of the streetlamps—not with tears, with . . . holy crap, with *passion*. He loped over to the car, yanked the door open, and stuffed himself in, glaring at me in concern. He smelled like cigarettes as usual, and I immediately rolled the window down.

"What happened, Titch?" His eyes widened. "With Skyler?"

"Nothing." I shook my head, hair fwapping across the bridge of my nose. But I could feel his eyes on me, and while I knew the tension coming off him had everything to do with Lucas and nothing to do with me or Skyler, it was still a *lot* to be near. "Okay, he tried to kiss me. *He* tried to kiss *me*. And I stopped him. 'Cause I'm *stupid*. And now I'm driving him to Seattle on Sunday, so you're gonna need to find a different ride to the airport." I glanced over at Armand, who was curled into the tiny seat, arms wrapped around his middle and his knees pressed together. "Like maybe *Lucas*?" I asked pointedly.

"Hnnrg." Armand shut his eyes briefly, taking a deep breath that made his massive shoulders shudder. "I'd rather not talk about that." He looked back at me again. "He tried to *kiss* you? And now you're running away to Seattle together?"

I bit both my lips and nodded. "He's going home to see his family, and I'm *finally* trying to be a good friend to him."

Armand was still watching me, looking—and I'd never felt more justified in using this word—*thunderous*. I gave him a tragic grin and shrugged. "I told Skyler I'd love to be his friend, i-if he'd have me." I sighed, flexing my hands on Camille's threadbare wheel and staring straight out into the dark parking lot. The light of the streetlamps made little yellow puddles that stretched out in a long row, curving across the hills. A few coyotes sang in the distance. "And I'm in the process of getting over myself. It's a work in progress, okay?"

Armand smiled at me hesitantly. "That's brilliant, Titch."

"Oh yeah, no, I feel *great*," I said dryly, wiping at my eyes and nose again—my voice was the only dry thing about me—but managed to smile back at him. "No, I know how lucky I am. And that I've been real shitty about this. Speaking of not being shitty." I raised my eyebrows at him. "You better say goodbye to him before you leave."

"I will." Armand huffed. "He's a good lad."

"He is," I agreed. Then I punched his arm. "Now tell me what the hell happened with Lucas!"

"Ow," Armand growled, trying to shy away from me but unable to since he was basically curled into a ball in the tiny space he had. "No! Bollocks! It is extremely none of your business!"

"You called me for a reason," I pointed out.

"Yes, er." He hesitated, then explained what he had in mind, only seeming to realize, as he said the words out loud, that his plans might be somewhat ruined by the fact that the business day was well and truly over.

"Don't worry about it," I told him, "I actually know a few places that are open twenty-four hours."

We pulled out of the Briars complex and started toward downtown. Armand was silent, still hunched in his seat, his hands worrying at each other. Finally, after we'd been driving for a few minutes, he grimaced at me. "I made an arse of myself," he said, and didn't expand on it.

I couldn't help it. "Well, that *is* what we do, isn't it?"

He frowned at me in confusion.

I widened my eyes slightly. "The *piners*, right? What was it? Die without dignity?"

"Stop," he groaned.

I chuckled to myself, already feeling a little better. Skyler might not feel sexual or romantic attraction, but he still *liked* me and we were about to spend a *lot* of time together in a confined space. And who knew what that might become? Given time, and patience, and the full force of my will . . .

Armand was giving me the side-eye, as if he could hear what I was thinking.

"We're working on it, right?" I equivocated, "No one gets over themselves all at once."

He nodded slowly, now staring off into the distance. "No, they do not," he said ruefully. His hands fisted and unfisted over his knees, that were all but tucked under his chin. "But the point is that they try. That *we* try." He worried his bottom lip for a while, his eyes looking haunted and his hands shaking just the slightest bit.

"You've been doing really well with the not drinking, huh?" I asked gently.

He winced and gave a noncommittal grunt.

We spent the rest of the ride in silence, and once we pulled up in the parking lot of the shopping complex, I shut the engine off and faced Armand fully. "I'm really proud of you. You know that, right?"

He went red and started trying to extricate himself from Camille. "Shut up, Titch."

"Love you too, Big Guy." I blew him a kiss, then followed him out of the car. Armand had made a lot of progress over the past month, but it still felt like a bad idea to let him attempt a business transaction on his own, downtown, after dark. My liaising skills were still required, clearly.

And Armand wasn't the only one who'd made progress—*look at me being all mature and enlightened.* I was going to be a good friend to Skyler, and who knew? Maybe one day I wouldn't be the worst person in the world.

56
LUCAS AT THE THRESHOLD

August 16th

I woke slowly, a smile stretching across my face. My skin still buzzed with last night's tension, and I kept replaying the look on Armand's face as I'd left him in the living room. It had been nearly strong enough to shatter my willpower.

Don't rush. We didn't even know what this was yet, and if I rushed, I might scare him off before we had a chance to figure things out. *But he's leaving. He's leaving and there's nothing you can do about it.*

I needed to talk to someone about this, and not just anyone. I reached for my phone, tapping against the sides for a long moment before dialing.

"Lucas, I'm so glad you called."

I knew I hadn't woken her up. Like me, my mother rose with the sun. "Hi, Mom. How . . . how are things at the ranch?"

"Well, we're finalizing the details for Grandpa Milkshake's memorial, and it's a lot of paperwork." She sighed. "But we can talk about that later. Are you okay? Everything good?"

"Yeah, I . . ." I sat up in bed, hugging my knees. "I wanted to apologize for being an asshole the other day. I know you've always wanted the best for me, and it's not your fault I was an idiot about Darren. I shouldn't have lashed out at you."

"Oh baby, it's okay." There was some shuffling on the other end, which was presumably her moving to a quieter spot. "You've been in pain, and I just wish there was something I could do to help."

I exhaled—I hadn't realized until this exact moment how much I'd hated fighting with her. Especially when all I wanted was to sit down and tell her all about Armand. "I finally met Mothman. In person."

Mom gasped. "Ooh, tell me about it! Is he young? Is he cute? Is he single? He's single, right?"

I coughed a laugh. God, I'd missed gossiping with her. "Um. Yes to all three. I mean, it didn't go as expected, but . . ." My eyes flickered to my bedroom door, my voice dropping a bit, as if there was any chance Armand would be conscious in his room at seven in the morning. "We've been texting a lot, and even before he met me he's been so sweet—and I know it's kinda soon after Darren, and maybe I'm actually a terrible judge of character after all, but . . ." I fiddled with the edge of my duvet. "I really like him, Mom. We went to dinner, and the whole time I was with him, I never felt . . ." I couldn't find the right word.

But Mom did. She always did. "Disrespected?"

It cut, but it was true. "Yeah. I felt . . . safe. Which, I should be suspicious about, right? Technically we just met and apparently now I have a track record—"

"Honey, honey." Strangely, she didn't sound patronizing or pitying. She sounded . . . pleased? Proud? "I'm not going to say not to be careful with your heart, I'd be a bad mom, but . . . at the same time, there's strength in putting yourself back out there, trusting people again. You've been hurt, and I'm sure one day you'll be hurt again, but for now your only job is to be happy. And if your cute awkward roommate who I am *so* relieved is not a serial killer makes you happy, then I'm over the moon."

I felt light enough to float away. Too jittery to stay in bed, I took the phone with me out to the living room, which had more space available for nervous pacing. "Yeah, I'm like, a little terrified, not gonna lie."

"That's how you know something's important." Mom let out an evil snicker. "I can't wait to meet him."

"Okay, well, we've had *one date*, so I'm gonna go ahead and say that's not super high on the priorities list right now because I'd very much like to not scare him away yet. Besides, he's flying out tomorrow, so I don't know—" I moved to open the living room drapes, when a flash of color caught my eye.

A bright pink Post-it note was stuck to the side of my fish tank. My pulse jumped.

There, swimming in the tank I had definitely left empty, were two female betta fish, happily chasing each other around the rock castle.

The Post-it note read, in Armand's messy but beautiful handwriting: *Hi, we're Timon and Pumbaa!*

A warm and fluttery feeling settled in my chest. "Hey, Mom, let me call you back," I said a bit shakily as my face stretched into a grin that hurt my cheeks. "Something just came up."

"Fine, but don't leave me hanging, okay? I love you, and the horses love you, and that boy is gonna love you—"

"*Okay, goodbye, Mother.*"

She was still laughing as I ended the call. I glanced back at Timon and Pumbaa, teetering dangerously between twirling around the living room and bursting into tears. I plucked the Post-it from the tank, walked to the kitchen, and grabbed a pen.

Then I paused.

I don't need to write him a note.

I set the pen on the counter and instead walked down the hall, coming to a rest outside Armand's door. I took a breath that felt too big for my chest, and knocked.

"Grmmff?" Another rumble and a shuffling noise later, and the door pulled open and Armand blinked blearily at me. "Lucas?"

I lost my breath. I'd almost thought that last night had been a beautiful dream and that my body was only imagining the lingering heat of his touch, the softness of his mouth—that Armand had already gone or had never been here in the first place. But here he was, as achingly handsome as I remembered, wide brown shoulders slumped with sleepiness. His chest was bare, he only wore a pair of tight black boxer briefs, and I thought for sure I would pass out.

In a blink, in an instant, something snapped, and I surged forward, cupped his scruffy face in my hands, and kissed him.

My mouth swallowed his yelp of surprise and the broken moan that followed, my legs threatening to liquefy even as his warm hands found the small of my back and clutched at me.

I pulled back gently, as I had last night, but it was only to catch my breath and stare into Armand's infinite dark gaze, which had lingered closed for an extra second, his lips chasing after mine.

"Thanks for the fish," I managed.

Armand stared down at me with hooded eyes that shone with heat and confusion. "The wha?" he croaked.

"Timon and Pumbaa." I managed to focus on what I wanted to say, even with Armand's fingers ghosting respectfully at the waistband of my sleep pants. "That was really sweet, you didn't need to do that."

"Erm," he responded eloquently, his already flushed face going redder. "I . . ."

My answering grin was instinctual. "You always know just what to say." I let my fingers trail across the smooth skin of his collarbone. "And yes," I teased, biting my lip and shivering as Armand's eyes dropped back down to my mouth, "*now* I'm taking the piss."

Maybe this was fast. Maybe we only had one day left and I might never see him again. And maybe this was new and frightening and so far outside my experience, but something bold and unfamiliar had bloomed beneath my rib cage, and I didn't realize I'd guided Armand backward into his bedroom until the light had dimmed and my head had filled with his intoxicating scent.

Somehow I managed to detach my gaze from Armand's in order to process the extent of the mess that was his room. The suitcase that he'd likely never seen fit to unpack. The piles of shirts and pants spilling out of it onto the ground. No wonder he'd injured himself on an inkwell—I could barely see the floor.

But the bit I could see . . .

"You cleaned?" I gaped at the mound of baking soda on the still slightly bloody and inky carpet near the foot of the bed.

Armand hummed some vague acknowledgment, his hands having found my arms and holding on to me like it was for dear life. "'S not perfect, and I know you're probably . . . ugh, worried about the deposit, but—"

"That was extremely hot of you," I interrupted, my heart flipping over at how easily Armand allowed me to sit him on the edge of the mattress. At how he almost instantly lay backward, pulling me closer until I was nearly straddling him. At how he waited, holding me gently, for me to decide what to do next.

"Is this—" I swallowed, the butterflies in my stomach mingling with a sudden burst of nerves. "Is this okay?"

God, the way he was staring up at me with parted lips, his hair curtained on the pillow, eyes dark and wide and fixed on my face as if—

As if I was something to be admired.

"This is bloody perfect," he murmured, stroking my arms. "We can do whatever you want. If anything."

"It's just—" I wet my lips. "Darren always wanted to be in charge, to decide what we did and when, and I . . . I've never . . ." Damn it, I was trembling. I didn't even know how to finish the sentence.

But Armand was sitting up, strong arms curling around me and easing me onto his lap. He brushed a strand of hair out of my face. "Tell me what you'd like," he said softly. His fingers hovered against my jaw.

What I'd like?

I inclined my head, slow enough that Armand could shove me away if he wanted, and lowered my lips to his neck.

His breath caught, warm against my cheek. He arched against me, baring more of his skin for me to access. As my lips inched downward, his hands traveled under my shirt, short fingernails pressing lightly into the skin of my back.

We were barely touching, and I at least was still fully clothed, but every inch of my body had sparked alive under his attention.

Emboldened by the thrill of his smell, his touch, the way he murmured semi-distinguishable words against the exposed lines of my skin, I nudged Armand down onto the mattress. I curled my fingers around his and urged them to the hem of my shirt, nodding to Armand as he silently asked permission before pulling it up and over my head.

It was more exposed than I'd ever allowed myself to be with anyone other than Darren, and for a strangled heartbeat of a moment, I froze.

"Lucas?" Armand's eyebrows furrowed in concern, his whole face open and genuine and attentive. There wasn't even a hint of expectation or pressure in the way his hands paused on my hips, his palms burning hot. "We . . . we could stop—"

The top of my head had been floating away, but I became instantly grounded, present in the moment. My chest clenched with a wave of such overwhelming affection I struggled to breathe. I didn't want to stop. I didn't want him to leave. I didn't want to waste any more of my life trying to please someone who'd never really wanted me.

And I wanted Armand. So badly it hurt.

I kissed him again, deeper this time, my self-control fracturing as he moaned. I rolled my hands down the unfairly defined muscles of his chest, the lined abs, the dusting of hair at the waistband of his briefs.

"I know we agreed not to do this," I said, startled at how low and rough my voice was already, "but you should know I don't think of you as a one-night stand." I paused only to take in his ragged breaths, hips trembling with the effort to not rock against my hands. "This means something to me." I pressed my lips to his, and he met me eagerly, our bare chests flush together.

"Me too," he whined into my mouth, as I freed him of his underwear and he did the same to me.

I took a breathless moment to admire the length of Armand's body, now entirely bare. My mouth went dry at the firmness of his muscles, the veins in his elegant hands, the all-encompassing heat of him. He grew hotter under my gaze, his skin like a live wire at every point we were touching.

"Do—" His voice was ragged, and he cleared his throat. "Do you want to—"

"Yes," I breathed. My fingers kneaded into the chiseled lines that cut down his hip, biting my lip at the whine he gave even as he reached for the bedside table.

When at last we both went boneless, sweaty and spent and utterly lightheaded, he fell sideways onto the mattress, pulling my back against his chest, cradling me like a weighted blanket. His lips lazily found the crest of my ear as we breathed each other in, my entire being relaxing into something safe and warm.

Through the blissful exhaustion, I shivered with pride. Armand had come completely undone because of me. I'd taken control rather than lying back and letting him call the shots. I hadn't had to struggle to find release past the constant reminder that I was just a means to an end, a dirty little secret.

I didn't have to worry that I wasn't good enough.

My eyes fluttered closed and I cozied back against Armand.

Mom was right. It was time I let myself trust again.

57
ARMAND TRIES AS HARD AS HE CAN NOT TO RUIN IT

August 16th - Time has lost all meaning

Consciousness arrived gradually, warmly, with the golden, soupy sunshine of late morning dripping past the blinds and onto the ceiling in lazy streaks and splashes. California sunshine. Still intimidatingly vibrant, but *genuine*. At some point during this past month, I'd stopped thinking of it as an enemy and had begun accepting the comfort and vitamins it offered.

Just as I was slowly coming to accept the waking world and the proceedings of the last few hours.

Lucas had . . . and then we'd . . .

Well.

We'd both fallen asleep, but not for long, it seemed; my muscles still buzzed with a velvety, heavy warmth that pressed me down into the mattress along with Lucas's weight. He remained nestled against me, one arm curled around my chest and his head tucked against my neck and shoulder.

I'd half-expected to wake and find him gone. *More* than half, really. It seemed impossible that he was still here, in my bed, smelling like California sunshine felt and *feeling* like a late-night wish gone solid.

These were stolen moments. He was asleep—he just hadn't had a chance to scarper yet. The moment he woke and realized what had happened, the regret would set in. He was a nice bloke, so he'd likely let me down easy, insist we remain friends, conjure up some lie about getting back with his ex—

Dear god, let it be a lie.

I shut my eyes tight and breathed in the warm smell of his hair, which was tickling the edge of my jaw. I tried to keep my body from stiffening, from giving away the game, waking Lucas early so that he'd leave me all the quicker. I could already feel the cold prickling along my arms, the sour knot below my sternum providing more than enough evidence that he should toss me away while he still could, like Ken had, like any rational person *would*—

"Shh."

It took me a moment to realize Lucas had spoken without opening his eyes.

"I—I didn't mean to wake you—" I began, not at all certain what I was attempting to communicate.

"Shh," he said again, landing a kiss—eyes still closed, breath still slow—on my collarbone. "Can we stay like this for a little bit?" He yawned, then nuzzled his nose against my chest. "I *never* nap during the day, but this is nice."

"It is nice," I managed. "We can stay like this for as long as you like."

"I'm not bothering you?"

I couldn't help it; I laughed. "No, hush."

He scooted up, and there was a gentle sensation of warm lips against my neck, and Lucas's soft murmur. "What about now? Am I bothering you *now*?"

His breath tickled, and I gave a louder, wheezier laugh. A delighted shiver ran through me as my body realized, once again, that it was both alive and conscious and, as a nice change, held me in contempt for neither. After all, there was Lucas. Still here.

And I was still here. If only for one last day.

And Lucas was speaking. Had already spoken and I'd missed it.

"Wha?" I rumbled—my voice had gone hoarse. "Sorry, was doing a bit of woolgathering."

He gave a happy little huff and pressed a kiss to my shoulder. "I was just saying that your phone's gone off twice and I was wondering if it was important maybe?" He levered himself up on one elbow and grinned down at me, strands of golden hair falling across his forehead and over his deep green eyes. "You really can sleep through anything, huh?"

Even after last night, after this morning, this closeness still made my face flare red. Being near him felt like huddling up to a heat source, like watching the stars come out in the country, like the rush of cool water on a sweltering day. My mouth pulled into a helpless smile. "Aye."

Lucas bit his lip, eyes twinkling at me in amusement, and moved in—at first I thought for a kiss, but then he reached past me to the bedside table and held my phone up in front of my face. "You're very cute, but I need you to make sure no one's trying to get hold of you about an emergency, okay?"

I blinked. Was this a good time to explain to him that I was not remotely the type of person anyone sought out during an emergency in which I was not directly involved?

It was Lakshmi. Of course it was Lakshmi. Calling to tell me it was over. That Drake House had officially decided not to renew our contract. I'd been so caught up in the joyful, hedonistic bubble of Lucas that I'd allowed myself to forget that the grim reaper stalked not far behind me. I'd forgotten to *momento* my *mori*. "It's my agent," I managed.

I had barely enough brain power to note that Lakshmi was attempting to commence a video call, and that I best keep my end audio only.

"Oi," I answered guiltily.

"Demetrio, you tosser." She squinted down at me. "Why's your camera off?"

"I'm in *bed*, Lakshmi." Not a lie. I took a deep breath. "What's the verdict?"

"You've not been online yet, have you?"

"No?" My stomach dropped. "What's happened?" Why wasn't she just telling me whether or not I still had a job?

"Nothing. Naught. You've gone *viral*, is all."

I stopped breathing. "What."

"You've been trending all night, pet," she explained, lighting a cigarette in the dark—her most default form. "You and your weird little penguin."

"What does that mean?" I sat up, and Lucas followed, cuddling up against me in a way that was distracting but extremely welcome.

"It means you're hot shit, Demetrio. It means Drake House can't *wait* to renew our contract." Lakshmi clearly couldn't help it, she was grinning at me like the sharp-lined, nocturnal predator she was. "Getting a bit stroppy about scant socials, though. We need to ride this wave. Make hay while the ruddy sun shines, yeah?"

I winced. "Aye. I'll . . . I'll post something."

Lucas leaned in close to my ear and whispered happily, "*Congratulations!*"

"Yes, you'll bloody post something." Lakshmi puffed a smoke ring toward the camera. "That reminds me, how did it go with the flatmate? I'm assuming he was the dishy blond at the con? You know, the one you couldn't take your eyes off?"

How did she—

Right. The cameras. The bloody livestream. I looked over at Lucas, who was watching me with intense amusement, stifling a snort. "Er. Aye," I said. "Lucas Barclay."

"Achcha," she said, businesslike again. "I've done a quick google, and it seems he knows his onions, actually." She stubbed out her cigarette and immediately reached for another. "Does publicity for horses or some suchlike, and brilliant portraiture. Any chance he does freelance?"

Lucas's eyes widened, and I raised my eyebrows in question. It seemed to take him a moment to realize what I was asking, and then he gave a quick nod.

"He does."

"Marvelous. He takes lovely pictures, so let him take you to the seashore or something. Eat an avocado. Once you're back across the pond, we'll hire someone full-time, at least for the next few weeks to ramp up for the anniversary issue— My word, you've gone *very* quiet. Is he there with you?"

I choked, then glanced over at Lucas in a panic. He was grinning brightly.

"Bloody hell, Lakshmi," I grumbled.

"Hii," Lucas trilled, bending toward the phone. "Nice to meet you!"

My agent *beamed.* "Hello, dear! *So* pleased we have this opportunity to chat. As you've likely discovered, Armand Demetrio is, bless him, a bit of a handful. He does great work when he *does* do work, mind you, but for someone with a platform and following as large as he has, let alone as he's *about* to have . . . Let's just say that his social media presence is next to nonexistent."

"I've noticed." Lucas giggled, being rather painfully adorable even as he conspired with my agent. "I could barely find a picture of him."

"So you see the problem." She raised a severe eyebrow. "Be my hero? We need to make sure the masses remember our boy, make use of that pretty face of his—get some intrigue going, if possible. I saw some of the cute bits you've done with your equine subjects, and that pretty white boy with the curls. Think you can drum up some pics for a hashtag or six?"

Lucas was already nodding along, smiling to himself while his eyes narrowed pensively. "Absolutely, I know we only have a day, but I'm sure I could think of something—"

"Wait," I cut him off, then barked at my phone, "give us a minute," before I hung up the call.

I set the phone down on the bed and faced Lucas, who, I was chagrined to realize, looked rather stricken.

"I'm sorry." He bit his lip. "I didn't even stop to ask if you wanted—"

"Come with me to London." Then I added miserably, "And I'm sorry I keep interrupting you. Come with me to London? Please?" I swallowed hard. "To do the publicity for the anniversary issue, I mean."

Lucas blinked at me. His hair was still tousled, the bedsheet pooled around his lap, and the broad, tan, peachy curve of his bare shoulders glowed in the muted light. His mouth had fallen open, and every nerve in my body screamed at me at once that if I did not kiss this man at once I would die.

"Are you serious?" His breath hitched.

"Regrettably, yes." I bit down on my knuckles, unable to meet his eyes. Instead, I focused on his hands: large and elegant and manicured and rough at the finger pads and palms. I couldn't help it, I reached for them, and nearly cried in relief when Lucas all but pulled himself into my lap.

"Come with me to London," I said again. "Take photos of me scowling at ducks."

He had one hand in my hair and tenderly gripped near the base of my skull, guiding my head back so he could peer into my eyes. "Why would you ever scowl at a duck? What did ducks ever do to you?"

I appreciated his willingness to follow me on this duck-related fantasy, but I couldn't help but notice that he hadn't answered yet. I swallowed thickly, searching that endless green and the teasing smile and the gentle raising of his brows. "If it's too much—" I began, but Lucas pulled me into a slow, languid kiss, his tongue brushing against mine and his lower lip catching on the scruff of my chin.

He bit down on my lip—not too hard, just hard enough really—then quietly whispered into my mouth. "Okay."

My body shuddered happily and I pulled him in closer, leaning back slowly until we were splayed across the bed again, Lucas's hips framing mine, the curve of his back filling my palms with strong, warm muscle. My shoulder landed on something cold and hard, and despite myself I broke the kiss to see what it was.

Lucas laughed softly and plucked my phone out from its vortex of sheets. He held it up playfully, so that the black mirrored side faced me. My reflection looked on in vexed disinhibition. "Shall we begin with a few glamour shots, Mr. Demetrio?"

My mouth pulled into a half grin, and I levered my hips, reaching for Lucas's shoulder and pulling him down beside me. "I actually wouldn't mind a quick selfie, Mr. Barclay."

He giggled and began sitting up again to take the photo, but I shook my head. "No, with *you*, love. Together."

Uncertainty crossed Lucas's face—unbidden, I remembered how hard it had been early on to find photos of Lucas that weren't heavily edited. To find any photos *of* him. He clearly felt far more comfortable on one side of the camera than the other.

"It'll just be for us," I whispered, "but we don't have to."

He seemed to struggle with himself for a moment, his gaze turning stormy, but then he gave a shy smile and lay down beside me again, holding the phone up above both our heads and pulling up the camera. "Wow," he breathed, presumably at the sight of himself—eyes bright, cheeks flushed, hair tousled, and all of him heart-achingly beautiful.

I was there too, unable to look away from him. I leaned in to nip at his neck as he took the picture, drawing out a delightfully surprised laugh. He snuggled up to me again, warm wet breath on my chest making me shiver and burn and melt into the mattress.

"London," he muttered against my shoulder, and I closed my eyes in bliss. However temporary.

Were we moving too fast? Likely so.

But if we'd learned anything from this entire debacle, it was that we could hardly rely on the universe's so-called natural order of things.

Let alone its poor sense of timing.

Dear Reader,

Thank you for reading Sylvia Barry's *Lessons in Timing*!

We know your time is precious and you have many, many entertainment options, so it means a lot that you've chosen to spend your time reading. We really hope you enjoyed it.

We'd be honored if you'd consider posting a review—good or bad—on sites like **Amazon, Barnes & Noble, Kobo, Goodreads, Twitter, Facebook,** Tumblr, and your blog or website. We'd also be honored if you told your friends and family about this book. Word of mouth is a book's lifeblood!

For more information on upcoming releases, author interviews, blog tours, contests, giveaways, and more, please sign up for our weekly, spam-free newsletter and visit us around the web:

Newsletter: riptidepublishing.com/newsletter
Twitter: twitter.com/RiptideBooks
Facebook: facebook.com/RiptidePublishing
Goodreads: tinyurl.com/RiptideOnGoodreads
Tumblr: riptidepublishing.tumblr.com

Thank you so much for Reading the Rainbow!

RiptidePublishing.com

ACKNOWLEDGMENTS

Sylvia Barry would like to thank the four winds, the ancient wisdom of her cats, and the ghost of her grandmother for inspiring her to write cozy queer love stories.

Maya and Anna, who made Sylvia up, would like to thank their families, and friends who have become their families. Emma: for your amazing photography and impeccable vision for our author photo. Liz: for graciously serving as our Sylvia body double and immortalizing her. Joey Dworsky, Madison "Honey" Hyman—you guys are the best cheering section any big sister could ask for. Alyssa Martin, Ella N'Diaye, Eric Berg, and Maayan Yuzuk: thank you for your lifelong friendship and brilliant minds. And, as always, thank you to Iliana Dworsky-Rocha Martinez—friend, roommate, wife—for putting up with us, and always lending a supportive ear and third pair of eyes. We love you muchly.

Thank you to the wonderful people at Riptide, especially L.C. Chase for the perfect cover design, Alex Whitehall for their eagle-eyed copy edits, and Carole-ann "Caz" Galloway for believing in *Lessons* while it was still a vaguely articulated idea, and helping us make this unformed thing into a clean, polished, rosy-cheeked book. Having a good editor is like getting glasses for the first time—everything comes into focus. Thank you for the hours and hours of effort to bring *Lessons* to its final form.

Thank you to anyone who picked up *Lessons in Timing*—we hope you enjoyed the fruits of our labor and we apologize for Armand. Just. In general.

Finally, we would like to thank Dr. Stephen Summers and Barry's Espresso Bakery and Deli for unknowingly inspiring Sylvia's namesake. Stephen, you united us in a love for literature and sideburns, and Barry's, you fed us soup and cookies.

2012 was a weird time.

Maya Dworsky-Rocha & Anna Catalano

ABOUT THE AUTHOR

Sylvia Barry is a waifish, seven-foot-tall witch living in an abandoned lighthouse.

She is in a long-term relationship with her five cats named Heathcliff, her sea-glass collection, and freshly baked bread. Sylvia is inspired to write queer romance stories because the world is a cold place, and love is warm.

She is also the invention of Maya Dworsky-Rocha and Anna Catalano, who can be investigated at sylviabarrybooks.com, should you desire a peek behind the curtain.

Enjoy more stories like
Lessons in Timing
at RiptidePublishing.com!

The Leaving Kind

Without heart, there is no art.

ISBN: 978-1-62649-984-3

Draw Me In

Jesse has a plan for love, and Brick isn't it.

ISBN: 978-1-62649-974-4